MAREK

GUARDIANS OF HADES BOOK 4

FELICITY HEATON

THE GUARDIANS OF HADES SERIES

Book 1: Ares

Book 2: Valen

Book 3: Esher

Book 4: Marek

Book 5: Calistos – Coming July 2020

Book 6: Daimon – Coming Fall 2020

Book 7: Keras – Coming Fall 2020

Discover more available paranormal romance books at:
http://www.felicityheaton.com

Or sign up to my mailing list to receive a FREE vampire romance ebook, learn about new titles, be eligible for special subscriber-only giveaways, and read exclusive content including short stories:
http://ml.felicityheaton.com/mailinglist

CHAPTER 1

He had never been one for believing in signs, but as Marek watched the skull made of bubbles slide down the glass shower screen, a bad feeling stirred deep in his gut.

He finished scrubbing the suds from his hair and slicked it back, running both hands over his head as his eyes strayed back to the skull now stretching and deforming into something resembling Edvard Munch's painting *The Scream.*

It meant nothing. Omens weren't real.

If the bad feeling came from anywhere, it was because things had gone too quiet since the wraith had broken into the Tokyo mansion and rescued the shapeshifter female he and his brothers had managed to capture. It had looked as if she was going to be a valuable source of information, that Esher could break her down and convince her to talk if he had enough time.

Marek and his six brothers had held her in their grasp for only a few hours before the wraith had used the memories he had stolen from Esher to penetrate the barrier around the mansion and had whisked her away through a portal.

Now, they were back to square one. They had an enemy and they had no clue how many were in their ranks or what they planned to do next. All they knew was that this band of daemons wanted to destroy the gates he and his brothers protected between the mortal world and their home, the Underworld, to merge the two realms into one they would control.

Keras was still annoyed about the fact they had lost their only source of information, as well as other things.

Marek couldn't remember the last time his oldest brother had said more than two words to him. At every meeting Marek attended, Keras spoke to the others about their reports and what he wanted them to do next, but when it came to Marek, all Keras dished out was the cold shoulder.

Marek cursed Enyo under his breath, not foolish enough to do it aloud in case the damned goddess of war was able to hear him. It was time she overcame whatever it was that stopped her from facing facts and his brother, before she ended up getting Marek killed. The next time she showed up on Marek's doorstep, *she* was getting the cold shoulder treatment.

Or he would damn well teleport to wherever Keras was so she was forced to see his brother again.

It was about time they both faced their feelings.

Keras was as in denial as Enyo was.

The skull continued to mock him. Marek swiped the side of his left hand across the glass, obliterating it, and shut off the water. He didn't believe in signs.

He made his own destiny.

The Moirai could tell him the future all they wanted, but what good were the seers when they couldn't tell him the details? He and his brothers had been stuck in the mortal world for two hundred years thanks to the fates and their sketchy facts. Their father, Hades, had banished them from the Underworld to protect the gates and await the attack the fates had foreseen, believing it would motivate them and give them reason to focus all of their effort on their mission so they could return home.

Two centuries of waiting and the enemy had finally made themselves known.

War was coming.

Marek couldn't wait.

His gut swirled with a dark hunger, one that had been steadily building over the last two weeks and pressed him to obey it. He flexed his fingers as his thoughts trod a dark path, feeding that hunger with images of beautiful carnage, of walls painted crimson, and blood rolling down his body as he stood amidst the aftermath of a battle.

The image wasn't one he had witnessed, but one that was to come. Marek could tell the future too in his own way. He could predict the result of a hunt—because he always won. Nothing stood between him and the high of victory, not when he was hunting. His blood burned with need as his hunger got the better of him, and he stepped out of the shower, unable to deny it any longer.

Tonight.

He would make that vision real tonight.

He dried off and scrubbed a towel against his dark hair, mussing the waves into curls as he stared at himself in the mirror. He wasn't surprised to find his normally brown eyes were black with the dark need to hunt, revealing the depth of his hunger.

He tried to keep his mind on other things as he tugged on his trunks and then his black combat trousers, and pulled on a tight black T-shirt, but his focus kept slipping, filling his head with pleasing images of fighting that roused another need in his veins, a trickle of pleasure that warmed him. His eyes slid shut as anticipation built, the thought of what was to come making him want to rush.

As always.

He clenched his fists, savoured the sting of his nails biting into his palms, and tamped down the urges, clawing back control. He would have his high soon enough. It was better he remained focused during the fight. Afterwards, when the twelve vermin he had been tracking for the last two weeks were little more than fizzing piles of flesh and bone, he could indulge himself and enjoy the bliss and satisfaction that came from killing them.

Vampires.

His father, Hades, would be angry with him if he discovered Marek's need to slay vampires, a species his father viewed as allies. His brothers would probably be just as furious. Knowing that didn't stop him. It couldn't stop him.

The vampires needed to pay.

He had tried to deny the hunger to kill them, and it hadn't ended well. The compulsion was strong, so powerful that it had driven him into his darker side—a side that came from Hades's blood in his veins—and he had lost all control, becoming a slave to it.

His second-eldest brother, Ares, had found him a week later, caked with blood and grime. Apparently, he had located him by following the trail of carnage Marek had left in his wake. By his brother's estimate, close to a thousand daemons had lost their lives to Marek's blade, and on top of that he had slaughtered five Hellspawn.

Hellspawn were what he and his brothers called the daemon breeds that Hades deemed acceptable, ones who still served him and were allowed to travel freely between the mortal world and the Underworld.

Hades had forgiven him for killing them.

He doubted his father would forgive him if he became aware of the thousands of vampires he had slaughtered since then.

All of them in cold blood while fully aware of what he was doing.

Marek stalked into his bedroom, the terracotta tiles cool beneath his feet despite the thick heat of summer. Insects buzzed and chirruped outside, their song a soothing melody as he breathed deeply to focus, centring himself as he prepared for battle.

He felt the earth deep beneath him, sensed it surrounding him, and he closed his eyes as he allowed his connection to it to calm him further, and push out the frantic need building within him. Patience.

There were a dozen vampires in that nest in Barcelona, and he was going to butcher every single one of them.

Nothing was going to stop that from happening tonight.

He rounded his oak double bed that stood against the wall opposite the bathroom and opened a drawer on the side table to its right.

His dark gaze landed on the one thing it contained and the hunger roared back to life inside him.

He swallowed and reached into the drawer, his eyes slipping shut and pleasure rolling in on the wake of his hunger as his fingers made contact with the leather hilt of the blade. It was smooth beneath his touch, worn from centuries of use. He bit back a groan as he curled his fingers around it and lifted the blade, felt the delicious weight of it in his palm. He opened his eyes and looked down at it, shivered as he drew the curved knife from its sheath and the silver blade caught the low lights, reflecting them up at him.

The beauty of it hit him hard in the way it always did, had him transfixed as he took in every nick in the razor-sharp blade and recounted all the vampires he had killed with it, using the silver it contained to send them to their final deaths.

The need to hunt condensed inside him, boiled and raged, pushed at him until he surrendered to it. He swiftly sheathed the blade and jammed it into the waist of his fatigues, and focusing on his destination, he summoned his ability to teleport.

Darkness whirled around him, consumed him as he took a single step forwards. Familiar sensation washed through him, his connection to the Underworld lasting only a heartbeat before he emerged from the teleport. It was comforting nonetheless, and the closest he had been to home in two hundred years.

He landed in a cobbled alley surrounded by old cream stone buildings. The air was thicker here in Barcelona than in Seville, heavy with moisture that made it hard to breathe as the stifling heat bore down on him. He gave himself a moment to adjust to the summer temperatures, and then silently moved along the alley, using the shadows as cover as he stealthily approached the arched entrance of the vampire nest.

His senses sharpened as he focused them ahead of him, eager to count the number of foes awaiting him.

Only it wasn't twelve signatures that popped up on his internal radar.

It was only five.

Marek cursed and moved faster, drawing his blade from its sheath at the same time. He could still eliminate these five, taking the edge off his hunger, and then he would wait for the rest to return. He reached the entrance of the building and stopped dead as the scent of spilled vampire blood hit him together with a feminine grunt and a hiss.

There hadn't been any females among the vampires.

Was it a vampire?

Or a victim?

He eased the heavy wooden doors open and slipped inside. His eyes rapidly adjusted to the darkness that clung to the ground floor of the building, revealing the courtyard.

And a woman.

She stood in the centre of the courtyard, the low lights reflecting off her caramel-coloured hair as it tumbled around her shoulder, shifting in waves as she turned her head left and then right, eyeing the four male vampires moving to flank her. If it hadn't been for the fact that she was facing off against the vampires, he would have thought her one of them with her tight dark clothing. She matched their style perfectly, calf-height black leather boots showing over her tight navy jeans and a form-fitting black tank revealing her toned figure.

A thin cut slashed up her left arm, a crimson trail from it reaching her elbow.

Darkness stirred inside him as she took in the vampires, her wide luminous hazel eyes bright with what looked a lot like fear.

A startling new urge blasted through Marek in response.

A need to protect her.

The dark-haired vampire facing her licked his fangs.

Not on Marek's watch.

Darkness rushed through him, sweet and addictive, dangerously seductive as it subdued his softer emotions, leaving only raw rage and a black hunger for violence behind. His nails sharpened into claws, canines lengthening to match those the vampire was flashing at the woman.

His would-be victim.

Marek leaned his weight forwards and readied his blade, his gaze locking onto the male; mind racing to calculate everything about him, from his weight and height, to which foot he favoured and any possible weapons he had concealed on his body.

Satisfied that the vampire wouldn't stand a chance, Marek pressed down on his right foot, intending to launch at the male.

Only the woman picked that moment to yell a battle cry and spin on her heel, a silver blur shining around her as she gracefully pirouetted.

And stabbed the vampire nearest Marek right through his heart with a short sword.

Marek rocked back on his heels.

She wasn't a victim.

She was a warrior.

Breathtaking as she ducked beneath the blow from the blond male behind her and lashed out with her leg in a fluid sweep that looked as if she had performed it a thousand times. She caught the male's ankles, toppling him, and spun back up to her full height as she brought her blade around.

It sliced clean through the throat of the vampire she had stabbed, cleaving his head from his body as he frantically clutched at the bubbling wound in his chest. The vampire slumped to land by what appeared to be the fizzing remains of another vampire, giving Marek a better view of the warrior as she took on the remaining three.

Part of Marek growled at him to intervene, to protect her as he had intended.

The rest of him was struck dumb by how gracefully she moved as she twisted and turned, blocked and attacked, undeterred by the way the vampires evaded her blows.

He had never seen anything like her.

It wasn't fear that flashed in her hazel eyes as she spun on her heel and jammed her blade into the gut of the blond vampire. It was excitement. Pleasure. The same thrill he felt as he watched her.

Who was she?

The hunger that had gone dormant inside him the moment he had set eyes on her returned with a vengeance, snarling a black demand in his head as he watched her fighting the vampires.

Fighting *his* vampires.

It didn't matter who she was. She was intruding on his battle, had ruined his plans for the night. These vermin were his to kill.

The woman slashed her blade across the leg of the blond vampire, cutting deep into his thigh through his black jeans, delivering another deadly blow of silver judging by how the vampire she had managed to kill was slowly melting away to nothing.

She leaned over and grasped the male by his hair, stared into his eyes as the silver consumed him, tearing pained hisses from between his clenched teeth as he convulsed.

Her first mistake.

A fatal one.

She had taken her eyes off the remaining two.

The tall dark-haired male grabbed her from behind, fisted her fall of caramel hair and pulled her head back, ripping a pained cry from her lips.

The vampire's eyes blazed red as he bent his head to pierce her delicate neck with his filthy fangs.

Marek growled from the shadows, the feral snarl pealing from him before he could contain it as the need to protect her roared back to the fore, stealing control of him again.

The woman tensed.

The vampires froze.

Their glowing scarlet eyes edged towards him.

Marek launched at them on a roar.

CHAPTER 2

Disgust rolled through Caterina and not for the first time that night. She stalked the streets, her blood on fire as she tailed two men, keeping her distance so she didn't rouse suspicion. She blended with the tourists whenever they stopped, snapped pictures with her phone and played the innocent, admiring the cathedral that towered at the edge of the gothic quarter in her city.

Barcelona.

Out of the corner of her eye, the men moved on. She broke away from the group of twittering tourists gathered on the broad paved pedestrian area and headed towards the trees that lined the buildings opposite the cathedral, where there were fewer people. She reached the intersection with one of the main shopping avenues and paused to seek her prey, ignoring the street vendors as they tried to sell her everything from things that squeaked when you blew air through them to illuminated mini-helicopters launched into the air using rubber bands.

The two men took a left, heading deeper into the gothic quarter.

She glared at their backs.

Vampires.

In her city.

She couldn't let that pass.

It was her mission to free Barcelona of their clutches.

Her heart ached as she thought about her older brother, Guillem. How many innocents in her city had fallen victim of these fiends, murdered or worse—turned as Guillem had been and left to face an eternity of suffering?

Rage burned in her veins, as fierce as the day it had ignited nine years ago when her brother had been turned, and condensed into a fire as eternal as her brother's suffering. She readied herself, harnessing that anger as she tracked the vampires up the sloping alley to the right of the cathedral, a path many tourists took.

She wouldn't let these two vampires hurt any of them.

Their reign of terror ended tonight.

She slipped her hand beneath the back of her black leather jacket and stroked the hilt of the short blade strapped to her back. The feel of it comforted her as she followed the men deeper into the warren of alleyways that branched off from the Carrer del Bisbe.

The streets grew darker, the lamps mounted on the walls of the old sandstone buildings spaced further apart as she left the more popular part of the quarter behind. She paused at a junction, flattening her back against the wall as she listened. Male voices carried along the street. More than two of them.

She peeked around the corner, a quick glance before she darted into cover again. There were four of them now, loitering outside one of the gothic buildings. She risked another peek and frowned. They were gone. She peered into the darkness at the other end of the alley and then looked both ways along the street where she stood. They couldn't have disappeared. They must have gone into the building at her back.

Caterina emerged from her hiding spot and studied the building. The lower windows were barred to protect them. She moved a few feet along the alley. An arched entrance stood where the vampires had been, the dark wooden door sealed shut. She doubled back and did a lap of the building, trying to spot another exit. None that she could tell belonged to the building where the vampires were hiding.

One exit and barred windows didn't bode well for her.

She cursed low.

Her stomach churned but she pressed her hand to it and breathed through the nerves as she walked back towards the front of the building. She wouldn't let it stop her. She couldn't.

One of the vampires inside the nest might be her brother's sire. Killing that vampire would free Guillem, she was sure of it. Her chest throbbed as she thought about him, about how pale and gaunt he was now, a shadow of the man she had once known. All because of a vampire.

She would free him of his curse, before it consumed him.

That need, that desire, kept her strong as she readied herself. Killing the vampire who had sired Guillem had to be the answer. *She was sure of it.* Everything else she had tried had done nothing to help him. This was her last hope. Their last hope. If she had to slay every vampire on the planet to save her brother, she would do it.

If she had to give her life for this cause, she wouldn't hesitate. Her brother meant everything to her, and he deserved to live again, without the sickness that plagued him.

Caterina pushed her leather jacket off her left shoulder and drew her blade from beneath it. She sucked down a deep breath, steeling herself for what she was about to do. Vampires had sharp senses, which meant she needed the element of surprise, and the only way to get that was to disarm them with the scent of blood. It was dangerous when she wasn't sure how many vampires were inside the building, but it was far less dangerous than just breaking in and attacking them. She might be able to cut down a few of them before they realised what was happening.

She drew the edge of the blade across her upper arm and hissed through her teeth as fire blazed in its wake. The scent of her blood was swift to permeate the humid air, turning her stomach as she sheathed her sword. She rubbed her arm, encouraging it to bleed, and pulled her jacket back up. Not wearing it so the vampires could get a good look at her wound would be better, but she couldn't risk them seeing her weapon. She had to keep it hidden until she was ready to strike.

Her phone vibrated in her pocket and she pulled it out. A message from Guillem. She opened it and stared at his picture, at the man he used to be, and tears filled her eyes, hot and stinging. She fired back a reply, telling him that she would be home soon, and continued to stare at his photograph, using the anger and pain the sight of it stirred to bring more tears.

Tears she intended to use against the bastard vampires.

This was going to be the performance of her life.

They wouldn't know it was all an act until it was too late for them.

She clutched her left arm and sniffled as she shuffled towards the arched entrance, keeping her head bent and bumping against the wall from time to time, in case they were aware of her. The weaker she looked, the better this would go for her. The vampires wouldn't think she was a threat if she looked close to passing out from blood loss and fear.

More tears came as her phone vibrated, no doubt with a reply from Guillem. He was weakening more each day now, running out of time.

She frantically banged on the wooden door, letting her desperate need to save Guillem get the better of her and colour her actions. The voices on the other side grew hushed and she waited, heart hammering in her throat as adrenaline surged, anticipation pushing her right to the edge. She breathed through it, calming her nerves and focusing on her act. She had to make it convincing.

She banged again. "Help me. Please. I heard voices in there. Please, help me!"

Footsteps echoed on the other side of the door and she tensed as it creaked open, revealing a handsome fair-haired man. He frowned at her, his eyebrows pinching hard above his dark eyes, and looked her over.

"What do you want?" he said in her tongue, his accent telling her that he was Catalan like she was.

A local.

How many other citizens of her city were vampires? They multiplied so fast she struggled to keep up with them. For every one she killed, another two were made.

"Please." She leaned towards him and peeled her right hand away from her arm, her brow furrowing as she revealed it to him. His nostrils flared, and crimson ringed his irises. She pretended not to notice his reaction, swayed a little and pressed the back of her hand to her forehead as she slurred, "I was attacked. A man... I think he's still after me. I heard voices and thought you could help me. Please, help me. I'm afraid he's going to find me."

The vampire's dark gaze drifted down to her arm as she wrapped her hand back around it, squeezing the wound beneath her leather jacket to tease more blood from it. That fiery corona rimmed his irises again, brighter this time as he stared, seemingly transfixed.

Completely under her spell.

"What's going on?" Another male voice came from behind him, tugging him out of his reverie, and he looked over his wide shoulders at his comrades.

She peered past him while he was distracted, quickly scanning the elegant courtyard and the arches that surrounded it on the ground floor where the building was set back a few feet on all sides, forming a covered walkway. The trio of vampires standing there eyed her, a flicker of hunger in their gazes as they took her in.

The blond nudged the dark-haired man and slid him a look, one that sent a shiver of disgust rolling down her spine. He thought her easy prey. He was going to find out how wrong he was about that soon enough.

"I'm sorry to have bothered you." She went to turn away but the vampire at the door grabbed her arm, the pressure of his grip firm enough to have the nerves she had tamped down rising back up again.

She shook it off. All vampires were strong. They were fast too.

But they had a vulnerability that evened the playing field.

They were highly allergic to silver.

It had sickened her the first time she had killed one with her sword and watched as the silver it contained had corroded flesh and bone, causing it to fizz and hiss as it melted.

Now, she was used to it.

"Come in. Until the danger passes. You'll be safe here." He smiled, revealing straight white teeth with no hint of fangs.

She wasn't the only one who was good at acting.

The shimmer of red in his eyes said that he wanted her blood, and the way he cast a black look at his comrades warned he didn't want to share. If provoked, would he fight his own friends so he could be the only one to taste her vein?

She filed it away as a back-up plan.

One she wasn't going to need.

He ushered her inside, all charm and warmth as he continued to smile at her. He shut the door, the heavy thud of it closing an ominous sound she tried not to interpret as a death knell.

She shuffled along beside him, casting fearful glances back over her shoulder from time to time for good measure. The door was closed, but it didn't look as if he had locked it. That was good. If things went south, escape might be possible.

A fifth vampire strode from a corridor off to her left and paused, his gaze immediately settling on her. "What do we have here?"

"I was hurt—" she started.

"We're going to take good care of her." The man holding her arm smoothed his hand along it, upwards towards her wound, a faint crimson glow lighting his eyes as he looked down into hers. "You will feel better before you know it."

She nodded, certain that she would as she casually slipped her right hand behind her and under her jacket.

The blond moved a step forwards, shadowed by the dark-haired man and the brunet. She shivered under the intensity of their gazes, sickened by the hunger that blazed in their eyes as they looked at her as if she was a five-course meal they couldn't wait to devour.

The fair-haired man edged closer.

Caterina pulled her sword from her sheath and had it buried in his gut before he could react, ramming it up into his heart. He hissed and shrieked, his fangs long white daggers as she yanked her blade free and leaped back a step, placing some distance between her and the others.

The vampire went down, clawing at his chest as blood soaked his T-shirt. She didn't watch as he crumpled into a heap, kept her eyes on the others as she circled them, tightly clutching her silver sword.

She ditched her black leather jacket, tossing it as she assessed her enemies. It was easier to fight in just her black tank, and she had the feeling she was going to need the freedom of movement it gave her.

The sound of footsteps on stones filled the thick silence, alerting her to the fact that there were more than these five vampires in the nest. She braced herself, expecting them to come join the fight. Seconds stretched into what felt like hours as she faced off against the remaining four vampires.

The others didn't appear.

Things were looking up.

The blond and the brunet vampire moved to flank her and she did her best to keep her focus split between all of them, aware that even a slip in it would be her downfall. The dark-haired male remained in front of her together with the other one.

He licked his fangs.

Caterina narrowed her eyes on him, silently showing him that this wasn't going to go down the way he thought it was—the smouldering pile of vampire remains on the flagstones to her left was testament to that.

She yelled to unleash the pent-up rage inside her and spun, digging the heel of her thick-soled leather boots into the paving as she brought her blade around in a low arc. She grasped the hilt of the sword with both hands as she came to face the vampire nearest the exit and shoved forwards, burying the point of the silver blade deep into his chest before he could stop her.

Caterina dropped hard as the air moved behind her, years of fighting honing her reflexes until they acted as an early warning system. The blond vampire's fist arced where her head had been and she swung her leg out, bringing it around in a low sweeping kick. Her calf connected with the vampire's ankles and she followed through, sending him slamming onto his back. She didn't stop. She used the momentum to propel herself upwards and brought her sword around at the same time, aiming it at the neck of the vampire she had stabbed in the chest.

She hid her grimace as it sliced through his throat and scraped across bone, and she didn't pause to watch as the vampire slumped into a heap near the remains of the fair-haired one.

Caterina twisted and ducked as the dark-haired vampire attempted to grab her, hurled herself forwards into a roll and came to her feet near the blond. She kicked him to keep him down and faced off against the brunet.

He snarled and flashed fangs, and she was quick to dodge when he slashed at her with his claws, ducking backwards and then to her right. His growls deepened, anger lacing them as she continued to evade him and jabbed at him with her sword, seeking an opening. He knocked her blade away each time. She lunged at him, determined to land a blow. He leaped back a step, brought his hand up to his mouth and ran it across his fangs. What was he doing? Blood rolled down his hand and he flicked it at her. She flinched away as it hit her in the face, and cursed herself for letting him distract her.

The blond made the mistake of getting up.

Caterina whirled to face him and stuck her blade in his gut. Excitement trickled through her as the number of foes dwindled to only two and she meant to leave the blond to die from silver exposure, but couldn't stop herself from lashing out at him again, pulling her blade from his stomach and slashing across his thigh to deal another fatal blow.

She knew it was a mistake the second she did it.

The air shifted behind her, the dark-haired vampire little more than a blur even to her trained eyes as he moved like lightning. She tried to turn, her movements sluggish compared with his, time seeming to slow as panic spiked in her veins, sending another sharp burst of adrenaline into her blood.

The vampire grabbed her hair, balling it in his fist, and yanked her head back so hard she saw stars. A cry burst from her lips as she bowed forwards, afraid he would break her neck, and the fear she had been denying roared up on her as he bent his head.

A vicious growl pealed around the courtyard.

She froze as ice skittered down her spine in response to that feral sound, the fear she had felt of the vampire growing tenfold as the man stilled behind her and the other vampire looked towards the arched exit.

Caterina looked there too.

Another vampire returned to join in the fight?

The darkness itself seemed to shift before her eyes, the ground quaking beneath her boots as the shadows suddenly parted to reveal the dark visage of a formidable warrior as he barrelled towards her and the vampire. Silver flashed in his hand as his eyes narrowed on the man holding her and the vampire came to his senses.

He spun with her, using her as a shield.

Her eyes widened as the newcomer threw his hand forwards, letting the silver knife he held fly. It came right at her as she flinched, sure this was it and her life was over.

The vampire behind her shrieked and staggered backwards, tugging her with him as he tripped across the courtyard. Heat bloomed on her neck and shoulder, the sickening stench of blood filling her nostrils and the bubbling hiss telling her what had happened.

The warrior had better aim than she had expected.

She wrenched free of the vampire and spared him a glance as he went down, clutching the knife protruding from his forehead.

The dark-haired warrior grabbed her arm and shoved her backwards, behind him. He planted a heavy boot against the fallen vampire's chest, gripped the hilt of his weapon and pulled it free, the sucking sound sending bile blazing up Caterina's throat.

"Keep back." The warrior's gravelly voice rolled over her, a pleasant belly-heating timbre to it as he moved to face the final vampire.

It distracted her enough that it took her a moment to realise something.

He was shielding her from the vampire, and he meant to fight the bastard alone.

She rallied and shirked his grip, because she was damned if that was happening. This was her nest of vampires.

The final kill was hers to make.

And if he stood in her way, she would cut him down too.

CHAPTER 3

The last thing Marek expected as he stared down the brunet vampire was the woman wrenching free of his grip and storming past him.

It surprised him enough that it took him a moment to realise what she was doing.

She spat a vicious curse in the Catalan tongue and raised her sword as she bore down on the vampire. Marek couldn't blame the male for looking as stunned as he felt. Blood flecked her face and drenched her sword, rolled from the places where she had been caught by more than one set of claws, and her hazel eyes were bright with the high of battle.

She was a formidable sight for such a slender, petite creature.

The vampire shook himself out of his stupor just as the woman reached him and dodged left, leaving her on a collision course with one of the pillars supporting the overhanging floors above the courtyard. She slammed her left hand into it and pivoted, using the momentum to her advantage as she pushed off, muscles flexing beneath her golden skin.

Marek leaped into the fray with her, partly because she needed his assistance with this vampire because Marek could sense he was stronger than the others she had managed to dispatch, and partly because he wasn't about to let her steal his quarry.

The vampire spotted him and put on a burst of speed, appearing behind Marek. Closer to the door. He meant to escape. It wasn't going to happen.

The woman noticed his intent too and turned on a pinhead to track the vampire, almost losing her footing in the process. Marek beat her to the male, using his own preternatural speed to cut him off before he could reach the door. The vampire almost barrelled into him, saving himself at the last second by back-peddling hard, his arms flailing as he fought for balance.

A flash of victory shone in the woman's eyes as she came up behind the vampire and Marek couldn't contain the growl that rolled up his throat as he realised he had driven the vampire right into her arms.

She gripped her sword with both hands and brought it up in a fast, brutal arc. The vampire bellowed as he arched forwards, blood spraying from above his shoulder as the blade swept upwards, delivering a vicious blow that was sure to be his end.

She swore again in Catalan, a not very complimentary curse about the vampire's mother, and spun on her heel as Marek watched, too enthralled by the bewitching beauty to move as she sang a siren's song to his heart.

It was hard not to find her alluring when she was doing his favourite pastime with so much grace and fire.

It was hard not to find her arousing.

The heat of battle was no place to be feeling pleasure from anything other than breaking bones, severing arteries and claiming heads, but it was hard not to feel it as he watched her decapitate the vampire.

Blood splattered over Marek's chest but he didn't notice, was too enchanted by how fire lit her eyes as she came to a halt, breathing hard, that delicious high of victory painted all over her face so vibrantly that he swore he could feel it, knew exactly what she was experiencing as she held her blade out at her side and watched the final vampire fall.

Gods, damn, she was incredible.

But also infuriating.

"That was my vampire," he said, voice a low growl that hid none of his fury as he looked down at the bubbling, smoking corpse between them. "This whole nest was mine."

She was swift to ready herself for a fight, bringing her sword down in front of her and bracing her feet apart. His heart beat a little harder, that wicked sort of heat she stirred in his veins burning hotter as she faced him, looking for all the world as if he was next on her dance card.

He wanted to be next on it, but the sort of dancing his body wanted wasn't the kind she had dealt these vampires.

He wanted to tangle with her.

Ached for it.

He had seen strong women before, Valen's beloved Eva being one of them, but they were rare and this female was a jewel among them, shining brightly and beckoning him. He wanted to possess her, and that made her infinitely more dangerous than the rest of her kind.

"So what?" she spat in heavily accented English, her chin jerking up as her features set hard, soft pink lips flattening and fine eyebrows drawing down over her bright hazel eyes. "You should have beat me to them then. Don't cry to me because you weren't quick enough and I bested you."

He raised an eyebrow at her as his blood heated another ten degrees. "Bested me?"

He almost growled, but then the irritating voice of reason chimed that she had beaten him to the kills.

He wasn't going to let it slide that easily though.

"There were a dozen vampires in this nest." He cast a glance around the bloodbath in the courtyard. Carnage that the woman stood in the middle of, a vision of crimson-splattered beauty. He tried to ignore the fresh bolt of hot lust that rushed through him on looking back at her. "I count only five bodies."

She swept her blade to her right, sending the remaining blood on it flying to the pavement, and slipped it into the sheath he had noticed strapped to her back. Did she no longer consider him a threat? Her second mistake of the evening.

Just because she was human, didn't mean she was safe from his wrath.

"I'll find the rest," she snarled as her pretty face darkened. "I'll scour the damned city until every last one of them is like that."

She nodded her head towards the vampire decaying between them, now little more than a bubbling pile on the paving slabs.

"I don't think so." Marek flexed his fingers around the worn leather hilt of his blade and her gaze flickered there. Her right hand inched behind her hip, edging towards the grip of her sword. She didn't need to worry. He wasn't going to attack her, but he wasn't going to let her have her way either. "You already killed enough of *my* vampires."

And the hunger he had hoped to sate was still riding him hard, unsatisfied by the single kill he had managed. He needed to find the others and deal with them, needed the high of battle that she was experiencing. The high she had stolen from him.

She huffed and planted her hands on her hips. "I didn't see your name carved on them. They're mine and you need to back off."

"That isn't going to happen," he growled and took a single step towards her.

Her right hand shot to the hilt of her sword, but she didn't draw it.

He stared her down, aware that the darkness was rising in his eyes again, provoked by his need to hunt, by the frustration now mounting inside him as he looked at the aftermath of the fight and could count only one of the kills as his own. The five vampires might have satisfied him.

Maybe.

Probably not.

It was taking larger and larger nests to keep his need to hunt the vermin quiet these days.

If he could track down the remaining seven, it might at least take the edge off.

He just needed to make sure the woman didn't get ideas about hunting them, so he had a clear shot at them, without worrying about her.

"You were almost killed tonight." He risked another step towards her and tried to keep the bite out of his voice as a replay of her held in the arms of that damned wretch flashed across his mind, his fangs poised to pierce her throat. Darkness rose within him again and he didn't tamp it down this time, let it flood his veins and his eyes so she would see it. So she would know what she was up against. "You're not strong enough to fight that many vampires alone. It's tantamount to committing suicide. Do you have a death wish?"

Anger flared in her hazel eyes, fire that stoked the one in his veins as he realised she was going to fight him on this. He wanted to tangle with her, just not in this way. If she wanted a fight though, she had it.

"I'm not afraid of death." The look in her eyes warned she meant that and told him that he wasn't the only one who had a reason to kill vampires.

She was driven by something, and from where he was standing it looked personal.

She stooped and grabbed a leather jacket from the ground, tugged it on in a way that screamed of the anger and frustration he could sense in her. Her eyes met his and she cast him a withering glare that let him know exactly what she thought of him, and then stormed past him.

He grabbed her arm, holding her back. "Where do you think you're going?"

She yanked free of his light grip, tilted her head back and glared up at him. "I'm going to find the vampires."

"You won't find them tonight. They will have gone to ground. It's going to take us a few nights to uncover the location of their new nest."

Her eyebrows shot up. "Us?"

He hiked his shoulders, cleaned his knife on his combat trousers and sheathed it. "I'm not going to let you hunt them alone."

Partly because she would get herself killed.

Mostly because he needed to kill them himself. Working with her seemed like a good way of getting her out of his way. Once they found the vampires, he could teleport her somewhere safe and return to kill them. She would be furious with him, but he found he liked that idea. He liked it when there was a bite in her tone and fire in her eyes.

"No one *lets* me do anything." She looked as if she wanted to hit him. "I'm not yours to control. I can find the vampires without you. I don't need your help."

He scoffed. "Is that so? Because from where I'm standing, I have the feeling I have at least two centuries of vampire hunting experience on you and I know every inch of this city in detail, can pin down at least a dozen locations I would check tomorrow night alone. Can you say the same?"

Her mouth flapped open and snapped closed. She was quick to recover and hit him with another glare that let him know exactly what she thought about him. If he was trying to get that spot on her dance card for a midnight tango, he was going about it the wrong way. Something about her made it impossible to play nice though. He had charmed his share of women over the centuries, could normally have them under his spell with only a few well-placed compliments and a little light flirting.

Something about her had him way off his game.

He didn't mean to be caustic with her, to push her buttons and rile her at every turn, but he couldn't help himself.

And he had the feeling it wasn't because he didn't want to share the vampire kills.

His mind whirled back to when he had first set eyes on her and the black, terrible need that had gone through him in that moment.

A dark urge to protect her.

He felt it even now, even as she levelled a black look at him, her eyes relaying the internal war she waged as she considered his offer despite the fact she clearly preferred working alone. Just the fact she was considering it didn't sit well with her, he could see that much.

He couldn't deny that it sat well with him. A little too well. The thought of working with her, seeing her again, had need rolling through him. Not a desire to tangle with her, but a desire to peel back her layers and discover what she hid beneath her beautiful, tough exterior.

Why did she hunt vampires?

He wanted to know the answer to that question.

The corners of her lips turned downwards and she looked away from him. "Fine. But only because it will speed things up."

Marek held his smile back, keeping his features flat and emotionless, so she couldn't see how much that pleased him.

He gazed down at her, tracing her profile as she gently brushed her caramel-coloured hair over her shoulder, causing the tumbling waves to catch the light and become threaded with gold. Her eyes slowly slid to meet his, stirring that wicked need in his veins again, quickening his pulse as he drank his fill of his enchanting vampire slayer.

He wasn't sure this was a wise idea. Duty waged war with desire inside him, the sensible side of him filling his head with everything that had happened over the last few months, how the threat from their enemies was mounting now.

Taking his eye off the ball could prove fatal.

Every battle-hardened instinct he possessed drilled that into him.

But another instinct pushed back against it, one that he had possessed from birth. An instinct she had awoken in him.

Not the vampire slayer.

But the vampire who had betrayed him.

He didn't miss the irony of that.

A vampire had awoken the dark, possessive side of his blood, had made him wild with a need to protect her and claim her as his forever, and she had killed that side of him too through a single act of betrayal.

Now, a vampire hunter had roused that instinct, breathing new life into it, and the fires of its rebirth felt as if they might consume him.

Completing this hunt without her was the most sensible course of action, but he couldn't do it. The side of him she had awoken needed her with him, where he could see her, so he knew she was safe. If he didn't meet her and hunt the vampires with her, there was a chance she would go off alone and do something as crazy as spilling her blood again to attract the vampires.

He touched her left arm, grazing his palm down the leather over the wound beneath it.

Her eyes leaped to his face and awareness of her narrowed the world down to only her, until she was all he could focus on.

Maybe keeping her safe wasn't the only reason he wanted to hunt with her.

He lifted his gaze to her face.

A hot bolt of lightning struck him as their eyes met.

He wanted her.

And nothing in this world, the Underworld, and all of Mount Olympus would stand in his way.

Darkness curled through his veins, sank tendrils into his heart and threatened to pull a growl from his lips.

He *would* have her.

CHAPTER 4

The fight had shaken her more than usual. Or maybe it was the mysterious warrior who stood before her that had her legs feeling weak.

Caterina tried to tear her eyes away from his rich, earthy ones. Eyes that had been black more than once during the fight and during their confrontation. He moved with the speed and fought with the strength of a vampire, but whatever he was, he wasn't one of their breed.

And he wasn't human like her.

According to him, he was older than two hundred years, something that might have sounded ridiculous or even incredible to her a decade ago. Now, she felt nothing. No sense of amazement. No desire to laugh in his face and tell him his joke was poor.

If vampires were real, then it stood to reason that there were other things that went bump in the night.

What was he?

A natural predator for the vampires? He evidently enjoyed hunting them, had been aggravated by the fact he had found her killing a nest he had earmarked for himself. He had seemed annoyed about offering to team up with her, even when it had been his suggestion.

In all her research, she hadn't heard of vampires having any predators. Everyone painted them as the top of the food chain. The great white shark of the immortal world.

She looked the man over. Where did he stand in that shadowy, secret world?

His fingers grazed her arm, up and down, a maddening caress over her jacket that seemed to reach beyond the leather so she could feel his touch on her bare flesh. Her breaths came shorter and faster even as she steeled herself against the effects of his stroking. She lifted her eyes to his, a demand to stop rising to her lips. It fell away as she fell into his eyes.

They brightened, mesmerising flecks of warm gold emerging against the earthy backdrop as they sparkled at her in the low light.

Heat swept through her, a wildfire that frightened her.

She had been so focused on her brother for the last decade that she hadn't been with a man in that time, hadn't even thought about indulging in such a thing. Now she couldn't think about anything else.

This dark warrior had stolen the whole of her focus, had her breathless and aching for him to do more than lightly caress her arm over her jacket. She wanted to feel his fingers on her bare flesh, ached with a need to have his large hands cupping her, kneading her, teasing her to the edge of insanity.

She swallowed to wet her parched throat and somehow found the strength to step back and break contact with him.

Her voice wobbled as she spoke, betraying how easily he shook her.

"I'll meet you in the Plaça Reial tomorrow night at dusk." Meeting in a very public square seemed like the most sensible course of action.

Something about this man unsettled her, and it wasn't just how easily he had her aching for his touch. She intended to question him before they went anywhere, learning more about him to set her mind at ease, something she couldn't do right now. She needed time to gather herself and build a wall, something to protect herself. He had her shaken, made her weak in a way she didn't like.

She took a step towards the exit and looked back at him. "I'll give you an hour but no more. If you don't show, I'm out of there."

He nodded. "Until then."

Caterina went to turn away from him, expecting him to follow her out of the building.

He disappeared in a swirl of black smoke and she stumbled backwards, her spine hitting the wall of the arched entrance as her breath left her in a startled rush. She stared wide-eyed at the lingering ribbons of darkness as they dissipated.

Cursed low in Catalan.

What the hell?

Her legs threatened to give out and she leaned more heavily against the sandstone wall for support, struggling to comprehend what had just happened.

Warning bells jangled in her head.

She tried to ignore them as she found the strength to walk out of the heavy wooden door and close it behind her, concealing the carnage on the other side.

There was more to the dark warrior than she had expected, and she didn't like it. For the last nine years, she had known what she was up against, had learned everything about her quarry so they couldn't surprise her, catching her off guard.

Now she had proposed working with a man she didn't know, one who had finally managed to stun her by revealing a power that did seem impossible. Laughable. A very poor joke.

He could teleport.

She tried to wrap her head around that as she walked from the scene of the crime, heading towards the nearest Metro station.

Walking felt good, had her legs growing stronger beneath her and her head clearing, although she couldn't shift the warrior from it, or how easily he had unnerved her. What other powers did he have?

She cursed again. Walking away from all of this was a good idea. Probably the best one she'd had all night. Before she ended up in deep trouble.

So why couldn't she do it?

Caterina pondered that as she exited the narrow, sloping shopping street into a small square with a busy road running through it and crossed it to the Metro station. Every moment with the warrior played on repeat in her head, every detail pored over, and every instinctive reaction he had triggered studied. Her attraction to him was obvious and she wasn't foolish enough to deny that it existed. But her instincts also labelled him as dangerous as the vampires.

Perhaps even more so.

Vampires she knew how to handle.

This warrior tied her in knots, had her pulled in too many directions, and she didn't like it.

She boarded a train and managed to find a seat thanks to the late hour, lost herself in thought as she waited for her stop deep on the outskirts of Barcelona, far beyond the tourist attractions that crowded the centre.

Not meeting him wasn't an option.

He knew the city and he wouldn't be deterred from hunting the vampires. Neither would she. Their paths would cross before the week was out and another confrontation would happen. Angering a man with unknown powers was probably a bad thing. It was better to go along with her original plan, presuming he showed tomorrow night, and learn as much about him as possible before they embarked on their hunt.

Although, she doubted he would enjoy a light round of interrogation.

She left the train and walked home, enjoying the quietness of the streets and how the air was finally cooling, the vicious grip of summer easing on the city for a few scant hours before dawn came and had everyone boiling in their skin again.

She loved her city, but hell, she hated it in summer. It was oppressively humid, the sun sending stifling air rolling in from the sea that bordered Barcelona and the nearby mountains trapping it over the city.

It was little wonder a lot of stores and businesses closed up for the hottest months, and many families headed to cooler destinations.

Sometimes, she and Guillem did that, picking another city in Spain as their base of operations for August, when the heat really hit. Vampires lived everywhere. There wasn't a city in the country where she couldn't find at least a few to hunt and eradicate.

She pushed the door to her apartment building open and headed up the stairs, keeping her footsteps light so she didn't disturb the neighbours. When she reached her apartment door on the third floor, she pressed her ear against it and listened. It was quiet on the other side, no sign that Guillem was awake.

He had been sleeping more and more recently, and it worried her.

She slid her key into the lock and eased the door open, trying to make as little noise as possible so she didn't wake him if he was asleep. He needed his rest. If she woke him, he would spend hours questioning her, and he might even argue with her. She didn't want that. She had argued enough for one night.

She silently closed the door behind her, removed her boots and socks, and padded barefoot across the living room, heading to her left past the kitchen towards her room. Guillem's room was beside hers, their beds stood against the same wall, but not their bathrooms. Hopefully, she wouldn't wake him as she washed the grime of battle off her.

She needed a long, hot soak.

Her bedroom door creaked softly as she opened it and she flinched. Waited, holding her breath. No sign of her brother came from the other room. She breathed a sigh of relief and stepped into her room, went straight to the bathroom on her left, and stripped off her jacket.

Long grooves darted across her chest near her left collarbone, and she frowned as she inspected them. They were already healing. She didn't remember any of the vampires landing a blow on her, but then in the heat of battle she rarely noticed her injuries. The sting of them didn't register at the time and everything happened so fast when fighting vampires. All of her focus was on surviving. It was only in the quiet aftermath that she grew aware of any bruises and cuts, and how close she had danced to death.

Her legs turned to noodles beneath her and she gripped the sink on the vanity unit, clutching it for support as she breathed through the crushing wave of panic. She was alive. She was fine. She cursed herself, how things always went like this even though she did her best to grow stronger, to overcome the debilitating onslaught of feelings that happened whenever she was home safe after a hunt.

Nothing she did stopped it from happening.

She stripped off the rest of her clothes, closed her bathroom door and stepped into the shower cubicle.

Caterina hissed in a breath as she switched on the water and a frigid blast of spray hit her. She shrank back, waiting for it to warm, holding herself as she willed it to hurry. She needed the soothing heat of the shower to wash away her burgeoning fear. It was ridiculous to feel it now, when she was safely locked in her apartment and the vampires were dead, but it always surged through her, a delayed reaction to the battle that she couldn't hold back.

The water heated and she stepped beneath the jet, tipped her head back and closed her eyes as she let it hit her face. A sigh escaped her as the hot water ran over her face and down her shoulders, stinging the cuts on her chest and the one she had made on her arm. The fear swelling inside her reached a crescendo and she let it come, let it wash over her just as the water did and let the water carry it away.

Time slowed as her entire world narrowed down to just breathing. In. Out. She was safe. The vampires were dead. The hunt would continue and for once she wouldn't be alone out there, walking the dark streets, fighting to keep them safe and to save her brother.

The warrior would be with her.

A soft knock at the door shattered the image of him building in her mind.

"Caterina?" Guillem's gentle voice rolled over her like the water to carry away her fear. He sounded stronger today. Had he been able to get some rest? Or were his spirits on the rise again? She hoped it was both. She hated seeing him so worn down and tired all the time. He rapped his knuckles against the door again. "Are you all right?"

"I'm fine," she hollered over the noise of the shower. "I'll be out in a minute."

Because she needed to see him, needed to see he was doing better tonight, and wanted to tell him about the warrior.

About the hope she had.

She shut the water off, stepped out of the shower and grabbed her dove-grey robe from the back of the door. She hastily donned it and tied the belt around her waist, cinching it tightly before she opened the door.

Guillem wasn't there.

Caterina snagged a towel and rubbed her hair with it as she walked through her bedroom to the main living area.

Guillem lounged on the couch, his black jeans and faded grey T-shirt baggy on his ravaged frame now when once they had fitted him perfectly. Her throat closed, eyes stinging as she looked at him, as he turned his head towards her and smiled at her over the back of the brown leather couch.

That smile didn't reach his hazel eyes.

They had been bright once, like hers. Now they were dull, constantly laced with fatigue and pain.

Fatigue and pain that she wanted to take away.

Would take away.

She took the seat beside him on his right as he flicked channels, twisted to face him and brushed her fingers through his dark hair, sweeping the overlong strands of it from his face. She would have to trim it for him soon. If she left him to his own devices, it would be down to his backside by now. He needed to take better care of himself.

"I met someone tonight… and I think he can help." She paused with her fingers against the side of his head as he finally looked at her again, taking his eyes off the screen of the television to her right.

"He?" Guillem's face darkened and the tightness in her throat increased as she saw a shadow of her brother, of the way things had been before he had been turned.

He never had liked her talking about men.

His need to protect her ran as deep in his blood as her need to protect him.

"He knows vampires. I took out a nest of them with his help." She left out a few details, like the fact the warrior had saved her. Guillem didn't need to know how close she had come to losing her life tonight. She had made the mistake of telling him everything in the early days and it had always upset him, and led to arguments.

He didn't want her to go hunting vampires for his sake.

She didn't care. She had to do it. For him.

"I'm going to meet him again tomorrow night to hunt some that got away. I'll question him while we look for them. I really think he can help, Guillem." She brushed another rogue strand of dark hair from his face. It had been as light as hers once, kissed by the sun. Now it was verging on black.

The result of his sickness?

She had never heard of it changing the colour of a vampire's hair, but then she hadn't exactly stopped to question any of the ones she had slain to find out all the details about their transformations. It was possible their hair changed colour, darkening to suit a creature of the night. Maybe the rest of them dyed their hair.

Maybe Guillem's was because he had never fed.

The same reason he was weakening, slowly fading as the years went on without her finding a cure for him. How much longer did he have before her inability to save him ended up killing him?

She shook that question away, because if she thought about it, the hope she was trying to hold on to would fade just as he was and she would slip back into depression. It was a daily struggle to keep that dark beast from her door. She wouldn't surrender to it again.

Guillem needed her out on the streets, searching for his sire so she could kill it, not holed up in her room, trapped in her bed by a crippling disease.

"I don't like the idea of you meeting with this man again. Who is he?" Guillem's eyes narrowed, the dullness finally leaving them as a flicker of fire lit them. It had been so long since she had seen anything other than resignation in his eyes that she wanted to cry. She squashed that urge and took hold of his hand, running her fingers over the bony back to soothe him. It didn't smooth the sharp edge from his voice as he frowned at her. "Is he a vampire?"

"No. Never. I'd never work with one, and you know that. He was hunting them. He's... something else. I don't know. I'll find out tomorrow." She squeezed his hand and smiled. "And I'll be careful. You know me. I never do anything rash."

She did rash things all the time. Like cutting herself to lure vampires into a false sense of security. She just didn't tell her brother about them.

It was better he didn't know.

She hated arguing with him.

Although she could see one building in his eyes as he stared at her in stony silence.

"I'll be careful. I'm not going to leave the Plaça Reial until I know more about him. If I get a bad feeling, I'll leave. All right?" She hoped it was enough to ease Guillem's worry, because it was all she could offer him, and she had doubts that she would actually go through with leaving the warrior and the hunt behind even if she did get a bad feeling about him.

She needed his help, because she needed to kill those vampires, and she had the feeling he was the fastest way to find where they were hiding now.

"I could go with you. You shouldn't go alone." Guillem's tone brooked no argument.

It didn't stop her.

"We're meeting at dusk. It's too dangerous for you."

"It's too dangerous for you," he countered, his features darkening in a way that warned they were going to argue if she let things continue.

"I'll be careful. I won't move a step from the square without being sure of him and that I can trust him, and if I feel anything is wrong, I'll head to the nearest police officers. There's always some hanging out there to keep an eye on the tourists." She brushed her hand over his, drawing his focus down to it, and the hard lines of his face softened at last.

He sighed and then reluctantly nodded.

She squeezed his hand again, gently so she didn't hurt him. "I know you worry about me, but I worry about you. He *knows* vampires, Guillem."

"He knows how to kill them," her brother countered, the bite still in his voice.

"I'm sure he knows more than that. I don't know what he is, but he's part of the same world as the vampires... as you." She hated herself for saying that, wanted to take it back straight away as Guillem looked away from her, his gaze straying to the window to the left of the TV.

He didn't need her reminding him of what he was, not when he was so weak, liable to head out into the night and do something rash. She wasn't the only one who had inherited their father's recklessness.

"Just let me meet with him. I'm confident he can help." Not a lie.

The more she thought about the mysterious warrior, the more confident of that she became.

He hunted vampires, sure, but that meant he knew the breed. He was part of their world, granting him access to information that was beyond her reach. If anyone could help her save Guillem, it was him. She just had to tap into that knowledge without revealing that her brother had been turned.

Because the warrior hunted vampires.

And the darkness that had been in his eyes at times left her feeling that he made no exceptions.

She looked at Guillem, filled with hope again as she thought about tomorrow, about the knowledge she might gain and how close it might bring her to saving him.

None of that hope was reflected back at her in Guillem's eyes.

They grew cold, hollow almost as he stared at her, and she could see him withdrawing, closing himself off from her again.

She tightened her grip on his hand, desperate to keep him with her even as she knew it was impossible. Whenever he changed like this, all she could do was cling to the hope he refused to have, for his sake. One of them had to hold on to it.

One of them had to remain strong.

Or both of them would give up.

It was hard with the weight of the last nine years on her shoulders, constantly threatening to break her, testing her strength at every step, but she wouldn't break.

She wouldn't.

Because she couldn't lose her only family.

For a moment, Guillem looked as if he wanted to say something, but then he slipped his hand from hers and stood.

Her heart wrenched into her throat as he looked over her head at the door and the distance between them yawned like a chasm, cold and forbidding, threatening to rip all hope from her.

"Guillem," she whispered, silently pleading him to stay with her.

He looked down at her and offered her a soft smile as he ruffled her hair. "I won't be gone long. I won't bite anyone, Caterina."

That smile gained a sorrowful edge as he rounded the couch and she twisted on the seat to track him.

He opened the door and murmured, "My fangs never seem to work anyway."

Hope began to deflate as the door closed behind him and she sank against the back of the sofa, the brown leather creaking under the pressure as she settled her chin on the top of it.

She clung to it, refusing to give up as Guillem had. Things were looking up, even if he couldn't see it, was so tired and jaded by the last nine years that it was impossible for him to find even a sliver of hope in what she had told him.

The warrior could help them.

She hoped.

She stared at the closed door, aching inside as cold swept through her together with a feeling that had her blood turning to icy sludge in her veins.

If he couldn't, she was going to lose her brother forever.

And she would follow him into the endless night.

CHAPTER 5

Marek shoved his dark brown linen trousers down and stepped out of them, picked them up and neatly folded them. He set them on the bed beside his combat gear and paused to stroke them, feeling the heat of the sun on their fibres. It had gone down almost twenty minutes ago, and the sunset had been glorious from the covered patio of his villa high on the hills above Seville. Golden light had kissed the entire valley, making the dusty ochre soil glow and bringing out the green in the olive trees. Birds had sung. Insects had joined them.

Peace had invaded every fibre of his being, despite how aware he was of what the sunset meant.

Dusk was coming.

He had spent the entire day thinking about the woman. He should have asked her for her name before *stepping*, a term he and his brothers used for teleporting since it only took a single step to move a great distance.

Getting her name was the first thing he intended to do tonight when he met her at the square in Barcelona.

The second thing he intended to do was dig into why she hunted vampires. The more he knew about her before they started their hunt, the better. He preferred to arm himself with as much knowledge as possible, whether it was about his enemy or a new ally.

He already knew she was reckless, and that she had been fighting vampires for some time given the skill she had displayed during the battle last night. She had a fiery personality, and she didn't like strangers, or perhaps men in general, trying to control any aspect of her life. She was headstrong, determined, and he had to admit, he found it more than a little alluring.

A slow smile curled his lips as he tugged his black fatigues on, barely aware of what he was doing as his mind replayed how they had come to verbal blows. She had intrigued him before they had started their intoxicating dance, exchanging barbs and subtly testing each other, seeking out how dedicated the other was to their cause.

He had concluded today that she was a force to be reckoned with, despite the fact she clearly didn't belong in his world.

He had also concluded that she had felt that same spark as he had when they had touched, when he had been looking into her eyes in that dark archway. Heat had flushed her cheeks, and the scent of desire had laced the air, teasing his senses and strengthening the need he felt for her as it provoked the side of him that had lain dormant for so long.

The dark need to possess her hadn't faded during their time apart.

Although that might have something to do with the fact that when he had managed to catch some sleep on the patio in the sunshine, she had been the star in a very wicked dream.

In it, it hadn't been the vampire behind her, twisting those waves of delicious spun caramel around his fist, bending her to his will as he lowered his lips to her throat.

Marek had been there, watching himself kiss her golden skin, watching the way pleasure flittered across her delicate features in response, how her breasts heaved with her quickening breaths and her lips parted on a blissful sigh.

He cleared his throat and adjusted his cock as it stiffened painfully, palming it into a better position. It had been too long since he had slept with a woman, and far too long since he had wanted one this badly. It was a recipe for disaster. He needed to get his body under control, because she was sure as hell going to notice how much he wanted her if he didn't.

His gaze strayed to the black T-shirt on the dark blue covers of his bed and then down at his groin. Maybe it was better he stuck with his black linen shirt. The tails were long enough that they covered his raging hard-on. It might spare him some embarrassment if he did fail to keep his cool around the woman tonight.

Although she would probably be able to see it in his eyes.

He twisted to face the bathroom and risked a glance at the mirror above the vanity. His normally deep brown eyes glowed with golden and emerald flecks, a sign of his hunger, the desire that pulsed inside him, running like quicksilver through his veins to drug him.

Desire wasn't the only thing that made his eyes shine like that. Anger did too. Could he make her believe it was anger or the thrill of the hunt making his eyes change if she asked about them?

A grimace tugged at his lips as he remembered that she had seen his eyes like this, when they had been in that strained moment in the arched entry way, both of them snared and held captive by the attraction that had blazed between them.

Not a chance she would believe that had been anger.

"Fuck, maybe it's better she knows what it is," he muttered and turned away from the mirror. "Might work in my favour."

She might help him scratch this itch he had for her. A midnight tango might be on the cards. He wanted her. What was the point in hiding that? It wasn't as if he was alone in his feelings. She wanted him too.

He started to grin.

Grimaced again when he felt a fierce tug in his chest.

The gate.

"Not now." He flicked a glance at the clock on his bedside table. Did he have time to deal with the gate?

Normally, he didn't mind when it called to him to do his duty, signalling that there was a Hellspawn waiting to cross between this world and the Underworld, or vice versa.

Normally, he didn't have a date with a beautiful vampire slayer.

He growled and pivoted, shoved his feet into his boots and quickly laced them before striding out of the bedroom. He crossed the living room, his boots loud on the terracotta tiles as he banked right towards the dark cream couches and armchairs surrounding the unlit fireplace. He took another right as he reached them, shoving the door to his office open, and swiftly closed the distance between him and the cupboards that lined the wall to his right, behind his desk.

The feeling came again, pulling at him, and he froze as something hit him.

The tugging sensation wasn't drawing him in the direction of the active gate.

It was pulling him towards that gate's twin.

A gate that hadn't been used in centuries.

"Shit," he growled, yanked the door of the nearest cupboard open and grabbed the silver and black circular medallion that was hanging on the brown leather and bronze shield mounted on the wall.

He slipped it on and tucked it into his shirt. It had come out that the circular amulets weren't the key to opening the gates when their enemy had stolen the one belonging to his older brother, Ares. Apparently, the Keys of Hades were Marek and his brothers, their blood containing the power to control the gates. Right now, the enemy didn't know that, and he wasn't going to be the one to reveal it to them by forgetting to bring his amulet.

Marek held his hand out behind him and focused. His mobile phone whipped into it from the desk behind him and he brought it up in front of him, fired off a group message to his brothers about his suspicions, and pocketed it before he stepped.

Darkness embraced him and then receded, revealing golden earth and olive trees that clung to a rocky hill that rose before him.

Silence stretched around him and he stilled, focused to sharpen his senses. Had he been wrong?

The tug was still there, deep in his chest, but it was lighter now, and it wasn't pulling him towards the main Seville gate on the other side of the valley, closer to the city. It was definitely the smaller twin gate that wanted his presence.

He followed the winding path up the hill to a bluff and scoured the land below, eyes charting everything in the fading light. The gate was down there, in a clearing among the sparse trees and brush. As far as he could tell, it was the only thing there.

Was it possible a Hellspawn was waiting on the other side for him to open it?

He eased down into a crouch at the edge of a flat rock. He doubted it. His father, the god-king Hades, never allowed anyone to pass through this gate. He had kept it inactive since Marek's only sister, the twin of his youngest brother Calistos, had been murdered. Upon discovering that he and his brothers were the Keys of Hades, Marek had realised the reason there were two gates in Seville.

One was bound to Calistos.

The other would have been bound to Calindria.

Now that she was gone, stolen from them, it was possible that Calistos had power over the gate, that the closeness of his blood would allow him to seal it if they had to go that route. It was a plan they had discussed more than once over the last few months since their enemy had made itself known.

The less gates they had to protect, the easier it should be.

In theory.

The problem was, the less gates there were to protect, the less gates there were to share the power that flowed between them, meaning the more dangerous and unpredictable they became.

His oldest brother, and self-appointed leader of their team, Keras, had decided that sealing any of the gates might prove catastrophic. Ares had agreed with him, and Esher hadn't been on board with the plan either. Marek and the others couldn't exactly argue when the oldest three of them were against it.

He reached down and pressed his hand to the earth beside his right boot, closed his eyes and focused on it, connecting to his element to give his senses a boost in case he had missed something and daemons were lying in wait at the gate. The call it had sent to him couldn't be caused by them, the gate responded only to Hellspawn, demigods, and gods or goddesses, but that didn't mean this wasn't a trap.

The enemy was strong. It was possible they had managed to get their hands on a Hellspawn and had brought them to the gate to make it reach out to Marek. In fact, it was the only explanation that made sense.

Although, he didn't see a Hellspawn in the vicinity either.

Maybe he needed to take a closer look. He wouldn't get too close to the gate. That way, it wouldn't manifest and be in any danger. He knew it well enough to be able to skirt the edge of it, far away enough that he wouldn't trigger it but close enough that he could get a good look.

He stepped, landing to the right of the clearing.

The olive tree in front of him wobbled and distorted.

Weird.

He blinked and shook his head. Teleporting shouldn't affect him. Heat haze?

"Marek?" The female voice came from behind him.

Sent fire and ice shooting down his spine and had him spinning on his heel, shifting to face her in another disbelieving blink of his eyes.

"Airlea?" He stared at the beautiful raven-haired female who stood before him, black diaphanous robes clinging to her curves, caressing the ample swell of her bosom and the tempting flare of her hips, cinched with silver at her waist.

Her dazzling green eyes shone at him, sparkled like emeralds as she smiled, her sweet cherry lips curving gracefully and making his heart skip a beat.

It wasn't possible.

On the heel of the wave of lust and heat that surged through him came anger and hurt so vicious and deep it sent him to his knees on the dirt. He clutched at the earth, growled and bore his emerging fangs at her as she tilted her head up and looked down her nose at him, as her smile turned wicked and cold, lips parting to flash fangs as sharp as his own.

"You cannot be here," he snarled and dared to look at her again. The pain beating inside him grew a hundredfold, morphing into an agony so fierce it stole his breath as his past flashed across his eyes, a thousand moments when he had been happy.

In love.

He struggled for air as he looked at her, as her expression softened again, ripping at the fragile remains of a heart that she had left in his chest after rending it apart with her claws.

With her betrayal.

An image of her standing on the elegant patio of a Georgian-style black mansion, illuminated by candlelight that chased over the creamy swell of her breasts and accented the delicate sweeps and lines of her face rose before him. His heart beat harder in response, thundered against his ribs as need, love and happiness poured through him.

And then she laughed.

Laughed in that way he would never forget as the three male vampires beside her spoke of him.

Stabbed him deep in his chest and ripped his heart to shreds as she spoke of him.

He didn't hear her words as he stared at her, the images flickering between the past and the present, the woman he had loved with every drop of his soul and the creature before him.

"You're dead." He focused on the one in front of him, managing to shatter the vision of his past.

He shook his head, clenched his teeth and snarled at her as tears stung his eyes.

"I fucking killed you."

Or at least he thought he had. The night he had managed to hunt her down was always a blur for him, the faces of the vampires he had slaughtered blending together into one bloody stream as the darkness he always fought to hold back had seized total control of him.

Was it possible she had survived?

Airlea edged closer, her soft green eyes pulling him dangerously under her spell as she held a hand out to him.

Gods, he wanted to take it.

Frigid cold blasted across his back, rocking him forwards as dust swirled past him and the longer lengths of his hair fell down to brush his brow.

Airlea's robes didn't move at all.

He frowned.

Voices wobbled around him, watery and distant, and he couldn't make out what they were saying, but they were familiar.

His brothers?

Airlea leaned towards him, stretching her hand out to him. "Take it. Return to me."

The agony boiling inside him reached a crescendo as he stared at her delicate hand, as his gaze flickered to her face and he saw the hope in her eyes.

The love in them.

His pain wavered, and his resolve went with it.

This was Airlea. His Airlea.

Returned to him.

Esher suddenly went barrelling through her, sending her spinning away from Marek. His older brother stumbled a few steps, his heavy worn black leather boots scuffing the ochre earth and sending dust up the blue jeans he wore tucked into them. He pivoted, the finger-length strands of his wild black hair falling down over his left eye as wind blasted him from behind. His blue eyes leaped around, darkening by degrees as he searched for something.

They settled on Marek and brightened, relief flooding them.

"Whatever it is you are seeing, it's an illusion." Esher swiped his hand across his forehead and glared at his surroundings, a shadow crossing his features as he skipped right past Airlea as if she wasn't there.

Because he couldn't see her.

Marek cursed. "Daemon."

The woman who had targeted Esher, desiring to turn him against his brothers and the entire human population of the world, had the power to create illusions so detailed it was almost impossible to tell they weren't real.

Marek looked at Airlea as she strode towards him, fury turning her eyes crimson as her claws lengthened.

She wasn't real.

The Airlea he had known would never have asked for him to take her back. She had too much pride.

And now that he knew this was an illusion, he could say with confidence that she had definitely died that night at the vampire stronghold. He hadn't left anyone alive.

It had been a bloodbath.

Another cold rush of wind battered him, and the sound of voices grew louder.

"Snap out of it." Esher grabbed his arm and hauled him onto his feet, his muscles flexing beneath the dark grey shirt he wore over a black T-shirt and causing the soft material to tighten across his arms and chest.

Marek shuddered as his blood vibrated in his veins where his brother touched him, feeling as if it was going to explode.

"Keep your head," Marek warned, his tone soft despite the gravity of his words.

If Marek lost his head, things got ugly.

If Esher lost his head, nothing survived.

Esher frowned at him and Marek was thankful that no trace of red shone in his brother's stormy blue eyes. Esher was in control, for now at least. Marek couldn't say how long it would last, not when they were fighting a powerful daemon and one who had managed to escape Esher's clutches.

It would probably only take her landing a single, wounding blow on one of his brothers to send Esher off the deep end.

"We're all good here, Esher." Marek kept his voice even, calm.

Daimon slapped him on the back so hard the air left Marek's lungs. "That's my line."

Marek wheezed in a breath and realised that it wasn't only the force of his younger brother's slap that had knocked the air from him. The spot where Daimon had touched was icy cold and his lungs ached as he dragged air into them.

"Sorry." Daimon grimaced and scrubbed a black-gloved hand over the soft white tufts of his hair, his pale blue eyes backing up that apology. As he lowered his hand to rub at the neck of his long-sleeved navy roll-neck, intricate patterns of ice glittered like diamonds on the black leather of his gloves. "You good?"

Marek nodded.

Looked for Airlea.

She was gone, and rather than an empty clearing, there were ten daemons and two more of his brothers.

And the gate.

A great twisting orb of fire swept past it as his older brother, Arcs, hurled his hands forwards, unleashing his power. It struck one of the daemons but the others were swift, easily dodging the attack. Marek wasn't sure what species they were. Right now, they appeared as human as he did, but there was a chance they had another form. Some were scaly and lizard-like beneath their human skin, and some could transform into beasts, and others resembled the images of vile horned and winged demonic creatures that humans equated with the word.

Marek despised those ones most of all.

Ares looked back over his wide shoulders, his tawny hair tumbling loose from the thong that held the top half of it back. "He good?"

Marek was beginning to wish people would stop asking him that.

"Think so," Daimon replied before Marek could answer for himself. "Got his illusion cherry popped so we get to interrogate him later about what he saw."

The way Esher glared at Daimon, his eyes darkening dangerously, said that wasn't going to happen. Marek glared at him too, because he was damned if he was telling them anything about what he had seen. His past with Airlea was his business and his business alone.

"It was a joke. Sheesh." Daimon stepped, appearing beside Ares.

The two of them joined forces, Daimon launching spears of ice at the daemons to drive them back from the gate as Ares formed a wall of fire around it to protect it. As much as Daimon and Ares fought and bickered, they were a formidable pairing.

Esher looked down at Marek, and he could read what his brother wanted to ask him.

"I'm fine." He dusted his knees off and huffed. "Give them hell."

Esher grinned, flashing the sharp tips of his canines, but didn't rush off to join the fight.

He casually lifted his left hand and curled his fingers into a soft fist.

Behind him, three daemons suddenly went down, convulsing violently.

Daimon was quick to teleport. Ares wasn't so fortunate.

Esher tightened his fist and the three daemons exploded, spraying black blood everywhere. Ares released a wave of fire, catching most of the blood before it could hit him, but the rest rained down on him, splattering his face and soaking into his T-shirt.

He tossed Esher a black look as his jaw set hard, the muscles in it popping beneath his tanned skin.

Daimon didn't miss a beat. He slowly raised his arms, his face etched with concentration as he reached deep below the dry earth with his power, drawing what moisture there was there to the surface. As his hands hit shoulder level, shards of ice shot up from the earth beneath two of the stunned daemons. The daemons shrieked and wailed as the glistening clear blue spears continued to rise upwards as Daimon gritted his teeth and strained to draw more water up, lifting them high into the air, and fell silent as a dozen smaller spikes of ice suddenly burst outwards from the main shard, ripping them apart.

Ares grinned and dodged as a daemon came at him, clearly enjoying tangling with them as he kept them from the gate.

Marek frowned as he realised the other brother he could sense hadn't moved.

His gaze tracked right, towards the gate, and he froze as it landed on Calistos.

His youngest brother's blond ponytail whipped around, the tails of his long black cotton coat flapping in the tempest that spun around him as he stared at the flat disc hovering a few feet above the earth in front of him. The dazzling vibrant colours of it reflected in his eyes as the concentric glyph-laden rings of the gate rotated lazily, flaring occasionally as it waited for a command.

Marek's gaze leaped back to Ares. "You brought Cal? What the hell were you thinking?"

That earned him a scowl from Ares.

Marek ignored him and focused on Calistos. "Cal, look at me."

Calistos didn't move, didn't acknowledge him as he stared at the gate, transfixed by it.

His eyes slowly darkening to black.

"It wasn't my damn idea." Ares broke away from the remaining few daemons, leaving Esher and Daimon to deal with them. "You messaged all of us!"

Marek cursed himself for that. He hadn't been thinking. He should have been thinking.

Calistos started shaking his head, slowly at first as Ares hurried to him, but he was frantic and clawing at his hair by the time Ares finally reached him, blasting straight through the gate and disturbing the concentric rings. Ares stepped the second he had Calistos in his grip, but Marek knew it was too late.

By the time they landed wherever Ares was teleporting them, Calistos would have succumbed to the darkness of his past and the night they had lost his twin sister.

And he wouldn't remember it or any of what had just happened.

And it would kill him.

"Damn it," Marek muttered beneath his breath, fury burning in his veins, all of it directed at himself.

Calistos suffered enough as it was because of the amnesia. He didn't need his own brothers triggering it for him.

Marek forced himself to focus on the gate as Daimon and Esher handled the remaining daemons.

If Ares and Daimon were a formidable pairing, then Esher and Daimon were a nightmare made flesh for any enemy that stood in their way. Esher preferred to use his power over water to make use of the abundant amount of it available in the cities when he fought, but here in the valley, the earth was baked dry from the summer heat and it hadn't rained in more than a month.

Not that it was a problem for Esher.

He had developed a rather disturbing ability to command liquid in any form, and he liked nothing more than exerting that power on his foes.

Another shriek pierced the night and Daimon swept his hand across the air in front of him. A wall of ice shot up from the earth to protect him, blue one moment and black the next, drenched in foul daemon blood.

"Rein it in," Daimon snapped. "I won't forgive you if I get even a drop of that shit on me."

"Rain it in?" Esher grinned.

The skies suddenly opened, rain pelting the earth from a cloud that hadn't been there a moment ago, sending the scent of it into the air.

Daimon smiled slowly.

Over the daemons, every drop of rain became a tiny ice spear. Two of the daemons tried to run, but there was no escaping the torrent as more clouds built above Marek, spreading to block out the stars as they started to emerge.

Marek focused on the gate and watched as the concentric rings gradually slowed and the disc shrank, the colours losing their brilliance as each band disappeared. When it was the size of his fist, it disappeared with a violent purple flash that made him flinch.

Silence suddenly fell around them, the rain ceasing as quickly as it started.

"The illusionist?" Marek held the gate closed as he jogged over to his brothers to survey the dead daemons.

All of them were male, and young. The enemy was recruiting. What had they offered these daemons to make them willing to risk their lives by attacking a gate?

The ranks of the enemy Marek and his brothers had fought in the past had revealed someone had offered them a slice of the realm that would exist if they succeeded in their plan to merge the Underworld with the mortal one.

Had these foolish daemons been offered the same?

Or had they merely wanted to go through the gate to the Underworld?

Many daemons craved that, even though they had never set foot in that realm. None of them were old enough to have lived in the time before Hades had banished the daemons from it after the last uprising. It didn't stop them from feeling as if the Underworld was where they belonged, and where they should be allowed to live.

While Marek understood why his father had banished them, he also understood why the daemons felt the way they did.

After all, Hades had also banished him and his brothers from the Underworld after the Moirai had gone to him with their prediction about the gates and the merging of the two realms. If they succeeded, they would be allowed to return home.

It had certainly motivated him and his brothers, even though it still stung to this day. Some of his brothers were less forgiving than he was. Valen still held a grudge against their father. Marek wasn't sure it would ever fade.

"She isn't here," Esher barked and pivoted away from the remains of the daemons. His deep voice grew as black as Styx. "She must have been here. Where the fuck is she?"

"Maybe she cast her illusions from a distance?" Daimon offered but Esher wasn't listening.

He paced, turning the slick ground to mud as his boots churned the earth, clawing at his black hair as he stared at a spot only a few feet in front of those boots.

Daimon went to move towards him. Marek held his hand out in front of him, not daring to touch his brother because he didn't want frostbite, but unwilling to let him disturb Esher. Their brother just needed a moment. He had been on edge for the last month, since the illusionist had escaped their grasp. He had probably been banking on recapturing her tonight.

The contingent of daemons she had brought with her had distracted them, keeping them busy while she had made her escape.

Marek was furious about that too, but there was nothing he could do to change what had happened.

"We will get another shot at her, Esher." He hoped it would soothe his brother and bring him out of his dark thoughts, before they got the better of him and had him slipping into thinking about what had happened in Tokyo.

Esher was handling it as best he could, but sometimes, it was all too much for him. Watching Aiko die still haunted him, and whenever he allowed himself to remember it, he always lost control.

And it always took her to bring him back to them.

The world didn't know the level of catastrophe it had narrowly avoided that day.

All three realms were lucky that Esher had managed to bring her back from the dead.

Esher nodded, shoved his fingers through his black hair and strode towards them. Daimon reached a hand out and hovered it over Esher's shoulder, keeping it from touching his dark grey shirt. The two of them had been close from the moment of Daimon's birth and nothing could change that, not even the fact that Daimon's power had manifested on Earth, affecting him physically.

"What do you think their plan was?" Esher asked.

Marek looked at the clearing where the gate had been.

"I don't know, but we need to call a meeting."

CHAPTER 6

Marek landed on the stone path outside the ancient Edo-period mansion in Tokyo. Some of the tension instantly melted from his shoulders as he saw it, as he felt the new wards he and his brothers had put in place around the white-washed walls trigger and cover him with their protective force.

Ares was waiting on the porch, the slender light of the approaching dawn revealing him where he stood beneath the overhanging roof of the single-storey traditional Japanese house. That same light caught on the grey glazed vertical ribs of the sweeping roof, drawing Marek's gaze up to the lightening sky.

"Esher." Aiko's soft voice, laced with desperation and relief, sounded so familiar now, a part of this place they all shared as brothers, as family, that a smile tugged at Marek's lips.

Esher hurried past him, closing the distance between him and the petite raven-haired woman in only a few strides. He met her where she waited barefoot on the wooden deck of the porch in front of Ares, and swept her up into his arms, burying his face in her neck for a moment before he kissed her. She brushed her fingers across the closely shaved sides of his head and then pushed them into the longer black lengths of his hair on top as she kissed him softly.

Ares muttered, "Get a room."

Clearly, Megan wasn't attending the meeting. Ares was always cranky when he couldn't bring her with him.

Valen appeared without his usual theatrics, and without Eva. He took one look at Esher and Aiko where they were still tangled in each other's arms and made a retching noise. Esher broke away from Aiko's lips and scowled at him over his shoulder.

Valen flipped him off. "If we aren't allowed to bring our ladies, I don't see why you get to have yours hanging around."

"She lives here," Esher countered, his expression darkening as he released Aiko and shifted to face Valen.

"She lives here," Valen parroted in a high voice, sneering at Esher, his golden eyes as bright as the lightning he commanded. He pulled a face and stomped past Esher, nudging him aside so he could pull his boots off, toss them on the deck and shove past Ares to enter the mansion.

"Someone's pissy today," Daimon muttered. "Eva must be working."

Valen always turned into a miserable, grouchy bastard when his little assassin was busy with work.

Well, he turned into a more miserable and grouchy bastard anyway.

Esher pulled Aiko inside with him and Marek met Ares's watchful gaze.

"How is Calistos?" Marek approached the porch, stopped on the step and removed his boots, neatly setting them down on the rack with his brothers' ones.

Daimon followed him.

"Annoyed. Frustrated." Ares folded his thickly muscled arms across his chest.

"He blacked out?" Daimon paused halfway through untying his right boot and looked up at Ares.

Ares nodded and swept the threads of his tawny hair from his face as he sighed. "I should have gotten him out of there the second he arrived."

"I never should have included him on the message. I wasn't thinking. I just wanted to get word out and get there to protect the gate." Marek offered Ares a tight smile when he looked as if he wanted to slap him on the shoulder, something that had become a habit when they had been in the Underworld, but would probably set Marek's shirt on fire if he did it now. He peered past his older brother. "Is Keras here?"

The grim face Ares pulled answered that question for him.

"Still annoyed with me?" Marek was growing tired of the cold shoulder treatment.

"I think he's cooling down at last. Just run away if she visits again, okay? You're not the only one who has to deal with him." Ares huffed, turned away and strode into the mansion.

"Not like I ask her to visit," Marek muttered.

"Don't envy you." Daimon grinned as he passed, flashing straight white teeth.

Marek used his powers to lift one of the pebbles from the carefully manicured front garden of the mansion and beaned Daimon in the back of the head with it. Daimon glared over his shoulder at him and then smiled again. Maybe next time Enyo visited, he would step to Daimon's house in Hong Kong.

That would wipe the smile off his brother's face.

The golden tatami mats that covered the floor of the expansive open-plan living area were rough beneath his feet as he entered the mansion, something he had always hated, but loved at the same time. It always felt good to return to the place they had once shared, before the world had begun developing at a rapid pace and his brothers had started finding places of their own.

Only Esher lived here now, his duty to protect the Tokyo gate and the city keeping him rooted in this mansion that their father had built with him in mind. Esher needed all the peace and tranquillity he could get. Surviving his time in the mortal world was difficult for him after everything he had been through at the hands of humans.

Which was why it was so strange to see him settled on one end of the cream couches that formed a semi-circle in the TV area to Marek's right.

With a human tucked in his arms.

Aiko sat on his lap, fussing over the few cuts her man had managed to pick up from somewhere, possibly from attempting to penetrate the illusion the female daemon had cast to weaken Marek.

He would have to thank his brother for that later.

He didn't want to think about what might have happened if Esher and the others had arrived any later than they had. The illusionist preferred to weaken her enemies with a vision from their past before attacking them, giving her the advantage as the illusion cloaked her from her victim's eyes.

He might not have been standing here if it wasn't for Esher.

Esher fussed over Aiko in return, paying attention to only her, and Marek could see the struggle in his blue eyes as he tried to regain control of himself and his thoughts, shutting out the ones that might prove a trigger and might awaken his other side.

The side that had been born in the bloody aftermath of what had happened to him centuries ago.

Marek hadn't been aware of it before the night Calindria had been murdered. Esher had gone off the rails when they had found her body, and the Underworld had suffered for it.

Valen slumped into the seat between Aiko's feet and Calistos, tipped his head back and sighed, causing his black T-shirt to stretch tight across his chest. He looped an arm around Calistos's neck, dragged him down and scrubbed a hand hard across the top of his head.

"Buck up." Valen wrestled with Cal as he fought him, trying to get free.

The two of them had resembled each other closely until recently, when Eva had dyed Valen's hair a neon shade of violet. The long bright strands hung over the left side of his face, leaving the right clear and revealing the puckered flesh that started low on his jaw and continued down his neck.

The place where his favour mark had been before Zeus had forcibly removed it from him.

Marek's own favour mark, the blessing of the goddess Gaia, warmed against his back in response to him thinking about it. He wasn't sure what he would do if he lost it. All of them valued their unique marks, and the favour of the god or goddess who had bestowed it upon them at birth.

Although he wasn't sure how much Keras valued his since Aphrodite had kissed his cheek as a babe and left a tiny black heart on it as his favour mark.

Marek had lost count of how many times people had said it made Keras look *girly*.

Mostly because Valen said it at least once a week to provoke a reaction from Keras.

Marek rounded the couch nearest the large flat-screen television that stood against the exterior wall of the house and sank onto it. Keras kept his profile to him, not even bothering to acknowledge him. Ares was wrong about him then. Keras was still angry with him.

Marek cursed both Keras and Enyo.

Keras needed to man up, grab hold of Enyo when she next visited, and tell her how he felt.

And then never let her go.

His thoughts leaped to the beautiful vampire slayer.

"Shit," he growled, gaining everyone's attention. He shrugged it off. "Just remembered something."

"About the enemy and the gate?" Valen stopped attempting to drill a hole in Calistos's head with his knuckles and both of them looked at him.

"Ah, no. I forgot something."

"Like the oven being on?" Calistos managed to extricate himself from Valen's grip and glared as he untied his blond hair, neatened it and tied it back again. "I forgot that once. Keras ripped me a new one."

Keras arched a black eyebrow at him.

"Yeah, go ahead and pretend I didn't get a lecture on the dangers of leaving the oven on." Cal's blue eyes glittered at their older brother.

The two were always a sharp contrast to each other. While Keras preferred to keep his black hair clipped short and neat, and wore impeccably pressed slacks and dress shirts with his fine Italian leather shoes, Calistos wore his hair long and paired form-fitting T-shirts, some of which had seen better days, with combat trousers and heavy scuffed leather boots. Keras had a refined air. Calistos was as wild and tempestuous as the wind he controlled.

Youngest and oldest.

The playful versus the most serious.

Marek was one hundred and ten percent certain that Keras was just a clone of their father. Same ridiculously good looks, refined air and haughty attitude. Both of them seemed to think the world should bow at their feet.

Not that he was going to let either of them know he thought that about them.

Keras would rip *him* a new one.

"We are not here to discuss the time you cremated dinner." Keras twisted the silver ring on his right thumb, idly spinning it around with his fingers.

"I'll start," Marek said, mostly because he wanted this meeting over with as soon as possible, now he had remembered his date with the vampire slayer.

A vampire slayer who was liable to leave without him if he didn't show soon. His leg twitched and he pressed down on it, stopping it from jiggling as he thought about her hunting the vampires alone. She would be vulnerable. In danger.

She was probably in danger right that second.

He needed to go.

He needed to see that she had waited despite what she had said.

He slammed a lid on that need.

What he needed to do was his duty, and that meant finishing this meeting. He had never been one to shirk his duties, and he wasn't going to start now. He left that sort of thing to Valen, who excelled at it.

"I felt the gate calling." He flicked a glance at Calistos to check on him. His younger brother's blue eyes were calm so Marek continued, although he would keep an eye on him to make sure he wasn't going to cause another episode. "I sent the message and then I stepped. I surveyed the area from a distance, and saw nothing unusual."

"Because of the illusionist. The whole area was probably already an illusion of the real thing at that point." Esher petted Aiko, brushing his fingers through her hair as she settled against him, resting her head on his shoulder.

"It would explain why the olive tree distorted when I stepped closer to the gate for a better look." Marek frowned as a thousand questions formed in his head, and wanted to growl when he realised that he could probably only get answers to around three of them. If that. "Can this illusion affect senses, like smell? I should have been able to smell all of those daemons."

He should have been able to sense them. Daemons caused a disturbing feeling in his gut, a swirling sensation that alerted him to their presence together with the coppery odour of them.

Esher nodded. "It's not so much the world she's affecting but your perception. That's how I see it."

"So she can strip us of our senses. That sounds like a bundle of fun." Valen snorted and then grinned, his golden eyes brightening dangerously. "I want a shot at her next time. Reckon a little lightning up her arse will stop her from casting illusions."

"Someone had to protect the European gates." Keras's tone didn't brook any arguments. It never did.

Valen looked at Esher. "Swapsies next time? Come on... please? Think of it as an early birthday present."

Esher flatly said, "No."

Attempting to get Esher to surrender a chance at getting his hands on the illusionist was like attempting to get his brother to go out and get chatty with the mortals. It was pointless, because it wasn't going to happen.

"I'll take gate duties next time. You can have your shot at her but you'll owe me." Daimon's pale blue eyes glittered like ice as he smiled in a way that said the favour Valen would owe him would be big.

"But then it's not a birthday present."

"Focus." Keras said the word calmly, his tone level, but he might as well have shouted it.

Everyone fell silent and looked at each other like kids who had just been told off by their father rather than men who had just been issued an order by their leader.

Ares came up to stand behind Keras, backing him up. "Get on with it."

The fiery edge to his brown eyes said he wanted to hurry things along for the same reason Marek did. He wanted to see his woman.

"So how did the gate call me?" Marek looked at each of his brothers in turn. "They were daemons at the gate... A gate that is closed to traffic. It shouldn't have called to me. It should have remained dormant."

Valen scuffed a hand over his violet hair, pushing the longer lengths back before he stroked the roughly chopped short sides. "The gate in Rome did something similar once and I was ambushed by daemons."

"And you are just mentioning this now?" Keras levelled him with a look that was almost a glare.

As close as Keras came to one.

Valen shrugged. "Didn't seem like much at the time. I fought the daemons and figured the Hellspawn who had been waiting for it had been scared off by them or maybe got bored waiting on the other side and left."

It was a reasonable explanation for what had happened in Rome, where the gate was used regularly.

But it didn't explain what had happened to the twin gate tonight.

Daimon said what all of them were thinking, but none of them wanted to ask.

"Is there a chance there's more than only daemons in our enemy's ranks?"

Marek really didn't want to consider that.

"Anything is possible." Keras spun the ring faster around his thumb, the action giving away his agitation even when his carefully schooled features and placid emerald eyes hid it. "Everyone is to report any unusual gate activity to me and Marek for study. Any incidents where the gate called and no one was waiting for you on either side when you got there. We need to know what we are dealing with, because there is a very real possibility we are dealing with more than daemons."

A shiver rolled down Marek's spine at the prospect.

Who in the Hellspawn world would turn against him and his brothers—and Hades?

What if it wasn't only Hellspawn involved?

He looked at his brothers and their grave expressions revealed their thoughts were traversing the same unsettling paths his were.

What if this went higher?

He only had to look at the history of his world to see there were a thousand grudges in play, and hundreds of people who might want to unseat Hades from his throne. Two attempts to do such a thing had happened in the past, the last one resulting in daemons being banished from the Underworld.

What if whoever was behind that uprising had been biding their time, waiting for this moment to strike and make another attempt?

"I'll hit the books and see what connections I can make," he said and Keras finally acknowledged his existence, nodding his head in Marek's direction. "I'll try to come up with a list of people who might possibly be involved."

And he was going to start with whatever few accounts of the last uprising in the Underworld existed in this world and in his library.

"We are on high alert. Be careful at the gates and be on your guard, especially you." Keras thawed a little as he looked at Marek, and Marek nodded, letting him know he would be careful.

The enemy wouldn't get the jump on him again.

"Call if anything happens in Seville, even something that seems ordinary like the main gate calling to you. Do not go there alone without backup. We need to face this threat together. We are at our strongest together." Keras reached across the gap between them and laid a hand on Marek's left shoulder.

Marek knew that, and was glad his brother did too. It was part of the reason he hated Keras being so cold and distant towards him. It weakened them.

They were strongest when they were a united force. They didn't need Enyo driving a wedge between them, not right now, not when there was so much at stake. They needed to remain united, not divided, and that meant Keras needed to keep his head.

He wasn't sure his brother could manage that where Enyo was concerned though.

She provoked his darker side, the possessive nature that ran as deeply in Keras's veins as it did in Marek's.

A possessive side that had Marek stepping to the front porch, jamming his feet into his boots and teleporting again.

Only it wasn't Seville that was his destination.

He landed in a shadowy alley near the square where the vampire slayer had asked him to meet her.

Hoping like hell she would be waiting for him.

CHAPTER 7

To say Caterina was annoyed was an understatement. She was fuming. She should have known better than to think the first man she had been attracted to in close to a decade would turn out to be punctual, respectful of her and her time, or interested enough in her to show up at all.

She should have left when she had said she would, but she had foolishly remained, wasting a further two hours in the hope the warrior would keep his word and join her on the hunt for the remaining vampires.

Had he gone without her?

She jammed her hands into the pockets of her leather jacket as she navigated the narrow alleys and swore under her breath, because if he had, she would never forgive him, not even if he apologised a thousand times over. She didn't need anyone protecting her. She never had.

When the police had started eyeing her where she had been waiting in the square for close to three hours, she had decided to call it. The warrior was a no-show.

It wasn't going to stop her.

She didn't know locations of possible vampire nests in the city as he proclaimed he did, but she knew where a vampire nest had been, and she might be able to get some information from it, possible clues as to other nest locations.

She followed the alleys into the gothic quarter, feet unerringly carrying her back to the building where she had slain four vampires last night. The warrior wasn't the only one who knew this city. She could have found her way to the old nest blindfolded.

Caterina checked the wider avenue when she reached the arched wooden door of the nest, scouting in both directions to make sure she was alone.

Satisfied that she was, she pushed the heavy door open and slipped inside, moving quietly in case any vampires had returned. She drew the blade from beneath her jacket and silently eased through the shadows towards the courtyard.

The vampires from last night were little more than ash swirling in the light breeze now, their dust spread around the worn flagstones.

She paused at the edge of the shadows and listened. Distant voices and the sounds of traffic on one of the main arteries were the only noises that reached her. She edged into the courtyard and checked all around it, her breath lodged in her throat as she checked every shadowy alcove beneath the walkway that ran around all four sides of it, columns and arches supporting the floors above. She kept her back to the wall and moved right, following that walkway around, listening the whole time. When she heard nothing other than the noises of the city, she moved forwards along the wall opposite the arched entrance, heading towards the corridor the vampire had emerged from last night.

As she neared it, the start of a set of steps became visible in the gloom. She swiftly closed the distance between her and them, and followed them upwards to the first level of the building. It was quiet, only the sound of her breathing breaking the silence as she took in the peeling crimson painted walls and the scant threadbare furniture.

She had seen more luxurious nests in her time.

This one looked as if someone had thrown it together in a hurry, forgoing luxury for the sake of having a modicum of comfort. A recent nest? Or perhaps these vampires had been young and poor, a new group that lacked the funds of their more established counterparts.

There was money in murder.

She had seen vampire nests filled with trinkets made of purest gold, sumptuous fabrics and expensive art and technology. She supposed that the dead had no need of money or whatever had been on their person, or in their house, when the vampire had killed them.

Caterina moved through the drawing room, heading for the next one. This one was in a better state, the eggshell-blue walls freshly painted where bookcases didn't line them. A desk stood to her right, with its back to the windows that overlooked the courtyard.

She hurried over to it, set her sword down on the worn mahogany top and rifled through the papers scattered across it, setting aside any she found interesting.

The air to her left shifted.

Caterina grabbed her blade from the desk and lashed out with her weak hand, panic lancing her as her heart rate jacked up and her mind screamed that a vampire had caught her off guard, something she had sworn would never happen.

The tip of her blade settled against the throat of the man towering over her.

His right eyebrow arched as his earthy eyes slid down to her sword, the flecks of gold and emerald emerging in them as he stared at it and then at her. He casually edged her blade away from his throat.

"Fast reactions you have there." His deep voice rolled over her, warming her despite her effort to remain unaffected by him.

Cold towards him.

She ignored him, set her sword down on the desk and continued her work, clinging to her mood as she found several interesting receipts but not much else. Apparently, the nest had placed a few orders for better furniture before she had killed some of them and sent the rest running. It looked as if they had been settling in for the long haul. Which wasn't in her favour at all.

She had been hoping this would be a satellite nest of a larger group of vampires, ones she had dealt with before, but it was looking more and more like a new group, recently formed, which meant the chances of finding them at any of the two locations of previous vampire nests she knew in Barcelona was slim to none.

"I am sorry." He moved around to the opposite side of the desk, into her line of sight.

She kept her focus on the papers, shifting another pile aside, refusing to give up even when she knew it was pointless. She wasn't going to find any information here.

The information she needed was in the head of the dark-haired man opposite her, the one who obviously wanted to get her attention as he leaned over and planted his large hands on the edge of the desk.

"Something came up."

She shrugged stiffly, trying to let those words roll off her. They sank into her instead, softening the sharp edge off her mood and threatening to make her lose her grip on it. He had stood her up. She had waited three damned hours for him, longer than she had ever waited for a man before.

"How long have you been here?"

Caterina shoved a pile of papers at him, forcing him to remove one hand from the desk.

He rose to his full height and sighed, the weary edge to it making her feel like a bitch. She was the one who had been put out, left like an idiot for all to see as they came and went from the square. She had tried to remain visible to make things easy on him, given how busy the square always was, had picked a spot beneath one of the towering palm trees that dotted it, close to the circular fountain in the centre. She had remained visible all right.

Several couples had eyed her on the way into the stunning rectangular square and on the way out again after they'd had a nice meal at one of the many restaurants that spilled into it. A few of them had looked at her with pity.

"I am sorry," he said again, softer this time and in Catalan, his voice warming her right down to her marrow.

He wasn't going to curry favour with her by speaking her native tongue rather than Spanish or English.

She grabbed her sword and sheathed it. "There's nothing here. I should have looked somewhere else. I'm just wasting my time in this place."

"I'm glad you looked here."

She lifted her gaze to him and frowned as she spotted a cut darting across the straight line of his jaw, visible through the fine layer of stubble. "Why?"

He smiled, one that warmed his eyes and curled lips made for kissing, turning his rough masculine features more handsome. "Because I found you."

She peered deeper into his eyes and saw the relief there. Had he been worried when he had reached the square to find her gone? It struck her that part of her had been worried she would never see him again. The part she tried to tamp down as she kept a fragile grip on her mood.

"You would have easily found me, if you had been on time." She moved around the desk, heading for the exit to her left.

He grabbed her arm before she made it more than five steps and spun her to face him. His eyes searched hers, intense and focused, sending a hot shiver through her as he palmed her elbow and drew her closer, until the heat of his body embraced her and she was aware of how tall he was, how strong he was.

How handsome he was.

"I meant to be on time," he husked, his gaze straying to her lips. "I really did. I have other duties, things I have to do."

"Things that take priority over hunting vampires?" She kept her gaze locked on his eyes as they brightened in that eerie way, gold and emerald flakes shining against the dark backdrop of his irises, refusing to look at his mouth because she was afraid of what she would do if she did.

The urge to kiss him was already strong, pounding as fiercely in her veins as it had last night when he had been this close to her.

He nodded. "If my brothers knew I hunted vampires, I would be in serious trouble."

Brothers. She filed that information away and seized her chance to learn more about him.

"They're like you?"

Another dip of his chin.

"And you fight what exactly?" When he glanced at her, a frown marring his brow, she added, "Your duty isn't hunting vampires, so what do you fight? It's obvious you're some sort of warrior."

"Warrior?" he chuckled and heat curled through her again as the rich timbre of it hit her hard. "I suppose we are warriors, with a vow to defend our home, but not from vampires. Vampires are your sworn enemy. Daemons are mine."

Daemons. She filed that away too, her curiosity growing as she wondered what other species existed in his shadowy world.

"Like with horns, and wings, and pointy tails?" A thousand images popped into her head, all of them very biblical interpretations of the creatures.

She had her upbringing to thank for that.

While she always wore a silver cross around her neck, it was more of a deterrent to vampires rather than a symbol of faith these days. She had witnessed too much darkness in this world to believe there was any light to balance it.

"Some of them have those things. What you would think of as a traditional demonic being. Others are different. Most appear human. It doesn't matter to me. If they have daemon blood, I kill them."

She narrowed her eyes on him. "Why are you telling me all of this?"

He grinned, a devastating one that blasted the last remnants of her anger with him into oblivion. "Because you already know about my world, so it seems pointless to lie to you, but more than that… because I am trying to make you like me again."

She shook her head at that. "Answer one question for me—no two."

He turned with her, ushering her towards the door. "While we move. I have a place in mind that I would like to check out."

She could go along with that.

She let him lead her from the building and paused on the street outside it as another question came to her, one she couldn't stop herself from voicing.

"You can teleport, can't you?"

He looked back at her and didn't hesitate to nod. "Among other things. Why, do you want a lift?"

A lift? He was offering to teleport her? She recalled the black ribbons of smoke that had swirled around him, making him look as if the darkness itself had devoured him in that instant he had teleported.

She shook her head. "I like my feet firmly on the ground, thank you."

He chuckled again and started along the street towards the Carrer del Bisbe. "You might change your mind when you realise how far it is to the vampire nest."

She hurried to keep up with him. His long legs made easy work of the distance, and although she was tall for a woman at five-nine, she struggled to remain beside him. The length of his stride and his pace meant one of two things.

Either he was in a hurry.

Or he didn't walk with women very often.

"And you're two hundred years old?" She let that one slip out casually, hoping he would laugh or something and reveal he had been joking about his age.

"Plus six hundred and fifty-six." His lips pursed as his eyebrows dipped low. "Bordering on fifty-seven."

Caterina's eyes widened. "*Déu!*"

He slid her a look. "I'm not that old. Three of my brothers are older."

Since when had eight hundred and fifty-six-going-on-seven not been old?

She felt like little more than a child at pushing thirty.

"I don't want to know." She waved him away when he looked as if he might tell her how old his brothers were.

"Were those your two questions?" He cast her another glance as they reached the main tourist route and he guided her right, towards the square at the other end where the elegant government buildings stood.

"No." She navigated her way around the groups of tourists blocking the narrow, cobbled pedestrian street, all of them snapping pictures of the sandstone covered walkway that formed a bridge between two buildings on either side of the Carrer del Bisbe.

The warrior took the other side, not bothering to ease around the crowd. He moved straight towards it and several of the tourists took one look at him and pulled their friends or family members aside to give him room to pass.

She wished she commanded that sort of respect.

It probably came with age.

Or possibly the fact he was six-foot-four of pure muscle squeezed into tight fatigues and a dark linen shirt that hugged his well-defined chest and arms.

"Fine. More questions, but first answer one for me." He joined her again on the other side of the crowd and she wanted to curse him when he picked up the pace again.

She hated crowds, but at least they had been slowing him down.

"What do you want to know?" She refused to chase after him as she took hold of the front of her black tank top and moved it back and forth, fanning herself as the stifling heat started getting to her.

Or maybe it was the warrior cranking up her temperature to an unbearable degree.

She watched as the distance between them grew as he hit the downward slope towards the square.

He looked to his left, where she would have been if she had been practically jogging to keep up with him, a frown crinkled his brow and he peered back along the street.

Caterina kept her pace reasonable, a level she could manage without becoming out of breath and sweating in a very unladylike fashion.

"I was walking too fast." Irritation flashed in his eyes and he smiled tightly. "I am sorry. I'm not used to walking, let alone having female company."

Another piece of information she filed away.

"If you want me to answer questions, I need to be able to speak." She reached him and he fell into step beside her for a change, his gaze on his boots and hers until he had her pace mastered.

He lifted his head, brushed a rogue wave from his forehead and tucked his hands into his pockets.

When he didn't speak, she said, "You wanted to know something?"

His eyes met hers. "What is your name?"

She stopped and held her hand out to him. "Caterina. I won't burden you with all my names, because it would probably take all night, but you can call me Caterina."

"Marek." He slipped his hand into hers, and the second they touched, lightning arced up her arm and heat bloomed in its wake, spreading through her as his large hand engulfed hers.

His grip was strong, but gentle. Firm, but light. As if he was afraid of hurting her, but he needed to feel the connection between them. She lowered her gaze to their joined hands and stared at them, marvelling at how something as simple as holding his hand could affect her so deeply, had her falling all over again, deeply aware of how attracted to him she was.

Her gaze drifted over his wrist and the thin, braided black band that encircled it, up the corded muscles of his forearm, to the rolled-up sleeve of his dark shirt. She let her eyes roam over his biceps, his broad shoulders, up to his neck.

There was a small red line where her sword had made contact before he had stopped it, barely a nick but it made her gut squirm and her eyes got stuck on it, even though she wanted to look at the rough, masculine perfection of his face and see how he was looking at her.

She wanted to know if that fire was in his eyes again, that hunger that echoed inside her too.

"Marek?" she whispered, a little breathless.

"Hmm?" He sounded as lost as she felt.

"I'm sorry I cut you."

His head turned, bringing the line of his jaw into view and then his bottom lip. He brought his free hand up, swept his thumb across the small cut, and brought it to his lips. Her heart pounded as she tracked it with her gaze, as she watched his lips part and his tongue swipe at the pad of his thumb.

"It's nothing. Don't worry about it." His soft chuckle heated her further. "You're the first person to surprise me like that in a long time... although maybe not a long time. Twice in a night. Must be losing my touch."

Who else had been able to attack him before he could defend himself tonight? The business he'd had to deal with before he had come to meet her? She wanted to ask, but held her tongue, because his irises had changed again, the colours growing muted as they verged on black.

And instinct told her that wasn't a good sign.

She slipped her hand free of his and started walking again, missing the heat of his touch as she thought about all the things she wanted to ask him.

"Why do you hunt vampires?" Marek fell into step beside her again and ushered her down another side street, towards a less touristy area of the quarter.

She studied the sculpture of a tower that looked as if it had been made with enormous chicken wire as they passed through another square, mulling over how to answer that question without mentioning her brother. She had the feeling Marek liked killing vampires, and that he wouldn't distinguish a good one from the rest.

And her brother was good.

As far as she knew, he had never bitten anyone since his turning. At first because she had begged him to refrain, and later because his fangs never seemed to work whenever the urge to feed became too strong to resist. That dysfunction had been a blessing in her eyes when he had first revealed it to her, something to grant her more time to find a cure for him. Now, there was a secret part of her that wished he could feed, because he was wasting away before her eyes.

"Personal reasons, to do with my family. I don't like to talk about it." She hoped he would let her leave it at that. She glanced across at him to gauge how he had taken it, and caught him frowning at the pavement ahead of them, his expression pensive and dark eyes narrowed. "Why do you hunt vampires?"

"Personal reasons." His tone gained a cold edge as his frown deepened and she regretted asking when his eyes blackened and she knew it wasn't the streetlights stealing the colours from them.

They walked in silence for what felt like forever as she struggled to find a way to voice the question she needed answering the most. Fear held her tongue more than once. Not fear that he would piece together that her personal reasons regarding her family were because one of them was a vampire, but because she feared what his answer would be.

When they reached a main artery, a busy multi-lane avenue with a tree-lined pedestrian walkway running along the centre of it, she mustered enough courage and steeled her heart.

"Marek?" she murmured, fear stealing strength from her voice. When he looked at her, she pressed on, not daring to hesitate because she knew she would lose her nerve. "I've done a lot of research in the time I've been hunting vampires, but there's something I've never been able to discover."

"What's that?" His step slowed and she slowed with him, could almost sense his curiosity as he studied her as she diligently kept her profile to him, her eyes on the next crossing on the avenue.

"Can a human who has been turned into a vampire be turned back into a human?"

She swallowed hard as she waited, heart rushing, nerves rising.

Marek tipped his head back and gazed at the trees. The silence between them stretched, tugging at her fears, giving them a stronger hold over her, and she was desperate for him to speak by the time he finally did.

"Maybe."

That wasn't much of an answer. Relief bloomed because it wasn't a definite no, but fear remained because it wasn't a definite yes.

"You've never met a vampire who had been turned and ended up becoming human again?"

His dark eyes slid down to meet hers and the coldness in them sent a shiver through her. "I've never met a vampire I haven't killed. Not in the last few hundred years anyway."

She frowned at him as something hit her. "That sounds an awful lot like a vendetta to me."

He shrugged his broad shoulders. "Call it whatever you want. The vermin deserve to die. I won't rest until every last one of them has been wiped from this realm."

Another shudder wracked her and she wanted to take a step back from him, wanted to turn and leave right that moment, because she could see in his eyes that he meant what he had said.

He wanted to kill every vampire he came across, because he despised them. Something had happened to him, something that had triggered a terrible need to hunt vampires, powerful enough that it demanded the death of every vampire in existence.

Or in this realm.

Her eyebrows knitted hard as she thought about that.

Strange choice of words.

He started walking again.

"This realm?" she asked as she looked at his back.

It tensed as he ground to a halt.

"Caterina," he murmured, voice low, the sound of her name spoken by him sending a devastating rush of heat through her that had her almost missing what he said next. "Some things about me and this world you're better off not knowing."

"No. It's too late for that sort of talk." She stormed towards him, refusing to let him get his way. "I never asked to be part of this secret world, but I'm part of it now, and the more I know about it, the better my chances of survival... So, I'm sorry. I need you to explain."

He looked across at her and she thought he would refuse to answer, but then the hardness in his eyes softened and he sighed as he lifted his hand and brushed a strand of her hair from her face, his touch light.

Almost tender.

"Fine," he husked. "But I'm only going to tell you this because you are right and there is a chance being armed with this information might increase your chances of survival."

And he wanted her to survive.

It was right there in his eyes as those mesmerising flecks of gold and emerald emerged.

As he swept his knuckles across her cheek in a soft caress.

"There are three realms. This one—"

She cut him off as her eyes widened. "Heaven and Hell. *Déu.* They're real."

He shook his head.

"They're not real?"

His expression grew guarded. "Maybe. I don't know. Realms overlap."

"Just how many realms are there? You said there were three." Were there more? Were Heaven and Hell real?

He shrugged. "I only have access to the realms of my world, but I know others exist. Valen, one of my brothers, is always proving that in Rome and Esher has trouble with the native gods in Japan."

Her head felt as if it was going to explode. Just how many realms was he talking about? And he was talking about gods as if they were real. Either he was delusional, or he was telling the truth.

She studied him. He had been honest with her so far, hadn't hidden anything because he wanted her to like him again. Which made her suspect that every crazy-sounding thing leaving his lips was, in fact, real.

"So which realms are the ones you were talking about."

That guarded edge to his expression returned and he looked closely at her, as if expecting her to faint or swear, or react negatively to what he was going to say.

"Olympus and the Underworld."

Caterina opted for swearing.

CHAPTER 8

Caterina was still having a hard time coming to terms with the fact that Mount Olympus and the Underworld apparently existed. Not only those two realms. As they had continued their walk, Marek had mentioned how the Roman pantheon of gods didn't get along with his brother Valen, and that his older brother who lived in Tokyo had a hard time convincing the local gods, tengu and oni that he didn't mean any affront by living on their land.

She had fallen silent after that, lost in thought as she tried to compute everything Marek had told her and make herself believe it. She was almost certain that he was telling her the truth about the worlds he walked in, it was just difficult to wrap her head around the idea that the shadowy world of vampires she had finally grown used to extended far beyond what she had thought possible.

Yesterday, vampires had been the biggest of her worries. Now, she knew about daemons, and apparently demigods and gods were real too, among other things. The history books were coming to life around her and she couldn't stop thinking about how many creatures of myth might be out there, as real as she was.

Marek paused at a crossing and checked the road before continuing onwards.

"Where do you fit into it all?" She tried to keep her focus on the quiet streets around them, and not only for vampires. This area of her city wasn't the best one, and although she could handle herself, it still paid to be cautious, especially so late at night.

Discomfort settled across his features. "That is probably a conversation for another night. We're close now. We should move with stealth."

He was changing the subject because he didn't want to tell her. Because she would find it as shocking as realising multiple realms she had thought were a myth actually existed?

Or *more* shocking?

The thought that she might find it more shocking made her want to press him for an answer, but he suddenly snatched her arm and pulled her behind a building. He pressed his hand to her stomach, pinning her back against the wall to his left, and leaned right to peer around the corner.

Caterina kept still, focusing on her breathing to keep it level and quiet as she listened. If frightening her was his way of stopping her from pressing him for answers, she was going to kill him.

Voices sounded, distant and male. She couldn't make out what they were saying, but their accent was local.

Marek looked at her and pressed the index finger of his free hand to his lips.

She nodded and waited, becoming increasingly aware of his hand on her stomach, how the heat of it seeped through her tank and stirred a wicked sort of fire in her veins. He leaned away again and she eased forwards, wanting to see what he was looking at. His hand pressed more heavily against her stomach, keeping her from moving, and he looked at her.

Looked down at his hand on her stomach.

Swallowed as he splayed his fingers, shifting the black material of her tank.

The flecks of gold in his eyes brightened.

He snatched his hand away from her and busied himself with checking his waistband.

And cursing like a sailor for some reason.

He twisted towards her and had her caged against the wall before she could blink, his hands pressing against it on either side of her head as his body hemmed her in.

He lowered his mouth to her ear and his warm breath sent a shiver through her as it caressed her skin. "Wait here."

He disappeared and she jumped, the suddenness of it startling her as she went from the delicious heat of his body to the cold touch of black tendrils of smoke. She swiped at them and moved to her left, placing some distance between her and the disturbing ribbons. They seemed to reach for her, and she hoped to God it was because she had moved, creating a shift in the air, and not because they were actually reaching for her.

Marek suddenly reappeared, right in the spot where he had been.

He frowned at the empty wall and then across at her as he whispered, "I told you not to move."

"No," she hissed low so the men didn't hear her. "You told me to wait here. I am here. I am not there because of *those*."

She waved her right index finger up and down, gesturing to the creepy black smoke that drifted around him, the tendrils of it curling around his arms and caressing his neck like a lover.

He looked as if he wanted to laugh. "It's harmless."

He brushed his right hand through one section of the smoke and held it out to her.

"See."

What she saw was the fact it seemed to writhe like a living thing in his palm, twining around his outstretched thumb as if it didn't want to leave him.

He sighed. "It's just the lingering effect of the teleport."

She shook her head, not interested in getting closer to it and not believing him. There was something sinister about that smoke. Something that set her on edge.

He shrugged, twirled the sheathed curved knife he held in his left hand and jammed it in the back of his combat trousers.

"That's what you went somewhere for?" She jerked her chin to the knife. "I have one you could have borrowed."

When she flashed the blade she kept in the inside of her jacket, he was the one who shook his head.

"Only this blade. I swore that a long time ago." He moved before she could ask who he had sworn it to and why. The more she knew about him, the more questions she had, and the deeper she fell into a dark rabbit hole.

Only unlike Alice, she wasn't falling into any Wonderland.

It was more of a world filled with nightmares.

Vampires. Daemons. Gods and goddesses. And who knew how many other wild and terrifying things lived in it.

She hung back as Marek stalked forwards, striding with purpose towards where the men had been and were now gone.

How wild and terrifying was he?

On a scale of one to ten, she could probably handle him turning out to be somewhere in the six to seven bracket. He clearly wasn't a daemon, judging by how harshly he spoke of them, and he obviously wasn't a vampire. Maybe he was just a daemon hunter. Or a form of immortal warrior.

He scowled over his shoulder at her.

Caterina hurried to him, eyes scanning as she closed the distance between them, checking every dark corner for a sign of the vampires.

Marek nodded towards a building at an intersection ahead of them, an apartment block that had seen better days. Independence flags hung from some of the balconies, but all of the plants on them were long dead. There were lights in the windows near the top floor.

"Sorry about this." He looked up at the illuminated floor, his noble profile to her. "It's either this or leaving you here."

Caterina didn't get a chance to ask him what he was talking about.

He snaked his arm out, curled it around her waist and hauled her up against him, and she grabbed hold of him with both hands as darkness whirled around her and the world spun into shadows. Cold slithered over her and she shuddered as she blinked in the inky black, desperate to see something as her senses were suddenly stolen from her.

There was only black. Only silence.

Only numbing ice.

And then there was light and voices, and the warmth of Marek's body pressing against hers.

Her head spun, twisting the world around her into a blur of colours, and the noises swam in her ears as her legs weakened beneath her, and bile rose up her throat.

"You'll feel better in a moment." Marek released her and something hissed.

A vampire?

Caterina slumped to her knees on the floor and gripped the tacky carpet, desperately clinging to it as if it would anchor her and stop the room from spinning.

"Needed the element of surprise." Marek's voice rang in her ears and then there was a grunt and another vicious hiss, and someone growled.

The light flickered as glass smashed, dimming and making everything more bearable. The spinning in her head started to slow, things coming gradually into focus, forming four black shapes.

Marek was one of them. She blinked and could make him out more clearly. He remained in front of her, blocking the path of the three male vampires as they swiped at him with their claws, all of them baring their fangs, their eyes vivid crimson.

The one to her right looked beyond her, taking his eyes off Marek for only a second.

Caterina looked behind her. The door there had locks on it. The only exit?

Marek had managed to teleport her into their nest and block the exit at the same time.

She would have been impressed if she hadn't wanted to vomit so badly.

She swallowed hard, trying to keep it down and keep it together, and exhaled hard. Marek glanced over his shoulder at her.

The vampire to his left sprang at him.

"Marek!" she screamed.

He was gone in a flash and the vampire stumbled through the black smoke he left behind. His red eyes narrowed, a frustrated snarl pealing from his lips as he realised Marek was gone, and then he looked down at her where she sat on the dirty grey carpet.

And grinned.

"Not so fast." Marek appeared behind him and thrust his knife into the vampire's side, spilling blood down his black jeans.

The vampire shrieked and tore away from him, ripping the wound open, so the flow of crimson became a waterfall that rapidly drenched the carpet and crept towards her.

The other two vampires attacked at once.

Caterina pulled herself together, and tore her leather jacket off as she shot to her feet. She reached around behind her, drew her blade and swept below the arm of the first vampire as he lashed out at her.

Leaving himself wide open.

She tried to land a blow on him, but the second vampire spotted her before she could get close. He kicked at her arm and she cried out as his boot connected, sending fire zinging along her bones.

Marek loosed an unholy growl and grabbed her by the strap of her sword sheath, and pulled her backwards as the black-haired vampire struck again. His boot shot through the air where her face had been. Marek twisted her around him, so her back was to his, and brought his hand around in a vicious arc, his silver knife a blur as it sliced through the air.

The black-haired vampire leaped backwards on a hiss, clearing the length of the room.

Marek's dark gaze swept around the room and he frowned at the same time as she did. This room was far too cluttered for a fight, the over-large sofa and coffee table getting in the way, giving the vampires objects they could hide behind to slow her and Marek down.

She had to clear some space.

Whether she could do that without losing her neck, or a pint of blood to the vampires, was another matter.

Marek tossed his knife to his left hand and swept his right one out before her, his palm facing the sofa and table. The large dark red sofa shot backwards, towards the mousy-haired vampire who had moved behind it for cover. He leaped over it, barely avoiding being pinned against the wall by it and landing with one booted foot on it before he gingerly sprang from it and towards her.

The coffee table suddenly shot up between her and the vampire and he ploughed into it. She flinched away, expecting both of them to hit her, curling into a protective position as she waited for the collision and the inevitable pain.

It didn't come.

Instead of hitting her, the vampire and the table flew backwards, slamming into the wall above the couch.

Marek muttered, "Breaking my own damned rules here."

He tossed his blade back to his right hand and glared at both of the vampires. The mousy one gathered himself, snarling as he tossed the wooden table aside and dropped down from the sofa. He wiped blood from his nose, his eyes fixed on her the entire time, as if it was her fault the furniture had suddenly attacked him.

Maybe it was.

Marek had somehow hurled the coffee table at the vampire to keep him away from her, something which had apparently broken the rules of engagement. She wasn't sure the vampires were aware of these rules as the black-haired one picked up a lamp and hurled it right at her, as if testing a theory.

Her warrior caught it and hurled it right back at him with enough force to leave a dent in the plaster when the vampire dodged it and it careened into the wall.

The vampire's slow grin said it all.

She was Marek's weakness.

They were going to attack her to provoke him, forcing him to lose his cool so he would make a mistake.

It wasn't going to happen. She was no damsel in distress. She didn't need Marek to protect her. She could handle herself.

She stepped up beside him, readied her blade and stared down the mousy-haired vampire as he edged around the room, heading towards the windows to her right, manoeuvring her between him and Marek.

No.

She realised that wasn't his intent as he leaned down to reach behind a worn armchair and metal dragged against the skirting board.

He straightened, revealing a length of solid steel pipe gripped in his right hand.

Caterina drew down a fortifying breath. Her sword was strong, but she wasn't sure it would stand up to the strength of a vampire combined with a thick length of steel.

Marek huffed.

She risked a glance in his direction, looked beyond him to the other vampire where he stood in the door to the next room, a huge kitchen knife in his hand.

"Hardly going to level the playing field." Marek twirled his blade, dark menace written in every line of his face as he braced his feet shoulder-width apart and hunkered down.

The black-haired vampire rolled his neck and eased his shoulders back. The one closest to her grinned and weighed his weapon. Marek might still like the odds, but she didn't.

They only got worse when the door behind them opened and another vampire walked in.

Froze as she took in the scene.

Launched at Marek on a vicious hiss.

He pivoted so his back was to Caterina's and slammed his fist into the female's chest as she flew through the air. Bone crunched, the sound twisting Caterina's stomach, and the female cried out as she fell backwards, hitting the floor in a sprawl near the door.

"Estel, run!" The black-haired vampire threw himself at Marek, swiping wildly with the blade he brandished, keeping Marek busy as the woman tried to pull herself onto her feet.

Estel clutched her chest and wheezed, staggered onto her feet and shook her head as she looked at the male, her eyebrows furrowing as fear flooded her crimson eyes.

He growled in response to that, the pain in it catching Caterina off guard.

They were lovers.

Hesitation beat through her for the first time ever when she had been fighting vampires. She had battled them countless times, had watched them from the shadows, but never had she witnessed anything like this. She had seen males and females together, but it had never looked as if what they were doing was anything more than casual, a sating of primal needs.

The way Estel looked at the black-haired vampire as he battled Marek, keeping him busy, pure fear written across every line of her face, said that what she felt for him was more than a primal need. More than lust.

It was love.

Caterina gasped when Marek twisted on his heel, rammed his shoulder into the gut of the male vampire, lifting him off the ground and knocking the wind from him, and hurled his blade at Estel at the same time.

It nailed her in the shoulder, burying deep and ripping a scream from her as she went down.

"Estel!" The black-haired vampire grabbed Marek, sinking claws into him, ripping long gashes in his dark linen shirt as he fought to get free of Marek's grip.

Marek kicked off, launching forwards, and slammed the male's spine into the doorframe, tearing a grunt from him. The vampire tore a grunt of his own from Marek, bringing his right knee up hard into Marek's stomach as he finally got a good hold on him. He kneed Marek once, twice, and then a third time.

Estel ripped the blade from her shoulder and hurled herself towards Marek on a vicious cry.

All sympathy Caterina had felt for the woman and her lover instantly dissipated.

She leaped into the brunette's path and swept her sword around. It connected with Marek's knife and the vampire's hand. Estel grunted as the silver sliced into her and dropped Marek's knife.

The knife didn't hit the floor.

When it was close, it suddenly shot past Caterina, coming close to grazing the shin of her calf-height leather boots. A male bellowed behind her and Caterina's heart leaped into her throat.

Marek.

She shoved forwards with her sword, driving Estel back, giving herself space to breathe so she could check on Marek. She cast a frantic glance over her shoulder and relief poured through her when she saw he was fine.

The vampire hadn't fared so well.

As Marek stumbled back a step, revealing the male, Caterina grimaced. The hilt of the short blade protruded from underneath the vampire's chin. His red eyes were glazed, dulling rapidly as he slumped against the wall and began to slide down it.

Marek gripped his blade and pulled it free, filling the heavy silence with a wet sucking sound.

Estel screamed.

Caterina blocked her before she could throw herself at Marek, pinned her back to his and fought the female away, lashing at her with her sword. The woman snarled, fangs flashing and scarlet eyes glowing dangerously as she hunkered down.

The mousy-haired vampire stared at his fallen comrade, his eyes wide as the male began to disintegrate, and then turned on Marek and Caterina with a low, rumbling growl.

Marek moved with her as the male attacked, blocking the vampire's steel bar with either his knife or his hand. Caterina fell into the fight with him, all of her focus shifting to surviving as Estel pulled a knife from beneath her short violet jacket. The blade flashed as the vampire attacked, her movements so swift that Caterina struggled to keep up with her as she jabbed and slashed, thrust and withdrew.

Heat blazed across her biceps and the left side of her chest and then across her right forearm, and she bit back the cry that wanted to leave her lips as the scent of her blood filled the air and fear crept up on her.

Marek growled and twisted with her, swapping positions so she was facing the male instead. He glared at her, red eyes narrowing as she brought her sword up between them, daring him to make the first move.

The heat that burned in her cuts became a fire that blazed in her blood as she fought with Marek at her back. She had never had a partner before, had never thought she would have one, but it felt good to know he was there behind her, watching out for her. She liked how they worked in tandem with each other, as if they had been made to fight together as a unit.

It was exhilarating.

A little bit thrilling.

She blocked the vampire's steel bar and swept her sword out, keeping him on the backfoot and trying to drive him into a confined space so she could finish him. The sound of the fight happening behind her threatened to distract her, but she somehow managed to keep her focus on her own opponent.

The mousy-haired male suddenly sprang at her and she reared, her back plastering against the solid, powerful heat of Marek's. He turned slightly and brought his arm up as the vampire swung, blocking the bar with his forearm and taking a blow that would have hit her in the side of her head. The vampire's eyes widened as he realised what had happened and Caterina didn't hesitate. She gripped her sword with both hands and brought it up in a fast arc, putting all of her strength and speed into it so he wouldn't have time to dodge it.

The blade slashed up his chest, slicing clean through his shirt and his flesh beneath it, the cut deep enough that she saw bone as he reeled backwards on a pained hiss.

Estel cried out at the same time and a thud sounded, but Caterina didn't take her eyes off her vampire, trusting that Marek could handle the female.

Had handled the female judging by the noises that came from behind her, bubbling and fizzing that filled Caterina's mind with a blur of memories, all of them blending together into one disgusting stream of disintegrating vampires.

The male in front of her hit the deck, his knees colliding hard with the carpet, and stared down at his chest, at the gaping wound that spilled crimson as his flesh began to blister and burn. He started babbling in Catalan, desperate frightened words that tore at her.

Caterina closed her eyes and swept her blade out, tensed as it met with resistance and he fell silent.

She exhaled, releasing the breath she had been holding.

It was over.

The usual fear that gripped her after a battle didn't come this time.

Her pulse remained fast, her blood buzzing as she breathed, as she felt the heat of Marek behind her. He took her sword from her hand and sheathed it for her, and placed her jacket over her shoulders, sending a shiver racing up her arms as he gently caressed them and eased her back against his hard chest.

His delicious heat sank into her as he banded his arm around her stomach, kept the cold at bay as he teleported with her. The stifling warmth of a summer night surrounded her, a breeze buffeting her as it swept in from the sea, carrying the scent of saltwater to chase away the horrid stench of blood.

"Are you all right?" Marek eased her to face him and she slowly opened her eyes as the weird swirling sensation faded and she was confident she wasn't about to fall to her knees or vomit.

The heat of battle kept it at bay, burned inside her as fiercely as it burned in his eyes as he checked her over, the gold and emerald flecks in his brown irises blazing brightly in the low light rising from the streets below them.

Caterina stared up at him, transfixed, unable to take her eyes off him as he looked her over, as he inspected her wounds with a tender touch and concern in his gaze.

The fire burning inside her grew hotter, brighter, consuming her from the inside out as it filled her mind with wicked thoughts, with a need that rapidly became impossible to deny as the fact she had survived sank in.

She was alive.

She wanted to feel it.

Marek lifted his head, his eyes locking on hers.

His voice was low, a belly-heating purr as awareness dawned in his eyes. "Caterina."

She didn't give him a chance to voice whatever doubts were building inside him, whatever attempt he might make to stop this from happening.

She grabbed him by the nape of his neck, pulled him down and kissed him.

CHAPTER 9

This was just adrenaline. A crazy post-battle high that was too powerful to resist. Caterina kept telling herself that as she kissed Marek, as his warm lips met and mastered hers, sending a sharp thrill tumbling down her spine and spreading over her limbs.

He turned with her and pressed her against a wall on the dark roof of the oceanfront building, the low moan that rumbled in his chest as their bodies came into contact pulling a groan from her own lips.

His large hands claimed her waist, slid up to her ribs and tugged her closer to him. The desperate clash of his lips with hers, a frantic and choppy meeting and parting of their mouths, spoke to her, telling her that she wasn't alone. The same fierce, undeniable need poured through him too.

A need that left her feeling as if she might die if she didn't satisfy it soon, easing this consuming hunger to have him, to feel his lips on every inch of her flesh and fulfil the attraction that had burned inside her from the moment she had set eyes on him.

He pushed the jacket from her shoulders and skimmed his hands down her arms, another shiver chasing in the wake of his light touch. His tongue brushed her lower lip just as softly and she opened for him, moaned as he angled his head and their mouths fused. His left hand claimed her nape, tunnelled into her hair and pulled her head back. He kissed her deeper, claiming all of her, his kiss a drug she couldn't get enough of as she surrendered to him.

Caterina placed her hands on his arms, heart pounding at her first touch, at the feel of his corded biceps beneath her palms. They were rock hard, tensed as he pulled her flush against him and held her there, as if he wanted her to know his strength. She was already deeply aware of it, of how powerful he was, and it spoke to her on a primal level where she wasn't quite master, had her arousal ratcheting up another ten degrees, until it was unbearable and all she could think about was how badly she needed him.

He groaned and trembled as she stroked her hands upwards, over the bulge of his shoulders to his neck, and lightly stroked there, teasing the short hair at the nape before ploughing her fingers through the longer lengths at the back of his head. She pulled him harder against her and stole control of the kiss, something deep inside her driving her to push him to the very edge, to the point where he wouldn't be able to think, let alone resist her.

Because she needed this.

And no way in hell was she going to give him a chance to back down.

She swore he could read her mind as he plastered one hand to her shoulder and eased her back against the wall, as he dropped his other one to the waist of her jeans and glared at them, his face etched with concentration as he unfastened them. His rough breathing filled the silence, mingling with her own panted exhalations as she focused on what he was doing, as she waited for that first delicious brush of his fingers over her flesh.

He didn't make her wait long. He shoved her jeans down her legs, dropped to his knees before her and tore off her boots. She kicked her jeans off, as eager as he was as the need spiralling through her coiled in her belly, heating it and making her restless.

Marek lifted his head and stilled.

His eyes blazed in the gloom, on fire with a need she ached to satisfy as his gaze slowly lifted from her hips, drifting over her stomach and her breasts before finally meeting hers.

"Marek," she murmured, unsure what to say, but needing to say something to let him know she was right there with him, as maddened by lust as he was, on the verge of begging him to do something to ease it.

He shot to his feet so fast she gasped. He swallowed that gasp in a kiss as he cupped her cheeks, backing her against the wall and devouring her. Her hands shook as he dropped his to her hips and skimmed them over her bare skin, his touch feather-light, a stark contrast to the hardness and ferocity of his kiss.

She moaned as he palmed her backside and lifted her, a deeper groan following it as she wrapped her legs around his waist and it finally sunk in that they were going to do this. That itch she'd had for him since they had met was going to be scratched at last.

Part of her wanted to slow things down, wanted to take a moment to explore his body, to do something to make this moment of madness last longer. She couldn't slow her kiss though, couldn't stop herself from rocking against his caged erection. The solid steel of it between her thighs as he ground into her only made the fire burn hotter, a blistering inferno that turned all of her control to ashes.

Caterina gripped his shirt, twisting both sides of it into her fists, and pulled it apart, ripping a low moan from Marek as buttons flew everywhere, pinging away into the darkness. She planted her hands against his bare chest, groaned and shuddered as she met firm, hot skin dusted with hair, and found each of his pectorals larger than her hands could cover. Sweet hell.

She rocked against him, faster now as she explored his chest, as she dropped her hands lower to his stomach and the heat pooled and coiled lower in response to the feel of his abdominals beneath her questing fingers. The man had the body of a god.

A warrior.

She shuddered and groaned, grabbed his nape and kissed him harder, wishing it was dawn so she could see his body, could explore it with her eyes as well as her hands.

It was his turn to shudder as she reached his navel and dipped lower, twisting her hand towards him and cupping the bulge confined in his fatigues. He slammed one hand against the wall beside her head and tightened his grip on her hip with his other one, clutching as she stroked him, exploring the rigid length of him.

"Caterina," he husked and she drifted her hand back up to the waist of his black trousers and tackled the first button.

Marek kissed along her jaw, dropped his lips to her throat and suckled it, licking the sensitive spot behind her ear and sending wave after wave of shivers through her as she freed his cock.

He stilled and shuddered again as her palm finally met bare flesh, as she stroked her hand from blunt tip to his balls.

Velvet on hot steel.

She trembled and ached, moaned as she ran her hand back up the length of him.

Marek gripped the waist of her black panties by her left hip and yanked, ripping a gasp from her as he tore them away. He ripped another from her as he filled her with one hard thrust, plunging to the hilt inside her and slamming her back into the wall. She trembled, quivered as her mind struggled to catch up as a wave of bliss rolled through her, the feel of him stretching and filling her scattering her thoughts, leaving only feeling behind.

He gripped her hips, withdrew and plunged into her again, thrusting deeper as he angled his hips, his pelvis brushing her sensitive bud as her hands flew to his shoulders. She dug her nails into them, desperate to anchor herself as he went to war on her, a battle she felt sure she would lose in only a few strokes as he curled his hips, driving her into the wall with each powerful thrust.

His mouth seized hers again and she lost herself in his kiss, in each wicked thrust of his hips, every meeting of their bodies that sent a wave of bliss through her. She tugged him closer, wrapped her arms around his neck and clung to him as she rode those waves, as he palmed her backside and quickened his pace.

Even then it felt as if he was holding back.

Was he afraid of hurting her with his strength?

That question scattered on the sea breeze as he deepened their kiss, a wild and desperate edge to it as his lips clashed with hers and their bodies met and parted. She dug her nails into his neck as she finally caught up, and satisfaction washed through her when she rocked her hips, rushing to meet him, and he moaned and shook, his hands trembling where they gripped her.

He hooked her right leg over his arm, did the same with her left one, and dug his fingers into her bottom as he thrust into her.

She cried into his mouth as his body slammed against hers and her release crashed over her, struggled to keep her grip on him as wave after wave of shivers shot down her thighs and up her spine, as she quivered around his cock. He didn't slow.

He growled and filled her again, the new position allowing him to push deeper, until she could feel every inch of him. She moaned as she gave herself over to him, as the haze of her orgasm began to pass and pleasure built again, the itch for him proving persistent as he thrust into her, moving faster now, his breathless moans filling her ears between kisses.

"Marek." She turned her head to one side, tipped it back and arched forwards as he thrust deeper still, his hips curling, his hard length hitting her in just the right spot.

He kissed and licked her neck, suckled it so hard she was sure he would leave a bruise as he plunged into her, slamming her spine into the wall. She held his head to her neck, closed her eyes and strained, desperate to reach another high with him.

She tensed around him.

He grunted and slammed into her, his cock pulsing and throbbing as he spilled and his fast breaths bathing her throat.

Caterina moaned as the feel of his climax had her joining him, her core quivering again as a subtler wave of pleasure rolled over her.

She sank against the wall, all of her strength leaving her as she savoured it, as she slowly came down from the rush of it all and awareness gradually returned.

Marek gathered her to him and rested his forehead against her neck, his rapid breathing filling the silence as she held him.

Refusing to regret what she had just done.

The post-battle high hadn't been responsible for this moment of madness.

She could see that now.

It had just been the perfect excuse.

She wanted Marek.

She wanted him in a way she had never wanted anyone before.

In a way that heated her blood to a thousand degrees, but chilled her at the same time.

Because she had never been in love before.

And she had the feeling she was going to fall hard for Marek.

And that was more frightening than facing a hundred vampires.

Because she wasn't sure she would survive this.

He would find out about her brother.

And then he would break her heart.

CHAPTER 10

Marek lifted the cool glass of juice to his lips and took a sip as his gaze scanned the screen of the laptop opened in front of him. He swept his right index finger over the touchpad, scrolling through the document. It had taken him months to transcribe every hand-written report he had stored in the basement of his villa, centuries of documents filed by his brothers, detailing every daemon they had come across and any unusual gate activity they had noticed.

It had been worth it.

Now, he had all that information at his fingertips, although it did take some searching and he couldn't begin to calculate how many hours he had spent in his office or on this recliner under one of the larger trees that were spotted around the main garden of his home in the hills.

There were two servers dedicated to patrol reports alone. Another where he stored information on every daemon they had ever encountered. And he had started a fourth recently.

That one held all the information they were gathering on their enemy.

Marek closed the file as he reached the end of it and opened another, scanning it for any mention of a time the gates had called his brothers and it had turned out there hadn't been a Hellspawn or higher present.

So far, he had only uncovered one incident, over a century ago. The Hong Kong gate had called Daimon to open it but when he had gotten there, only daemons had been present. Marek switched to that document and read it again. Daimon had disposed of the daemons, but had noted that two had been shapeshifters and there had been one from the demonic breed.

He pulled up the more recent report from Valen, one his brother had belatedly filed yesterday, recounting all the details he could remember about what had happened at the gate in Rome.

There had been a shapeshifter and a demonic male then as well, together with daemons Valen had labelled as 'bloodsuckers'. Not vampires, because his brother would be able to recognise their scent.

If they had been rogue vampires, it would have easily explained things. As a recognised breed of Hellspawn, vampires were allowed to pass through the gates, if Hades granted it.

Was it possible one of them had been a mixed breed, part vampire and part something else, with enough Hellspawn blood to be allowed entrance to the Underworld?

Marek almost laughed as he immediately discounted that.

His father wouldn't allow a mixed breed into the Underworld. Purebred vampires only. Even turned vampires had to age to at least a century and prove their lineage and loyalty before Hades considered allowing them access to his realm.

He closed the two reports and kept scanning, humming as he sifted through another ten documents, taking the odd break to rest his eyes and sip his drink. The day was wearing on, the second that had passed since he had last seen Caterina.

His focus wavered as she filled his mind, as the taste of her and the way she had felt in his arms tugged at him, flooding him with a need to see her again. He should have asked for her number, shouldn't have let her leave with only a promise that he would see her again. She had been distant when she had parted from him, asking him to meet her again in three nights.

When he had pressed her to tell him why he couldn't meet her the next night, she had clammed up and said that she had something she had to do.

What did she need to do that took three nights?

Marek had pondered that question far too much during their time apart. It kept intruding, demanding an answer and distracting him from his work.

Which set him on edge.

If his brothers saw him like this, unable to focus on his research, they would immediately know something was wrong. The last thing he needed was his brothers probing into his life, and not only because it might lead to them discovering his penchant for killing vampires.

He growled and clenched his teeth as he thought about Caterina.

About his brothers wanting to know about her.

Demanding to meet her.

Caterina was his, and he would keep her that way. He wouldn't let his brothers near her. If they didn't drive her away with their overbearing protectiveness, they might make a play for her.

She was beautiful.

Gods, she was beautiful.

One of them was bound to want her as their own.

They couldn't have her.

His mood took a dark turn and he glared at the screen of his laptop as his fangs emerged, the black need to protect Caterina and keep her at his side, his alone, flooding him with a terrible urge to fight.

Not vampires.

Not daemons.

He wanted to fight his brothers.

The heat of summer suddenly gave way to icy cold that lasted only a heartbeat.

That heartbeat of time was enough for him to react, to fix his gaze on the one who had created it and snarl at her.

Enyo arched a fine black eyebrow at him. "Someone is in a mood."

"Someone doesn't need this shit," he snapped and set his laptop aside as he sat up on the wooden recliner. "Go bother someone else."

Her jade green eyes brightened, the black that ringed them seeming to grow thicker as she glared at him.

Normally, he took the hint and backed down, not wanting to provoke her into killing him by being rude to her, but this time, he was more worried about Keras killing him because she had visited him.

"Leave, Enyo." He shoved to his bare feet, slipped them into his sandals and stormed towards the white-washed villa.

She stepped into his path and stared him down as he halted, her six-foot frame bringing her level in height to him as she stood on the edge of the terracotta patio near the door, slightly up the slope from him.

The light breeze stirred the tips of her sleek black hair as she held his gaze, brushing it away from the right side of her face.

"I have information. I thought you were the one who dealt with such things."

Trying to sweeten him up? He wasn't the only one who liked to get their hands dirty with research, happy to spend hours glued to a chair poring over every tiny detail in the hunt for the one clue that would give them a lead they could work on. All this to eliminate their enemy and fulfil their duty.

Keras enjoyed it as much as he did.

Marek debated mentioning that to provoke a reaction from the goddess of war, and then thought the better of it.

He looked her over, from the thick black cloak that hung from her shoulders, to the silver and black chest piece, and the short black strips of leather that passed as a skirt, to her knee-high black leather boots and the silver filigree that decorated them.

She had come armed for war again, right down to the black and silver vambraces that protected her forearms.

The only thing that was missing was her sword.

But then the war she was armed for wasn't a physical one. It was an emotional battle, and she wrapped herself in the trappings of her duty in order to avoid waging it.

In order to protect herself.

Her green gaze flicked beyond him, to the recliners positioned beneath the tree. "You should stop sleeping in the sunshine, Marek."

He frowned at her. If she wasn't going to play nice, then he wouldn't either.

"Go and talk to another brother. Try Keras. He is our leader. All information you have, you can pass it to him."

The air chilled and the sky darkened, clouds forming above the villa to blot out the blue.

He was pushing his luck.

"Perhaps I should pass on information about what I witnessed in my last visit to you," she snapped.

He growled at her as an image of her sitting atop a stack of crates, surveying the aftermath of a battle he had waged against vampires, flashed across his eyes and his blood ran cold. "You would not dare."

At least he hoped she wouldn't. He had never figured her for a fan of blackmail, but clearly she was determined to get her way and avoid Keras, and she didn't care if she had to trample Marek emotionally in order to get it.

"You tell *any* of my brothers what you saw, and you will regret it." Marek squared up to her. He wouldn't win in a fight against her, mostly because he would pull his punches so Keras didn't kill him, but he wasn't going to sit back and let her threaten him.

"What about if I tell your father?"

He stepped back, bracing himself as that verbal blow hit him, and clenched his fists as the momentary shock passed and regret flared in her eyes.

"I would not," she said before he could find his voice. She looked away from him, down the sloping garden towards the valley basin, and wrapped her right hand around her left biceps. Her voice dropped to a whisper. "Let me relay the information to you, Marek."

Seeing such a powerful goddess, one who had been all smiles and laughter once, looking on the verge of tears had him relenting and easing back another step. He sighed and turned away from her, sat his arse back down on the recliner and waited.

"Fine, but if I get killed, it's your fault. I want you to know that." He reached around and grabbed his laptop, balanced it on his knees and opened a new document.

He was going to capture this information verbatim and file it to his brothers via email. It seemed safer than meeting Keras in person to hand it over to him.

He might be able to avoid the worst of the fallout.

"Ares, my brother, sent me this time." Her hand fell from her arm and she slowly recovered, straightening as the seconds passed, her eyes gaining that confident edge that had always been there whenever they had met in the Underworld.

Before Keras had been sent away to the mortal realm with the rest of them.

She twisted the braided length of hair that hung from her left temple, twining it around her fingers as she frowned. "The feeling returned. It is stronger this time, and there are rumours that others on Olympus are experiencing it too."

Marek didn't bother to write that down. Enyo had already warned him that her brother could sense something coming. Something powerful.

"The twin gate activated." As those words left his lips, her green eyes widened. He looked down at his knees. "I know. It came as a shock to us too. When I went there, only daemons were waiting. Our enemy. We suspect that a Hellspawn, or possibly even someone like a demigod might be involved. Ridiculous, right?"

He kept hoping it was nothing more than a wild theory, but everything was pointing towards it being a very real possibility, and that had him worried. What if this was more than a few daemons taking a shot at claiming the crown?

Daemons they could handle. Hellspawn and demigods would prove more of a challenge, and they couldn't be sure some of them weren't already in the Underworld, working right under his father's nose to manoeuvre the pieces into place to cause his downfall.

Enyo was silent for a long time, so long he had to listen to the song of the insects and the birds to calm his nerves. He wanted her to say his theory was foolish. Impossible.

He willed her to say it.

"Whoever Ares can feel… they are growing stronger each day," she said and he closed his eyes.

That wasn't good.

"It seems unlikely though. Who would dare implement such a plan against Hades?"

He shrugged. "Father does have his enemies. The two previous rebellions proved that. I have a theory that this relates to one of those times, but that would mean whoever is behind it was alive then."

"And that would mean they are not a daemon." She crouched at the edge of the patio.

Marek averted his gaze, bringing his hand up to block his view for good measure, just in case Keras decided to take a peek at his memories later. "Exposing way more than I want to see, Enyo."

"I am wearing undergarments."

"I know that, but I do not want to see them. I like breathing."

"I would not kill you."

He huffed and muttered, "You might not. Someone else will."

"Is this more acceptable?"

He wasn't sure it was wise to risk looking at her, part of him expecting her to be in a worse position now, one that was sure to sear itself onto his mind and therefore get him killed.

He cracked one eye open and gingerly peeked over his hand.

She was sitting on the edge of the patio, her knees firmly shut and absolutely nothing on show.

He nodded. "If you are going to insist on coming to see me, please wear more clothing."

"Do you find my armour exciting?" She glanced down at herself, a crinkle forming between her eyebrows.

"No. I find it terrifying." It was strange being so candid with her. "It's like facing a death sentence and you never know quite when it's going to happen, but you feel sure it will at some point."

He blamed Caterina.

Amazing sex clearly loosened his tongue.

Either that, or it had fried his brain. He did still feel a little frazzled. He shook himself back to Enyo, before his thoughts could traverse paths that would only make him look as if he did find her armour arousing.

"Can you do a little digging for me?" Changing the subject seemed like a sensible course of action, one that might keep him alive. "Any information you can get would be greatly appreciated. Just listen in on conversations or try to get more out of your brother. We need an inside man... or woman... on this one."

She nodded. "Of course. With all the tension on Earth right now, I can come and go quite easily. Would you like me to do some... *digging*... in the Underworld too?"

He thought about that. "If you can manage it without alerting my father to our suspicions. You know Hades. The last thing we need is him finding out there *might* be more than daemons involved."

She smiled. "He would probably evict everyone from the Underworld."

"And our enemy would go to ground. We need them to think they're on course to achieve their goal. If they go to ground, it could be centuries before they resurface." And Marek had been in the mortal world for centuries already. He wanted to go home.

Caterina spun into his mind in a blur of silver, her sword swinging as she fought invisible foes in the dark, mesmerising him.

Maybe he didn't want to go home.

Not yet.

He could stand to live here a little longer.

But he wanted it to be his choice.

There was a vast difference between being stuck in the mortal realm, banished from his home, and choosing to live here while being able to visit the Underworld and his parents, free to come and go between the two worlds.

He wasn't sure he could live with another two centuries of this.

Not only because he missed home.

If Caterina became something to him, the only way to make her live as long as he needed her to would be to take her to the Underworld.

Which would mean parting from her while he was trapped on Earth, protecting the gates.

That would probably drive him mad.

Ares and Megan would face the same fate too, separated by duty, and so would Valen and Eva. Valen had only just started becoming more bearable, some of his rougher edges smoothed off by his woman. Marek could live without him becoming caustic and quick to fight with everyone again.

"This troubles you greatly," Enyo said, and he cursed himself for getting lost in thought, forgetting she was there.

He nodded. "It troubles us all."

"I will do my best to find out who is behind this, Marek. You have my word on that." She stood slowly, and he was thankful she was careful to keep her underwear hidden, smoothing her skirt down as she rose to her feet.

"Thank you." He waited for her to teleport.

She lingered.

Rolled her lower lip inwards as if she wanted to bite it but had thought the better of it.

Her gaze drifted away from him, roaming towards the distant hazy hills across the ochre olive tree spotted valley.

"How is your brother?"

Those words, softly spoken, laced with a wobble of uncertainty, told Marek how difficult that question was for her to ask.

He smiled, hoping to calm her nerves as she glanced at him. "Which one?"

She scowled. "You know which one."

"Why don't you ask him yourself?" He meant that playfully, but grimaced as she looked away from him, her brow furrowing.

She turned on her heel.

Panic lanced him and he shot to his feet. "Wait."

She looked over her shoulder at him, green eyes filled with emotions. Hope. Despair. Pain. Love. It was all there, mingled with other feelings, ones that seemed to increase the strength of some and weaken the rest.

Marek was going to get into trouble for this, but she needed to know.

"Keras hasn't been the same since leaving home. You should go and see him. I'm sure he would like to see you, Enyo."

A swift shake of her head was exactly the response he had expected.

Her words, however, were the opposite.

"He would not want to see me."

He found that hard to believe. "You want to bet on that? My brother won't admit it, but he's lonely."

And he constantly played with the ring Enyo had given him.

"Lonely?" Her eyebrows rose high on her forehead. "Keras could have any mortal he chose."

Her voice wobbled on his brother's name, betraying how deeply saying it had affected her, together with the way the pain in her eyes grew stronger.

Although maybe that had something to do with the fact she clearly and wrongly believed his brother had been unfaithful to his feelings for her.

"He hasn't touched a single one, Enyo. Maybe he doesn't want any mortal. If you would just go and—"

Her eyes narrowed and the world swiftly darkened, night seeming to close in as black clouds boiled overhead. "You presume too much. Do not think to meddle in affairs that do not concern you, *boy*."

She was gone in a flash of white-blue smoke that lingered in the air where she had been.

He presumed too much? He laughed. Did she think he was the only one who had noticed that she loved Keras? The only one who was blind to it was Keras himself. Neither of them had a clue about the other's feelings.

Or maybe they did and they had stupidly been waiting for hundreds of years for the other one to make the first move.

Marek looked at his laptop, pursed his lips and shrugged.

Maybe Keras and Enyo just needed a damn push.

He pulled his phone from the pocket of his black linen trousers, fired off a message and then stepped, landing on the porch of the Tokyo mansion. The warm light from the huge stone lanterns spaced along the path at his back illuminated the white walls and darkened the ancient wood to black. He looked over his shoulder at the garden and the wall that surrounded it, breathed in the cool night air and steeled himself for what was to come.

This was foolish. Insane. Reckless.

But someone needed to make Enyo and Keras face their feelings, and he felt sure that Keras wouldn't kill him if all their brothers were present.

At least, he hoped he wouldn't.

Maybe this was a bad idea.

He considered stepping back to Seville and then stopped himself, the curious part of him demanding he stay and see it through.

He had provoked a reaction from Enyo tonight. He wanted to provoke one from his brother too. He wanted confirmation of Keras's feelings to see whether they really did match the ones Enyo had revealed.

He toed his sandals off and set them on the rack, taking his time about it as a series of high giggles rose from the other side of the door, together with a few husky murmured words.

A phone jingled. The giggling ceased.

A snarl cut through the late-night air. "Fucking Marek."

Charming.

Although, Marek would have been angry too if someone had disturbed his alone time with Caterina.

Caterina.

Gods, he wanted to see her again.

The urge to track her down was strong, rousing a fierce need to obey it. He wanted to kiss her again, wanted to hear his name on her lips as she found release, but more than that, he wanted to fight at her side, with her at his back, chasing the ultimate high.

The one that came from slaying vermin.

Someone slapped him on the back, jerking him forwards.

Calistos laughed. "Not like you to space out."

Marek shrugged it off. "I'm just tired. Research is taking longer than expected."

Ares eased around both of them to place his leather boots down on the rack to the right of the porch. "You're causing a queue. Any reason you're standing out here?"

"They were... uh." Marek tried to think of a delicate way to put it.

"Doing the nasty," Valen chimed in, a grin in his voice. "Makes me shudder. Thought of my big bros going at it like rabbits."

"You're one to talk." Ares tossed Valen daggers, his eyes faintly glowing as his mood shifted. "I'm not the one who has angry sex."

Calistos covered his ears. "This is so disgusting. I don't want to know about any of this."

"Virgin." Valen shoved Cal in the shoulder, sending him into Marek, and then went flying across the garden, narrowly avoiding clipping one of the lanterns. He jerked to a halt an inch from the wall, his head whipping backwards and the longer lengths of his violet hair flying upwards before falling down over both of his eyes. They narrowed on Calistos and burned gold. "Keep pushing me, brother. See what happens."

Calistos flipped him off. "Keep calling me a virgin and see what happens. I've had my share of women and I'm getting sick of you all treating me like a kid."

Valen dropped to the gravel as Calistos released his hold on him and casually dusted his black combats and T-shirt off, even though no dirt had gotten on them. "Don't tell me. You met all these girls at camp and they live in another state?"

Marek wasn't sure what that meant, but it firmly pressed Calistos's buttons. He flew at Valen.

Keras appeared in his path, pressed his palm to Calistos's chest and stopped him dead.

"Temper." Keras looked over his shoulder at Valen, his green eyes looking black in the low light from the lanterns. "If I have to tell you one more time not to provoke him, we will fall out, Valen."

Valen waited until Keras had his back to him again before he pulled a face at him, mocking their older brother.

Keras looked from Calistos to Marek, and Marek braced himself.

It wasn't the light from the lamps that made Keras's eyes look black as they narrowed on Marek. The storm raging in his brother's eyes passed quickly though, disappeared in a blink that left them green again.

That was disappointing.

Keras strode to the porch where Marek stood and he waited, sure his brother would say or do something.

"You have information to report, I presume. Let us not waste time." Keras removed his black polished shoes, placed them neatly on the rack and moved past him, entering the mansion ahead of everyone.

That bad feeling Marek had felt in the shower days ago returned, unsettling him.

He looked at Ares as the others filed past him, meeting his gaze and catching the concern in it. He wasn't the only one who had expected more of a reaction from Keras, and he wasn't the only one unsettled by how easily Keras had let it go.

Ares jerked his chin towards the open door behind him. "Give him another go."

"Why?" It sounded like suicide to Marek, although maybe not.

He wasn't sure what to feel as he thought about it. Barely an hour ago, he would have stepped back to Seville rather than making another attempt to get a reaction from Keras, afraid of his older brother losing his temper. Now, part of him needed to push him.

He needed to get a reaction from him.

"Something is wrong." Ares looked beyond him. "I don't know what it is... but I know it's wrong."

Marek risked a glance over his shoulder, into the long room where his brothers all waited on the crisp golden tatami mats, deep in discussion already.

His gaze tracked Aiko as she hurried from the kitchen to the left with a tray of drinks for everyone, Esher hot on her heels.

The daemon that had managed to escape them, the one they called the illusionist, had imitated Esher in order to get to Aiko.

He shifted his focus to Keras.

"It can't be the illusionist. The wards are new, unknown to them." Marek looked back at Ares.

His brother shook his head, his deep brown eyes solemn as he ran a hand through his tawny hair. "I don't think it's that. I don't know what it is… but something is up."

"Are we having this meeting or not?" Valen barked as he leaned forwards to peer through the door at Marek.

"Sure." Ares came up beside Marek, and his voice dropped to a whisper. "Just don't push too hard."

Marek nodded, unsure this was a wise idea but onboard with it. Keras hadn't reacted to the scent of Enyo on him, not really. With their blood, a passing flash of darkness was nothing in their world. It certainly wasn't on par with the reaction Marek had gotten the last time he had come to a meeting fresh from a visit by Enyo.

He followed Ares into the house, nerves rising as he joined the circle of his brothers in the centre of the main living area.

Keras stood opposite, his green eyes clear and calm, no trace of emotion in them. "What new intel do you have?"

"I checked the files, some of them. So far, I've turned up nothing." He hesitated and Ares gave him a look that told him to get on with it as he came to a halt beside Keras. Marek focused on Keras, watching closely, seeking a reaction in case it was as subtle as before and he missed it. "Enyo reported that her brother is no longer the only one who can feel something coming, and that whatever he is feeling, it is getting stronger every day."

Keras's eyes remained eerily flat and empty. "Very well. Anything else?"

What the hell?

He was tempted to take a step towards his brother and ask what was wrong with him, but kept his bare feet planted to the mats. Beside Keras, Ares looked worried, his gaze on his brother's profile and his brow furrowed.

Marek tried again. "I told Enyo our theory and asked her to help us, and she agreed. She will keep an eye and ear open on Olympus, and even offered to scout the Underworld."

Keras still wasn't affected.

Ares was right—something was wrong.

It was almost as if whatever feelings Enyo visiting normally evoked in Keras had been numbed or crushed out of existence, which couldn't be right. He knew that Keras felt something powerful for the goddess. The fallout from the last time she had visited was proof of that.

So what had happened between then and now?

He studied his brother in silence as they all discussed theories and how Enyo might be able to help them, not missing how Keras's eyes remained devoid of feeling the entire time, or how his voice was too calm, distant almost.

Keras slipped his hands into the pockets of his black trousers and that strange calmness seemed to grow.

Ares wasn't the only one who looked concerned now. Valen stared at Keras, and then at Ares and finally at Marek, the look in his golden eyes telling Marek that he had noticed Keras had changed too.

Marek subtly looked at everyone and caught the same worry in their eyes.

Had he pushed Keras too far, causing him to withdraw into his thoughts?

Or was there another reason he felt as if he was looking at a shadow of his brother?

CHAPTER 11

Caterina jostled the bags of groceries, swapping hands to stop her fingers from going numb. Guillem had promised to try to eat something, so she had gone to the store via the butcher and purchased him a container of pig's blood. It was the best she could do, although she doubted that it would help him.

The last time he had tried to drink pig's blood, he had ended up vomiting it all over the table.

It had been cold that time. Perhaps if she warmed it. The thought of warming blood in her microwave turned her stomach and she shoved it out of her mind as she shouldered the door to her apartment building open and worked her way up the stairs.

She looked down at the bag that contained the blood when she reached her apartment door. It had to work. Even if it only staved off the worst of the effects, buying Guillem more time.

Time she badly needed now that Marek had filled her head with doubts.

She had done her best to cling to hope, but it had been fading over the last two days, withering away just like her brother was.

She had tried to talk to Guillem about it, but every time she had found her voice or the right way to word things, she had ended up saying something else, anything else to avoid disappointing him. She needed to talk to him though, couldn't let it go on any longer, because she didn't only want to talk to him about what she had learned.

She also wanted to talk to him about Marek.

She needed her brother's advice about what she had done.

Had it been wrong of her?

It hadn't felt wrong. It *didn't* feel wrong.

But Marek wasn't human like her.

"Guillem." She pushed the door open and frowned when he wasn't in the living room.

He had been there when she had left an hour ago, watching one of his favourite TV programmes on Netflix. Maybe he was in the shower. He had talked about wanting one before she had left.

"Guillem?" she called again and listened. She couldn't hear any water running.

She turned towards the kitchen, thoughts drifting to Marek and what she had done. It had been good at the time, but the more she thought about it, the more she felt as if she was getting in too deep into a world she knew little about.

Falling down that dreaded rabbit hole.

That feeling only intensified as she pushed the kitchen door open and found Guillem standing on the other side of the table they had squeezed into the limited space.

And he wasn't alone.

A beautiful woman stood behind him, almost as tall as he was, her long fall of dark violet hair shimmering black beneath the harsh lights. Her quicksilver eyes lifted to meet Caterina's gaze. The woman smiled, her black painted lips curling softly, and her irises shifted, the silver in them swirling.

Her slender pale hand gently gripped Guillem's throat, her black nails a stark contrast against his ashen skin. He kept his chin tilted up as his dull hazel eyes fixed on Caterina.

"Guillem," she whispered and slowly lowered her bags to the tiles, afraid that if she moved too fast that the woman would spook and hurt him. "Please, let him go."

"She will not hurt him." The deep male voice held a note of authority, a command that drew her focus to its owner.

He sat at her small square kitchen table, casually reclining in one of the wooden chairs, his feet resting on the oak surface and the scuffed soles of his black knee-high riding boots facing her.

His hands rested in his lap, as pale as the moon against tight onyx trousers, and the long coat he wore spilled from his hips to pool on the floor. She followed the trail of silver buttons up his chest to the tight collar and forced her gaze to keep moving as nerves began to rise, awakening the need to run.

Because she was more than getting in too deep.

She was already down the rabbit hole.

And at the bottom, a monster had been waiting.

His violet eyes held hers, rendering her immobile, stealing all her focus.

"I need you to do me a favour." His regal accent sent a shiver tumbling down her spine, his calm tone setting her on edge for some reason.

She flicked a glance at the woman holding her brother. Not a vampire. She was something else.

Her eyes leaped back to the violet-eyed black-haired man. He was something else too.

Something dangerous.

Every instinct she had honed over the last decade screamed that at her.

They were both dangerous.

And they had her brother at their mercy.

"Guillem, are you all right?" She glanced at her brother again and he gave a strained nod, only able to move his head a few millimetres as the woman tightened her grip on his throat. Caterina's gaze shot down to the man seated at her kitchen table. "You hurt him and I'll..."

She trailed off when his eyes narrowed slightly, in a way that screamed he wanted her to finish that sentence with the impotent threat that had been on the tip of her tongue.

"And I won't do anything for you." She hated how weak and defeated she sounded as she uttered those words rather than the threat of violence she had wanted to throw at him.

She wanted to say that she wasn't interested in doing them a favour, but she knew in her heart they weren't giving her a choice. If she didn't do what they wanted, they would hurt Guillem.

Or worse.

And then they would probably kill her.

Her eyes lifted back to Guillem, her heart aching with a need to set him free, to get him away from the woman and this man. Guillem's eyes remained dull, his gaze distant, as if he wasn't quite here in the room with them. A bad day. Her brother always looked like that when the hunger became too much for him, always withdrew and ended up passing days without uttering a word. It broke her heart. He had looked so well the other night that she had fooled herself into thinking he was getting better.

"We just need you to do something." The man's calm tone, each word spoken carefully, set her on edge.

Caterina locked gazes with him again. She hadn't meant to, had only intended to glance at him, but something about those eyes made it impossible to look away from them. They brightened, holding her, and she struggled to keep her focus as she fell into them.

Her brother was in danger.

That sharpened her senses again, allowing her to claw back some control of herself.

"What will I get in return?" she said.

The man smiled, a spark of amusement igniting in his eyes. "To live?"

Caterina tensed.

His smile widened, grew charming as he theatrically waved his hand towards Guillem where he stood behind him, still held by the beautiful woman. "You clearly love your brother. Do you need any other motivation? We have been watching you since we first saw you with him."

She frowned. "With my brother?"

"No." His smile turned cold. "The wretched god."

"God?"

"Do not play dumb. You know who we are speaking about," the woman snapped, each word lashing at Caterina, driving them deep into her mind.

Until a thought crystallised.

She did know who they were talking about.

She just hadn't expected Marek to be a god.

"Your brother is sick," the man continued, his shrewd gaze leaving Caterina in no doubt that he knew more about her than he was letting on, and that he knew she was aware the man she had slept with was no man at all. "Do this for us, and we can make him better."

Her heart leaped at that before she could stop it and she feared he had seen it as his eyes narrowed slightly, the corners of his lips curling in response.

She told herself not to believe him, not to let him blind her with hope just as she had lost it. There would be a catch. There always was in this sort of situation. She had been losing hope and this man had appeared to offer her everything she had been fighting for this last decade. No way there wasn't a catch, and it wouldn't be a huge one. Life just wasn't that kind to her.

"I see doubts in those eyes of yours." He leaned back further and dropped his feet to the floor, sitting up and commanding all of her focus again. "I assure you, I can make Guillem better. You just need to do this one thing for me and then you can have what you want—your brother well again. You do want that, do you not, Caterina?"

The silky persuasiveness of his voice made it hard to remember that he was holding her brother hostage, and that he wasn't here out of the kindness of whatever black heart lurked beneath his tight coat.

It lulled her and had her falling into his eyes all over again.

She snapped herself out of it and looked at Guillem, seeking her strength there in his eyes, in the way he was still looking at her, trusting her to save him.

"More than anything," she whispered, aching to go to him as he shook, his eyes glazing as hunger got the better of him.

Hunger she had hoped to assuage with damned pig's blood when she knew that wasn't what he needed. What he needed was help, and that was the one thing she couldn't give him.

Hunting vampires wasn't going to save him.

She could see that now.

All she had been doing was fooling herself, burying her head in the sand because she didn't want to face facts.

She was going to lose the only family she had left.

"How do I know you can help him, though?" She looked back at the man, the desperation building inside her lacing her voice for him to hear. She was too tired to hold it back and hide it, too low in spirits to pretend she still had hope.

Marek had burst that dam and it was flooding out of her now.

"I know his breed better than anyone." He parted his lips and revealed short canines that slowly extended, becoming white daggers. "I can save him, Caterina. You only need to do as I ask."

"You're a vampire."

He shook his head. "No. I am not one of that breed, Caterina. I know it well enough though."

Well enough to save Guillem?

"There's no cure," she whispered, testing the waters, determined to discover once and for all whether it was possible for Guillem to be freed of his curse. Marek had told her it might be possible. What would this man say? She studied him as she steadied her nerves. "He told me that much."

His face darkened. "The wretched god does not know of your brother's situation. If he did, Guillem would be dead. He does not know how you suffer, desperate to save him. I know, Caterina. I know and I can help him. I can free him of this curse. I have done it for others."

The shattered fragments of her hope slowly pieced themselves back together in her heart as she listened to him, as she saw the conviction in his violet eyes, the belief that he could help Guillem.

She looked at her brother again.

She knew what the man wanted her to do. He wanted her to pick between her brother and Marek. She was attracted to Marek and had thought things between them could have grown into something given time, something more than explosive passion.

But if she had to choose between him and her brother, she would pick her brother every time.

She forced herself to nod, schooled her features and refused to let the man or the woman see how much this hurt her. Her stomach squirmed and she resisted the urge to touch it, to rub it and get it to settle as she waited for the man to speak. She silently apologised to Marek. She had no choice.

This was Guillem they were talking about.

Her brother.

"Lure the god under your spell and into a trap for me." The man eased onto his feet, coming to tower over her brother and the woman. "We have tried this before, but the fool failed. With this brother, we will do it right. Find the wretch, cast your spell, and cast it well. I will tell you the next step once I am satisfied the hook is set."

Caterina didn't like the sound of being bait for Marek, not the way the man painted it, wanting her to continue growing closer to him. She wasn't an actress. When she felt something, it showed ninety percent of the time. Her mother had always said she wore her heart on her sleeve when it came to her deeper feelings. Even when she was facing vampires, she found it hard to conceal her true feelings in order to deceive them and allow her to get the jump on them.

Could she pretend everything was fine between her and Marek?

Could she even be around him without risking falling for him?

If the man spoke true, then they had attempted this ploy with one of his brothers. Surely that meant Marek would be on alert, wary of women or people attempting to seduce him in case it was a trap.

Although, he hadn't been at all wary of her on that rooftop in the dark.

She didn't want to think about that moment. Not only because it stirred heat in her, had the attraction she felt towards Marek rising to the fore again to fill her head with a need to see him, but because she feared the man before her had witnessed it all.

That was the reason he was here now.

He had seen what she had done with Marek and felt sure she could carry out this task for him. Could she?

Whenever she thought about luring Marek into a trap, the churning in her stomach worsened and war erupted inside her, a battle between what she felt for Marek and her love for her brother.

Guillem suddenly bowed forwards and struggled against the woman's hold. She was quick to subdue him again, wrestling him back under control as Caterina's gaze leaped to him.

His eyes were bright and wild as he stared at her, his chest heaving with each hard breath he sucked down.

"Why are you hesitating?" he spat in Catalan, the venom in his voice shocking her. "I'm your brother. He's nothing to you… nothing. You love me. You can do this for me… for us, Caterina."

His breaths came faster, his nostrils flaring as he strained towards her, fighting the woman as she gripped his chest and throat. If he didn't calm down soon, he would pass out.

She took a step towards him.

The violet-eyed man held a hand up, a warning she found difficult to heed as Guillem clawed at his dark hair and gritted his teeth, snarling through them.

"I'm sick of this," Guillem muttered and as quickly as his strength had returned, it faded. He sagged against the woman, his breaths shallow and uneven. "Sick of it."

"Guillem." Caterina reached for him, her brow furrowing, chest tightening as his eyes dulled again. Her gaze darted to the man and then the woman, her pulse racing in her ears as fear got the better of her. "He needs to rest. Please."

"Lisabeta, take the young man to rest." The black-haired man regally waved his hand and the beautiful silver-eyed woman nodded gracefully, and led Guillem away, ushering him towards Caterina.

When he neared her, Caterina reached out and brushed his hand with hers, met his gaze and hoped he saw in her eyes that it would all work out. Everything would be fine. She would save him, just as she had promised all those years ago.

Although she wasn't sure she would be able to live with herself.

Marek had done nothing wrong in her eyes, he had done nothing to deserve what she was going to do to him for the sake of her brother. She tamped down her rebellious feelings and focused on Guillem, on fulfilling that promise. She had to do this.

The man withdrew a slender wooden box from his coat pocket and opened it.

Her pulse jacked up as he carefully lifted a syringe from its bed of black velvet. The dark liquid it contained was thick and syrupy as the man turned it so the needle was pointing towards the ceiling, and rested his thumb against the bottom of the syringe.

"What is that? The cure?" She found herself leaning forwards as that thought struck her, the hope he had pieced back together growing stronger as she convinced herself that it was.

Saving her brother was there within her reach.

The man disappeared in a plume of violet and black smoke that sparked with purple lightning, and she gasped as he reappeared behind her, his free hand closing over the front of her throat before she could move.

"No," he purred into her ear. "An insurance policy."

She flinched as he stabbed her with the needle, the world going silent for a moment as her ears rang, and then panic flared, adrenaline crashing through her as her mind caught up and screamed at her to get away.

She struggled against his hold, elbowing him in the ribs with her left arm, but he tightened his grip on her throat. She choked and gasped for air, her eyes watering as her throat burned and a strange cold ran outwards from the point where the needle had pierced her arm.

"This is just in case the feelings you have for the god grow stronger than the love you have for your brother... or you develop a conscience." He eased his grip on her throat as she gave up fighting him, his voice as smooth as honey, sweet enough to soothe the edges of her fear as he withdrew the needle. "Only I can cure this infection."

Her pulse spiked right back up, her eyes shooting wide. "Infection?"

The man stroked her throat, slowly, gently, and the cold that had been rolling through her turned to warmth. She tried to pull away from him but he caged her against him, and she was glad for his hold on her when her legs buckled, suddenly giving out beneath her.

"In my experience, people tend to care more about themselves than anyone else." He banded one arm around her waist and manoeuvred her onto a wooden chair at the table. When she was settled on it, he crouched before her and looked deep into her eyes, his leaping between them. He touched her forehead and she shivered, the cool touch against her burning flesh sheer bliss. "This way, you will do as I want."

"I was going to do what you wanted anyway!" She shoved at him, knocking him back a step, and regretted it when the delicious cool of his hand left her skin and she burned up all over again.

"The male is resting." Lisabeta stepped into the kitchen, looked between her and the man, and frowned. "It is done?"

He nodded.

Her face blackened. "You said you would not do it alone. Did you lay hands upon her?"

He smiled, a mixture of amusement and irritation in it. "Dear Lisabeta, you know my heart belongs to you. I only did what I had to for the cause."

Caterina wasn't interested in their lover's spat. She stared at the empty syringe on the table, panic mounting again as she thought about the dark liquid that had been in it and was now in her. Sweat dotted her brow, and she swore someone had turned the temperature up. She swiped the back of her hand across her forehead and swallowed, unsuccessfully attempting to wet her parched throat.

She needed water.

She tried to stand and collapsed onto the floor at the man's feet.

He sighed, picked her up and set her back down on the chair. "Things are progressing more swiftly than she believed they would. This is concerning."

"What did you give me?" Caterina slurred, shoving both of her hands against his chest to push him away from her.

This time, he didn't budge. Not because he was exerting any strength to resist her, but because she was too weak. Her hands shook violently against his chest and it took all of her strength to keep them there and stop them from falling limply onto her lap.

"A cocktail of blood, donated from various daemons in our collective." His words wobbled in her ears but she understood them enough that a chill swept through her, a brief reprieve from the fire that was blazing in her veins, burning up her skin. He pressed his hand to her forehead again and she leaned into it, desperate for the coolness of his touch, her eyes slipping shut despite what he said next. "It will not be long before you start exhibiting symptoms. Best you get moving, Caterina, because the one thing I know about this god—he despises daemons just as deeply as his brothers and his father."

She shuddered as his words swam in her ears, the warning they contained not lost on her because she had witnessed Marek's hatred of daemons. It had shone in his eyes when he had spoken of them.

It ran as deep as his hatred of vampires.

"The daemon infection might kill her if I do not draw it out of her soon. The dose was too strong. She messed it up." The man looked at Lisabeta, a flicker of what might have passed as concern in his eyes. Caterina doubted the concern was for her. He was worried that Marek might see what she was becoming before she could do as he wanted and lure him into a trap. His violet gaze shifted back to her and hardened again, even as his voice softened to lull her. "You must work fast, Caterina. What will happen to your brother if you die?"

Caterina shook as she imagined Guillem alone in this world. He would lose his way, would slip into the darkness like the other vampires. He needed her to be strong, brave, and to do whatever was necessary to save him. She would be all those things for him. She would do what was needed.

She didn't know Marek.

Not really.

She kept telling herself that, but it didn't settle the sickness brewing in her stomach.

The man rose to his feet and held his hand out to Lisabeta. She slipped hers into it and stepped up to him, her black lips stretching into a satisfied smile as he wrapped his arm around her. Behind him, purple-black smoke swirled, spreading outwards like clouds laced with green and violet lightning until it was taller than he was and wider than both of them.

"Move swiftly, Caterina." He stepped backwards with the woman into the smoke, his voice lingering in the room as it dissipated to leave her alone in it.

Her stomach twisted, every muscle in her body spasming as she bent over and retched, dry-heaving between her knees. She wrapped her arms around herself, her teeth chattering as she struggled to hold herself together. She was falling apart. She swore she could feel it as pieces of her fell away.

A voice sounded in her ears, or perhaps she was imagining it. Her hearing was distorted, nothing more than white noise as she held on to herself.

She didn't resist as arms lifted her, cradling her aching body against a cool chest. She slumped into it, seeking the cold to ease the burning in her blood. A cry rolled up her throat as her muscles spasmed again, cramping so hard she felt sure her bones would break. Her breaths shortened with each terrible shudder that wracked her, which left her feeling more brittle, on the verge of dying.

"Shh, Caterina." Guillem's sweet voice. "I'll take care of you."

Tears lined her eyes, hot against her skin despite the fact she was burning up, and she sagged against him.

"Rest now."

Those words were black magic, reaching deep into her soul to loosen the part of her that was clinging to consciousness.

She dropped into the welcoming darkness.

CHAPTER 12

Caterina's stomach cramped despite the two burgers and large fries she had devoured. She rubbed it through her black tank, trying to ease the cramp even when she knew it was impossible. After waking from what Guillem had told her had been a three-day sleep, she hadn't felt at all as she had expected based on how she had felt before she had passed out.

She felt strong.

And ravenous.

No matter how much she ate, it only ever took the edge off her hunger. It never satisfied it. It never tasted right. Juicy steak. Tapas of every variety. Fast food. She had tried it all and all of it lacked whatever it was her body now demanded.

She craved something else. She wasn't sure what, and part of her didn't want to contemplate it.

She moved along the Ramblas, a broad street that cut through the heart of Barcelona, stretching from the huge Plaça de Catalunya in the centre of the main tourist area down to the harbour. The hour was early, the stores that set up along the wide tree-lined pedestrian avenue that ran along the centre of it still open and doing business. Cars passed along the single-lane roads on either side of her, the pavements beyond them busy with tourists and locals. The heat of day was breaking as night closed in, and everyone seemed determined to take advantage of it.

Which had drawn out more than just the local pickpockets who lurked beneath the trees and blended with the crowd, determined to take their fill tonight.

She had spotted at least one vampire lurking in the shadow of a building, avoiding the weak evening light. The woman had been watching the crowd as it moved across the entrance to the market.

Caterina had studied her for a while before moving on. She wouldn't find her quarry by tracking a single vampire.

Marek would be hunting for a group of them, the ones who had been at the nest that night they had met. They had killed five of them that night, and a further three the next night. That left four from the original nest.

She scanned the crowd, sure they would be hunting tonight. It was so busy on the Ramblas that it was like a buffet for the vampires. They could easily pick out some prime prey to follow down one of the many roads that led off the main avenue, and there were plenty of dark corners on those roads, perfect for pulling prey into for a quick bite to eat.

A multi-coloured haze suddenly appeared over all the people around her and she stopped dead, her heart hammering so fast she felt sick as she blinked.

The colours didn't disappear as expected.

Caterina pressed her hand to her head and moved to the nearest tree, rested her back against the rough bark as she breathed, waiting for the weird spell to pass.

It grew stronger as she settled, and the panic started to fade as she began to track a few of the passing people and realised something.

The colours changed as they spoke to their friends, the shimmering haloes that surrounded them shifting as their expressions altered, and sometimes when they didn't.

Was she seeing... *emotions?*

She shook her head at that. It wasn't possible. She was just tired still, overwrought and stressed out because she was a walking carrier of daemon blood, and getting her life back depended on her finding a man who she had stood up several days ago, one who probably never wanted to see her again now.

The colours remained, mocking her. They continued to change, one hue morphing into another. Red. Green. Blue. Violet. Even a shadowy sort of black. That one clung to a man who was loitering on the other side of the pedestrian area to her, his eyes scanning the crowd. Could she see evil intent?

What daemon had this ability come from?

The man had given her a cocktail of them apparently. How many abilities could she expect to experience before she finally got the cure, or died?

Caterina sucked down a breath. "Not necessarily die. He said I *might* die."

Which meant she might live.

Her body might be able to absorb all these new abilities and she might emerge from the process as something new.

But something that was no doubt going to be a daemon.

So just rolling with the punches wasn't going to happen. She needed to find Marek and get the cure, and save her brother. She was not going to become a daemon, not when her brother was going to emerge from the darkness at last, free of its stain and able to live his life again.

As a human.

Caterina forced herself to keep moving. She was wasting time. She needed to find Marek and, well, she wasn't sure what her plan was. Finding Marek was step one. She was sure step two would come to her once she had achieved step one.

She wasn't even sure he was in Barcelona.

She took a left, crossing the road to follow the pedestrian shopping street that would take her to the Plaça Reial. When she reached it, she slowed her steps, scouting the corners of the busy square. She did a lap, ignoring all the street vendors who tried to sell to her, and the waiters offering her dinner. She wasn't hungry. Not for food anyway.

She idly rubbed her stomach as she left the square and headed back towards the nest.

The wooden door was ajar when she reached it.

Caterina paused and listened.

And heard *everything*.

Her eyes widened as a cacophony of sounds reached her ears. People talking. Cars moving. Creatures scurrying. Someone breathing.

She heard it all as if it was happening right next to her.

Heat bloomed in her face, rapidly building into an inferno, and she reached out to her right and pressed her hand to the wall to steady herself as her head spun. This wasn't good.

Voices came from behind her and panic set her feet to autopilot. She stumbled inside the nest, closing the heavy door behind her and resting her back against it as she breathed, focusing on each one in an attempt to settle herself. She was strong. She could survive this. She cursed the man, cursed him again when the first one didn't satisfy her in the slightest.

The dose had been too damned strong.

How was she meant to get anywhere with Marek when she felt as if she was going to collapse at any second?

"Caterina?" His deep voice rolled over her, and she thought she was imagining it at first, was hearing it because part of her was desperate to see him again.

And not because she wanted to get her cure and save her brother.

He hunted daemons. He could tell her what the man had done to her, what she could expect to happen.

She crushed that thought.

She couldn't tell him. Not because telling him would mean no cure for her or her brother.

But because he would kill her.

She was becoming a daemon now.

It made things easier for her in a way. There was no point in falling for a man who would hunt and kill her if he knew what she was becoming.

"You never showed." He had moved closer, his voice louder now, holding a hard note that spoke of irritation and disappointment.

She slowly opened her eyes, wanting to know what colours those emotions were. Apparently, they were no colour at all, or her new ability was broken.

"Sorry," she murmured and resisted the temptation to peer more closely at him to see if she could make the colours appear. "I didn't mean to."

Maybe she could switch it on and off? She pushed away from the door. Her legs were steadier and the heat that gripped her was breaking. That was good.

Maybe he wouldn't notice something was wrong with her.

"Your cheeks are flushed." He inched closer, his dark eyebrows drawing down as he pointed to her face. "Are you sick?"

She nodded. More sick than he knew. More sick than she wanted him to know.

She pressed the back of her hand to her right cheek. "I've been under the weather. It's the only reason you beat me to these vampires."

She didn't look at the two bodies that were fizzing just behind him, one slumped over the other.

Marek did. He cast them a black look. "They were foolish enough to return. One even gave up another location for us to check."

Caterina clung to that word. Us. Marek wasn't going to push her away because she had stood him up. That was good, wasn't it?

So why did part of her want to scream at him that he needed to get away from her?

She shut that part of her heart down and tried not to let it affect her. She had to save Guillem.

She did look at the slain vampires now.

106

If she didn't, Guillem might end up like them, killed and left to rot away and turn to dust.

Slaughtered by a god with a vendetta.

She could recognise one when she saw one. She had been treading the same angry path as him. Was still treading it. Even if she managed to save Guillem, the compulsion to destroy vampires would still have its claws in her. She knew that.

Even if she managed to save Guillem?

She frowned.

When she saved Guillem.

She stared at the decaying bodies, fear snaking black tendrils around her heart as they rapidly disintegrated, as Marek cleaned his knife on the clothing of the one on top and sheathed it.

Would Guillem stay home tonight as she had asked? She didn't want him visiting the bars as he often did, drawn to them by the overpowering need for blood. She didn't want him out in the city when Marek was in it.

What if they crossed paths?

She shook at the thought, limbs trembling as the tendrils of fear became icy claws that sunk into her heart.

"If you are sick, you should be resting." Marek's palm brushed her cheek, the sudden heat of him sending a wave of panic crashing over her.

She hadn't noticed him closing the distance between them.

She slapped his hand away, the fear sinking so deep into her now that she wanted to bolt. She couldn't let him touch her. She had let him touch her. Did he know what she was now?

Her eyes leaped to his, despite the part of her that was afraid of what she might see in them.

He frowned at the hand she had smacked away, and then his rugged features softened as his gaze drifted to meet hers, his eyebrows furrowing slightly.

"I might make you sick," she stuttered, latching on to that excuse and hoping he bought it.

"I can't get sick." He curled his hand into a fist and lowered it to his side.

"Because you're a god," she whispered, and regretted it when his face darkened, his eyes shifting towards black as suspicion formed in them. Damn. She needed to explain herself and fast, before he called her on the fact she knew what he was when he had never told her. "You talked about the Underworld and Olympus, and about gods and things. I thought perhaps because you hunt daemons, you were a god. You seem strong enough to be one."

And clever enough to see right through that weak compliment to the truth she was trying to hide.

He said nothing, just kept looking at her, scrutinising her as she sweated. She rubbed her forehead again, grimaced as her hand came away slick.

The weird colour haze popped into existence around him, a red shimmer with dashes of black and gold. She had no clue what that meant. Was it a bad sign or a good one? The damned bastard who had done this to her could have at least given her a breakdown of what to expect. This could be a power that would be handy in her mission to lure Marek for him.

She wanted to vomit at that thought.

Or maybe she just wanted to vomit.

Her stomach cramped hard.

She doubled over.

"Caterina, you are sick. You must rest." Marek reached for her and hesitated before placing his hand on her shoulder.

It was only a brief pause, but he had hesitated to touch her. She was already screwing this up, pushing him away when she was meant to be drawing him closer.

Because now that she was with him again, there was a part of her that wasn't sure she could go through with it?

That didn't want to do this to him.

He rubbed her back, gentle soothing circles over her tank that had her breath coming more easily and the pain subsiding as she focused on them.

"It'll pass." She hoped.

She braced her hands against her black-jeans-clad knees and gave herself a moment. It had nothing to do with how good it felt to have Marek's hand on her, his light touch filled with concern. She closed her eyes and hung her head, so her fair hair concealed her face from him and she could wage war with herself in private, without giving everything away.

She had to do this. It was Marek or her brother.

Caterina straightened and Marek's hand slid to her shoulder. He helped her up, held her as she waited for a dizzy spell to pass, and did his best to make this all so much harder on her as he smiled, worry shining in his dark eyes.

She looked away before she could fall into them and under his spell. "Two more to go then."

His gaze didn't leave her face. "More than two according to the intel one of them gave to me in the hope I would let him go. He mentioned fresh recruits and some more rolling in from the countryside."

"Why are so many of them gathering in the city?" She risked meeting his gaze again and the heat that swept through her this time had nothing to do with the daemon blood in her veins. "I've never seen activity like this before."

Marek pivoted away from her and crossed the courtyard to the decaying corpses, his boots loud on the flagstones, filling the silence that felt too tense to her.

He squatted next to the dead vampires and studied them. "Sometimes rats gather together. Maybe they think there's safety in numbers?"

He chuckled, the sinister sound sending a chill tumbling down her spine as something dawned on her.

He relished the fact the vampires were gathering.

Because it made it easier for him to kill them.

"Why do you hunt vampires?" She couldn't stop that question from leaving her lips as she stared at him.

He didn't look at her as he stood, his eyes remaining locked on the vampires lying dead at his feet, a place he clearly believed they belonged. His eyebrows drew down, and that aura that flickered around him shimmered with shades of crimson, tinted with flares of blue.

And then it went pitch black.

He turned cold eyes on her, ones that revealed none of what he was feeling. "I have to go."

"Meet me tomorrow, here, at eight?" she blurted, afraid she had done something wrong and was going to lose her chance to save her brother.

Afraid she wouldn't see Marek again.

He hesitated.

Nodded.

Looked down at the vampires and then at her, and she felt sure he wanted to say something.

He disappeared, leaving wisps of black smoke behind.

Caterina sagged against the door, her breath leaving her in a rush as her tension bled out of her. She mulled over what she had learned tonight. The man hadn't lied to her. Marek was a god. He hadn't denied it when she had called him on it.

What sort of god was he?

She doubted he was anything like the man who had done this to her. There was darkness in Marek, but that man had been cruel, a twisted sort of dark that still set her on edge even now and had her doubting that he would keep his word even if she did what he wanted.

Another wave of nausea hit her and she breathed through it.

Would the sickness ever pass?

Did she want it to?

If it passed, it might mean she was a daemon now, no longer just a human with an infection that could be cured.

She looked down at herself. What sort of daemon would she be?

She had pondered that question more than once since waking to find Guillem watching over her, preparing herself for the worst in case the man had lied and couldn't cure her.

Her brother had asked her what had happened, and she hated herself for lying to him. She didn't want him to worry about her. That didn't stop him. He had fussed over her every night since the man had visited them, had tried to keep her from going out. When she had explained that she had to go or she couldn't save him, he had relented.

Whenever she returned from searching for Marek, Guillem questioned her all over again, and she went to bed with guilt churning her stomach to burning acid that wouldn't let her sleep. Not only because she was lying to her brother, but because she was doing something terrible.

She killed monsters.

And now she was going to help them?

The man and Lisabeta were monsters. She was sure of that. They were evil. Marek was darkness, a warrior born of shadows, but he was nothing like them.

How was she meant to hand him over to them?

She closed her eyes and thought of Guillem.

She would do it for him.

And when he asked her tonight where she had been and what she had been doing, and why she was still sick, she would lie to him.

Because she had to protect him and she felt sure that if he knew what she was involved in, he would try to protect her by getting involved.

Which would put him in Marek's firing line.

And she knew in her heart what would happen then.

Marek would kill him.

And that would kill her.

CHAPTER 13

Leaving Caterina last night had been difficult, but Marek had done it for her sake. If he had stayed, she would have wanted to hunt the other vampires, and as far as he could tell, she had been in no fit state to fight. She would have been vulnerable, and would have ended up injured or worse.

He leaned back in his leather executive chair and stretched, reaching his arms above his head as he stared at the three monitors mounted on his desk. His back ached from sitting for so long, muscles stiff from hunching over the keyboard, and for what? He was no closer to discovering if there was a Hellspawn among the ranks of their enemy.

Esher and Daimon had filed their nightly reports, both of which had amounted to one line. No activity at the gate. Tokyo and Hong Kong had passed a quiet night. The fourth in a row. That was unusual in itself. It was rare to go more than a night without a Hellspawn wanting access to the Underworld or the city on the mortal side of the gate.

Several of the gates had been too quiet. New York was heading towards a week without any activity, not even daemons sniffing around when Ares had gone to check the gate still worked.

Marek didn't like it.

Keras wasn't interested in listening to any theories on the matter though, not when traffic through the Paris and London gates was at an all-time high, and Valen was experiencing more than one call out a night too.

The Seville gate had been quiet last night, but the three previous nights it had called him to it and a Hellspawn had been waiting for him to open it. No daemons in the vicinity either.

It was almost business as usual.

Which set Marek on edge.

It felt as if someone was trying too hard to make them relax their guard.

It wasn't going to happen, not since the enemy had somehow activated the twin gate in Seville. Marek wasn't letting his guard down again, not until this was all over and his enemy was no more, and the threat to his world and this one was eradicated with them.

He pushed to his feet and padded barefoot from his office, banking left as he reached the living room and heading towards his bedroom. He looked at the combat clothing he had laid out on his bed, the black almost blending with the dark blue covers. It had been another hot day, and according to the weather report he had watched, it was sweltering in Barcelona.

Marek looked down at his charcoal linen trousers. He really didn't want to gear up tonight, when all he planned to do was some light recon work. The material of his fatigues was heavy, the cotton so thick it would trap his body heat and probably make him feel as if he was slowly boiling to death in his own clothing.

He turned away from the bedroom, headed towards the back door beside the unlit stone fireplace at the other end of the living room, and grabbed his sandals. He slipped them on, fastened them and scrubbed a hand over his hair, neatening the wild waves so he didn't look as if he had been running his fingers through them all day, worrying them as he had carried out another long stretch of sifting through files on the servers, looking for clues.

He fastened a few more buttons on his black linen shirt, debated unrolling the sleeves, and then blew out his breath and stepped.

Caterina gasped and whirled to face him, putting her back to the arched wooden door. "Déu! You frightened me."

"Sorry. I thought I would be first here." Since he had left a good thirty minutes before they had agreed to meet.

He tilted his head back and looked up at the clouds that were beginning to gather threads of gold and pink as the evening encroached. He was definitely early. He looked back at Caterina.

A hint of rose climbed her cheeks. "I wanted to take another look around."

She had been as eager as he was to get going.

Or had she been eager to see him again?

He had been eager to see her.

He closed the distance between them, brushing off the lingering ribbons of black from the teleport as he went, aware of how much she didn't like them. They were gone by the time he reached her, by the time he lifted his hand and swept his fingers across her cheek.

"You look better today." He stroked his fingers down to her jaw, pressed two beneath it and gently tipped her head up. "Although, you are still a little pale."

"It's just flu or something." She pulled away from him.

"I told you I can't get sick. You don't have to worry about passing it to me."

She muttered, "That must be nice."

She rubbed her hand against her bare arm and he frowned as he noticed that she wasn't wearing her leather jacket, or her sword. She wasn't planning on fighting tonight either? That eased his mind. He was glad she knew her limits and wasn't as reckless as he had thought.

"Where do you pop in from?" She glanced at him. "When you teleport."

"Seville." He didn't see the point in hiding things from her, not when she already knew he was a god.

"I've fought vampires there before." She moved past him but he didn't miss the way she looked him over.

His blood heated at that subtle sweep of her eyes over his body and he found it hard not to give her the same, long and leisurely look over.

"To think, I could have run into you on my turf." He turned to track her as she meandered around the courtyard, traced her profile as she tilted her head back to gaze at the sky, her long caramel-coloured hair falling from her slender shoulders to brush the back of her black tank. "We could have met years ago."

"I would have liked that." Her faint smile had him taking a step towards her as concern washed through him.

He had thought her brighter today, recovering from whatever sickness weakened her, but she looked so sombre as she stared at the evening sky, felt so distant from him.

And resigned.

"Caterina." He slid his hand along her elbow and gently cupped her left arm. She glanced down at his hand and then up at his face, a myriad of feelings in her eyes that were impossible to decipher. Other than that terrible resignation he didn't want to see in them. "Is something wrong?"

She stared at him for long seconds.

Then shook her head.

Forced a smile.

"I think I'm just tired. This infection is taking its toll on me. I'm sorry, I'm not much company."

Infection? She had said it was influenza before. Influenza was a virus, not an infection. Perhaps she was just more tired than she looked and was struggling to think straight. That had him wanting to take her home and make her rest, to tuck her into his bed and sit with her until she had recovered. They could talk, while away the hours by learning more about each other. He would like that.

"Are we hunting vampires tonight or not?" Caterina breezed past him, paused at the wooden door and looked back at him. "I want to get going."

"It's a long walk to the location I was given. I could teleport you." He went around in circles, debating that in his head. Was she strong enough to survive a teleport?

Her cheeks were flushed again as she stared at his body, and he wasn't sure whether it was because she was sick or because she was recalling the last time he had teleported her somewhere.

To a dark roof where they had made love.

"I'll walk. I need the air." She held her hand out to him. "Come on. I want to get away from this place."

He walked to her and she dropped her hand to her side as he reached her. Not that he had intended to take it and hold it or anything. He looked down at it as she exited the courtyard. Did she want him to take it? Would she find it comforting?

He made the mistake of glancing up at her and his gaze caught on her breasts, on the fine sheen of sweat that glistened on her modest cleavage as she fanned herself with her hand.

"The city is too damned hot tonight," she muttered and took hold of the front of her tank top and waved it back and forth as she walked along the alley.

Gods, she would be his undoing.

He spotted a convenience store ahead of them on the road and hurried towards the refrigerated cabinet near the entrance. He grabbed two bottles of water, tossed the cashier some money, and was back outside before Caterina had reached the door.

He held one of the ice-cold bottles out to her.

"My hero," she murmured, a genuine smile curling her lips as she took the water from him.

She closed her eyes, tilted her head back and pressed the bottle to her neck. The half sigh, half moan that left her lips transported him back to the dark rooftop.

She stilled and slowly opened her eyes. They locked on him and a flush touched her cheeks. Nothing to do with her sickness this time. She was remembering that moment too. It was there in her hazel eyes as her pupils dilated, darkening them.

An unsettling swirling sensation formed in his stomach.

The coppery odour of daemons hit him.

Marek's focus whipped to the one standing at the other end of the street, her glowing yellow eyes fixed on Caterina. He reached out with his senses, sharpening them as he slowly reached for Caterina's arm. His internal radar pinged three daemons, all of them strong.

"Damn it." He looked at Caterina. He couldn't teleport her, not when he wasn't sure she would survive it.

He couldn't fight where he was either, exposed to the eyes of too many mortals.

And he couldn't leave her behind, because the daemons had seen her with him and were sure to target her.

He scooped her up into his arms, tearing a gasp from her, and launched into a dead sprint towards the opposite end of the alley. Two more daemons stepped out in front of him and he barrelled past them. He banked sharply right as he hit the small square beyond them and hoofed it down the busy road, trying not to jostle Caterina too badly.

Mortals paused to stare as he ran past them, as he dodged and weaved through the cars to reach the other side of the road, hoping that it would slow the daemons down.

"Marek?" Caterina sounded panicked as she gripped his shoulders and pulled herself up.

He glanced down at her, finding her looking over his shoulder.

"They're closing in." Her eyes darted to his, wide and luminous pools that reflected the fear he could feel in her. "They're not vampires."

"Daemons," he barked as he kicked off and launched over a car, landing on the roof before pressing down hard with his foot and leaping again.

"They look human." Caterina clung to him, her fingers digging in hard.

He landed in a clearing between a car and a bus, fielding a lot of shocked looks from the occupants, and growled as he pushed himself harder, reaching for a little more speed.

Just enough to get Caterina somewhere safe without the daemons noticing.

If he could hide her, he could fight them without worrying about her safety. She was a liability as it stood right now, a distraction he couldn't afford in a fight against three daemons.

Caterina shrieked, the sound a knife through his heart, and his senses blared a warning. He dodged right, cutting in front of a van, and a muffled grunt and the screeching of tyres was like music to his ears.

The daemons had to be some sort of higher form of shifter, possibly one of the ugly sorts who wore human skin to hide their scales, horns and pointed protrusions that made them resemble lizards.

He would find out if he could land a blow on one.

He focused on the ground beneath him, on the sand and earth hidden below the stone pavement, summoning his connection to it. It flooded him with warmth, the lingering heat of day. Each step he took shook the earth, had the pavement bucking as he left it behind, forming a jagged surface in his wake that he hoped would slow the daemons down.

Salt laced the thick air, and he frowned as people screamed ahead of him and behind him, rushing for cover as the buildings shook and the ground bucked harder. Car horns blared. Dogs barked. One slipped its leash and bolted past him.

Marek didn't care.

All he cared about was that he was running out of road.

The ocean loomed ahead of him.

Golden streaks chased over the waves.

He grinned.

The daemons were strong, but were they strong enough to handle a direct dose of evening sunlight?

The area where they had ambushed him had been a network of alleyways, providing them with enough shadows to move without fear of the setting sun. The beach was another matter. It stretched before him, a golden swath of sand that had looked like a dead-end at first, but now looked like the perfect battleground.

Even if the daemons could withstand the fading light, they would be weakened by it.

Giving him the advantage.

Hiding Caterina took a backseat as he put his new plan into action. He focused on the path before him, sending a shockwave across the earth to shake the pavement in all directions, right down to the sea.

The humans scattered as planned, several of them leaving their vehicles to run for cover.

The streets emptied.

Perfect.

He broke out into the light and switched his focus to the daemons, tracking them as they pursued him, waiting to see what they would do. Only one of them hesitated as they reached the edge of the shadows. The other two stayed firmly on his heels.

"They're still close. Can you go faster?" Caterina breathed in his ear.

He arched an eyebrow at her. "I could drop some ballast."

Her eyes widened and she clung to him. "Don't you dare."

Marek tried not to savour the feel of her arms around him or how she held on to him, trusting him to protect her and revealing that she wanted to remain close to him.

Tried and failed.

His feet hit the sand. He pivoted to face the daemons, lowering Caterina at the same time. The blonde female's yellow eyes fixed on her and she hissed as her claws extended, flaring from her fingertips like talons.

Marek gripped Caterina's hip and went to guide her behind him.

A brunette female appeared right next to her.

Everything slowed as he grabbed Caterina's right arm.

As he pulled her towards him.

As the daemon's claws cut across Caterina's left arm, slicing through the healing scar that darted over her biceps.

Her cry ripped at him, the pain that crumpled her face tearing at his heart and stirring the darkness within him, whipping it into a tempest that had a snarl pealing from his lips as he launched a hand out at the daemon.

Caterina stumbled backwards, clutching her arm, and the sight of the blood seeping from between her fingers pushed him over the edge.

He raised his right hand and a hundred spears of sand burst from the beach, each jagged shard razor-sharp on two sides. The blonde daemon nimbly dodged them all, fast on her feet, but the brunette didn't fare so well. One of the blades cut up the side of her thigh, spilling her vile black blood.

The stench of it had the darkness pushing harder, stealing more control from him. He focused on the brunette, casting a wave of sand at her. She brought her arms up to protect her face but the weight of it took her down, burying her in a pile at least a foot deep.

He turned on the blonde, not surprised to find she was alone.

The third daemon had turned back, fleeing for the shadows.

Marek needed to wrap this up fast, before darkness fell and that daemon joined the fight again, and so he could check on Caterina. She muttered curses behind him, the sound of them reassuring him that she was fine, but a little angry.

"If I had my blade," she growled and he tossed her a look that said even if she had been armed, he wouldn't have let her fight.

Not this time.

Vampires were strong, but these daemons were stronger and they had built-in weaponry. The blonde lashed at him with her claws, driving him back towards Caterina. So she could get a shot at her? It wasn't going to happen.

Marek used telekinesis to throw sand in her face.

And his power to summon a wall around Caterina, one that closed her in on all sides and was three feet of baked-solid earth, far too tough for a daemon to penetrate.

"What the hell?" Caterina's voice rose over the high wall. "Marek?"

"I'll explain later. Little busy."

The daemon recovered, launching herself at him on a vicious snarl that flashed twin rows of sharp teeth. Her lips peeled back from them, her smile so wide it almost reached her ears as they grew pointed. He backhanded her, sending her tumbling into the second daemon as she managed to claw her way out of the sand.

No longer looking human.

Dark burgundy scales covered every inch of her, a contrast to the pale bony protrusions on her elbows and shoulders, and the line of spikes down her spine, and the three horns that flared back from either side of her head.

Her tongue flickered out, forked and black, and her yellow eyes dimmed as a film closed over them from the outer edge of her eyes towards the twin holes that now passed as her nose.

At least he knew for sure they were one of the lizard-like shifter breeds.

Which meant conventional means of attacking them was out of the window. They possessed the ability to harden their scales, protecting them from blows that would otherwise sever a limb or pierce an organ.

But they could only shield small areas at a time, not the whole of their body.

So he just needed to hit them with an attack that would rip through every inch of them and then he was sure to deliver a fatal blow.

Or he needed to knock them out.

Marek focused on the blonde as the other daemon made a break for the high wall he had built around a now furious Caterina. She hollered abuse at him, banging on the thick curving wall.

He dodged the blow the blonde aimed at him and teleported behind her, grabbed her from behind and got her into a chokehold. He gripped his wrist, pulling hard on it so his forearm dug into her throat. She wriggled and snarled as he heaved backwards, lifting her feet from the sand.

Sharp pain shot in a line down his chest.

"Son of a—" He tossed her aside and gritted his teeth, fury building inside him as he looked down at his shirt and found a series of holes in it.

And his body.

The female rolled into a squat and hissed at him, baring fangs as the spikes down her spine retracted.

He scuffed sand into her face and followed it as she reared up to avoid it, barrelling into her and lifting her from the ground. She clawed at him and he wrestled with her, managed to get hold of both of her wrists and slammed his forehead into hers. Stars winked across his eyes and he was sure his skull had just cracked, but the attack had the desired effect.

The blonde hung limp from his arms.

Marek released her and swiftly brought both of his hands up. A huge spear of earth shot up, pierced her chest and lifted her with it as it grew in size and impaled her. She dangled from it, arms and legs splayed, head tilted back and unseeing eyes fixed on the darkening sky.

The other daemon halted her attempts to break through the earth wall and looked across at her fallen comrade.

Her yellow eyes grew impossibly large and she shrieked, the keening sound hurting his eardrums. He flinched away. She was on him before he could recover, claws shredding his shirt, cutting close to his face. He clenched his jaw and grappled with her, and when catching hold of one of her arms didn't stop her, he twisted and slammed her into the sand. Her breath left her on a fetid rush, carrying the scent of her foul blood.

Marek shoved a knee into her chest, pinning her down, and gripped both sides of her head as she struggled and twisted hard.

Bones snapped.

The daemon went limp.

He rose to his feet, sucked down a breath to shut down the pain from the lacerations covering every inch of his chest, and exhaled, his shoulders sagging with it as he sensed that he and Caterina were alone.

The third daemon was long gone.

Not a soul other than him and Caterina was in the vicinity.

His gaze slowly tracked to the wall that shielded Caterina. She had gone quiet. His senses fixed on her, the need to hear her heart beating and her panicked breaths, to know that she was alive and had survived the fight, overwhelming him. He crossed the stretch of sand between him and her, his pace quickening as he lifted his hand and focused on the thick earth wall.

"Marek?" she whispered, fear lacing her voice, tugging at his heart.

She worried for him.

He couldn't remember the last time a woman had worried about him.

A time long ago flashed into his mind and he barely bit back the need to snarl, because that woman hadn't really cared about him. It had all been a lie. A manipulation. Her betrayal had proven that.

"I'm fine, Caterina." He couldn't stop those words from leaving his lips, the need to reassure her and soothe her fears pulling them from him, straight up from his heart.

A heart that beat with a need to see her, to see that she was fine too.

The earth wall cracked, fissures forming as he exerted his will on it, and Caterina gasped as it crumbled before him, a whole section falling away to land with a hard thud on the sand between them.

Her eyes leaped from it to him and the relief that washed across her face flowed through him too.

Until he noticed that she was still holding her arm.

The blood was dark on her skin, turned his stomach and had his chest tightening as he held his hand out to her, needing her to come to him. She stepped over the remains of the wall and picked her way over the boulders of baked earth, struggling for balance whenever one of the pieces wobbled beneath her weight.

Marek met her at the edge of one of the larger sections and took her left hand, holding it gently so he didn't hurt her as he guided her down to the sand.

By the time she reached him, the light had faded, but he could still see well enough that he cursed when he removed her hand from her arm and saw the two lacerations that cut across her arm.

"Fucking daemons," he snarled and ghosted his thumb over the wounds, a black need to hunt blasting through him as he stared at it. "They are vermin worse than the vampires. I will hunt the third one down, and when I catch it, I will tear it apart with my bare hands."

Caterina took a step back, the scent of her fear increasing as she covered the wound on her arm again. Her hand shook against it. No. Not just her hand. The need pounding in his veins grew darker, more demanding as he realised the whole of her was shaking.

"Caterina," he murmured, an apology in it because he was sure he was the one who frightened her now.

He stepped up to her, cupped her cheek and stared down into her eyes, fighting for the words he wanted to say to her as feelings collided inside him, a tangle of relief and anger... and need.

That need built rapidly as he looked at her, as he saw that she was all right, until he could no longer deny it.

He dropped his head and pressed his lips to hers, and the rage burning in his blood gave way under the sweet relief that rushed through him when she kissed him back, her mouth playing against his, the softness of her kiss chasing the darkness from his heart and filling it with light.

Marek sank into the kiss, drew her closer and deepened it.

Her tongue tangled with his.

A strange sensation swept through him and he frowned as it grew stronger, unsettling him even when he couldn't put his finger on what it was that was wrong.

He frowned as he kissed her, as she pressed closer and took hold of him, her hands trembling as she gripped his biceps. Her need rolled through him, drugging him with the thought of satisfying it for her, of satisfying both of them.

But the weird feeling grew stronger.

And stronger.

And then it hit him.

She tasted different.

Wrong.

He pulled back as every instinct fired inside him, grabbed her by her arms and shoved her away from him. The scent that had been building around her, triggering one of his deepest instincts, grew so strong that he couldn't deny it, even when part of him desperately wanted to, was seeking excuses even as the truth hit him like a one-two punch in the chest from a gorgon.

Marek stared at her arm where he gripped it, at the blood that eased from between his fingers and trickled down her arm.

She couldn't be.

He brought that hand away from her, turned it towards him and stared at it in the low light. It shook, trembling so badly he couldn't focus on it as he splayed his fingers, as he drew down a deep breath to catch the scent of her blood.

Three words ran around his head on repeat. *Please be wrong.*

He lifted his hand to his face and sniffed.

The vile edge to the coppery scent of her blood was unmistakable.

"Daemon!" He shoved her backwards, sending her staggering over the mounds of earth blocks.

She stumbled and fell, landed hard on her back on the sand, her breath leaving her on a pained cry that ripped at his heart. He slammed the door to it shut, refusing to let her affect it.

Tears glistened on her cheeks as she struggled to her feet, the hurt in her hazel eyes threatening to break down the barriers the darker side of him had constructed around his heart, and built between them. She brushed the tangled waves of her caramel hair from her face and the pain that had been in her eyes morphed to fear and then something else.

"You didn't seem to care about it a moment ago." Her words lashed at him, fury making each one as sharp as a blade, and they cut him deep, severing the part of him that had foolishly clung to the belief that his instincts were mistaken and she wasn't a daemon. She clenched her hands at her sides, her fists shaking as she stared him down. "Unless that moan had been a protest?"

She mimicked it.

Marek snarled at her, baring his teeth as his canines began to extend, the darker part of him coming to the fore as his entire world seem to crumble around him. A voice deep within mocked him, hurling images of his past at him and all the lessons he should have learned back then.

Never trust women.

Never let one into your heart.

He felt weak as he stared at her, as he fought the feelings that still burned inside him, refusing to die even as he tried to vanquish them. They weren't real. Everything between them had been a lie.

A manipulation.

And he had fallen for it all over again.

His heart caught fire, the flames as black as midnight, rapidly consuming it and replacing his softer emotions, his weaker self, with emptiness that morphed into a rage so deep he lost control.

On a vicious growl, he stepped and appeared right in front of her.

He launched his bloodied right hand out and gripped her throat, tore a terrified gasp from her as he lifted her feet from the sand and held her aloft. He stared into her wide eyes and shook her, an anguished snarl pealing from between his clenched teeth as he fought for control, some command over the pain devouring him as it dredged up a thousand memories he wanted to forget and connected them to the woman before him.

Her face crumpled as she fought for breath, her face reddening and legs flailing, her fear hitting him hard and threatening to overwhelm him. He fought it too, because he wouldn't be weak again.

Never again.

She lifted her hands and gripped his forearm.

"You dare touch me, daemon?" He went to tighten his hold on her, a grip that would choke the last of the air from her lungs.

"You. Touched. Me." She squeezed each word out, the hoarse wheezy sound of them hitting him hard and rattling him.

His eyes leaped to his hand.

Widened as he saw black claws pressing into her delicate flesh, spilling blood down her neck, and the dark rings of bruises beneath his fingers.

He reeled, blinking hard as he dropped her to the sand and stumbled backwards. His ears rang, the darkness that had been consuming every part of him losing its hold as cold swept through him, a numbing sort of iciness that had him close to falling to his knees.

Caterina choked down breaths as she rubbed her throat, as tears cut down her cheeks and glistened in the brightening moonlight.

Marek reached for her, driven by a need to comfort her, but stopped himself. She was a daemon. What was he doing?

As her breaths grew stronger, she slowly straightened, and the coldness in her eyes as she fixed them on him sent another wave of chilling ice through his blood.

But it was the other feelings he could see in them that had his resolve wavering, his lingering feelings for her breaking through the restraints he had placed on them, fighting every instinct he had and demanding he go to her.

Reproach.

Hurt.

Fear.

Her brow furrowed and for a heartbeat, she looked as if more tears would come, but then she swallowed hard and scrubbed a hand across her cheeks, and glared at him.

"You kissed me." She held her throat as she spoke, each hoarse word another blade in his heart, a reminder of what he had done.

She was a daemon.

Everything had been a lie.

A manipulation.

He clung to that, used it to stoke his fury back to life, until his darker side stirred again, rising to push back against the feelings she was trying to evoke in him. It was a lie. She was still manipulating him, bending him to her will. She was a daemon.

His sworn enemy.

She sucked down another shuddering, wheezing breath.

Her fine eyebrows furrowed, the fire in her eyes fading as she looked at him.

"I wanted to tell you. Doesn't that count for something?" Her eyes searched his and he made damn sure she saw only darkness in them, only the side of him that hunted her kind, because it was all she deserved to see. She managed another breath and looked down at her bloodstained hand. Tears cut down her cheeks. "I don't want this. I don't want to be this. I didn't have a choice."

Marek frowned at her.

She shook her head, sending more tears tumbling.

"I just want things back to how they were," she whispered, and he wanted to tell her that wasn't possible, because it had all been a lie constructed by her, a daemon. She curled her fingers into a fist and before he could line up the words, she yelled, "I just want this damned blood out of mine!"

She disappeared.

Marek blinked hard, mind reeling from the shock of seeing her teleport and what she had said.

He stared at where she had been, feeling cold from head to toe now that she was gone, even when he had wanted that. Hadn't he?

He had wanted her away from him.

She was a daemon.

Her words taunted him.

She wanted the blood out of hers.

He frowned as he lowered his gaze to the sand just in front of his feet and tracked back over the last two days. She had said she was sick, and tonight she had called it an infection. She had been distant, had withdrawn from him more than once, not wanting him to touch her.

Because she had feared he would discover the daemon blood in her.

Blood that wasn't her own?

Was it possible someone had infected her?

His gut twisted at the thought that it might be, the violent way he had reacted to her replaying in his head to twist it tighter still, until he felt sick.

The way she had looked at him in the moments before she had somehow teleported were branded on his mind, and seared on his heart. The pain in her eyes had been genuine, and the fear hadn't stemmed from what he had done to her or what he might do to her.

She was afraid of what was happening to her.

Her voice echoed in his ears, a desperate declaration that she had wanted to tell him.

But she hadn't, because she had known how he would react.

He clenched his fists and relished the pain when his short claws cut into his palms because if his suspicions were right, he deserved to feel it.

He wasn't sure he was right though, or whether this was all another lie, an elaborate one designed to make him believe her so she could get close to him again.

Marek shoved his fingers through his hair and pulled it back.

He wanted to believe her, and that was a problem.

He was too close to this, to her. He couldn't think objectively, was blinded by his feelings for her but also jaded by his past, and a slave to his instincts. The three sides of him made it impossible to look at all the facts without being affected by at least one of them.

Which meant one thing.

If he was going to discover the truth, he was going to have to do something that might only make things worse.

He was going to have to tell his brothers.

CHAPTER 14

Caterina sank to her backside as she appeared on a dark roof close to the beach, shock and adrenaline combining to turn her legs to rubber beneath her. She sat there, thoughts spinning, entire body quaking as she stared blankly ahead of her at the horizon.

Had she just teleported?

She found that hard to believe, even when all the evidence pointed to yes as the answer to that question. She could teleport now.

She moved onto her hands and knees and shuffled to the edge of the roof, not trusting her legs. Her head was fine, wasn't spinning as it did whenever Marek teleported her, but her body felt weak, as if she had just used up every drop of energy in it in one go.

The lights along the promenade made it difficult to see the beach. She focused on the sand in the direction she thought she had been. The lights seemed to dim and the beach brightened. Another power? She peered deeper into the shadows and stopped when her heightened sight revealed Marek where he still stood on the sand, his back to her.

Her chest tightened, as painful as her throat as she rubbed it and looked at him.

Her mind whirled again, replaying everything that had just happened as she struggled to catch up. One moment she had been in heaven, wrapped up in his arms and the heat of his body against hers, lost in the moment, and then she had been in hell, chilled to the bone by how Marek had reacted to her.

Flooded with despair and hurt that cut her so deep she wasn't sure she could recover from it.

Did he think this was easy for her?

She wanted him so much, and even though she knew it was impossible now that he was aware of what she was becoming, she still wanted him.

But he hated what she was becoming—a daemon.

He had shown her that tonight, giving her a terrifying, and up close and personal look at the hatred that burned inside him. Her ability to see emotions had chosen that moment to reveal his, showing her the darkness of his feelings in a black aura laced with crimson and green, colours she presumed signalled fury, loathing, and disgust. She wished that power had remained on the fritz, sparing her to a degree. Hearing the hatred in his voice and seeing it in his eyes had been bad enough.

And she hadn't been able to stop herself from reacting, lashing out at him just as he was lashing out at her, a vain attempt to protect her own feelings even when the damage had already been done.

She kept rubbing her throat, trying to ease the pain that burned in it.

For the first time in her life, Caterina truly hated the world.

Because tonight it had hit her that she bore the blood the man she was falling in love with despised above all else.

That she was becoming one of those things he had fought.

She sank against the low wall that edged the roof, all hope bleeding out of her as something else dawned on her too.

Marek would never allow her near him again.

How was she meant to fulfil the task the man had given her if Marek hated her now?

How was she meant to save her brother?

To rid herself of this damned blood?

The tears she had been holding back burned her nose and stung her eyes, but she still refused to let them come. She refused to give up, even when she desperately wanted to do that.

She had been so afraid when she had been cut tonight and had seen her blood was darker than before, almost as black as the liquid had been in the syringe. She had feared Marek would notice it when he had inspected the cut, had been terrified of showing it to him, even when she had known he would insist and wouldn't rest until he had checked the wound.

When he hadn't noticed the change in colour, she had been so relieved.

Had thought everything would be fine.

She curled up and stared at him, wishing it had been, wishing he hadn't somehow discovered what she was when he had been kissing her of all things. She could understand his reaction, even when she didn't want to, when she wanted to be furious with him for lashing out at her.

Daemons were his enemy.

She couldn't blame him for thinking she was one of them.

But that didn't make it hurt any less.

She watched him as he turned to look around him, the need to go to him so strong that she had to hold the wall to anchor herself, had to keep telling herself that it would be a mistake. He wouldn't listen to anything she had to say.

And she couldn't tell him everything anyway.

If he learned who had done this to her and what they wanted her to do, he would hate her even more.

It didn't stop her from wanting to go to him.

He ran his hands over his hair and his broad shoulders lifted in a deep sigh.

How had she ever thought she could do this?

She couldn't.

She wouldn't.

She didn't want to hand Marek over to that man and the woman who had been with him. She couldn't bear the thought of doing it, or the thought of what they might do to him. Being the instrument of his downfall, seeing him suffer because of her, would destroy her.

He heaved another long sigh and then disappeared.

Caterina slumped against the wall, resting her chin on it as she stared at the dark sea.

But what choice did she really have?

It was Marek or her brother.

Only one of them would survive this.

And that broke her heart.

CHAPTER 15

Marek had forced himself to sleep on everything before bringing it to his brothers. Now, dawn was coming and he hadn't gotten a wink of sleep, had paced through the night, tormented by what he had done to Caterina, enraged by what she had done to him.

He huffed and stalked into the open-plan kitchen next to the living room, poured himself a glass of juice from the refrigerator and downed it. Wearing a groove in the terracotta tiles of his floor wasn't going to solve anything. He was getting nowhere, had gone in circles about Caterina all night. He was finding it harder to think straight now than he had after she had disappeared from the beach.

He needed to speak with his brothers.

He had written a message to that effect and had almost sent it three times, but each time his thumb had hovered over the send button, he had thought about Caterina and what his brothers would do to her if they discovered what she was.

Which tied him in knots.

He was meant to hunt her kind, defending the gates from them, protecting his home from them.

Why couldn't he hate her as he hated the other daemons?

His heart supplied that he knew the answer to that question—because Caterina was different.

Wrong.

She didn't affect him like other daemons did. When he had been with her, he hadn't felt that strange sensation in his gut that warned him when a daemon was near him, and she hadn't smelled like a daemon when she had been cut.

Which gave him hope.

Hope that Caterina had been telling the truth and that she was somehow infected.

He just wasn't sure if that was possible.

He pulled the phone from his pocket, brought up the message and hesitated over the send button again. Was it better he took this to everyone, or just one of them?

One brother questioning him sounded infinitely more palatable than having six brothers questioning him.

He immediately discounted Keras, in case his older brother had finally reacted to Enyo visiting him and was in a foul mood. Ares seemed like the best choice.

Although Ares would tell him what he already knew in his heart.

It was best he took this to all of his brothers, just in case it had something to do with their enemy.

Just in case?

It had all the hallmarks of their enemy, there was no use denying that. He didn't want Caterina to be a daemon, and he didn't want her to be working with his enemy, but when had he ever gotten what he wanted?

He pressed send on the group message, pivoted on his heel and went to his bedroom. He grabbed the T-shirt from the clothes still draped over his bed, went into the en-suite and stripped off his ruined shirt. He tossed it in the bin and washed his chest. The cuts were all healing now, little more than scars.

Were Caterina's wounds healing as rapidly?

He meant to think about the one on her arm, but instead was hit by an image of her throat, black with bruises, spotted with blood where his claws had pierced her.

Marek leaned over the sink, gripped the edges of it and squeezed his eyes shut.

He had dealt her more than just those physical wounds if she had been telling the truth and she was somehow infected with daemon blood. He had dealt her emotional blows too, ones that had hit their mark, cutting her deeply judging by the hurt that had been in her eyes and how she had verbally lashed out at him.

Would she ever forgive him?

He wasn't sure he would deserve it.

"Marek?" Ares's deep voice boomed from the living room.

"Just a minute." He splashed cold water onto his face and steeled himself as he dried off, as he donned the T-shirt and ran his fingers through his hair.

He should have called this meeting hours ago, before he had twisted himself in knots that were so tight and tangled that he couldn't see the ends to pull to loosen them, or had any hope of freeing himself from them.

He wouldn't mention Caterina. He would keep his brothers from her.

But if she was a daemon?

He didn't want to think about what would happen then.

Ares was in the kitchen when Marek found the courage to emerge from his bedroom. His big brother bent over the refrigerator, humming to himself as he picked through the contents.

"Looking for anything particular?" Marek leaned his backside against the rear of the dark cream couch that stood near the fireplace with a matching armchair, facing his brother.

"Anything high in carbs." Ares grinned as he glanced at Marek, but there was an edge to his dark eyes that spoke of pain. Possibly agony. "Megan is on a health kick. No pizza."

Marek shuddered at the same time as his brother. "That is sacrilegious."

Like most of his brothers, Marek craved pizza like a fiend, although he shared Valen's love of pasta too, and enjoyed the local cuisine. He could never get enough of Iberico ham and chorizo, and some of the seafood in Spain was to die for.

But pizza.

Pizza was godly.

"I told her that." Ares shrugged his broad shoulders, rolling them beneath his black dress shirt, and jammed his hands into the pockets of his equally dark jeans as he leaned near the sink, giving up his search. "She doesn't care. Something about watching her weight. Which means I get to suffer, because she's cranky as hell and I get an earful if I dare to bring pizza home since she refuses to eat it."

"An enforced diet. Have you tried eating it before coming home?"

Ares rolled his eyes. "She can smell it on me. Reacts like I've been with another woman or some crazy shit like it."

Valen appeared and slumped into the armchair. "What's up?"

"Discussing Ares's new diet plan." Marek twisted to look over his shoulder at his younger brother.

"Megan is on a diet, so I am too," Ares grumbled. "No pizza."

"Shit, that sucks." Valen mussed his violet hair and sank deeper into the chair as he yawned. "Have you tried convincing her you two can just work off the calories?"

"Believe me, it's our main source of exercise." Ares grinned now and folded his arms across his chest. His expression sobered. "Not that it's any of your business."

The door beyond the fireplace opened and Daimon poked his head around it.

"I thought you would be outside." Daimon shut the door behind him, leaving frost glittering on the knob that rapidly turned to dew. He pulled down a breath and sighed it out, his eyes closing and a blissful look crossing his face. "Damn, that feels good. How many BTUs is that?"

Marek had cranked up the air conditioning after he had worked up a sweat pacing a trench into the tiles and had forgotten to turn it down.

Before he could answer his brother, Daimon continued.

"Esher isn't coming. Moon and all that." His white-haired brother waved at the ceiling. "It's been a rough night."

"Not a problem. I should have thought about it before messaging everyone." Marek was doing that a lot lately, messaging before considering all the angles.

First, he had summoned Calistos to the Seville gate, and now he had probably made Esher feel bad for not being able to leave Tokyo. The full moon wreaked havoc on his brother, pulling at his powers as fiercely as it did the sea, only it turned Esher unpredictable and dangerous.

Or at least more unpredictable and dangerous than usual.

"Is Aiko watching him?" Marek nodded when Keras and Calistos appeared and was surprised when Keras bowed his head in return, a very civil greeting.

Still not mad with him?

Something was definitely up.

"Yeah, but I promised I wouldn't be long." Daimon drifted to the AC unit, his pale blue eyes expressing all the pleasure he took from having it blast cold air directly on him.

The Tokyo mansion didn't have such a luxury, and the city was in the grip of a heatwave.

Daimon was probably melting while he took care of Esher.

Marek wanted to offer to let him go back to Esher, but he had the feeling his brother would wave him away. He was enjoying the reprieve from the heat too much. Of course, Daimon would be cooler in Tokyo if he wasn't wearing a roll-neck long-sleeved navy top, leather gloves and black jeans.

Old habits died the hardest.

Like reacting badly to the presence of a daemon.

132

Marek cleared his throat, lined up what he wanted to say and waited for Calistos to get comfortable on the couch. His youngest brother looked tired, his blond hair in disarray as he stacked all the pillows at one end of the sofa and lay back on them. His blue eyes were stormy as he looked up at Marek, as he scrubbed a hand over the stubble coating his jaw and sighed.

There were numerous healing cuts on his face and neck, and a bandage around his left arm, peeking from beneath the sleeve of his khaki T-shirt.

Keras had a few scratches of his own, including one that darted down his cheek, almost perfectly in line with the neatly clipped angle of his sideburns. That cut sliced into his black hair too, above the slightly pointed tip of his ear.

Keras's green eyes narrowed on him, a silent warning to get on with it.

"I don't have any fresh intel on our possible Hellspawn problem." It seemed like a good place to start, although it had Daimon, Keras and Ares frowning at him. He didn't give them a chance to start asking why he had summoned them for a meeting. "I have a question, and I need you all to answer it."

"Marek has a question?" Daimon's white eyebrows shot up and he looked to Ares. "How is that possible? Marek knows everything."

Marek scowled at his younger brother.

"Not everything. He never said he knew everything. He knows *most* things." Ares moved past Keras where he still stood in the centre of the room, his green eyes fixed on Marek.

That earned Ares a black look too. "I'm being serious."

"Of course you are… because you're asking for help, and it's weirding me out." Valen used his boots to push some magazines along the wooden coffee table and rested his feet on it.

"It's weirding *you* out?" Calistos tipped his head back to look at Valen upside down. "I never knew him before he attained the knowledge of the ages through rigorous and tedious reading. I've never known him when he was *learning* shit."

"This is serious," Marek snapped, and regretted it when everyone fell silent and stared at him as if he had sprouted another two heads.

Daimon and Ares looked as if they weren't sure how to handle his outburst.

"This is serious." Valen looked from Calistos to Daimon, his tone mocking, laced with faux shock. "Quick guys… hit the books! They're just in there. Off you go. I'll wait here."

He jerked his chin towards Marek's office.

Keras sighed just as Marek was about to lose his temper.

It was enough to have the rest of his brothers turning deadly serious.

When Keras sighed, everyone behaved themselves. Even Marek. It was the same effect Hades had when he sighed, because that simple sound was laced with exasperation and a hefty dose of danger even when it was done lightly, what would be a regular sigh for most people.

It was a warning that if things continued as they were, someone was liable to lose their head.

And that someone wasn't Keras.

"Continue." Keras waved his hand towards him.

"Is it possible for a human to turn daemon?" Some of the hardest words Marek had ever had to say, and he watched his brothers closely as they left his lips, gauging all of their faces, waiting for a reaction.

Keras arched a single black eyebrow. "Perhaps. A vampire can turn a human, infecting them with blood to force a transition from human to vampire."

Marek schooled his features, holding back the scowl that wanted out as his brother spoke casually about vermin and without even a shred of disgust in his voice.

"A daemon can be born of a corrupted soul." Keras's eyebrow lowered and both of them knitted above his green eyes. "I have never considered it before, but it might be possible for that corruption to occur while the soul is still within a living vessel."

"A living vessel," Marek murmured, the knots twisted inside him pulling tighter as he thought about that.

For humans infected by vampires, death was the catalyst of their transformation.

What if it was the same for whatever infected Caterina?

"What's this all about?" Calistos sat up and hit him with a worried look. "Do you think daemons are trying to recruit humans by doing something to their souls?"

Marek looked at all of his brothers, deeply aware of how far south this might go but needing to tell them more, because he needed them to convince him that Caterina had been telling the truth.

"I ran into a mortal female during some patrols." He left out the fact he had been in Barcelona and he hadn't been hunting for daemons, because that way led to more questions, and he needed to keep everyone's focus on Caterina and her possible problem. "Yesterday evening, I met her again. She had been sick since the night before that, and had told me it was nothing, possibly just influenza."

"What happened?" Ares inched closer, coming to stand beside Valen where he still lounged in the armchair.

"We were attacked by daemons and I dealt with them, but afterwards... I was checking a wound she picked up and her blood smelled daemon. I had the sense she was a daemon." He left out a few details there too, like the fact he had been kissing her when that sense of her being a daemon had struck him.

"Is it possible daemon blood got on her?" Ares's deep brown eyes held his.

Marek shook his head. "No. I encased her in a wall. She was hit by a daemon's claws and then I made sure she was protected."

"So, your girlfriend is turning daemon?" Valen's eyebrows pinned high on his forehead. "Bummer."

"She is not my girlfriend," Marek snapped, ignoring the part of himself that pointed out he had been hoping she would be that and so much more to him. He really didn't need his brothers knowing that.

"How did you take it?" Daimon's eyes narrowed on him as they paled, turning almost white, a warning that his brother was probably mulling over how he might have taken it if he had been in Marek's shoes, and was either enjoying it or not liking it at all.

Marek didn't dare ask which it was.

"Badly. I..." He huffed and shoved his fingers through his hair. "I took it badly. Instinct kicked in."

Ares tipped his head up, his eyebrows rising as he said, "Ah."

Valen grimaced.

"But if she's a daemon, what does it matter?" Calistos shrugged as everyone looked at him. "Daemon. We kill daemons. You all forget that?"

"What if she isn't really a daemon?" Daimon countered. "I hate them as much as the next guy, but if she was mortal..."

Calistos's face darkened, his eyes turning stormy. "Wouldn't have stopped me."

Valen kicked him in the knee. "You get a woman of your own and say that if it happens to her. Thinking about that happening to Eva... Fuck. I don't want to think about it."

He dropped his feet to the floor, leaned forwards and buried his head in his hands, his violet hair falling to cover them.

"She definitely didn't give you the heebie-jeebies before?" Ares started pacing, his eyes not straying from Marek.

Marek shook his head. "It isn't just what I felt. It's what she said. She was sick, Ares. She was afraid of me touching her and I thought it was because she didn't want to make me sick... and she grew distant."

He rubbed his forehead and started pacing too, needing to work off some energy as he thought about everything, and about what he had done.

"I attacked her." Saying that out loud made him sick to his stomach, as if admitting it suddenly made it real when he had lived it, had stood there with his hand around her throat trying to choke the life out of her. It hit him hard and he swallowed, covered his mouth with his hand and cursed. "When I realised what I was doing, I let her go... but I hurt her, and what she said... I don't... I don't think she was always a daemon."

"You believe that?" Calistos tossed him a thunderous glare. "She's a daemon. They're all liars and bastards."

"No. She's not a daemon. She's becoming one. There is a damned difference." He stalked towards his youngest brother, the ground shaking beneath his feet with each hard step, and Calistos leaned back, attempting to distance himself as Marek bore down on him. "She told me she wanted to tell me. She said she didn't want it and she didn't have a choice."

He stilled and his shoulders sagged as the words she had hurled at him before disappearing hit him all over again.

He whispered.

"She said she wanted the damned blood out of her own."

Keras's green gaze drilled into him. "Out of her own?"

Marek nodded. "Those were her exact words."

It wasn't as if he could forget them.

Or the fact she had disappeared from his life right after hurling them at him.

"And then what happened?" Ares again.

Marek closed his eyes. "I think she teleported."

"Teleported?" Daimon barked.

Marek braced himself, waiting for one of them to point out that she was definitely a daemon then, and definitely powerful, because the ability to teleport was rare in her kind and only manifested in older daemons.

Which meant she had definitely been lying to him the whole time.

"Amaury could teleport," Ares put in, his words carefully weighed and softly spoken, and Marek dared to look at him.

Because he hadn't even thought about that.

Amaury had been the first of their enemy they had encountered, a daemon with the ability to teleport and also the power to steal abilities from another. He had taken Ares's fire the night Ares had met Megan, but his ultimate goal had been to take Megan's power to heal.

So he could act as the medic for the enemy.

"So, your girlfriend isn't a fully-fledged daemon but she is working for the enemy? Is that what I'm getting here?" Valen lifted his head and twisted on the armchair to look over the back of it.

Marek wanted to point out again that she wasn't his girlfriend, but it would get him nowhere, and he was getting tired of his brothers thinking Caterina was the enemy.

When from where he was standing it looked as if she was the victim in all of this.

"She wanted the blood out of her. She said she had no choice... And she wanted to tell me." He swallowed. Hard. "I think... I think this is my fault. The daemons attacked the gate here, which means their focus is on me. I got her pulled into this."

And gods, he had thought he couldn't feel any worse than he already did, but there it was.

Rock bottom.

"Marek," Keras started and Marek shook his head, because he didn't want coddling or excuses.

"They must have seen her with me. I put a target on her back." He turned on Keras and his throat closed as reality hit him hard. "Now she's been infected with daemon blood and it's all my fault, and I attacked her because of it."

He sank to his backside on the arm of the couch next to Calistos, rested his elbows on his knees and hung his head.

"You're such a dick." Valen was as helpful as always. "I probably would've flipped my shit too."

That wasn't any comfort. Valen flipped out around once a week, and often about something trivial.

"What are you going to do?" Keras this time, and his deep voice held a note of what sounded a lot like concern to Marek.

He lifted his head and met Keras's gaze as he replayed his last moments with Caterina, as he saw all over again how terrified she had been and it hadn't been fear of him that had gripped her.

She was scared of what was happening to her.

But she didn't have to deal with it alone.

"I'm going to find her."

CHAPTER 16

Finding Caterina had sounded easier than it turned out to be. Marek had visited the beach, the vampires' nests, and had even patrolled the entire gothic quarter of Barcelona for two nights straight.

So far, there had been no sign of her.

He paused for a rest on one of the benches beneath the trees that lined one side of the wide-open paved area in front of the Cathedral and tracked the people with his gaze, studying each of them in turn.

Had she gone into hiding?

Or was she too sick now to move?

Marek shoved that question aside before he could contemplate it, because he couldn't bear the thought of her getting worse when he had seen she was getting better. He knew nothing about this sort of thing, and he felt it as he sat watching the couples moving around the square. Even if he could find Caterina, he had no way of saving her.

His entire plan revolved around apologising and then asking her about what had happened to her, and the more he thought about it, the colder it sounded. She was infected, and he wanted to interrogate her about who had done it and what it was they wanted her to do.

Because he doubted they had done this to her just to get to him and weaken him.

He singled out a couple, a dark-haired man dressed in a black T-shirt and worn blue jeans with a woman wearing navy jeans and a cream spaghetti-strap camisole.

The woman's caramel hair drew his focus to her and he ached inside as he pictured it being Caterina, saw her turn and look at him with that warm smile she had bestowed on him once or twice, a smile that had heated him right down to his marrow.

Gods, he missed her.

The woman turned towards the dark-haired man, lifting her face towards him.

He had to miss her more than he had thought, because now he was seeing Caterina in that woman, in that soft smile she offered to the man as she took his arm.

Marek frowned as he slowly rose to his feet and took a closer look at the woman.

It *was* Caterina.

Darkness poured through him as his focus shifted to the slim man beside her, the one she was looking at with light in her hazel eyes as she talked to him.

Who was he?

The darkness coiled around his heart, twisting tightly to squeeze it as he began following them, and it hissed into his ear, whispering words about betrayal, about how another woman he had been foolish enough to feel something for had acted just like Caterina.

Fawning over another man.

He clenched his teeth to deny the growl that wanted to roll up his throat and fought back against his darker nature, against the side of him that wanted to rip the man apart for just touching what was his.

Caterina wasn't his.

He kept telling himself that as he stalked them through the warren of narrow pedestrian streets and watched them walk into a bar, passing the patrons milling around outside it at small tables.

He stopped outside on the pavement, stared in through the glass to Caterina as she took the seat the man offered, as she smiled and touched his hand.

A black snarl pealed from his lips.

The humans outside the bar scattered.

Marek was storming into the building before he was even aware of what he was doing, shoving people aside as they dared to get in his way, and coming close to baring his emerging fangs at more than one of them.

"Caterina," he growled as he reached her.

She stood sharply and swung to face him, her hazel eyes enormous. "Marek."

Her heartbeat was off the scale, thundering in his ears as the scent of her fear hit him.

"Didn't expect to be caught?" He stepped up to her and she tossed a panicked glance at the man, confirming his worst fears.

She had betrayed him with this man.

She felt something for him.

Did she feel nothing for Marek now? Had he killed it all that night on the beach? He wanted to turn away and leave, but he bottled that weak side up and clung to his fury, the jealous side of his blood that demanded retribution. He could feel like hell later, when this was all over, could lament what he had done and how badly things had gone, and nurse the fractured heart that pounded against his ribs as he glared at Caterina.

As she stood her ground and faced him, her eyes hard and daring him to attack her again.

"What's going on?" she said, far softer than he expected, and the rigid line of her shoulders relaxed.

"That's my line. Who is he?" Marek jerked his chin towards the man.

He hadn't bothered to stand, was still seated at the table with his dull eyes fixed on Marek, a watchful and wary edge to them.

"I can explain." Caterina's voice shook as she edged towards the man.

Away from Marek.

"I don't need an explanation," he barked and took a step back. "I think I've seen enough."

"It isn't like that." Her eyes grew wild and she leaned towards him, went to lift her hand and let it fall rather than reaching for him. "You're overreacting."

Marek didn't think he was, and worse, he couldn't blame her for moving on, finding a man who wouldn't treat her as terribly as he had. His gaze flickered to her neck, to the fading bruises on it.

He had never been one to burn bridges, but he wanted to torch the fragile remains of the one between him and Caterina.

Partly to protect her from his instincts that even now labelled her as a daemon.

Partly because she really did deserve better.

He held his tongue though, because he was meant to be helping her and getting answers from her. If she had been infected by his enemy, then it was his fault. The least he could do was find a way to fix it for her, to free her of the grip of his enemy and the daemonic blood running in her veins.

Even if she didn't end up with him.

"Caterina." He dared a step towards her.

She glanced at the man to her left, a fearful look that had Marek's focus leaping to him. Was she afraid of this man?

As his senses locked onto him, something hit him like a freight train.

Darkness surged through him.

"Vampire," he sneered, unable to believe it even as everything clicked into place. "Did he do this to you? Is he with them?"

A Hellspawn might be a member of the ranks of his enemy, and he was looking right at one.

And Caterina's silence said she had known what he was.

Marek lunged for the bastard.

Caterina stepped in his path, blocking his way to the vampire as she stretched her arms out. He slammed to a halt and stared at her, blinked as he struggled to take in what she had done. She was protecting him.

She was protecting the vampire and there was love and fear in her eyes as she did it.

"You were conspiring against me all this time," Marek snarled, his blood thundering in his ears and his fists shaking as he clenched them, as he looked between her and the vampire, waiting for her to deny it.

The words that left her lips, softly whispered, weren't a denial.

But they did send him reeling.

"He's my brother."

Marek could only stare at the man as he placed his hands on Caterina's slender shoulders over the straps of her cream camisole.

She tensed.

"You don't have to protect me." The man lowered his head towards her ear but didn't take his eyes off Marek. "I can handle this."

She threw a frantic look at him. "No, Guillem. Not this... this is mine to handle."

She lifted her left hand and placed it over his on her shoulder as she smiled, a gentle one that did nothing to soothe Guillem's evident hunger to fight.

"I'll be just a minute. Will you wait here?"

Guillem didn't look inclined to agree to that, but then he reluctantly released her and sat back down at the table, and glared at Marek.

In a fight, Marek would destroy him. He was weak, looked as if he hadn't fed in months. Was he the reason Caterina fought vampires?

The reason she had asked Marek about a possible cure?

Caterina scowled at Marek as she stormed past him, her shoulders tensing up again with each step, and he could sense the fury building inside her, the rage that would explode from her as soon as they were alone.

He had his own dose of rage to level at her.

She turned on him the moment he stepped out into the stifling evening heat.

The fire that had been building in her was quick to die and resignation flooded her hazel eyes as she took a lunging step towards him.

"Please don't kill Guillem." Her fine eyebrows furrowed and she gently shook her head as tears filled her eyes. "What happened to him wasn't his fault, and he's never bitten anyone, I swear. You told me you were meant to hunt daemons... and I'm one of those things, right? So, take me, but just... just let Guillem live."

Marek stared at her, stunned as he listened to her, as he saw the desperation in her eyes, and sorrow too.

That same emotion filled him, born of two things. She would sacrifice herself for her brother. She honestly believed Marek had come here to kill her.

He wasn't sure what to say to that.

He knew what half of his brothers would say. She was right, and she was a daemon, or at least becoming one, and his duty was to hunt and kill their kind.

But just as she clung to some crazy hope that she could turn her brother human again, he clung to a crazy hope that he was wrong about her and she had told him the truth on the beach.

She hadn't chosen this and she wanted to be human again.

He clung to the hope that he could find a way to make that happen.

"I didn't come here to kill you, Caterina."

Something like relief crossed her eyes. "What do you want then? You made your feelings about me abundantly clear on the beach."

Her hazel eyes darted to a group of people coming towards them along the narrow street. Afraid they would hear things they shouldn't? He wasn't. In his experience, mortals tended to forget hearing things that sounded too far-fetched to be real, or too frightening.

"I... shouldn't have reacted like that." He diligently kept his eyes off her neck and those healing bruises.

She dragged his focus to them by touching them. "Well, you did and I figured I would never see you again. But here you are, and I'm finding it difficult to believe you didn't come to take another shot at me."

"Caterina," he said in a low voice, hoping she would hear the warning in it. "I didn't come here to fight."

But if she kept provoking him, the darkness he was fighting to hold at bay might slip free of his control. That darker side of him labelled her as a daemon, something to eradicate. He kept telling himself that she wasn't. Not yet anyway.

He wasn't sure he could kill her even if she did become a fully-fledged daemon.

She hadn't chosen this. It had been forced upon her.

"I hate this," she whispered, frustration lacing those words, mingling with the pain that shone in her eyes. Tears lined them, tearing at his heart, and she scrubbed them away, turning her profile to him. "I hate what's happening to me. I hate what they want me to do. I hate that I was going to do it."

Her gaze drifted to meet his.

She shook her head.

"I hate that we can't be together."

He clenched his fists, denying the urge to reach out and feather his fingers across her cheek.

He hated it too.

As he stared at her, he realised that neither of them knew what to do. She was only part daemon, but it was still enough to have most people in the Underworld after her head, and his father would kill him if he so much as touched her.

Hades would probably kill him several times over if he knew that Marek's feelings for her hadn't changed in the slightest. His instincts might view her as a daemon to be dealt with, but his heart only saw Caterina.

His beautiful, courageous and reckless Caterina.

"You need to go." She stepped up to him and pressed her hands to his chest, shoved him backwards as her eyes turned wild and desperate again. "If you aren't near me, you're safe."

Marek shook his head. "I'm not going anywhere, not until you tell me everything. What happened, Caterina? How did this happen to you? Who did this? I need answers."

Because he needed to help her. That need had been strong in him before, after she had teleported from the beach and he had cooled off a little, able to look at things objectively again. It had grown stronger during his meeting with his brothers.

Now, it burned inside him.

A compulsion that demanded he obey it.

He had dragged Caterina into this, and he could pull her free of it.

He wasn't sure how, but he would find a way.

"Marek—" she started.

Thick fog rolled through his head and she wobbled in his vision. He blinked and reared back, gritted his teeth and grunted as heat spread outwards from his right shoulder, burning a path across his flesh that had him close to doubling over as his strength left him and the world grew dim.

It hit him that he had just been stabbed in the back.

Literally.

He stared at Caterina, into her wide eyes, catching the shock in them as she looked beyond him.

"You never said you were going to hurt him!" Those words leaving her lips cleaved his heart in two and unleashed cold fire that blazed through him, consuming all of the softer parts of him, the weak parts that had brought him to this place.

That had made it possible for this to happen.

He tried to keep his focus on Caterina as he snarled, as he fought the heaviness invading his mind and his body, weighing his limbs down.

Her eyes shifted to him, fear shining in them, fear he refused to believe was real. None of this had been real. It had been a lie. A manipulation. And he had fallen for it, believing she felt something for him, that she had been pulled into this because of him, and that he could save her.

He had been betrayed.

Again.

Fool him once?

Shame on the vampire bitch.

Fool him twice?

He was going to kill the fucking lot of them.

CHAPTER 17

Cal wove through the late-night traffic on the Victoria Embankment, the street lamps dotted between the towering trees on either side of the four-lane road flashing over the visor of his helmet. A visor that dampened his vision, but he was sick of Keras berating him about road safety. His older brother needed to get a life, or a hobby.

A hobby other than making Cal's life hell.

It was bad enough he was stuck with Keras as a partner, couldn't shake the bastard no matter how hard he tried. Keras was perpetually stuck in big-bro mode when it came to him, so Cal was perpetually trapped in the lowest, worst level of the Underworld.

At least it felt that way.

Worse were the times all his brothers treated him like a kid.

He huffed and swerved left, slipping the motorbike between a double-decker bus and a shitty electric car that was so compact, he wasn't even sure how the driver fitted in it. He revved the engine as he pulled up beside it. The pretty brunette behind the wheel glanced at him, a frown marring her delicate features.

Cal flicked his visor up and grinned at her as he kept pace with her, slowing to a boring speed, one that had him sure he was going to fall off his damn bike. He revved the engine again, the purr of it sending a shiver of pleasure through him, together with the sweet vibration of it beneath him.

The brunette cracked, her scowl becoming a smile as she slowed to a halt at a set of traffic lights.

Cal stopped beside her and tapped on her window.

She shifted her right hand from the steering wheel and the window whirred downwards.

"Hey, beautiful," he leaned towards her, resting his left elbow on her door and planting his boot on the road to keep the bike from toppling over and making him look like a fool. "Want to ride?"

He patted the sleek fuel tank wedged between his thighs, stroking the metallic lime green and black paint.

"I can go fast or slow. Whatever revs your engine."

A blush scalded her cheeks.

"I really shouldn't." She cleared her throat, her blush deepening as her eyes dropped to his hand as he stroked it closer to his hips. "I... uh... I have a boyfriend."

He shrugged. "Whatever. Not like I'm asking you to marry me. Just offering a ride to a pretty girl."

Her eyes darted between his hand as he rested it on his inside thigh and his face, a war erupting in them.

The traffic lights changed.

The bus driver hit the horn like it was going out of fashion.

She tensed and panicked, fumbled with her steering wheel. "I should... I have to go."

For a moment, she looked as if she was going to crumble.

"I have a boyfriend," she blurted and put her foot on the gas, creeping forwards at her mundane speed.

"Your loss." Cal slammed his visor down, gunned the engine on the sleek Kawasaki Ninja superbike and peeled away, the front wheel lifting off the tarmac as he passed the woman, tearing down the narrow gap between the two lanes of traffic.

There were plenty of other fish in London, and one of them was bound to take the bait tonight, so he could blow off some steam.

Patrols had gone quiet, gate activity hitting a boring zero in the last two nights, as if someone had flipped a switch. It was weird, but he wasn't going to sweat it. Daemons would pop up soon enough and he could blow off steam that way too.

He darted through the vehicles for fun, grinning whenever one of the humans tooted their weedy horns at him, cutting close to the more expensive sportscars to rile their owners. One of them even wound his window down to holler abuse at Cal.

Cal flipped him off over his shoulder.

Applied a little pressure to the air inside the guy's tyre and laughed as it burst.

He hit a stretch of empty road as he made it ahead of the traffic and slowed to a more reasonable fifty miles per hour, taking in the broad swath of the Thames as it glittered to his left, reflecting the lights from the London Eye and the buildings on the other side.

Parliament loomed ahead on his side, signalling the end of his fun unless he did a U-turn and went back the other way.

He was debating it as a weird sensation crawled over his back and head. The same sensation he had been having for a while now. It wasn't his ability to sense daemons kicking in. This was something else.

Cal pulled the bike over to the side of the road and cut the engine. He looked around him, trying to find the source of the feeling of being watched. It was starting to unsettle him now, because over the last week, it had felt different.

There was no malevolence in it.

Not like there had been before.

His phone vibrated. He unzipped his black leather jacket, reached inside and pulled it out. The light from the screen reflected off his visor, but he could read the message. A meeting in Tokyo.

He stuffed the phone back into his jacket, zipped it up and focused as he gripped his bike. Shadows wrapped around him and darkness surrounded him, and then light as he landed in the large garage he had added beneath his townhouse. He pulled his helmet off, set it down on the fuel tank and kicked the stand down. He tugged the bike up onto it and eased off it, ran his hand over the leather seat and cursed his brothers for ruining his night.

He looked over his shoulder at the line of bikes parked along the wall at a diagonal, their jewel-coloured paint gleaming under the bright strip lights in the white room.

He had wanted to take each of them out for a spin.

Maybe the meeting would be over with quickly and he could get back to riding.

He didn't bother to remove his leather jacket before teleporting, landing on the porch of the old mansion. The wooden deck creaked beneath his weight as he removed his boots and kicked them into the corner, next to the rack where his brothers had neatly placed theirs.

He shoved the door open.

"Well, all we know is what Zeus said." Valen's voice rose above the din of voices, coming from Cal's right as he stepped into the long room. "When Calindria died—"

Cal didn't hear the rest as he was whipped back through time, to a dark bluff on a mountainside, to her screams and his desperate bellows as he tried to break free of his bonds and help her.

He fell to his knees, clutched the sides of his head and screamed with her.

Hands grabbed him and he fought them, but they wouldn't relent. They were too strong, overpowering him, binding him as he thrashed against them, desperate to break free of them just as he had tried to break free of his bonds.

He wrestled, lashed out with his legs and his elbows, managed to catch one of them with his head. Pain spider-webbed across his skull and his vision dimmed, the muffled grunt that left his opponent's lips not bringing the satisfaction he had thought it would. He kept fighting them, the need to reach his sister hitting boiling point as her screams continued, as she pleaded the bastards to have mercy on her.

On him.

As she offered her life in exchange for his.

He snarled through his tears, begged her not to do it, begged the bastards not to listen to her, to listen to him instead. His life for hers. She was precious. She deserved life. The world couldn't lose her.

One captor remained, his grip so strong Cal couldn't shake it, no matter how many blows he landed or how fiercely he struggled. A hand clamped down over his forehead, the pressure of it pleasant as the riot in his head slowly dulled and darkness encroached, creeping in from the corners of his mind to steal everything away.

He slipped into it, welcoming it as he became aware of what was coming, escaping the past before the inevitable moment when his entire world had changed.

The darkness devoured him just as she started to scream.

He drifted in it a while.

Made a wish to stay there forever.

Light burst around Cal, bright and blinding, and he shot up, blinked as he looked around him and found he was sitting on the floor. Golden tatami mats. Tokyo. He swallowed and frowned, looked at the feet surrounding him.

At the arms holding him from behind.

His strength left him in a rush and he sank against Keras's chest.

"I was on my bike. There was a pretty woman in a car." He growled and clenched his teeth as he tried to remember the rest of what had happened but it wouldn't come.

Keras stroked his forehead, that touch soothing the raging headache building in his temples, keeping the darkness at bay.

"You're fine," his brother murmured softly in his ear.

"I was chatting up a human." He clenched his fists and his face crumpled. "She was pretty."

"I know," Valen said as he eased to crouch before him, his golden eyes warm and tender. "And now you're here. Nothing vital happened."

"You don't know that," he snapped and pushed Keras away when his touch became stifling, twisting his insides and making him feel as if he couldn't breathe. "What if I forgot something important? What if something triggered it and I forgot it?"

Keras gently placed a hand on his shoulder.

"You haven't." His brother hesitated, conflict reigning in his green eyes, before he added, "We were talking about her."

Cal's eyes slowly widened and all of the fight rushed out of him. He sagged where he sat on the floor, his gaze falling to rest on it as the fear and frustration became sorrow that threatened to devour his heart.

"I see." He couldn't bring himself to look at his brothers, not now that he knew why he had blacked out. He didn't want to see the pity in their eyes, didn't want to see how weak they thought he was because of his affliction.

It was bad enough that they constantly coddled him because of it, treading on eggshells around him.

Keeping things from him.

Keras squeezed his shoulder.

Cal jerked out of his grip and shoved to his feet. "I'm fine."

He paced away from his brothers, towards the panels that had been slid open to reveal the elegant courtyard that filled the space between the three sides of the mansion.

Bright sunlight warmed the pale gravel and birds flitted between the neatly clipped pine trees, dancing among the twisting branches to the perfect ovals of green needles at the end of each of them.

The stepping stones that wound between them led his eye to the koi pond that separated the courtyard from the main garden, to the vermillion arched wooden bridge that crossed the water to the other side, where mossy boulders and trees tangled together in perfect harmony.

She would have loved this place.

He wanted to remember her again, he wanted to remember what his brothers had been talking about before his episode, but he didn't dare risk it. It would only trigger another attack and this time, he might pass out. It had happened before, in the early days when he had tried to remember, foolishly believing that if he pushed himself it would all come back to him and he could help his sister by recalling what had happened.

By remembering who had killed her.

The last time he had tried that, he had been out cold for five days.

He couldn't allow that to happen when the gates were in so much danger.

This battle needed all of them on the front line if they were going to win it.

He turned around and looked at his brothers.

And realised one was missing.

"Where's Marek?"

Keras's expression grew grave. "We don't know. We tried contacting him but he isn't answering."

"He wasn't in Seville when I checked," Ares said and jammed his hands into the pockets of his black jeans.

Daimon glanced at Esher as he began pacing, his bare feet carrying him swiftly across the mats.

Cal hoped like hell nothing had happened to Marek, because if it had, Esher wouldn't be the only one going nuclear.

He would be right there with him.

CHAPTER 18

Marek's back hurt like a bitch.

He shuffled to the wall of the dark empty room, struggling to crab-crawl with his hands bound, keeping his bare backside off the oak floor. His heightened vision revealed the space to him, one ability the daemons hadn't taken from him.

Maybe they couldn't.

They had shut down his power over the earth and his ability to teleport, and his telekinesis wasn't working either.

When he reached the wall, he rubbed his back against the pale green plaster, a desperate attempt to make the burning stop. A grimace tugged at his lips as he twisted his hands behind him and manoeuvred into a better position, one where he could itch the point on his left shoulder.

The floor was cold beneath him, the air in the room frigid despite the fact it was high summer, and he chuckled as a thought pinged into his head.

This was probably Daimon's version of paradise.

The air conditioning unit whirring above the door had to be industrial meat-locker grade.

The daemons were intent on keeping him docile, using the cold to steal more of his strength and make him sluggish. Dehydration and the cold would take care of that. His muscles were stiff already, his joints hard to move.

The relief that hit him when he managed to find the itchy spot on his shoulder was sweet and almost drugging, and he fell into an easy rhythm, rubbing against the wall until heat bloomed and trickled down his back.

The smell of his own blood was strong in the air, together with other things that Marek was not about to admit came from him. He wasn't sure how long he had been out before coming around to find himself naked in what had turned out to be his prison cell, but he had been awake for more than a day now.

Not that he could really tell.

Someone had nailed boards over the tall windows, blocking out the sunlight.

"Fucking daemons," he spat and kept rubbing, drawing more blood, working up more heat.

Whatever the bastard had carved on his back, it had done a number on Marek's powers.

A ward?

He had no doubt now that the wraith was behind his capture, and what had happened to Caterina. If he could believe her anymore. He wanted to, but it was hard as he shed more blood, leaving the wall behind him red with it as he waited for the daemon to decide to fuck around with him again.

The illusionist had brought Caterina into this room and made her stand there watching him for almost an hour. The dark-violet-haired daemon had been forced to hold her arm the entire time to keep her upright. Whatever was happening to Caterina, it was getting worse again.

She had looked better when he had found her in Barcelona, but the last time she had been brought to him as some weird form of torment, or perhaps a test to see if he would react to her either violently or sexually, her skin had been as white as snow and she had been shaking, and sweating profusely.

And Marek had foolishly wanted to tell the daemon bitch to undo whatever the fuck it was they had done to her because they had him now.

He growled at himself and stoked the anger, the darker side of him that was more than happy to point out what a gigantic idiot he had been to trust a woman again.

Especially after what had happened with Valen.

Eva had been hired by their enemy to seduce him and lure him over to their side.

They had tried the same crap on Marek and he had fallen for it, although he doubted they wanted him to fight on their team. They had grander plans for him.

Ones he wasn't going to stick around to find out about.

He kept rubbing, until his shoulder was raw and burned from it rather than the symbol they had carved on him.

It had to be a ward.

The wraith had taken Esher's memories through a fragment of his soul he had stolen with his blade, the same blade he had used on Marek to knock him out. Which meant he also had some of Marek's memories now.

And he knew a whole host of wards that could easily be implemented even by a daemon.

He thanked the gods that when they had created new wards around the Tokyo mansion that they had chosen to do it all away from each other, and that he only knew the ward he had made. Breaking one ward wouldn't allow the enemy to penetrate the barrier around the mansion, which meant it was still a safe place for his brothers and their women.

Marek leaned to his right and tried to peer over his shoulder at the ward carved into his flesh. All he could see was blood. He couldn't tell whether he had managed to make it deep enough yet to disrupt the power of the ward.

His healing ability wasn't helping him.

Whenever he thought he was making progress, that ability kicked in, undoing his work.

The daemons could have been kind enough to lock that one down too.

He looked around the room again, a futile endeavour since it was empty and he had checked every crevice of it for something he could use to either pry open his bonds or carve a damned hole in the ward.

The green walls were growing more red by the hour, and patches of dried blood now decorated the wooden floor, dark against the polished oak.

But he was getting nowhere.

The only way to get rid of this ward and get his powers back was to destroy it, and that meant getting his hands free and on a blade or something sharp.

The door opened, throwing light across him, and the illusionist slinked into the room, her long black dress flowing around her feet to conceal them. She halted in front of him, but he kept his eyes on the open door, on the freedom it taunted him with, a glimpse of a cream corridor and a side table that had an elegant crystal vase on it.

"It will not work." Her honey-sweet voice dripped in his ears as she leaned towards him, dragging his focus to her. Her breasts threatened to spill from the low vee of her dress.

He curled a lip at her.

She sighed and looked to her right when he glanced there, at the door.

"No escape that way." She eased down in front of him, her silver eyes swirling as her black lips curled into a faint, satisfied smile. "How infuriating it must be to have your powers bound."

She pouted, pulling a face of mock pity that tore a growl from him.

Because it hit him that this was payback.

He and his brothers had put her in Esher's cage when they had caught her. The enchantments on it stole the powers of those contained within it, rendering them weak. Esher used it when the full moon hit a lunar perigee, the point in the year when it was closest to the Earth. Daimon had to lock him in the cage because what he became was dangerous, a beast more savage than anyone could imagine, thirsty for violence and controlled by a need to shed human blood and watch them suffer.

The cage kept Esher and the world safe from that savage, dangerous side of him.

This daemon had been given a taste of the cage, and now she wanted him to experience what she had.

Or perhaps it was the wraith who wanted him to suffer as she had, a gift to her that evidently pleased her as she observed Marek and he couldn't hide how much this was annoying him, how much he despised being without his powers, left at the mercy of his enemy.

"The female did well to bring you to us." The woman canted her head, causing her glossy straight dark violet hair to fall away from her shoulder. "We should reward her. Perhaps we should complete our end of the bargain and take care of her brother's problem."

Caterina had been telling the truth about the vampire being her brother then, and about her reason for doing what she had done to Marek. It didn't make him feel any better. It only made him feel worse, because it confirmed that she had betrayed him. She had chosen to save her brother by condemning him.

He bared his short fangs at the daemon as they emerged, as he felt the darkness pouring into his veins turning his eyes black. The illusionist's eyes narrowed as her smile widened.

"A reaction at last." She leaned closer. "He will be pleased. It seems the little female got to you just as he suspected. He was right to bring her into the fold. We had thought you would be the difficult one. It was disappointingly easy to capture you."

Marek spat in her face.

She flinched, her face twisting in disgust as she brought her hand up and delicately wiped the spit away.

She looked at her hand.

Struck him hard across his right cheek with it and sent him falling onto his side. His head spun, vision twirling, and he rolled his eyes, trying to shake off the blow before she got any ideas about following up with another one.

"Weak creature." She snarled and pushed to her feet to tower over him. Her silver eyes glowed as she glared down at him. "We will break you. By the time we are done with you, you will be on your knees telling us everything we want to know."

She swept from the room, slammed the door, and he closed his eyes as the sound of metal scraping against metal filled his ears. He listened to her as she stormed away from him and it stoked the fire inside him, refusing to give in as she wanted.

She wouldn't break him.

He was going to get free of this place, and this damned ward, and then he was going to destroy them.

His vision wavered out of focus.

But first, he was just going to rest his eyes.

When he opened them again, he was on his back, his hands numb beneath him. He groaned and rolled onto his side, onto his front, and shoved his face against the floorboards to push himself up. He shuffled his knees beneath him and grimaced as he sat up. Every muscle on his torso protested and cramped in response, but he managed it.

His stomach growled.

His parched throat screamed for water.

Marek looked at the boarded windows. How long had he been out?

He tried to look at his shoulder but he could only see the start of the mark carved on it.

It was fully healed again.

"Damn it," he barked and wriggled backwards, towards the wall.

The cold fire that had burned inside him since the night he had been taken blazed colder still as he remembered everything the daemon had said about Caterina and his darker side latched onto it.

She had betrayed him.

She was going to pay for that.

No one betrayed him and got away with it.

The need for retribution mingled and entwined with the darkness and he gave in to it as he started rubbing against the wall, harder this time, the hunger for vengeance a driving force within him, filling his head with pleasing images.

He would start with Caterina, knew she was in this building somewhere. He would get rid of this ward, break free of his bonds, and he would find her. Once she had paid for what she had done to him, he would regain his strength and bring hell down on this house and its occupants.

The thought that he had been weak again taunted him, giving the darkness a stronger grip on him. He sank into it, relished it as it gave him strength, a purpose. He wouldn't be weak again.

He had let her past the barriers again, when he should have kept them slammed shut against her. He shouldn't have tried to find her. He shouldn't have cared that she might be turning into a daemon. He should have called it quits long before he had realised her brother was a vampire.

He shouldn't have let his ridiculous feelings for her blind him.

She was a daemon. Maybe not in body, not yet, but she had proven herself just as vicious and vile as their kind, willing to lure someone to their death.

The darkness inside him writhed, hungry to be fed, for the carnage his mind was swift to imagine as he kept scrubbing his shoulder against the wall.

Rapid footsteps sounded on the other side of the wall to his left.

Followed by something hitting it hard.

He stilled right down to his breathing and reached for his powers. A curse pealed from his lips when they didn't come and he listened to the heartbeat rushing in his ears.

Not his own.

It belonged to whoever was on the other side of the wall.

Metal scuffed, the doorknob jiggled, and another attempt was made, the sound of the metal scraping against each other grating in his ears.

A burst of light.

He flinched away from it and glared at the silhouetted figure in the doorway.

The petite shadow blurred as it moved, refusing to come into focus as adrenaline pushed his already fatigued body right to its limit.

Was it the illusionist come to break him?

He feared he might do just that as she entered the room, coming towards him.

He frowned and amended that.

Stumbling towards him?

That frown deepened when his damned vision finally cleared and he could make out the woman who hit the floor just a few feet from him, collapsing in a heap.

Caterina.

She recovered swiftly, throwing a panicked look over her shoulder.

"Drop the act," he growled, not wanting to play this game anymore. He looked at the doorway. "Come out, I know you're just trying to fuck with me. I know you're there."

No one appeared in the doorway.

It was a struggle to get his senses functioning properly, but when he managed it, he found only two signatures in the immediate vicinity.

Caterina.

And him.

"Have to be quick." Caterina's voice was low, hoarse, and weak.

She crawled towards him.

"Get away from me." He reared back, kicked at her with his left leg and caught her right arm.

She went down hard even though he had barely touched her, face-planting on the floor. She lay there a moment, her breaths uneven, fast in his ears.

Finally, she moved, pressing her palms to the oak boards and wobbling as she pushed herself up.

"Trying to help." She pushed each word out with an evident struggle as she wavered on her hands and knees. "Don't have long. They don't leave for long."

"Who doesn't leave for long?" Marek told himself not to fall for this. It was another ploy, a lie constructed to weaken him again, to make him trust the daemon crawling towards him.

He would never trust her again.

"The daemons," she whispered and whimpered as she stopped, as she hung her head and clutched her stomach, banding one arm around it.

His stupid heart jerked in his chest, panic flooding him as he waited to see if she was going to pass out.

She was sick. Her hair was damp, hanging in tendrils around her face as she lifted it, revealing a sweat dotted brow and dull eyes.

"Be quick."

He wasn't sure she was talking to him now as she inched forwards. She muttered things beneath her breath, Catalan words that sounded a lot like a prayer. Her breath sawed from her lips, each one cutting him despite how fiercely he tried to remain immune to her.

When she finally reached him, she gritted her teeth and eased up on her knees. He tensed when she reached behind her and pulled a knife from the waist of her navy jeans. It fell from her fingers as she cried out and doubled over, clutching herself again.

Another prayer fell from her lips.

Marek stared at the knife on the floor.

"You here to kill me?" He kept still, conserving his strength in case he needed it.

He was in no state to fight, not with his strength and powers bound, and his hands tied behind his back, but Caterina wasn't in any state to fight either. He could almost feel her weakness as she held herself, as hoarse sobs burst from her lips and she shuddered.

When whatever terrible pain that wracked her had passed, she inched her hand towards the blade, using her fingers to drag it towards the hilt. They shook as she pulled it towards her, and her grip was limp as she finally closed her hand around it.

"Turn." She breathed hard, struggled into an upright position again and looked at his waist.

"So you can stab me in the back again?"

Tears glistened on her cheeks as her brow furrowed. "Trying to... free... you. Maybe... pick... lock."

Is that what she had done with the door? She hadn't been picking the lock then. No. She must have used the knife and her limited strength to break it open, draining herself in the process.

"Forget the bonds." He hoped he wasn't going to regret this.

It wasn't trusting her again. He kept telling himself that as he shuffled so his back was to her, trying to make it easier on her. He was using her this time.

Not just to get free either.

She had been a guest in this house and would be able to give him information on it, and on her hosts. Or should he say her allies?

"See that mark on my back? Slice through it."

"What?"

He found it hard to believe that horror in her voice was genuine.

"You already stabbed me in the back once. Just do it again." He didn't miss the way she glared at him and he didn't repent either. She deserved everything she got from him as far as he was concerned.

Her throat worked on a hard swallow as she stared at his back.

She was going to bottle out.

"Do it. Do it or I'll hunt your fucking brother down and slaughter him," he snarled, his voice darker than he had ever heard it.

She gasped.

He let it bounce off his back, because he was done being nice to her. She had burned that bridge between them before he could get there and do it for her.

"I'll help," she murmured weakly. "Don't hurt... Guillem."

"I bet that's what you said to them too." He couldn't keep the venom from his voice as the cold fire in his heart turned white-hot with an emotion he didn't want to contemplate.

He wasn't jealous of the lengths she would go to for her brother, revealing how deeply she loved the vermin.

He wasn't.

He grunted when she suddenly stabbed him in the back, hard enough to jerk him forwards, and gritted his teeth as she drew the blade down, slicing right through the heart of the mark carved on his shoulder.

"You... deserve... that," she spat and then something thudded on the floor. The knife?

He looked over his shoulder as heat spread through him, bringing strength in its wake, and the power of the ward dissipated.

Caterina lay on her side, out cold, her damp caramel hair spilling across the floorboards and the hilt of the knife balanced on her open palm.

He felt nothing as he looked at her.

He closed his eyes and turned away. He felt *nothing*.

His heart called him a liar.

Marek waited for more of his strength to return and then focused it all on his arms, on his wrists as he pulled them apart. The chain linking his bonds snapped, the sudden release of his arms flinging him forwards. He slammed a hand into the floor to stop himself from hitting it and slowly looked back at Caterina.

He felt nothing.

Telling himself that didn't do shit as he moved onto his knees and went to her, as he canted his head and looked down at her, studying every dark hollow on her pale face.

Even out cold she was breathing too rapidly and shaking.

Had the daemons done something else to her?

He gathered her into his arms and stumbled onto his feet, and paused as he looked at the door. She had said the daemons didn't stay away for long. If he waited, he could deal with them now.

He looked down at Caterina. She was burning up, her trembling growing worse as he held her tucked against his bare chest. He wasn't sure there was anything he could do to help her, but gods, he wanted to try.

Setting himself up for another fall?

Probably, but he just couldn't convince himself to hate her, to hold her responsible for what had happened to him. He couldn't bring himself to believe that she had known what would happen that night in Barcelona when he had found her with her brother.

"Idiot," he muttered to himself, a name he more than deserved, and one that was far nicer than the ones his brothers were going to use when they discovered what he had done.

He reasoned that he was in no fit state to battle two strong daemons on their own turf and that the best warrior armed himself with knowledge first, and then steel.

Caterina was a vital weapon in this war, one he intended to use to its fullest. She would tell him everything.

And if she refused?

He would let his brothers handle her.

He turned away and stepped with her, reappearing in a dark-wood-clad vestibule. He leaned back as his strength wavered, the grey stone arch that surrounded one of the leaded windows cool against his burning shoulder.

He needed to get Caterina to the basement, but teleporting again would be a mistake. He couldn't afford to pass out, not before he had her contained anyway.

Marek slowly crossed the vestibule of the castle, his body warming as the heat of day met it and he passed the shafts of sunlight that washed into the room from the row of arched windows to his left. He passed a corridor and kept going, took a right near a shadowy section of the hallway and headed that way, towards stone steps that led downwards.

He carefully picked his way down the spiral staircase, doing his best not to damage Caterina as she slumbered in his arms. The light and heat of day gave way to chilling darkness, an echo of where he had spent the last gods knew how many days.

He tried not to let it affect him as he banked right again at the bottom of the steps. The cold flagstones chilled the bare soles of his feet as he carried Caterina to the first cell in a row of three, opened the solid iron door and took her inside.

He set her down on the cot that had seen better days and hesitated as he looked down at her.

When his brothers learned what she had done, they would want to hurt her. Could he let them do that, when he honestly couldn't say whether she had betrayed him or not? It felt like a betrayal, but he was jaded, his view coloured by his past.

The darkness he had managed to push back and contain rose within him again as he looked at her, as his shoulder burned and the shackles around his wrists weighed them down. It condensed into a malevolent force, a hunger that wouldn't be denied.

Marek turned away from Caterina, exited the cell and closed the door. He slid the bolts across, sealing her in the dark room, and peered through the small window of bars at her where she lay on her back, every inch of her shaking.

She was safer in there, away from him.

At least until he was back in control of himself.

Although regaining that control was going to take her telling him everything. Only then would he be able to even begin believing her.

He trudged away from her, his feet heavy as the darker part of him grew restless, filling him with a need to turn back and watch over her. Not because he didn't trust her this time.

She was sick.

Weak.

And he feared she wouldn't last the day.

He moved up through the castle, forcing himself to place some distance between them as he fought to untangle what he really wanted. The darkness within him wanted to hurt her, but it also wanted to take away her pain.

It wanted her to suffer.

And wanted to protect her.

He laughed mirthlessly as he shoved his hands through his hair.

What was wrong with him?

He gripped the rail of the thick mahogany banister on the main staircase and followed it up to the first floor, where he and his brothers had their rooms. His gaze strayed to the arched windows that lined the grey stone wall to his left as he passed along the corridor. Sunlight rippled across the loch, lapping against the rocks that formed the shoreline around the castle. Beyond the deep water that surrounded the island, mountains rose, golden and pale green, laced with patches of pink where the heathers bloomed.

How long had it been since he had visited this place?

He and his brothers kept it as a safehouse now, a place only they knew about and one they could escape to if everything went wrong and they lost their stronghold in Tokyo.

Sometimes, Marek came here to enjoy the solitude.

He pushed the wooden door to his room open and headed for the bathroom, stopping in front of the cream marble sink. He turned the tap on and waited. A few minutes passed before the system kicked in. Air hissed and gurgled from the tap and then water. A trickle at first.

He ran his hand under it and shuddered at the icy coldness of it.

He would need to fire up the boiler if he wanted it warm. A shower was out of the question until then. He was lucky the electricity hadn't gone out like it had the last time he had visited. It had taken him a day to fix the wiring once he had found where the local creatures had chewed through it.

They had eaten their way through half the contents of the larder too.

Marek filled the basin and splashed the water on his face. He hissed as he washed his shoulder, the cold water stinging the cut. He was going to need Keras to remove the ward for him, before the wound healed and it kicked back to life.

Keras was not going to be happy.

His focus drifted to Caterina as he washed himself off, shuddering whenever the cold became too much. How was he going to keep his brothers from killing her once they discovered what had happened?

He had been missing for days. By now, they would be frantic, and he didn't want to think about how Esher was handling it.

He needed to get word to his brothers and ask them to meet him, Esher excluded. He couldn't risk his brother coming to the island and realising that he had Caterina locked in the basement.

He might be able to talk reason into the others, convincing them that she was a valuable source of information but was too weak for any rough interrogation tactics they might have in mind. Talking reason into Esher wasn't going to be an option.

His brother would kill her on sight.

He tensed when noise sounded below him, grabbed a pair of dark grey sweats from the dresser in his bedroom and pulled them on. He moved stealthily from the room, easing along the corridor, straining to hear who it was.

The daemons?

The wraith could use portals, but there was no way he could have tracked Marek to this location, or entered the building without triggering the wards.

"You here, old man?" Ares's voice boomed up the stairs, tugging a smile from Marek.

"That's my nickname for you." Marek looked over the banister at the top of the stairs.

Ares tilted his head back and relief filled his dark eyes.

"Thought it might get a response." All the light and warmth left his older brother's eyes. "Where the fuck have you been?"

"Are you alone?" Marek knew an opportunity when he saw it.

Out of all of his brothers, and regardless of what many people who knew them thought, Ares was the most liable to keep his head in any given situation.

Even one like this.

Ares nodded. "So, you want to explain yourself before the rest arrive? I'm getting the feeling you weren't off on vacation with your girlfriend."

Marek didn't even bother to correct him, because it was going to become blindingly apparent Caterina was anything but his girlfriend when he explained what had happened to him.

He made his way down the stairs, to the turn that brought him face to face with Ares where he hadn't moved off the bottom step. He sank to his backside on the landing there.

And sighed.

Where to begin?

"I found Caterina in Barcelona. We had a little confrontation. She thought I was going to kill her brother."

"Why? He a daemon too?" Ares frowned and gold sparks lit his eyes, an indicator that his mood was heading south.

Marek cringed inside. He shouldn't have brought the brother up, but he knew Caterina would when she came around and his brothers all spoke to her, so there was little point in trying to pretend he didn't exist.

Or that he wasn't a vampire.

Ares didn't know about Marek's habit of hunting vampires, so the fact her brother was one wouldn't matter in his brother's eyes. Although, there was a chance he might draw the same rash conclusion that Marek had and believe he was the Hellspawn involved with their enemy.

Marek didn't get a chance to see what Ares would say.

Keras appeared beyond him, swiftly followed by Calistos.

"Shit, it's been a while since I came to this gloomy place." Valen's voice echoed along the corridor from the vestibule.

Daimon's deep voice joined him. "Never did like it here either. Except in winter. It's nice in winter."

"You would think that." The third male voice made Marek freeze up faster than a touch from Daimon.

Esher.

Marek launched from the stairs.

His first mistake.

Esher took one look at him, at the lines of the mark that reached the top of his left shoulder, and his eyes blackened.

Narrowed as he drew down a deep breath and snarled.

"Where's the fucking daemon I can smell?"

CHAPTER 19

Keras seized Esher before Marek could reach him, holding him in place and weathering vicious snarls as Esher tried to break free of him. Crimson ringed Esher's deep blue irises, a warning sign that Marek wasn't going to take lightly.

"Get him the fuck away from here," he snapped at Keras, because if he didn't, Esher was going to rip Caterina to shreds.

Marek couldn't let that happen.

"A fucking daemon." Esher bared fangs at Keras, the scarlet band in his irises growing as he kicked at Keras's legs, leaving marks on his black slacks. "She hurt him. She hurt—"

Keras and Esher disappeared in a swirl of black smoke.

All of the tension that had been building inside Marek flooded out of him and he reached out to his left and gripped the newel post next to Ares to keep himself upright.

Ares just looked at him, giving him the same one that Daimon, Calistos and Valen were levelling on him.

"She has information." It was a reasonable excuse for Marek wanting to keep her out of Esher's claws. "He would have torn her apart."

"She in the basement?" Daimon looked beyond him, to the junction in the corridor that led down to it.

Marek nodded. "She's out cold."

"I'll wake her up." Valen cracked his knuckles.

Ares tossed him a black look. "No violence. She isn't liable to talk if we're rough with her."

"She isn't liable to talk at all. You don't understand." Marek moved into the corridor to block the way to the basement, because he needed his brothers to know what they were dealing with, he needed to see they understood everything.

Not just the fact Caterina was sick.

But that pushing him right now was dangerous.

He wanted to hurt her, but he needed to keep her safe. Right now, he was torn in two directions by the same instinct. He wasn't sure what he might do if his brothers laid a hand on her, and he didn't want to find out.

"I think she's infected with daemon blood. I still don't get the feeling that she's a daemon. It just isn't there. My gut doesn't react to her as it does with daemons, but sometimes my instincts kick in when I'm near her. When father's blood in my veins is at the helm, I can feel the daemon in her." Marek looked between his brothers, and Daimon and Valen exchanged a look.

Calistos leaned against the wooden wall. "I don't feel it either. If you told me there was a daemon in the basement, I wouldn't believe you."

"Esher would say otherwise," Daimon put in.

"Esher reacted because he saw I was hurt and because the darkness is always at the helm with him." Marek was confident of that. "You told him about Caterina, didn't you?"

Daimon gave him a sheepish look. Ares huffed. Valen shook his head.

"There was a reason I didn't want him to know, Daimon. Not yet." Not until he had figured out the truth anyway.

He still wasn't sure what he would do if it turned out she had been telling him the truth all along. She was becoming a daemon. Fraternising with a daemon was a huge no-no in his father's eyes.

Falling in love with one might just see him banished from the Underworld and exiled from his family forever.

Although the warmth and understanding in Ares's eyes said he might not lose everyone if he did lose his heart to Caterina.

"You want to tell us about that mark on your back?" Ares nodded towards it, his dark eyebrows dipping low as his lips compressed. "Because from where I'm standing, it looks like a ward."

Marek tried to look at it. "It is a ward. The wraith carved the damned thing on me with that blade of his. The illusionist seemed pretty pleased to have me as her guest, with a ward scrawled into my skin."

Daimon moved closer and peered at his back. "If that is a ward and it was written by the wraith, then we need it off you. Esher can feel the wraith when he's close because of what happened to him, and I'm guessing that means you'll probably experience the same pain as he does now whenever the wraith is nearby. I also have a theory that it works both ways."

"The wraith will know when he's close to Marek?" Ares looked as if he was chewing a wasp as he said that, and the gold and red in his irises blazed like the fire he commanded as he glared at the mark on Marek's shoulder.

"It's just a theory," Daimon said, his voice level but not enough to hide the note of concern in it.

Marek wasn't going to dance around the subject. "If the wraith can feel me and possibly the ward, and let's just agree he probably can, then I need it off me as soon as possible."

Because the wards around the castle were strong, but they weren't designed to repel daemons, making it impossible for them not to enter the grounds. They were designed to weaken daemons and alert him and his brothers when the wards were penetrated, giving them a heads up so they were ready for a fight.

He looked at Ares as something hit him. "You knew I was here."

His big brother shrugged. "I felt the wards trigger."

"We all did." Valen leaned his right shoulder against the wall. "Figure it was because you brought your girlfriend here for a dirty weekend."

Marek levelled him with a black look. He was getting tired of Valen constantly poking that sore spot.

"She isn't my girlfriend." His black look became a full-blown glare when Valen just shrugged that off, and he wanted to punch him for it. "She still doesn't feel like a daemon to me. There's daemon blood in her for sure, but I'm beginning to... well... I'm not really sure what I believe anymore."

He went in circles about it, and it was getting tiring.

"The wards on the cells are still in place?" Ares sounded worried.

Marek could understand why. He had brought Caterina to this place, one he and his brothers hadn't visited as a group in a long time, one they had thought the enemy didn't know about.

And now there was a potential enemy in the basement.

Gods, he hoped she wasn't one of them, but what did he know? He couldn't trust her. She had helped him escape, but it could have all been an act, one designed to bring them closer together or make him trust her, or do something to endanger everyone.

Like bringing her to a stronghold where all of his brothers would come to see him.

A stronghold that didn't have the defences of the Tokyo mansion.

"Valen, Cal, we need to shore up the wards here." He looked at both of them, making sure they were listening because both of them had a tendency to misread the gravity of a situation and treat it lightly.

Daimon sighed. "I'll go with them."

"Thanks." Marek watched them go, listening to them teasing each other about who could make the best wards.

When their voices disappeared, and he was alone with Ares, Marek's focus shifted to the floor beneath his feet, and beyond it to the basement. Was Caterina all right? She was weak enough already, and the thought of the wards draining her strength further because of her daemon blood had his gut churning, heart aching with a need to check on her.

He hardened it.

For all he knew, she was the enemy, and this was an attempt to infiltrate their ranks.

"We need to get that off you." Ares moved around behind him and Marek could feel the heat of him as he leaned closer to get a better look at the ward.

Marek nodded. "I can feel it healing again, dampening my powers. Damned thing will stop me from teleporting soon. I might need to rely on you guys if anything goes down."

Ares nodded. "Valen and Cal will have your back. If it's an emergency, I'll step with you."

Marek wanted to say something about taking Caterina too, but held his tongue. Ares wouldn't agree to that. His brother had heart, and clearly understood what Marek was going through, but there was no way he would allow any threat to come with them to somewhere else where they might be tracked again because of her.

"When Keras returns, I'll have him draw the power out of it and undo it." He reached over his shoulder and pulled on it as he twisted his head, trying to see the extent of the damage. He scowled when he saw several of the curving slashes had cut through his favour mark, into the dusky branches of the circle of trees. "Bastards."

"It's not as bad as it looks." Ares gave him a tight smile. "It will heal up nicely once we get rid of the ward. There is another less elegant way of doing it. I can burn it out."

Marek's stomach turned at just the thought of his brother searing his flesh deeply enough to destroy the ward. It would do the job, and Marek would heal from it, but he was damned if he was going to pick it over waiting for Keras. What Keras would do would hurt enough. What Ares proposed would be agony that would last for hours, and would probably have him waking in a cold sweat each day for months after reliving it in his sleep.

Ares had burned something off him before, ink that he'd had done on his right forearm in the heat of the moment, before the vampire bitch had betrayed him.

He wasn't sure he wanted to go through that hell again, feeling as if his entire body was about to catch fire and burn to ashes, smelling the stench of his own burning flesh, seeing the guilt on Ares's face as he hurt him.

"I can wait." Marek turned to face him and smiled, hoping his brother would see that he didn't want to put him through that again.

"How did you break the ward to get here?"

He sighed and his focus slipped to the basement again. "Caterina came to me. She had a knife. I didn't trust her at first, but she seemed... I don't know. I don't know whether I'm meant to trust her or treat her like the enemy."

And it was tearing him apart.

"Had she really wanted to help me or is this all another lie?" He looked to his brother, needed him to answer that question for him because whenever he tried, his answer kept changing.

Ares lifted his hand and looked as if he wanted to lay it on Marek's bare shoulder, and then his face crumpled and he scrubbed his hand over his tawny hair instead, tugging some of the overlong strands from the thong that held it tied back.

"I don't have the answer to that question. I wish I did. The one who can answer it for you is dealing with Esher."

Marek frowned and then his eyes slowly widened. Why hadn't he thought of that? Keras could read Caterina's mind.

But Keras was also the only thing standing between Caterina and certain death right now.

As much as Marek wanted him here, to look into her memories and to remove the ward on his back, he needed his brother in Tokyo more. Keras could stop any of them from teleporting with nothing more than a touch and a flex of his powers, and he was the only one who possessed that ability.

He was going to have to attempt to uncover the truth the traditional way, by questioning Caterina and looking for a lie in every word she spoke, and in the way her body reacted. His senses were strong enough to detect spikes in her heartbeat, or tremors in her voice.

Although she was sick.

And the wards on the castle were probably draining what little strength she did have.

Could he really tell if she was lying to him?

He hadn't been able to tell up to this point, so what made him believe he could detect a lie in her now?

He was still blinded by his feelings for her, both the side of him that viewed her as a daemon he needed to eradicate, and the side that desperately needed to protect her and believe her.

He was too close to this.

Ares's expression softened, a hint of concern colouring it. "You don't need to be there."

Marek shook his head. "I do. She's weak. I don't want her pushed too hard and she will be if she's faced with all of you."

And no him.

It would panic her, and gods, he couldn't bear the thought of her becoming overwrought with fear. She was too weak from whatever was happening to her. It would probably kill her.

Valen and Calistos returned, looking almost like twins in their standard black T-shirt, fatigues, and heavy boots. Only Valen's new shocking-violet hair colour made them stand apart, and the colour of their eyes. They jostled and grinned at each other, clearly amused by something.

Daimon trailed along behind them, tugging at the collar of his navy roll-neck.

A roll-neck that was wet.

Marek looked his younger brother over, from his wet white hair that stood up in haphazard spikes as if he had run his fingers through it, trying to make it look as it normally did, to the navy long-sleeve and black jeans that stuck to his skin.

"What the hell happened?" Ares looked him over too.

"Someone tried to make a ward on the rocks, you know the ones near the southern end of the island?" Calistos grinned as he looked back over his shoulder at a disgruntled Daimon. "They were a bit slippery."

"Hey, maybe he just wanted to cool off and have a swim." Valen pivoted on his heel and walked backwards, facing Daimon. "Although, you certainly cooled off with all those ice chunks forming around you."

"That's enough." Ares pushed past both of them and shook his head as he looked Daimon over. "You want me to dry you off?"

Daimon burrowed into the collar of his top. "I'll change, thanks."

He took the wooden stairs two at a time, heading upwards, and disappeared from view around the corner.

Valen smirked.

"Not another word." Ares scowled at him. "You've had your fun."

Valen looked as if he wanted to fight Ares on that. Marek braced himself for the usual explosive outcome of Ares exerting some command over Valen.

Cal eased back a step, clearing room for the fight.

Valen frowned, and then huffed and shrugged it off. "Whatever."

That was anticlimactic.

Marek stared at Valen, not sure what to make of this new version of his brother. He wanted to tease him about the effect Eva was having on him, levelling out his mood and smoothing his sharper edges, but he knew that if he did that, Valen would bring up Caterina and call her his girlfriend again to taunt him.

He was beginning to doubt she would ever be that for him.

Even if she was telling the truth.

Daimon trudged back down the stairs, dressed in a pair of navy sweats and a long-sleeved dark grey T-shirt. His gloves glittered with frost that cracked as he curled his fingers and flexed them.

"I don't have a spare pair," he muttered to Ares as he reached the bottom step.

"Come here." Ares held his hands out. "One dryer coming right up."

A heat haze rose from Ares's hands as his eyes brightened, the flecks of red and gold in them shimmering. Daimon held his hands out a good six inches above them, turning them over several times to dry all of his gloves.

When they were done, Daimon stared at them, a distant look in his pale blue eyes. "Toasty."

When was the last time Daimon had felt warm? Years ago, he had confessed that even in the high heat of summer, he was wracked with chills from time to time, and that the warmth didn't feel right to him. It felt cloying, choking.

Did he ever feel warmth like Marek and his brothers could? Was it ever pleasant to him?

The look in his eyes said that Ares's heat was pleasant, and that he enjoyed it.

"Are we going to meet your girlfriend?" Valen grinned when Marek scowled at him.

"No violence." He looked at each of his brothers in turn and waited for them to nod.

Daimon was the last to do it.

Marek turned away from his brothers and led the way down the spiral staircase, his breaths loud in the narrow space as he fought to settle his nerves. He had only left her barely half an hour ago, but he wasn't sure what to expect.

When he reached the door, he peered in through the small barred window again.

Relief crashed through him as he found her curled up on her side, her eyes open and her breathing rapid but steady.

"Caterina," he murmured.

She tensed and her gaze jerked to him. "Where am I?"

Her voice sounded stronger. The relief flowing through him grew stronger with it.

He slid the bolt on the door across and opened the heavy iron panel. He entered slowly, aware of her gaze on him and that her heart was picking up pace. Fear tainted her scent. Her eyes leaped to beyond him.

He looked back at Ares and Daimon, and glared at them as he subtly shook his head. She needed time to adjust to where she was, and to him. She didn't need four warriors piling into the room with him, not when Daimon looked ready to deal some violence, even when he had sworn not to.

The overhead light buzzed on, flickering and making a plinking sound. Caterina squinted up at it and then covered her eyes.

"You're safe, Caterina."

"I don't feel safe." She curled into a ball and then suddenly exploded into a sitting position, her eyes wild. "Guillem."

Her face crumpled and tears dashed down her cheeks as she sagged, rolled forwards and hung her head between her legs. The shaking started again, but he knew that this time it wasn't because of the daemon blood in her veins. She was worried about her brother.

She should be worried about herself.

Marek eased to a crouch a few feet from her, keeping enough distance between them that she couldn't reach him before he could move. Not that he expected her to attack him. She was too busy holding herself together and the strength that had shot through her was quick to wane again, leaving her trembling violently as she stared at him.

Something fierce slowly built in her wild hazel eyes, something fuelled by a desperation that he could sense in her. She was skirting the edge, liable to work herself into a frenzy before they could get any answers if he let her continue.

He needed to keep her in the room with him, focused on him, and not on whatever terrible things she was imagining.

"Caterina, I need you to tell me everything. Starting with what the wraith and the illusionist wanted you to do."

Her eyes leaped to his and she lunged forwards, which had Daimon and Ares suddenly in the room, towering over her as they flanked him. She looked up at them, gaze leaping between them, her fair eyebrows furrowing as she shrank back.

She pulled her feet up onto the cot and pressed her back to the dark stone wall.

Her focus slowly fell back on Marek.

"Why did you help me?" Marek held her gaze, part of him wanting to tell his brothers to back off, the rest of him deeply aware of how much he needed them there, right beside him.

A reminder that this was an interrogation, and that his mission was to uncover information on their enemy and his loyalty was to his family, not to Caterina.

She looked at his brothers again where they loomed over her.

Her lips compressed and she swallowed hard.

"Why did you help me?" He tried again.

She looked back at him, something dawning in her eyes, the same wild need that had made her lunge for him and that made sense as she spoke.

"Help Guillem," she husked in Catalan and eased forwards, the look in her eyes revealing how much she wanted to reach for him, wanted to take hold of him, because she needed to know he was listening to her. "Help Guillem, and I'll tell you... whatever you want to know."

He could see how important that was to her, how much she loved her brother and feared for him, and it struck him that she had risked a lot by helping him. If she had actually helped him and it hadn't been another trick.

"They said," she hiccupped on a sob, switching to English now as she flicked a glance at all his brothers. "They would save him. But now... if they... they'll kill him. I know it."

Had she done all of this because she had wanted to cure her brother?

If she had, then she had jeopardised everything to save Marek. Presuming her rescue had been real and not another trick. Gods, he hated that he thought that whenever he started to believe something about her.

He cursed Esher. If his brother hadn't flipped his switch, Keras would have been here and this would have been so much smoother. Keras could have taken a look into her mind and told them everything.

"Who's Guillem?" Daimon looked down at him.

Marek didn't take his eyes off Caterina. "Her brother. He's a turned human."

"A vampire?" Disbelief laced Ares's deep voice.

Marek nodded.

Caterina rocked forwards, wrapped her arms around her stomach and grunted. Her face contorted and sweat beaded on her brow as her cheeks flushed deep red.

"Is she sick? She looks sick." Cal sounded concerned.

"It's the daemon blood." Valen answered for Marek. "Probably fucking her up royally."

Marek really hadn't needed to hear that, not when he was struggling to keep it together, awareness of his four brothers building inside him, pulling at the side of him that felt compelled to protect Caterina whatever the cost.

"Caterina, why did you help me?" He tried for a third time.

She shook her head and lifted it, pain shining in her eyes as she wheezed, "Help Guillem. Give you my address. Bring him... here. Then... I talk."

She doubled over again and cried out, and it took all of his will to keep himself where he was and not go to her as he wanted.

He couldn't do what she wanted. He had risked enough by bringing her to this safehouse. He couldn't bring her brother here too, not when he didn't know whether or not he was working for the enemy. They suspected a Hellspawn was among their ranks, and he was one of that breed.

But he had to do something for her brother, because she was serious, and she wouldn't talk unless she knew her brother was safe.

Part of him said to wait for Keras. Keras could brute force her mind and get the information out of her, although Marek wasn't sure she would survive such an assault in her weakened state. There was a chance she would resist, and that would cause her pain. Keras wasn't exactly gentle when extracting information, and with Caterina turning into a daemon, his brother was liable to be rougher with her than normal.

"Cal will go and tell him to get away from Barcelona," Marek offered, hoping it would be enough.

She immediately shook her head and bit out, "No. Bring... here. I won't tell anything... until I see... my brother. Need him safe. Need him here."

Her head lifted and the hurt and fear in her eyes cut at his restraint.

"They'll kill him."

Tears streaked down her cheeks.

Damn it.

Marek looked to Ares. Ares studied Caterina for a moment, his fiery eyes narrowed and intense, sharp as they took her in, and then they slid down to Marek. He nodded.

"Cal," Marek said without taking his eyes off Caterina. "Go to this address."

He nodded to Caterina. She recited her address.

"Got it. I know a place near there I can land." Cal's voice cut off at the end, and Marek didn't need to look to know his brother had stepped.

Caterina started to rock, holding her stomach. Her face paled, her eyes growing unfocused as she stared right through Marek.

She was getting worse again. Fear for her brother was stripping away the strength she needed to survive the assault of the daemon blood on her body. He could only hope that seeing her brother again would restore that strength, giving her a shot at surviving the night.

The sound of boots hitting the stone floor had Marek looking over his shoulder.

Cal's expression was grave as he looked down at him. "He wasn't there."

Caterina lunged from the cot and collapsed into a heap on the flagstones. She muttered desperate things to herself, clawed towards him and froze when Ares stepped in front of Marek, blocking her path to him.

She looked up the height of Ares at the same time as Marek did.

"I won't... talk. Find... Guillem."

Ares's face hardened, his eyebrows dipping low and the corners of his mouth turning downwards. He stared down at Caterina, but his words were meant for Marek.

"Get some air."

Marek swallowed hard, the more rebellious part of himself screaming at him to deny that order and stay right where he was. The rest of him didn't want to witness what was about to happen. Time was up for Caterina.

Daimon's eyes glittered with white, as hard as diamonds as he frowned down at Caterina and closed ranks with Ares.

She tossed Marek a panicked glance as his brothers formed a wall between them.

Marek stared at her, his brow furrowed, the war raging out of control inside him. He knew what needed to be done, but the thought of his brothers forcing her to talk, the thought of her being alone with them, had him dangerously close to slipping into a black rage.

"I'm out of here. I can't stand here and watch this going down." Calistos moved back a step, into the corridor, and Marek was glad that he wasn't the only one who was against what Daimon and Ares were about to do.

Even when he knew in his heart it was the only way.

They needed information, and it was better she gave it up herself, without Keras forcing his way into her memories. There was a better chance of her coming out of Ares and Daimon's interrogation than there was of her surviving Keras's intrusion into her mind.

"Valen, come shoot some pool with me in the games room like old times. Leave the older brothers to deal with this shit."

Valen scoffed. "I'm older than Daimon!"

"Yeah, but you don't act like it. Daimon is like eight thousand in spirit age. He acts older than Dad."

Marek caught the glare Daimon levelled on Calistos over his shoulder.

"Sure," Valen said. "But only because I'm going to run some errands first. We need food and water. She needs it. We'll get the place up and running."

Marek looked at Caterina.

She needed sustenance, but she needed water most of all. They hadn't offered him anything to eat or drink when he had been captive in that house, and he doubted Caterina had been treated any better.

"I'll get her water and food." Marek pushed to his feet and backed away from her, each step agony as she stared at him, her eyes growing wild again, fear brewing in them. "I won't be long."

He couldn't bring himself to look at Ares and Daimon as he turned away at the door, his heart heavy in his chest, sinking deep into his stomach as he heard the iron door closing.

He hurried up the stairs after Valen and Calistos, thankful that both of them were silent, as deep in thought and as uncomfortable with what was about to go down as he was.

When they reached the top of the stone spiral staircase, Valen stopped and looked at him, placed a hand on his bare shoulder and squeezed it.

"I'll step to the nearest town and get supplies. Get some air. It'll do you good." Valen's golden eyes softened, revealing a side of him that rarely showed. "Believe me, I know how shitty this is... Fuck, maybe I don't. Eva had Megan there with her when Keras questioned her."

And Eva hadn't been turning into a daemon.

Caterina was alone with two gods she didn't know, warriors who had a duty to eliminate the threat to the gates, and who were deeply protective of Marek.

"I need to go back to her." Because he couldn't let her face them alone.

He went to turn, but Valen held him firm, stopping him.

"Just get some air. Give them ten minutes. As long as it takes for me to bring some water back. Then you can go back down there and intervene. If she hasn't started talking in ten minutes, she won't start talking."

Marek had to force himself to nod. It went against everything he wanted, but he made himself move further away from her, trailed out of the castle as Valen teleported and Calistos went to the boiler room.

He pushed the heavy wooden door open. The scent of salt and peat hit him, laced with seaweed and heather. He breathed deeply of it as he paused in the late afternoon light, letting it ease the chill from his bones. The sea lapped at the sloping dark grey rocks that formed the edge of the small island, a sound that was strange to him now after spending so long in the hills near Seville.

Rather than insect song, the call of seabirds rang in his ears, cries that sounded as desperate as the one that had left Caterina's lips.

Marek followed the path to the right of the entrance, where it gave way to grass that was soft and damp beneath his bare feet. He walked along the side of the long tall grey castle, passing the arched windows, heading towards the rear where the grass gave way to rock.

He stood on the point of the island and stared across the water that stretched between two hills, forming an entrance to the loch from the sea. Beyond the hills, in the distance across the dark water, the isle of Skye was hazy despite the clear blue sky.

Marek scanned the horizon, trying to focus on it rather than what was happening behind him in the small Scottish castle. To his left, the sun was slowly easing lower, on a direct course to set behind Skye. To his right, beyond the mountains, the sky was rapidly darkening, storm clouds rising high into it, catching the golden light.

He tracked the building storm. It was heading towards them, coming south on cooler air. A lightning storm.

Valen would love it.

He sensed his brother return.

Marek pivoted away from the rocks and walked back around the castle, pushed the door open and swung it hard as he entered, so it slammed behind him. He took the bottle of water that Valen offered him, not slowing as he made a beeline for the stairs to the basement.

He braced himself when he reached them, steeling his heart against whatever he was about to hear, knowing it would be bad. He couldn't let it get to him. Caterina had valuable information that they needed. He was sure that Ares didn't take any pleasure from what he was doing, although he couldn't say the same about Daimon.

He paused at the top of the steps. No sound came from below. He frowned and ventured downwards, clutching the bottle of water so tightly he felt sure it would burst before he reached her cell.

Marek hit the floor and rounded the corner, his heart beating faster now, a sickening hammering against his ribs as he focused on breathing, the anticipation of what he would find clawing at him, close to tearing him apart.

Daimon stepped out of the cell, gave him a grim look and strode past him.

Marek blew out his breath and forced himself to keep moving forwards.

He stepped into the room.

Ares pushed to his feet and looked at him, his body twisting to reveal Caterina where she sat on the cot.

Unharmed.

The conflict reigning in Ares's eyes told him what he needed to know. Neither he nor Daimon had been able to make her talk, and neither had been willing to hurt her.

"Give me a minute." Marek moved aside when Ares nodded and walked towards him.

Caterina's gaze tracked his brother.

He kept his focus on Caterina as his brothers left them alone, as he moved into the room and sank into a crouch in front of her.

Her hazel eyes, red from her tears, finally left the open door behind him and came to settle on him.

"I'm listening." He set the water down beside him, eased onto his backside in the middle of the floor, between her and the door. "It won't be long before Keras comes back. If Ares and Daimon scare you, then what Keras will do to you…"

He couldn't bring himself to say it.

Not when she tensed, that fear that seemed to be a constant in her eyes rapidly building again.

Marek picked up the water and played with it, needing to do something with his hands. Her gaze dropped to it and her tongue poked out, flicked over her lip as she stared at the bottle as if it was her salvation.

She was mistaken.

Her salvation was the one holding the bottle.

But he could only save her if she started talking.

"Whatever you have to say, Caterina, now is the time to say it."

CHAPTER 20

Caterina watched Marek playing with the water, wrestling with herself, torn between telling him what he wanted to know and demanding once again that he find Guillem.

His brothers hadn't been cruel to her, but they hadn't been kind either. Not like Marek was. They had threatened her, had spoken about taking her outside for a swim in the sea, one where she would be held under the water to see how long a daemon could hold its breath. They had talked about seeing whether the waning sunlight would burn her now.

Somehow, she had stood firm throughout it all.

But as she looked at Marek where he patiently sat before her, worry shining in his rich brown eyes, dark crescents beneath them speaking of his fatigue, she wanted to talk.

She wanted to tell him everything because she didn't want him to hate her, not as his brothers clearly did.

"Can you save Guillem?" she whispered, her thoughts returning to her own brother. Where was he? Had the man and Lisabeta taken him captive?

Was he already dead?

She couldn't contemplate that.

Couldn't bear it.

Marek sighed. "He's a vampire, Caterina. I don't think there's a way to reverse vampirism."

"There has to be. They said they could save him." She burst forwards and regretted it when her head turned, causing her to sink back against the wall.

Marek looked as if he wanted to come to her as she pressed a hand to her forehead. "Whatever they told you... it was probably just—"

"Don't say it," she interjected, because she couldn't bear the thought that he was right and they had only said what she had needed to hear to motivate her to do what they wanted.

She couldn't bear it because if it was true, then she had done this for nothing. She had ruined everything she could have had with Marek for nothing.

"You might be able to save yourself," he husked softly.

She closed her eyes and shook her head as she buried it in her knees, drawing them up and hugging them. She refused to believe him. He was just trying to hurt her because of what she had done to him.

"They swore they could save him." Her voice was muffled, but she knew he could still hear her clearly. "I can't have done this for nothing."

A new feeling burst to life inside her and she lifted her head and stared at Marek over her knees.

"I have to go back. Maybe if I go back, I can make—"

"There is no going back, Caterina." He cut her off this time. "They are going to know you assisted in my escape."

She shook her head so hard her brain hurt. "I'll make them see it isn't the case. I'll say you took me captive."

He chuckled, a low and cold sound that shredded her hope. "They won't believe you escaped from me, or that we didn't kill you. They will think you're a mole sent there by us to infiltrate them."

Oh God, could it get any worse?

"You can't save your brother." His deep voice was colder than she had ever heard it, sent a chill down her spine as she tried to shut out his words, desperate not to listen to them. "I'm not sure you can save yourself either."

She sagged into her knees, rested her forehead on them and fought back the tears.

Resignation swept through her, extinguishing the last of her fire.

"I don't want to be saved then." She didn't want to live without Guillem. She didn't want to live as a daemon.

She sank into the mire of her thoughts, drowning in them, choking as they closed in around her.

In the darkness, a tiny spark flickered.

"No," she whispered and gripped her knees so hard her hands shook. "I won't believe you. There has to be a way to save Guillem. There just has to be."

Caterina wearily lifted her head and fixed her gaze on Marek.

"I promised. I swore." She tried to get to her feet, but her legs buckled beneath her and she struck the side of the cot as she went down, sharp pain lancing her right hip and shooting up her back, ripping a cry from her throat.

She gripped the bar of the cot and pushed up, refusing to give up, determined to save her brother.

No matter the cost.

Her breaths came faster, sawing from her lips as desperation and fear collided inside her, as pain tore through her bones and she felt as if they were going to break. The heat that had abated scalded her skin as she tried to walk, as she set her sights on the door. She could reach it. She could get away from this place and help her brother.

She needed to help him.

She wasn't sure what she was saying as she inched her feet forwards, as she wobbled and her vision wavered, darkness encroaching at the edges. She only knew that she had to reach that door.

She had to save her brother.

Her right leg gave out and she staggered sideways, hit the wall and flinched as her head cracked off the stone. The darkness grew stronger, a throbbing, pulsing wave of heat accompanying it now, radiating across her skull.

Marek grabbed her arm.

She shoved him off her. "No. I need to go. I can save him."

She swayed to her left, but Marek was there, blocking her path to the door. His voice swam in her ears as she pushed at his bare chest, as she weakly pounded her fists against it, putting all of her strength into each blow.

"I promised." She gasped as her throat closed, as she fought for air and to push back against the rising wave inside her, one that felt as if it was going to destroy her when it broke, crushing her beneath the tremendous force of it. "I swore."

She couldn't breathe.

She wheezed, frantically attempting to get air into her lungs.

"Caterina," Marek whispered and it tore away the last of her strength, because she couldn't understand how he could still say her name with so much warmth, so much kindness, after what she had done.

She deserved his anger.

His hatred.

She broke down, the world spinning around her as she sank into the gloom.

Because there was no saving her brother.

And there was no saving herself.

CHAPTER 21

Marek caught Caterina as she collapsed, her desperate gasping breaths grating in his ears. She kept talking, repeating words about saving her brother, pleading him to let her go.

He carefully pulled her into his arms and pressed his right hand to her forehead. She was burning up. He palmed her slick brow and focused, calling a power that he never used. It was weaker than the one Keras possessed, but he hoped it would be strong enough to help him with Caterina.

Because he feared she would hurt herself if he couldn't stop her, or worse, she would manage to escape somehow, mustering up enough strength to make it outside the wards and teleport, and she would get herself killed.

"Sleep," he murmured softly as her struggles slowed, as her words slurred together.

He kept channelling that compulsion into her, trancing her into a deep sleep, one he hoped would be restful for her and would give her weak body and fragile mind time to recover from her ordeal.

Marek grew aware of someone behind him as he lifted Caterina into his arms, satisfied that she wouldn't wake for a few hours. He ignored them and set her down on the cot, focusing on her even as part of him waited for his brother to say something about what he had just witnessed.

He covered Caterina with a thin blanket, brushed her damp caramel hair from her dirt smudged forehead and cheeks, and drank her in for a moment, waiting until he was sure she wouldn't stir before he finally broke contact with her.

He turned and looked at Ares.

His big brother filled the doorway, a shadow in his black T-shirt and jeans, formidable as he folded his thickly muscled arms over his broad chest.

"Did you learn anything new?"

Not the words he had expected to hear leaving Ares's lips. Marek wanted to fool himself into believing his brother hadn't noticed what he had done to Caterina, but awareness of it was there in his dark eyes, laced with a hint of surprise.

Marek was sure he wasn't the only brother other than Keras who had a power other than the ones they all had in common. Maybe Ares hadn't inherited any of them from their parents. Keras had managed to get all of them.

"Nothing." He split his focus between Caterina and Ares, unable to give his brother the whole of his attention, not when he was worried about her.

Not when he felt useless, unable to help her.

What she needed was to know her brother was safe, and that was the one thing he couldn't give her. All he could do was ask Calistos to try again, and again, but he didn't have much hope that eventually Guillem would appear.

If it had been Marek in the wraith's shoes, he would have taken Guillem captive the moment he had discovered Caterina had escaped with his enemy. Guillem was now leverage in a very dangerous game, and Marek felt sure it wasn't going to end well for the turned human.

Or Caterina.

"I have to go back to New York, but I'll check in later." Ares glanced beyond him to Caterina before his dark eyes shifted to the ceiling of the damp cell, drawing Marek's focus there. "Daimon has gone to help Keras with Esher. Cal had to return to London to keep an eye on the gates now night is falling. Valen has agreed to deal with Rome and Seville, and I'll lend him a hand if he needs it."

Now that his brother had mentioned the others, he realised they were gone.

"You've got maybe half a day tops." Ares turned away from him. "It's all I could buy you. Make it count. I won't be able to delay Keras for longer than that."

With that, Ares stepped, the swirls of black smoke that he left in his wake hanging in the air for long minutes as Marek stared at them, slowly processing what his brother had done for him.

Ares had sent his brothers away so Marek could have time alone with Caterina, a shot at getting her to talk without his brothers looming in the shadows, frightening her.

His brother would never know how much Marek appreciated that.

He looked back over his shoulder at her. Although he was sure she wouldn't be waking any time soon.

Not naturally, at least.

He could bring her up from the deep slumber he had tranced her into any time he wanted, but for now he would let her rest. If she didn't wake before morning, he would rouse her, and hopefully she would be stronger, well enough to talk to him without working herself into another frenzy.

He needed to give Keras something to go on when he arrived. If Keras knew the memories he was looking for, there was a chance he would be gentler with her, and the mind probe wouldn't hurt her too much.

Marek shut the door behind him, slid the bolt across and pressed his hand to the cold iron that separated him and Caterina.

She had suffered enough because of him.

The sight of her on the worn cot, in a damp cell, played havoc with him. He wanted her somewhere more comfortable, but none of his brothers would be pleased if they arrived to find her outside of the cell. Keras would rip him a new one.

As much as he hated it, she had to remain locked inside it, at least until he had discovered the truth. He couldn't trust her again until he knew she wasn't working for the enemy.

He closed his eyes and checked the wards on the cell. When he found a vital one was missing, he let the darkness inside him rise to the fore so his fangs would emerge and used one to slice his finger. He drew the mark on the stone wall in his blood, focusing on each stroke of the elaborate pattern to infuse his power into it, forming a new ward.

One that would stop Caterina from being able to teleport while inside the castle. The ward would spread to affect all adjoining stones, a ripple effect that would see to it that every inch of the castle was bound by it.

It wasn't strong enough to stop his brothers from teleporting, but it would stop a daemon.

He stared through the door at Caterina, forming a mission plan in his mind as he watched over her.

She would rest until dawn, and then he would wake her if she hadn't arisen already, and he would see to it she was fed and had water.

And then he would convince her to talk.

He wasn't sure how he was going to achieve that, but he would make it happen, somehow.

Marek forced himself to leave her, trudged back up the spiral staircase to the main floor of the castle, and busied himself with unpacking the groceries Valen had brought as promised. He checked the refrigerator. It was cool, but not cold, the device still settling in after being turned on for the first time in years. He was surprised it worked at all.

He checked the stove next, watching the metal ring heating until it glowed red, and then switched it off.

The bags Valen had dumped on the island in the middle of the large kitchen contained everything he needed, and not only things like water, soup, milk and bread. There were things for females too. Deodorant. Soap. A pink washcloth. Even a matching pink toothbrush and toothpaste.

And a hairbrush.

Marek shook his head at them. It was Eva's doing. Softening those edges. Bringing out the side of Valen that everyone thought had died with their sister.

Marek appreciated the hell out of it though, because he hadn't even thought about getting Caterina the basic necessities. Her cream camisole was dark with filth, and her jeans had been dirty in places. Maybe she would feel better if she was washed and dressed in warm, clean clothing. He added finding her something to wear to his list, and rifled through the store cupboard where he and his brothers tossed everything that didn't have a regular place in the castle.

In the back of it, on a low shelf, he found a metal basin that was deep enough to hold a good amount of water, and a matching jug. He took them out and washed them, preparing them for Caterina.

He selected a can of soup and a bottle of water, and lined them all up on the kitchen island with some liquid soap and the washcloth. He went to his bedroom, turned out half of his clothes and realised none of them would fit her, and stalked up the hallway to Valen's bedroom. His brother wouldn't mind him borrowing some sweats for Caterina. He found a suitable black pair, carried it back to his room and added a light grey T-shirt from his own clothes, because he was damned if Caterina would wear all of Valen's things. He wanted her dressed in something belonging to him. Possessive? Absolutely. Foolish? Probably.

He ran the water into the basin in his bathroom, pleased to find it was warm now, and washed his face. He pulled another T-shirt from his drawers and tugged it on, and grabbed a pair of socks too. Dressed and feeling more like his old self, he picked up the clothes for Caterina and took them downstairs. He placed them into one of the empty grocery bags together with the metal bowl and went down into the basement. He unlocked the door and opened it, and set the bag down just inside the door, quietly so he didn't disturb Caterina.

He paused and studied her, listening to her steady soft breathing, reassuring himself that she was still sleeping soundly, getting the rest she needed to rebuild her strength.

He headed back upstairs and warmed the soup, poured it into a thermos he found in a cupboard, and set it on a tray with a bottle of water and a plastic bowl. He filled another thermos with hot water he could use to make tea or warm the water in the basin so she could wash.

Satisfied that everything he could do was done, he took his haul to the cell and placed it next to the bag. He meant to leave, but one glance at Caterina had him staying.

He closed the door and sank to his backside, pressing his shoulders against the cold iron panel as he stared at Caterina.

What was he going to do now?

She was turning into a daemon, and she might have betrayed him, but he still felt something for her.

He wasn't sure that anything could change that.

He lost track of time as he went in circles, aware that he was never going to figure out what he was going to do but unable to stop himself from thinking about it as he watched Caterina sleep.

As bird song broke the thick silence that hung over the castle like a shroud, Caterina finally stirred.

She moaned and rolled onto her side, her face scrunching up as she curled into a ball.

Marek waited, watching her, keeping an eye on her in case the panic that had gripped her before he had sent her to sleep seized her again, and preparing himself to go to her and offer her what little comfort he could.

Her eyelids fluttered and then lifted, and sleep-filled hazel eyes slowly settled on him.

"Caterina," he murmured softly, not wanting to scare her or panic her.

She blinked and frowned, took in her surroundings and the grogginess in her eyes suddenly lifted.

He was before her in an instant, his right hand on her bare arm. He stroked it softly.

"You're fine. Safe." He caressed her, watching the flare of panic subside as she looked at him. "Can you eat something?"

He didn't wait for her to respond. He went to the tray and brought it over to her, setting it down on the cold stone floor near her head. He opened the bottle of water for her and then the thermos of soup.

"It's chicken noodle. It's meant to be good for making humans feel better." He poured the soup into the bowl and lifted it so she could see it.

She stared at it blankly, her voice small and leaving him feeling lousy as she spoke.

"I'm not human. What does a daemon eat to make itself feel better?" Her eyes lifted to lock with his, filled with resignation and laced with sorrow. "Blood? Souls?"

She swallowed hard.

"Children?"

Tears lined her lashes and she looked away from him.

Marek stroked her arm, unable to deny the need to comfort her.

He focused on her, on where they touched, on her scent and her racing heartbeat, and waited.

The coppery odour of daemon didn't pour from her. The gut swirling sensation of a daemon being near him didn't hit him.

She smelled like Caterina. Felt like Caterina.

Was Caterina.

"You don't feel like a daemon to me." He watched his fingers as he stroked them down her bare skin, feeling no revulsion or need to hurt her. The darker part of him remained docile, relaxed by her presence even, by the fact that she was looking better again.

"But I am one," she croaked.

He couldn't deny that she was becoming one, not when he had seen her teleport, but that didn't make her a daemon right now. "There's still time. Maybe we can reverse this infection and cure you."

"Maybe." She chuckled mirthlessly, a cold and hollow sound that matched the bleak look in her eyes. "And maybe your brothers don't hate me because of my tainted blood. Maybe you don't hate me."

The laugh that left her lips was bordering on hysterical this time.

"Maybe Guillem is going to be just fine."

Marek lowered the soup, set it down on the tray and fought to find the right thing to say. This was all too much for her. It was right there in her eyes.

It hit him that he did believe her. He believed everything she had said to him. She hadn't wanted to become a daemon, and she hadn't wanted to hurt him. She didn't want to be a daemon.

Anger surged inside him, burning up his blood, because there was nothing he could do for her.

Except maybe take her mind off things and show her that he didn't hate her. She should hate him. He was the reason they had done this to her. It was his fault that she was turning into a daemon and her entire world had been turned upside down.

She had asked him things when he had met her, things he hadn't wanted to tell her because he hadn't told them to anyone, but if he could take her mind off what was happening to her and could form a new connection between them again by lowering the barriers, he would do it.

He would put himself through that pain.

For her.

CHAPTER 22

"You asked me once why I hunt vampires. Do you still want to know?"

Caterina nodded. It was subtle, but the interest that flared in her eyes wasn't.

He was really going to do this, wasn't he?

Marek wasn't sure how she would react to some of the things he had to say, but he needed it out there now, no longer a secret he closely guarded just like his heart. He wanted her to know this about him. He craved that connection with her again.

"A few centuries ago, I made what had to be my greatest mistake." He twisted to sit on his backside beside the cot. "I fell in love with a vampire. Airlea. She was beautiful and I was young, and an idiot. She wooed me, seduced me, filled my head with compliments from the moment we met at a social gathering in one of the regions of the Underworld where the vampires live."

He did his best to ignore the way Caterina scowled at him, because he was too afraid he would read into it and fool himself into believing she felt things that were no longer true.

"I fell hard for her." And he had fallen even harder for Caterina.

"Were your family angry?" Caterina slowly sat up, a small frown forming a crease between her eyebrows. There was a smudge of dirt just above that crease, darting towards her hairline on the left side.

Marek shook his head. "Vampires are accepted by my father."

"But daemons aren't." Her voice was small again and she looked away.

He wanted to tell her that it would all work out, but he didn't want to lie to her. He didn't know what happened now, and even though he wanted to set things right for her, he didn't know if he could. The one who would know for sure was his father, and he wasn't about to ask him whether Caterina could be cured. Hades was liable to kill her on sight, or possibly even kill him. At the very least, Marek might end up incarcerated in one of the unsavoury areas of the Underworld for a century or two, until Caterina was long dead and his father believed him free of her taint.

"What happened... with her?" Caterina's gentle voice lured him out of his dark thoughts and back to her. "Something terrible must have happened to make you spend centuries hunting vampires."

"We had been together for years and I had come to the decision that I wanted her to be my wife. I went to ask her as much." He closed his eyes and did his best not to relive that night. "When I reached her family home, I saw her on the patio with three males, all vampires. All of them were clearly familiar with her in an intimate way. I was furious, ready to tear them to pieces for touching what I considered mine... my wife."

He opened his eyes and sighed as he looked at the damp stone floor, as her high laughter rang in his mind and seared his heart all over again.

"I was about to intervene when she started talking about me. Discussing how she was sure I was close to being completely hers and they were going to get what they wanted. Not that she was going to get what she wanted... but that the four of them were." He tipped his head back, deeply aware of Caterina's gaze on his face as he lost himself in his past. "It turned out that she had been playing me all along, telling me what I wanted to hear so she could secure me and in turn secure the wealth and privilege that came with me, and an entire estate that was as large as the realm where the vampires resided."

He lowered his gaze to Caterina.

"She intended to set up buildings on it for the three vampires, houses where they could host grand parties during my absences, debauched gatherings at my expense that I would never know about." He rubbed his forearm where the ink he'd had done to honour her had once been, the self-hatred he tried to keep at bay bubbling up inside him as he forced himself to continue so Caterina would understand him. "She never loved me. I was a game to her, a way of achieving something for the men she did love. She hated me. She hated it when I touched her. She hated it when I..."

He couldn't bring himself to say anymore, not when the anger and pity, the rage and despair built inside him so swiftly he wanted to scream.

"What happened?" Caterina edged closer to him, concern in her eyes that brightened them, chasing away some of the sorrow and resignation.

At least he was taking her mind off her own situation, giving her some respite from it.

"I lost it when she spoke of drugging me to keep me compliant, to ensure I didn't notice what was happening around me and keep me under her spell. I don't remember much—only pain, and raw fury, and blood. I killed the three men, and I killed her. I killed that entire nest of vampires and it wasn't enough. She had revealed their true nature to me and it birthed something inside me... or maybe awoke something." And that something had been born of his father's blood in his veins.

No one betrayed Hades and lived to tell the tale.

"You've hunted vampires ever since?"

He nodded and hesitated, because while hunting vampires was one thing, what he was about to admit was something entirely darker and he wasn't sure how she would react.

Marek swallowed hard. "It's a compulsion. A sickness."

It was strange to call it that, to admit that what he had was a disease, an affliction that he was now certain had no cure.

"I can go maybe a few weeks at most before the need to hunt and kill vampires becomes too much and steals control of me. If I don't obey it, if I don't satisfy it... it's like an itch I have to scratch and I would go mad if I didn't do it."

He had managed to make it to six weeks once, and he had felt as if he had been losing his mind, hadn't been able to recognise the thing he had become. It had been a foolish attempt to break the cycle and it had almost broken him.

"That was why you were so angry that night, when we met." She pulled her knees up to her chest and hugged them, the dark blanket still in place over them. "I ruined your hunt and killed most of the remaining vampires, and you didn't get to scratch that itch."

He nodded. "When it has me in its grip, I... I don't like who I am. I enjoy it while it's happening. The hunt. The fight. The kill. I love every second of it. In the aftermath... it's like a high... but there's a part of me that knows it's a high that will only get harder to find the more I hunt vampires. At first, I was satisfied with one or two kills when the need gripped me. Now I'm only satisfied if I can kill ten or twenty vampires. How long before I'm only satisfied when I kill thirty?"

He wasn't sure he wanted to find out the answer to that question.

He needed to find a way to let go of his pain before it reached that point, because it wasn't healthy. It wasn't healing him. It was keeping all of his pain alive inside him, a writhing black and terrible thing that was slowly destroying him.

"I'm sorry," she whispered.

Marek frowned at her, confusion sweeping through him. "For what? That I'm compelled to kill vampires. You suffer the same compulsion. Maybe that's what I wanted to show you. That we aren't so different."

She shook her head and her brow furrowed. "I'm sorry I betrayed you too."

The tears that had been threatening began to fall as the strength and fire he admired in her crumbled under the weight of everything that had happened.

"What they wanted me to do... I meant to go through with it, and I'm sorry about that."

"You meant to go through with it," he murmured, mulling that over, and shifted so he was facing her. "What made you change your mind?"

"When we fought the daemons... when you kissed me. I wanted so badly that you would keep kissing me like that, even though I was becoming something you were born to kill." She picked at the blanket covering her knees, her eyes on her fingers now.

And instead of continuing to kiss her, he had lashed out at her.

Tried to choke her.

"I'm sorry about what I did, Caterina," he husked and didn't hesitate to reach out and place his hand on her knee, between hers.

She stared at it now and gods, he wanted her to take it. He wanted her to show him that he hadn't fucked everything up with her.

He wanted to laugh at that.

It was already all screwed up.

He wasn't even sure he could un-screw it.

"After what happened, I realised I couldn't do it. I couldn't pick between you and my brother." She closed her eyes, tilted her head and rested her cheek on his hand.

Heat swept through him, the warmth of her soft skin invading his bones, easing the tension from his muscles as he savoured the way she was trusting him and seeking comfort from him.

Maybe there was hope for them after all.

"What's going to happen to Guillem?" she whispered.

"I don't know. I'll go again later to see if he's come back. I'll do whatever I can to get him away from my enemy." He didn't hold out much hope of finding Guillem though.

"Why do they want to hurt you?" She edged her hands towards his and his eyes slipped shut as she made contact, as her thumbs brushed his skin.

"They want to destroy the gates I protect with my brothers. If they can manage it, they will merge this world and the Underworld to create a new realm they intend to rule." He opened his eyes and looked off to his left, to the small window in the door of the cell and beyond it. "If it happens, it would be a hellish world. I can see it sometimes, a curse from the Moirai… the three goddesses of fate. Their method of keeping myself and my brothers focused on our mission. We can see what will happen if we fail."

"Don't fail." She wrapped her fingers around his and pressed her cheek to the back of his hand. "This world can be cruel, and humans are intent on ruining it, but it has beauty too, and kindness."

She frowned at his hand.

"Is your world hellish?"

He shook his head. "No. It's a dark realm, carved from obsidian in most places, but it has beauty and kindness too. The good souls go there as well as the bad. There are incredible valleys that are as green as anything in this world, lush with nature of a different sort. Mother sees to that."

"What happens to a daemon soul when it dies? Does it go there?" A tear slipped from her cheek, hitting his skin and burning him.

Marek lifted his other hand and brushed his fingers over her hair, sweeping it back from her face. "Don't think about dying, Caterina."

Because he couldn't bear it.

Just the thought of her dying had his heart ready to break.

"I feel like I'm dying," she murmured.

He pressed his hand to her brow. "You're not burning up anymore and you seem brighter, more lucid. I think the daemon blood hits you in waves and when the storm recedes, you are changed a little more. Is teleporting your only ability?"

She shook her head against his other hand and edged her eyes up to settle on his face. "I can see colours too."

"Colours?" It was an odd thing to say.

"Like black when you were angry with me, and red at times. I saw them on people. When they were talking the colours changed. It's weird and I don't like it." She lifted her head and toyed with his fingers. "I think I'm seeing emotions."

"Emotions." He mulled that one over too and could only think of one explanation. "Where did the blood come from?"

"He said it was a cocktail of their blood."

A cold shiver danced down his spine on hearing her confirm his suspicions.

"They had a daemon who could teleport. He died. The one who gave you the daemon blood killed him before we could get anything out of him." Marek slowly eased his hand out from beneath hers, hating himself for fearing she might have inherited other powers from Amaury's blood—the power to steal

Marek's command over the earth. "There was a succubus too. It might explain the ability to see emotions."

"A succubus?" Her eyes widened, horror flaring in them. "Like something that feeds on…"

A blush climbed her cheeks.

"Something like that." He ignored that heat that scalded his own face and recalled what Valen had told him about Jin. "She had other powers too. She could cast a barrier."

Which would be useful for Caterina. Together with the ability to teleport, she would be able to protect herself well.

"There's also a woman we call illusionist. She was with the wraith—"

"Lisabeta?" She cut him off and he frowned at her. "She has weird eyes and dark purple hair that's almost black."

He nodded. "That's her. She's called Lisabeta?"

"The man called her that. What can she do?"

He could see the cogs and wheels turning in her mind as curiosity shone in her eyes. She was trying to figure out what other abilities she might gain as the daemon blood took hold in her.

"She can shift to appear like other people, can mimic them right down to their voice and scent." Which was another handy ability that would keep her safe if she could master it.

"And the man?" She moved the blanket off her legs and scowled at her dirty cream top and jeans.

"He's a wraith. I brought you clean clothes and some things so you can wash." He moved to the bag and opened it, took out the sweats and the T-shirt. "I won't look."

He turned his back to her and busied himself with filling the basin with the hot water and mixing in some cold. The sound of material rustling behind him had him aching to peek, but he somehow found the will to resist.

Caterina didn't make it easy.

The cream camisole hit the stone floor just beyond the tray and her jeans followed it, quickly enough that it was obvious she was now only in her underwear.

Marek swallowed hard.

He topped up her soup, hoping to warm it with the remains in the thermos.

"Done." Caterina sounded even brighter and an arrow of pride shot through him, an unfamiliar satisfaction that he found addictive. He had done something for her, something that had made her feel better.

He turned towards her.

And she was wearing his T-shirt.

It was too large for her, dwarfing her slender frame, but gods, he liked the sight of her wearing it.

He offered the soup and she took it this time, chased the noodles around the bowl with the spoon and took little bites.

"What powers does a wraith have?" She paused and looked at him over the bowl. "He had fangs."

"He's like a vampire, but he needs souls for nourishment, not blood."

She shuddered and pulled a face. "I hope I don't develop any of his abilities then."

He offered her the water and she handed him the bowl. He set it down on the tray and thought about the wraith, about the abilities they knew he possessed.

"He can make portals too, and can steal memories from fragments of a person's soul."

Her fair eyebrows drew down. "When he... do you think he..."

He shrugged. "Most likely."

She didn't want to mention that the wraith had stabbed him in the back and most likely had his memories now, and he didn't really want to talk about it either. He had been enjoying just being with her, without thinking about what had happened.

He idly rubbed his left shoulder, feeling the grooves of the ward through his T-shirt. He needed Keras to look at it as soon as his brother arrived, because it was almost healed. He doubted he could step now if he needed to do it, and he could feel his connection to the rock and earth around him had waned, was weak now. It wouldn't be long before it disappeared, locked down by the ward.

His strength would probably follow it.

He tensed as his senses spiked and looked at the ceiling. One of his brothers had just returned. Another followed, and then another.

"What is it?" Caterina lowered her water to her lap.

"I have to go for a while. My brothers are here." He stood and brushed his damp backside down, went to turn and hesitated. He looked down at Caterina, not liking the way she curled into herself again, drawing the blanket up to her chest as her eyes lifted to the ceiling, a flicker of fear emerging in them. "Try to eat some more."

She lowered her gaze to the thermos and the bowl she had taken barely two mouthfuls from. "Why? What do you really care?"

That resignation was back in her voice, and he hated it. He cursed his brothers. She had been doing fine before they had returned, had been growing more comfortable around him. Now, she was drifting away again, closing herself off to him.

Because she feared his brothers would hurt her.

And that he would side with them.

If it came down to it, what would he do?

He pondered that as he walked to the door of the cell, as he opened it and focused on Caterina and his brothers, torn between them.

He closed the door, because any delay would see Keras coming down to confront her now, and he wanted her stronger before that happened.

Marek lingered, his hand on the bolt as he finished sliding it into place, and looked in at Caterina, meeting her gaze, wanting her back with him and needing her to know that she wasn't alone. Whatever went down, he would be on her side.

So he put it all out there and refused to regret it, no matter what happened.

"I care. Seeing you like this is killing me."

CHAPTER 23

The moment Megan's black sneakers hit the wooden floor, she swallowed hard and breathed slowly, struggling to keep down the bile that shot into her throat. The wood-panelled kitchen whirled around her, cabinets blurring together as she struggled to focus.

"Sweetheart?" Ares rubbed her lower back as she leaned forwards and braced her hands against her knees.

"I'm fine." She shook her head and managed a smile for him, but it didn't lift the concern from his dark eyes as he frowned down at her. She gave him a thumbs-up. "Just peachy."

He didn't look as if he believed that, and she couldn't blame him. She had been doing her best over the last month, trying to keep up with everything that had happened and keep everything between them as it had been, but it was hard.

Impossible.

There was too much swirling around her mind, a thousand thoughts and fears that kept her awake while Ares slept beside her, had her tossing and turning, and distant from him. She wasn't sure how she had thought she could keep her worries from him until she had figured everything out. He had been able to see right through her to her heart from the moment they had met, had the ability to strip away her layers to reveal the things she wanted to hide from him.

He stroked her back and leaned forwards as she straightened, his focus wholly on her, as if his brothers didn't exist as Marek appeared in the kitchen doorway and everyone began talking.

She squirmed under Ares's scrutiny, guilt churning her stomach worse than the teleport had as she wrestled with herself, hating keeping things from him. He was her partner. Her husband.

Her everything.

She shouldn't have any secrets from him.

She didn't want to pretend everything was peachy when it wasn't.

It felt as if her whole world was falling apart around her and she hated herself for trying to cope with it alone, when she knew Ares would be there for her, would be the strength she needed right now and would see her through it all.

Pressure built inside her as she struggled to find the words, had her tensing up in a way that Ares noticed.

He lifted his hand to her face, his brow furrowing as his eyes leaped between hers.

Heck, she just needed to say it.

Why couldn't she say it?

She just had to throw it out there and Ares would see to it that all of her fears, all of her hurt and doubts, became something else.

Something she wanted to feel.

Happiness.

Excitement.

Joy.

The pressure reached boiling point and she couldn't hold it back as she looked into his eyes, as she saw the worry in them.

The unconditional love.

"I'm late," she blurted.

Everyone fell quiet, the air in the room thickening until she wasn't sure she could breathe as she waited for the bomb to drop.

"Silly." Ares grinned, one that melted her heart. "We're perfectly on time. Valen was last in. You worry about the strangest things, sweetheart."

"No. *I'm* late."

His expression gradually changed from innocent confusion to shock, his eyes widening as his eyebrows rose high on his forehead and his lips parted.

"Late late?" He stared at her, paling by degrees.

She nodded, hyper-aware of the other six men in the room as they gaped at her.

"Baby late?"

She twisted her fingers together in front of her blue jeans and pulled a face. "Yes."

She was sure of that at least, had taken what felt like three thousand tests over the last few weeks.

The verdict had always remained the same.

Pregnant.

Her man finally smiled, cracking a grin that was accompanied by a strained laugh, and she melted as tears formed in his eyes.

Eyes that shone with love so deep she felt as if she might drown in it.

His hand shook against her face, and she smiled as tears filled her eyes now, seeing Ares so overwhelmed by her news touching her deeply, chasing away some of the fears that had plagued her.

"I'm going to have a son." He looked from her to his brothers, his grin holding, even as he was paling further.

She laughed too, a short bark that seemed so out of place in the moment, but it seemed her body wasn't quite sure how to react to the whole situation. "It could be a daughter you know? There are two sexes."

Ares just continued to grin at his brothers. "Who'd have thought one of us would be a dad before we were one thousand?"

Her stomach dropped, the smile falling from her face as one of her deepest fears loomed before her. "I don't even want to think about the complications involved in this."

Ares tossed her a confused look.

"I'm mortal." She waved her hand up and down Ares, from his heavy boots, up his black jeans, to the T-shirt that stretched like a second skin over his chest. "You're a god. You live for thousands of years—"

"And so can you," Keras interjected and she looked across the kitchen island at him. "With regular visits to the Underworld, you will gradually become like us. We are a product of our environment as well as our breeding. Time in the Underworld will change you. Your aging will slow. The same will happen to your child. In the mortal world, you will age faster, but not noticeably so."

Ares slung his arm around her shoulder and pressed a kiss to the top of her head. "It'll work out, sweetheart. When I told you I wanted forever with you, I meant it."

She twisted and looked up at him, blamed her hormones when tears spilled onto her cheeks and warmth filled her. She had never seen him looking so proud.

So happy.

She had been afraid he wouldn't want the child, or that something would prevent her from having it, some sort of incompatibility between them, but the way he was looking at her said all of her fears had been for nothing.

"I'll send a message to my parents right away." He smoothed another kiss across her brow. "They'll want to know."

Another wave of fear swept over her, this one with the force of a tsunami, and she stared blankly at Ares's chest as she reeled from it.

"This is all suddenly a little too real." Her ears rang and she lowered her hand to her stomach, not hearing anything as she thought about everything. Not only was she pregnant, but she was carrying the child of a god, and the grandparents were the god-king of the Underworld and his wife, Persephone, a goddess of nature.

She wasn't bringing a baby into the world.

She was bringing a demigod into it.

"Breathe." Ares's voice broke through the ringing, and she stared at him as he leaned over in front of her, bringing his eyes level with hers. His handsome face softened, love and concern in his eyes that called to her and told her to trust him, to believe in him as she always had. He would take care of her, and the baby. He slowly smiled, threatening to send the tears in his eyes dashing down his cheeks. "It's going to be great. You'll see. I'll be the best damned husband and dad the world has ever seen."

She nodded, couldn't stop herself from throwing her arms around his neck and kissing him. He banded his arms around her, clutching her close, and kissed her deeply, pouring love into it that chased the fears away. She leaned into his kiss as he lifted her, as he cradled her gently, tucking one hand beneath her backside to support her.

When he finally broke away from her lips, he looked down and pressed a hand to her stomach, pride shining in his dark eyes as they glittered with sparks of gold and red.

The heat of his hand seeped into her T-shirt, a gentle warmth that made her feel loved as he kept control of his fire, holding it under his command so he wouldn't hurt her.

"Congratulations," Keras murmured.

That heat bloomed on her cheeks as Megan remembered that they weren't alone. She looked at the men gathered before her, taking in the range of their expressions, everything from happiness to shock.

Ares sobered as he looked at Marek where he stood near the door, his wild dark hair a mess of waves that looked as if he had been running his fingers through it all night.

Megan sobered too, cursed herself as she looked at him, into his tired brown eyes. His handsome face was sombre even as he smiled, and she could see he was forcing himself to be happy for them.

This wasn't the time to be celebrating anything.

"I'm sorry," she said and he waved her away, but she refused to hold her tongue and let him have his way. "I didn't mean for it to come out like this... now. I should have waited a little longer."

Because Marek had the weight of the world on his shoulders and he didn't need her adding more to it.

Esher suddenly spoke. "A babe?"

He stared at her stomach, his blue eyes rapidly darkening, turning stormy as they narrowed and his black eyebrows met hard above them. His hands shook as he curled them into fists at his sides, arms trembling beneath the long sleeves of his black shirt he wore over a grey-marl T-shirt.

The water that had been dripping into the sink behind him suddenly slowed, drawing her focus there as a perfect orb of it hung in the air.

"Esher." Daimon went to him and Ares lowered Megan to her feet and moved in front of her.

Which seemed to be entirely the wrong move to make.

Esher growled and moved left, trying to see past Ares.

"We have to keep her out of sight," Esher snarled and took a hard step towards her before casting a panicked glance around the room at his brothers. "The enemy cannot know she is pregnant. We have to take her from this place... from that vile abomination in the cells."

"Watch your tongue, brother." Marek's voice was darker than she had ever heard it, the fury that laced each word managing to draw her focus from Esher as Keras went to him and gently clutched his shoulder to keep him in place. "What happened to Caterina wasn't her fault. It was mine."

"But the babe—" Esher started, black ringing his irises as he threw a worried glance at Ares.

"I will keep Megan safe." Ares cut him off, his deep voice gentle and low, and she appreciated his attempt to ease Esher's mood and his mind.

It had become apparent to her over the last month or two that Esher had come to view her as family, and that meant the protective side of him that needed to know his family were safe now extended to her, and also to Eva and Aiko. Esher's family was growing, and Ares had warned her that it meant the chances of him losing himself to his other side was growing with it.

And now she had announced that she was bringing a baby into his family.

She could see in his eyes that it was too much for him as he looked between Daimon, and Ares, and her. He was thinking bad things, dwelling on the negatives just as she had been.

Megan stepped out from behind Ares, so Esher could see her and could see that she was fine. She slipped her hand into Ares's right one and Esher looked there.

"Nothing will happen to me," Megan said softly, hoping to calm him. "Ares will take care of me."

"We all will." Ares looked at each of his brothers in turn. "We'll all keep Megan safe."

Everyone nodded.

Except Daimon.

He had backed off into the corner of the kitchen, his pale blue eyes cold and distant as he stared at her in a way that chilled her and left her feeling something was wrong with him.

He looked as if he had seen a ghost.

She lowered her hand to her stomach and tried to focus on the conversation as it flowed around her, but she couldn't shake the feeling that something was wrong with Daimon even when he smiled and his eyes brightened, whatever had been bothering him seemingly forgotten as he congratulated her and Ares.

Was it because he shared Ares's problem and was unable to touch anyone because his power had manifested when he had come to this world? Now Ares not only had her, someone he could touch without fear of harming them, but they had a child on the way. Was that the reason Daimon had looked so cold and distant?

Or was there something else that haunted him?

CHAPTER 24

Marek kept a close eye on Esher as the meeting moved from waves of congratulating Megan and Ares, and discussing what would happen for both of them now, to discussing Caterina and their enemy.

Esher's eyes had darkened again the moment someone had mentioned her.

Marek was damned if he would let his brother get near her. He couldn't teleport right now, but he was still strong enough to take Esher down if he needed to do it.

Or at least he hoped he was.

"Keras, can we discuss this while you do something for me?" Marek pulled his T-shirt off, earning a growl from Ares that his big brother apologised for with a sheepish smile when Marek glared at him. He wouldn't hold it against his brother.

If Ares whipped his top off in front of Caterina, if any of his brothers revealed their bodies to her, he would react in the same way, the possessive dark side of his blood filling him with a need to drive them away from his female.

Keras nodded, his green eyes grave as he moved around the kitchen. "This will hurt."

Marek pulled one of the stools from beneath the counter on the island and settled himself on it. He rested his elbows on the dark marble top and tried to focus on what he had learned from Caterina as Keras came to stand behind him.

The second Keras's palm made contact with his shoulder, fire blazed across his back and burrowed deep into his bones.

Marek gritted his teeth and grunted as he dug his fingers into the marble, a vain attempt to brace himself against the pain spreading through his body.

Megan gave him a concerned look. He scowled at her, gaining a black look from Ares.

He didn't need anyone coddling him.

"Are we dealing with the thing in the basement?" Esher bit out.

Marek bared teeth at him. "No one touches Caterina. I have her talking."

He grunted when another searing wave crashed over him and he felt as if his bones might burn to cinders.

"This is impressive work." Keras shifted his hand, tracing fingertips that burned like acid over the mark.

"Is it right to be impressed by something a daemon did?" Calistos voiced what was clearly on everyone's mind judging by the way they all looked at Keras as if he had gone crazy.

"I have never seen a ward created by a daemon before, and it did entirely shut down Marek's powers."

When Keras put it like that, Marek was a little bit impressed too. The wraith had skills, powers that they hadn't known about before or even thought possible for a daemon to possess.

"I think it comes from his power to steal memories." Marek leaned forwards, obeying Keras as he nudged his shoulder. The burning started again, but this time a tugging accompanied it, a weird sensation that made him feel as if Keras was trying to physically pull something from him and that something didn't want to leave.

"Stands to reason. He took Esher's memories and now yours. He has pieces of your knowledge, enough to cobble together a ward." Ares leaned towards Marek and peered at his shoulder, his eyebrows rising as he tried to get a look at the mark.

"This is more than cobbled together," Keras countered and the tugging sensation grew fiercer, until Marek couldn't stop his shoulder from lifting with it. "This runs deep. A ward like this takes skill. He deciphered how to do this from whatever memories he managed to take from you two. That takes intelligence."

"So, the wraith is the Marek of the enemy?" Calistos hopped up to sit on the counter on the other side of the island to Marek and opened a cylindrical packet. He tossed one of the cookies in his mouth and pulled a thoughtful face as he ate it.

Valen reached over and swiped one for himself. "What else do you think he knows?"

Marek had a suspicion that the wraith knew a lot more than he was letting on, things that could prove vital to their enemy in the battle ahead.

"He knows enough. He was able to break our wards to take the illusionist back and that makes him a threat." Keras tracked one of the lines on Marek's back and the whole thing lit up, ripping a pained snarl from Marek's lips as white-hot fire lanced him and he doubled over, breathing hard.

His vision wobbled, lights winking across it as he fought for air, to shut down the pain ricocheting through his bones.

"All done." Keras patted him on the back.

"Lisabeta," Marek murmured, his mouth and brain still fixed on what he had been about to say before Keras had attempted to kill him.

"I thought her name was Caterina?" Calistos said.

Marek swallowed hard. "Lisabeta. The illusionist. Caterina called her that."

"We have a name at last then. Think it might be of use?" Ares didn't sound sure and Marek wasn't either.

A name was nothing to go on. He had pored over the knowledge in their servers when the illusionist had first made an appearance and he had no records of one of her kind.

"Did you see her when you were being held captive?" Keras edged into view, his green eyes still sober, revealing nothing.

Marek nodded.

"I think all of this… it's revenge." He pushed up into a sitting position. "At least, what the wraith did to me was."

"A ward to take your strength and powers. He wanted you to suffer like she did." Daimon cast a worried glance at his shoulder. "Does it feel better now?"

Marek rolled it and focused on his body, and slowly nodded as he felt his connection to the earth inside him, felt the strength flowing through his veins.

"Did anything happen while I was away?" He hadn't had a chance to ask them when they had been at the castle before, because he had been too preoccupied with Caterina.

Was still preoccupied by her as his focus drifted to the wooden floor at his feet.

She was down there, close to him. Was she able to hear what they were discussing? He hoped not, but some breeds of daemon did have heightened senses, including hearing.

"Daemon activity at the gates is increasing again." Keras casually folded his arms across his chest, causing the sleeves of his black shirt to tighten over his muscles. "There have been several instances in the last forty-eight hours where we have encountered multiple daemons near each gate."

Which judging by the looks on his brothers' faces was unnerving everyone.

"We have to face facts here," Ares put in as he drew Megan closer to him, curling his arm protectively around her shoulders to tuck her against his side. "The otherworld is looking worse again, daemons are attempting the gates more than once a night, and I'm worried. I can't be the only one."

Daimon and Esher nodded in unison.

Calistos lowered a cookie from his lips. "I don't like it."

"I preferred it when it was quiet in Rome, just the odd stupid daemon." Valen stole the cookie from Cal. "Now I can't go a single night without killing double digits. Eva is helping as best she can, but it's only getting worse. How long before it's ten daemons at each attempt? Twenty?"

Marek hadn't realised things had gotten that bad in his absence. "If all the daemons hiding in the cities come crawling out of the woodwork, then we are going to be in trouble. Taking down a few daemons is one thing, but an entire horde of them? They could use sheer numbers alone to overwhelm us."

Ares stroked Megan's arm. "They must be being drawn out by the activity of our enemy. They're gaining confidence. The daemons I'm seeing are older. Stronger. It won't be long before something goes down. I can feel it brewing."

Marek wanted to mention that he sounded like the real god of war now, but held his tongue, aware that talking of Enyo's brother might end with Keras finally losing his temper again.

"We will devise a plan," Keras said and his gaze shifted from Ares to Marek. "Perhaps we can get some information from Caterina?"

"She's awake. I left her eating, but she's weak. Whatever is happening to her, it's taking its toll physically and emotionally." He flicked a glance at Esher to check on his brother and found him glaring at the floorboards, murder in his eyes. "I can take you to see her, but she won't talk with this many of us around."

It seemed like a valid excuse to get rid of some of his brothers and he was glad when Keras nodded.

"I want to take Megan home so I can get a Messenger to relay the news to our parents." Ares shuddered, and he wasn't the only one. Valen and Calistos both joined him.

"Creepy bastards," Valen muttered beneath his breath. "Always popping out of thin air."

Marek couldn't agree with him more. While he and his brothers could teleport, there was something about the way a Messenger did it that disturbed him. Their appearance didn't help. Messengers were all male and all shared the same appearance, as if they had been cloned, their short black-blue hair and heterochromatic eyes, one green and one blue, and their defined features making it impossible to distinguish one from the other.

One second you were alone, the next there was one of them right next to you.

Their ability to know the exact location of whoever they were to contact was what made their teleporting so unnerving.

And they had zero boundaries.

One had even appeared while he had been in the shower once.

"Plus, I have to get you home to rest." Ares swept Megan up into his arms and she scowled at him, her dark eyes and soft features hardening as she huffed.

"Don't get overbearing straight away." She pouted and stroked his shoulders, working black magic on his brother judging by how Ares instantly softened, the determination in his eyes morphing into something else. "Can't we just enjoy this?"

Ares grinned. "I know a way we can celebrate."

Daimon glowered. Calistos retched. Valen smirked.

"Esher, return to Tokyo and cover it and Hong Kong." Keras was all business as usual as he crossed the room, passing Ares and Megan as they disappeared. "Cal, take care of London and Paris."

"I'll cover Rome and Seville." Daimon stepped, leaving black swirls of smoke behind him.

Cal and Esher both nodded and teleported too.

Leaving Marek with Valen and Keras.

Marek could live with that.

He relayed everything Caterina had told him to Keras, and everything that had happened, filling him in as Valen demolished the rest of the packet of cookies.

When he had brought both of his brothers up to speed, he led the way down to Caterina's cell.

He gripped the bolt, his pulse pounding faster as he looked at Keras and Valen and grew aware of what was about to happen. This wasn't going to be easy, but he needed to let Keras near her and he needed to let his brother do his thing. He had to stand by and watch without interfering, even if Caterina was hurting.

Interrupting Keras and severing their connection would only cause her more pain.

He pulled the bolt back and stepped into the room, and Caterina's gaze leaped from him to his brothers as they entered behind him.

"Caterina, this is Valen and Keras. Keras is going to take a look at your memories." Marek stepped aside to let him pass.

Caterina shot backwards, her spine hitting the stone wall as she clutched the blanket to her. "He's going to do what now?"

He wanted to go to her as she stared wide-eyed at Keras and shook her head.

Valen shoved him in the back, propelling him towards her.

Marek focused on her rather than the urge to glare at his brother for intervening. He eased down to kneel beside her, by Keras's feet.

"We just need to see that everything you've told me is true. You don't have anything to worry about. I'll be right here." Marek resisted the desire to place his hand on the cot beside her, tempting her to take it, mostly because Keras was watching him, observing him closely.

It struck him that hiding what he felt for Caterina was pointless.

Keras would see it soon enough.

Through Caterina's eyes.

He was jealous of his brother as he realised that Keras was about to find out exactly what her feelings for him were, how she felt whenever she looked at him, what she thought about him. He knew his brother wouldn't focus on such things, not when he was looking for the truth about their enemy and her involvement, but it still grated.

Keras crouched in front of her and she kept her eyes fixed on Marek, even when his brother spoke.

"Caterina, I need you to look at me."

She shook her head and squeezed her eyes shut.

Marek lifted his hand and placed it over hers where it clutched her knees. "It'll be fine, Caterina. Relax. If you relax, it won't hurt. You won't even notice it happening."

If she didn't relax, it was going to hurt like hell.

Both her and him.

"Can you do this for me, Caterina?" He squeezed her hand.

Her eyes slowly opened and locked on him, and he didn't hide how much this meant to him, how badly he needed to know that she had been telling the truth about everything.

That everything had been real.

"What if he sees things I don't want him to see? My memories are private. I'd like to keep them that way." She swallowed hard and looked as if she wanted to glance at his brother as her heart rate spiked in Marek's ears. "I don't want him prodding around in there, but I'm getting the feeling I don't get a choice."

He couldn't blame her for being nervous, or upset. He didn't like the thought of Keras poking around his head, and he had been angry the few times his brother had done it without permission.

"You're right. Your memories are private." He caressed her hand, his eyes lowering to it, locking on his fingers as he stroked them along hers. "And it's hard for me to ask you to do this... but I need you to do it, Caterina. I need to know everything was... is... real."

Her eyes leaped between his and her features softened as understanding dawned in them, and then resolve bloomed in their hazel depths and her fear faded. She shifted her hand beneath his, feathered her thumb along his fingers, and held his gaze, staring so deep into his eyes that he felt connected to her.

She nodded, lingered for a few seconds, and then shifted her eyes to Keras.

The moment she met Keras's gaze, she relaxed, her hands going lax beneath Marek's touch. Her lips parted and her eyes dulled, losing focus. Marek kept up with the pressure of his hand on hers, hoping she could feel that he was there with her still, even as she felt the presence of Keras in her mind. He was still here for her and he wouldn't let anything happen to her.

As the minutes trickled past, Valen started pacing, his boots loud on the stone floor.

It did nothing to help Marek's nerves.

He kept his focus on Caterina's face, on her eyes as she stared at his brother, her pupils gradually dilating until they devoured the earthy hazel of her irises. She slowly leaned forwards, towards Keras, as if she was experiencing that same powerful pull Marek had when Keras had been removing the power of the ward carved on his shoulder.

Marek bit back a growl when Caterina kept leaning forwards, her hand falling from beneath his to press against the bar of the cot as her legs fell open. She moved closer to Keras, and then closer still, until their faces were only inches apart.

Too damn close for comfort.

Marek did growl when she leaned further forwards, looking for all the world as if she was about to kiss his damned brother.

Keras eased back and Caterina blinked, and looked herself over, a confused crinkle forming between her eyebrows before she quickly sank back against the wall.

Marek glared at his brother.

Keras toyed with the ring on his thumb, twisting the band around it, his handsome face etched in pensive lines as he stared at Caterina, his eyes shining like emeralds.

He blinked, and when he opened them again, they were fixed on Marek and were dull again, back to their normal colour.

Marek braced himself, preparing for the worst, for all of his fears to come true in the next instant.

"She is telling the truth about everything." Those words rolled over Marek and it took him a moment to realise his brother was telling him something positive.

The complete opposite of what he had feared.

Caterina muttered things in Catalan under her breath, calling his brother a devil, stating that he was the daemon as she clawed at her dirty hair, pulling it back from her face.

He wanted to go to her and comfort her, but Keras wasn't done.

"We can use her." Keras pushed to his feet. "She is a valuable asset. She will be able to get us information."

Marek shot to his feet as fire blazed through him, burning up his blood. "No!"

Keras slowly turned to face him, a shadow passing over his features that had Caterina whispering a prayer and had Marek regretting what he had said. He hadn't been able to stop himself. Caterina had been through enough.

She proved that by falling on her side, her arms draped over the edge of the cot in a tangle.

Marek eased down beside her and checked on her, his heart thundering in his ears as he made sure she was still breathing and had only passed out.

"I was not making a suggestion," Keras snarled, onyx invading the edges of his irises as he rose to his full height and glared down at Marek. "I was making a decision."

Marek had to be an idiot, because he stared his brother down, unwilling to go along with that decision just because his brother had lost his temper again.

"She may be able to get us information about Calindria." Keras's features hardened, his eyes glittering like green diamonds as he narrowed them on Marek. "The wraith is the one handling her. She can get close to him."

Marek burned with a need to know what had happened to their sister's soul too, but at the risk of losing Caterina? He wasn't sure he could do it. There had to be another way.

He clenched his fists and cursed himself for thinking that. Keras was right, and Caterina was their best option. She could get close to the daemon. She could bring them information, and then once they had a solid lead, they could finally break everything to Calistos.

He hated keeping their youngest brother in the dark about everything, but he knew deep in his heart that it was necessary until they knew exactly what had happened to her soul and how they could find it again. If they told him now, it would only make things harder on him. He had succumbed to his affliction after he had been to the twin gate.

How badly would he react if he discovered they knew what had happened to Calindria?

"Don't go along with it." Valen stepped into the room, dragging Marek's focus to him as light flickered from his direction. Tiny sparks of lightning chased around his fingers as he glared at Keras. "It's a death sentence and you know it. Look at what happened to Eva when she went double agent for us."

Marek's stomach turned.

Eva had almost been killed.

He looked between Keras and Valen, a war erupting inside him as he thought about asking Caterina to infiltrate the enemy. Benares and Jin, the incubus and succubus siblings, had been dangerous enough, but the wraith was even more dangerous, and far more intelligent. He had proven that.

"They will know Caterina helped me escape." And that was the main reason he couldn't go through with it. "Someone would have seen her."

"You said yourself that the illusionist saw you had been trying to break the ward and that she had brought Caterina to you more than once. It is possible she will believe you broke the ward and took Caterina hostage when she tried to come to you." Keras sounded less than sure about that.

Which was not a comfort.

"I can go back. Alone. I teleported out of that house, I can get back in." Marek glanced down at Caterina where she lay on the cot, out cold. "I can draw him out or something."

Or something was far from a solid plan.

It wasn't like him to want to rush in like this, but the alternative was Keras getting his way and sending Caterina in. He couldn't let that happen, so he would come up with a plan on the fly for once. No careful preparation. No pulling up of blueprints and scouting the location, studying every aspect of it.

He would just pull a Valen or an Ares and make it up as he went.

The look on Valen's face said he knew what Marek was thinking, and that he wouldn't be alone if he did decide to go with the flow for once.

"The wraith will be on his guard now. He won't easily be drawn out, Marek." Keras's deep voice was smooth, one of reason.

Marek had always admired the level head his brother had on his shoulders. Now he hated it.

"So Caterina will be in even more danger if we just send her in there." Marek paced away from her, unable to keep still any longer. "I can't do it. The wraith will know she helped me. Even if by some miracle he doesn't, how are we going to convince him that I took her captive? How exactly is her escape going to look real?"

"Valid points." Valen looked from him to Keras. "Got a counter point?"

A soft voice croaked behind Marek.

"I'll do it."

CHAPTER 25

Caterina was aware that she had passed out at some point. She rested on her side, the sound of male voices filling her ears as she drifted, thoughts spinning into a blur. What had Keras seen?

Enough to clear her name apparently.

She remembered that much from before she had passed out.

The talking grew louder.

More like arguing.

She tuned into them, until the spinning in her head slowed enough that she could make out what they were talking about.

Her.

She listened harder.

Something about using her to infiltrate the enemy just as the enemy had wanted her to infiltrate the brothers.

Keras was for it. Valen was against it.

And Marek?

Vehemently against it.

"So Caterina will be in even more danger if we just send her in there," Marek snarled, warming her heart and chasing the chill of having her mind read from her skin. "I can't do it. The wraith will know she helped me. Even if by some miracle he doesn't, how are we going to convince him that I took her captive? How exactly is her escape going to look real?"

"Valid points." Valen paused. "Got a counter point?"

Caterina thought about everything she had done, about Guillem and what was happening to her. She didn't have much hope left, and her body was unreliable, and there was a high chance Marek was right and the wraith he spoke of would kill her, but if she could help Marek, she would do it.

"I'll do it," she croaked and pushed herself up.

The room wobbled into a dark blur and she squeezed her eyes shut. When she opened them again, Marek was beside her, holding her shoulders and helping her sit up.

"No." He brushed his thumbs over her skin, his touch offering comfort that she stole and savoured.

She looked at him, catching the horror and fury in his dark eyes. Fury he turned on Keras.

"She isn't doing it."

"I'm doing it." She lifted her hand and placed it over his right one where it gripped her arm. "I can do it."

"You'll need to make it look convincing," Valen said, earning a glare from Marek that held disappointment. Because Valen was switching sides? His violet-haired brother shrugged it off. "I'm just saying. It's going to take a public fight to convince the enemy that she was a prisoner not a guest, and it's the only way of making her escape look real."

"I said no." Marek frowned at all of them when Keras continued as if he hadn't spoken.

"It cannot be one of us then. The enemy would know we are pulling our punches."

"I can handle myself. Although, I do feel a little weird and weak," she put in, tired of them not including her when she was the one who would be heading into enemy territory.

She frowned. When had the wraith and Lisabeta become *their* enemy? The answer to that question stoked the fire in her blood into an inferno, and made her restless to get going.

When they had pulled her into this and threatened her brother.

"What makes you think you can handle fighting a god?" Valen arched an eyebrow at her.

"I hunt vampires. It's how I met Marek." She looked up at Marek.

He went remarkably still as both of his brothers looked at him.

She cursed. His vampire hunting was meant to be a secret.

"It is not as if I did not see it... among other things we will be discussing in private before the day is over." Keras slid a look at her and she glared at him.

Because he had seen in her memories the time Marek had spent with her in this cell, and now he knew Marek's secret, one he had guarded and entrusted to her.

Marek looked less than pleased at the prospect of having to talk to Keras about what his brother had seen.

214

"I still think it's a shit idea to have one of us fighting her." Valen sounded a lot like he was trying to shift the focus away from Marek and his troubled past in an attempt to make Keras forget about it.

At least, Caterina thought it had been an attempt at helping Marek.

She couldn't be sure.

Because all it did was anger Marek.

"No one is touching Caterina," Marek snarled, the vicious sound startling her. She looked at him and a shadow crossed his features, blackening them as his eyes turned onyx. "No one lays a damned finger on her."

Valen jerked his chin towards her. "You're laying fingers on her right now."

The joke was lost on his brother.

Marek shot to his feet, seized Valen by his throat and slammed his back into the wall beside the door, every muscle in his arm straining and bulging as he tightened his grip. While Valen was slimmer than Marek, his muscles less pronounced, Caterina wasn't confident Marek would win in a fight.

Something about Valen left her feeling he was the sort of man who fought dirty.

Valen just smiled.

There was something seriously wrong with him.

He frightened her more than Keras did when he smiled like that, as if he was enjoying what was happening to him.

She re-evaluated her opinion of him when Marek suddenly jerked and shuddered, and sparks leaped from around Valen's hand where it touched his wrist. He didn't just frighten her.

Valen positively terrified her.

He could somehow channel electricity.

Marek released him and staggered backwards, shaking his head at the same time.

"Calm your tits." Valen shoved away from the wall and shook his hand at his side, until the sparks leaping between his fingers had all disappeared. "None of us will touch her. We can have Eva do it. The enemy knows she's on our side now and she's human so it would appear authentic."

"I still don't like the sound of this," Marek grumbled and rubbed his arm.

"It appears it is happening whether you like it or not." Keras adjusted the ring on his thumb, a silver one that resembled a wedding band. "We will discuss it later, once you and Caterina have had time to rest. When was the last time you slept?"

Marek shrugged. "Does passing out count?"

Her gut squirmed as an image of him doing just that flashed across her mind. Watching him go down in that street outside the bar had utterly destroyed her. She had somehow forced herself to remain where she had been, resisting the need to go to him and check on him, aware that if she revealed her feelings for him that the wraith would hurt her too.

Every time Lisabeta had brought her to Marek and she had seen the state of him, the fear that they would hurt her had compounded, and the guilt had grown stronger.

She wasn't aware that Keras and Valen had left, and she was alone with Marek, until he came and crouched before her, drawing her out of the past.

Plunging her back into the present.

Helping Marek and making amends wasn't the only reason she wanted to become a double agent, as Valen had called it.

Now that the daemon fever had lost its grip on her and she was thinking more clearly, she knew that the wraith had her brother and that was why Marek's brother hadn't been able to find him.

Guillem had been leverage before, and now he would be leverage again. The wraith would use him to lure her out and force her to do as he wanted.

But she wouldn't.

Not anymore.

"You don't have to do this," Marek husked, his voice going low as he reached up and brushed a strand of hair behind her ear.

"I do." She stared deep into eyes that held warmth, and something she dared to hope was real, because it echoed inside her too, even when she knew it was hopeless.

There wasn't any way to save herself. She could see that now. But she could still save her brother—and she could save Marek.

Because she cared about him.

More than cared.

She had fallen in love with him, and he would never know, because whatever happened next, he could never truly love her, not now that she was a daemon.

But she was still going to do this for him.

"I'm sorry about everything." He stared at his fingers as he brushed them down her cheek. "All of this happened to you because of me... and I'm sorry. It would have been better if you had never met me."

She didn't understand how he could think that.

Or believe that he really meant it.

216

If she'd had her way, things would have been different, but she couldn't bring herself to wish they had never met.

She was glad that she had met him that night. That for a brief, beautiful moment her crappy life had been wonderful. She had met a man who could understand her, who had been more than attracted to her, and who she had fallen in love with.

"I'm not sorry," she whispered, her voice lacking the strength and conviction she felt in her heart.

She shuffled to the edge of the cot and he moved backwards to give her room, his eyes darting between hers as he frowned.

"I'm not sorry we met."

She lifted both of her hands and framed his face, relished the warmth of his golden skin beneath her palms and how he looked at her with all the love in the world in his eyes, tinged with confusion and a lot of pain.

"I'm only sorry that things didn't turn out the way I wanted."

She tried to smile but it wobbled on her lips as she looked into his eyes, as she tried not to think about tomorrow or what was to come, or what would happen if she somehow survived.

Because there was no hope.

She had thought life was cruel to her, but she had been mistaken. Her parents' deaths, her brother's turning, a decade spent desperately trying to save him, it had only been the warm-up act.

It had only been the build-up to this.

Life hadn't been her main enemy.

Love was.

Love was crueller, filled her with despair and pain, and yet she couldn't stop it from pouring through her whenever she looked at Marek.

Couldn't stop it any more than she could stop her own heart from beating.

Even when it was hopeless.

Marek cupped her cheeks in his palms, his gaze searing her, filled with the conflict and hurt running rampant inside her, revealing that he didn't know what to do either.

He opened his mouth, his brow furrowed, and he shook his head and pulled her into a hug that was so tight she wanted to cry.

She cursed the world instead.

She cursed it with all the venom she could muster.

Because the one thing she wanted was right here in her arms, but he would never be hers.

The world spun into a cold darkness.

CHAPTER 26

When the darkness faded, Caterina pulled away from Marek and looked around her, curious as to where he had taken her.

A colossal black building that resembled a temple from ancient Greece towered before her, thick towering fluted columns lining the façade to support the triangular pediment. There were two rows of them at the front, but only a single row along the sides, forming a walkway that ran around the temple.

Beyond it, a low roofed walkway lined with columns connected it on either side to smaller temples that were set back from the main one.

Beyond them?

The blackest mountains she had ever seen speared a dull grey sky, fault lines in their cragged faces glowing gold and illuminating the smoky clouds that swirled across them.

"Marek." She seized his arm, her heart racing and lodging in her throat as cold realisation slid down her spine.

This was the Underworld.

He had brought her to the Underworld, a place where daemons weren't allowed.

Why?

A thousand doubts filled her head, fear gripping her tightly as she let them come, didn't have the strength to deny them while she was staring at the ominous black temple.

The bright, colourful garden that surrounded it was so out of place, and did nothing to soften the terrifying image of the buildings. The whole place reeked of power, malevolence that seeped into her skin and made her want to teleport away.

Only she didn't know how to teleport. She had managed it once by pure chance, and a hundred attempts after that she still hadn't managed it again.

"I don't like it here. Take me back." She shook Marek's arm, jerking him back and forth as he stared at the entrance of the temple.

"I can't take us back... I didn't bring us here," he murmured, voice distant, as if he wasn't quite with her.

"You can teleport. Just do it." She squeezed his arm, digging her fingers into his biceps. "I said I would do what your brother wanted. I don't need to be convinced."

"I'm not trying to convince you." He turned a frown on her and shook his head. "And believe me... I would never bring you here, even if I could enter this realm. I was banished to Earth. I can't teleport to this realm until that banishment is lifted."

"If you didn't bring us here... who did?" Her hands started to shake as she considered everything he had said and drew a terrible conclusion.

Ice skated down her spine, a sensation that someone was watching her. That feeling of malevolence grew until it was choking, had her shaking Marek again, on the verge of begging him to try to teleport.

She stilled, frozen right to her marrow as awareness washed over her.

They weren't alone.

She slowly inched her head to her left, towards the main temple as metal clanked against marble, the sound like a death knell in her ears.

"Marek," she whispered and stepped back, releasing him even as she wanted to edge closer to him instead.

She didn't dare, not when her eyes landed on a tall slender figure in the doorway of the temple, dwarfed by the height of it. Black shadows appeared around him, swirling with streaks of blue and deep red. Caterina wished with all of her heart that her flaky new powers hadn't chosen this moment to reveal emotions to her.

Because she had the dreadful feeling those were the colours of anger and hatred so deep nothing could alter it.

The man strode into the light of one of the torches mounted on the columns at the front of the temple, and she swallowed hard.

Warm light chased over the black armour that hugged the man's lean frame and the spikes that rose from his short onyx hair. A heavy crimson cloak hung from his shoulders, swirling around his ankles with each step, drawing her eyes down to the pointed tips of his boots. They scraped on the marble with each step, and she couldn't stop herself from imagining how he might use them in battle.

Although, the claws that tipped his gauntlets were infinitely more terrifying.

He tucked his arms behind his back, carrying himself with a regal poise as he tilted his head up and narrowed red eyes on her.

The colours surrounding him turned as black as the temple behind him.

And then suddenly winked out of existence.

Caterina wasn't sure whether to be relieved or worried by her newfound ability failing her again. She might have been able to use it as an early warning system, turning it to her advantage.

Although, she doubted she would have a chance to escape if this man made a move.

It would be over in a blink of his crimson eyes.

If it wasn't for those eyes, she would say it was Keras who stood before her, dressed for war.

She had the terrible feeling this man was a far cry from the one she had met in the cell, the one who had proposed she help them and had cleared her name with Marek.

This man wanted her dead.

It was right there in his eyes as he stared down his straight nose at her.

"This is bad," Marek whispered beside her.

She risked edging closer to him.

The man's eyes narrowed, freezing her in place.

"Who is that?" She really didn't want to know the answer to that, because she already knew and she wanted to keep pretending that this wasn't happening.

"Father." Marek stood his ground when the man's eyes shifted to him. "The god-king Hades."

Oh. This was very bad.

If Marek and his brothers hated daemons, then this god-king despised them with a vengeance.

And he had summoned her.

A daemon.

It was all going to end here.

She had thought she had given up all hope, but some foolish part of her must have been clinging to a tattered thread of it because now that she was facing death, she realised she had still believed she had a shot with Marek.

And now whatever chance she might have had was going to die with her.

Hades shifted his crimson eyes to her again and his nostrils flared as he drew down a deep breath, as his black eyebrows knitted hard and his lips compressed. Disgust shone in those scarlet eyes. Disgust and hatred.

And violence.

She instinctively brought her hands up to her chest, a vain attempt to shield the heart he could easily rip from her if he wanted it. She was no match for him. His power was palpable, thickening the air and pressing down on her.

If he wanted her dead, she wouldn't stand a chance against him.

Marek moved in front of her, placing himself between her and Hades. She stared at his back, reeling and struggling to believe what he had just done.

He was shielding her.

Protecting her from his father.

"You would do well to apologise for bringing this *thing* into my presence." The ground seemed to tremble in response to that deep voice rolling over the land, the tension in the air growing as each word left Hades's lips.

"You brought her into your presence," Marek countered and then his back stiffened, his shoulders going rigid, as if he regretted speaking out of turn to his father.

Or maybe he was as afraid of him as Caterina was.

No. She wasn't afraid of him. She wasn't going to let him scare her. Marek was right and he had brought her to the Underworld, and if her life was about to end, she was going to go down fighting, not cowering behind someone.

She stepped to her left, so she could see Hades, and clenched her fists as she stared him down.

Because she was damned if he was going to talk about her as if she was something so far beneath him that she was akin to the dirt he scraped off his boot.

"I didn't exactly choose to be infected by a daemon." Her hands shook as she spat those words, as she weathered the glare he turned on her. Her heart thundered, so fast that she felt sick as she fought to remain where she was and not slink behind Marek again.

"I would never bring such a foul creature into my realm." Hades turned that glare on Marek.

She could almost read Marek's mind as he frowned at his father, his handsome face awash with confusion that echoed in her.

If Hades hadn't brought them to the Underworld, who had?

"Do not treat our guests so poorly, darling." A soft female voice came from behind Caterina, as gentle as a summer breeze, filled with warmth that was a strange contrast to the bleak lands around her.

It evoked images of sunlight and greenery, of flowers and crystal-clear rivers.

And Caterina swore the crimson in Hades's eyes faltered, a flicker of blue shining through as he looked beyond her to the woman.

Marek looked over his shoulder, his face softening, his dark eyes gaining glimmers of gold and green as they tracked the woman.

She came around Caterina's left, slowly drifting into view, and Caterina couldn't take her eyes off her. The long black dress she wore, layers of gauzy fabric that seemed to float as she moved with incredible grace, blended with the black earth, but her eyes were the clearest green and her hair was scarlet, flowing over her pale shoulders in gentle waves.

"Mother," Marek whispered, the love in his eyes showing in his voice as he looked at the beautiful woman who didn't appear a year older than he was.

She smiled serenely and held her hand out to him as she glided towards him, all elegance, a regal edge to her that was markedly different to the one Hades had. His was commanding, that of a king who expected absolute obedience and ruled with an iron fist. Hers was gentle, that of a queen who would do whatever was needed in order to ensure her people were cared for, were safe and would live long lives, filled with peace.

A queen who loved all equally.

Marek took her hand, bowed and pressed a kiss to it, his eyes slipping shut as the waves of his dark hair fell forwards to caress his brow. He lingered, breathing her in, as if he couldn't bring himself to release her.

If he wasn't allowed to enter this place, how long had it been since he had seen his parents?

Caterina was always aware of the hole the death of her parents had left in her life, a void that would never be filled again, but she couldn't imagine what it would be like to be exiled from your home by your own parents, always aware they were alive but never allowed to see them.

Marek finally, reluctantly released his mother's hand and stepped back, close to Caterina.

"Why have you brought this thing here, Persephone?" The gentle way Hades said that didn't hide the hatred that seeped from him as he stared at Caterina.

Persephone rounded Caterina, brushing Marek aside. He took another step back and Caterina wanted to move, to close the distance between them again. While Persephone felt like light and warmth, Caterina was still deeply aware of the woman's incredible power, and the fact she was a daemon in a world where she wasn't welcome.

Assessing green eyes skipped over every inch of Caterina, and she swore she could feel them, was aware of them even when Persephone was behind her. What was she looking for? Had she brought Caterina here to simply sate her own curiosity?

Or to judge her?

Persephone glided back into view and stopped just in front of her.

She reached a slender hand out towards her.

"Stop," Hades boomed, the sound cracking like thunder around them, shaking the black earth.

Persephone froze, her fingers bare millimetres from Caterina's arm.

"I am a goddess of creation and life," Persephone said softly as she slowly turned towards Hades. "I only wished to see if I could reverse what was done to this poor child."

Reverse it? Caterina didn't dare hope that was possible. Marek didn't believe it was, she knew that. He had spoken of finding a way, but there had been no shred of hope in his voice.

Blue flickered in Hades's eyes again, concern surfacing in them as he gazed at his wife.

"I will do this with or without your permission." Persephone turned back to face Caterina.

Hades huffed and scowled at her back. "Very well. If you feel the slightest tainting of your powers, you are to release the creature."

She nodded regally. "Of course, my love."

The look in her green eyes as she held Caterina's gaze said she had no intention of obeying that order. Caterina glanced at Marek. He didn't look at all surprised that his mother was willing to disobey his father.

Was she so assured of her power over him?

Caterina looked beyond the crimson-haired beauty to the towering god-king.

And caught the love and concern in his blue eyes as he gazed at Persephone before he noticed Caterina staring.

His irises blazed scarlet.

He bared his fangs at her.

"It is not wise to test him," said the woman who was doing just that, her soft voice like a melody as it embraced Caterina, chasing some of the chill from her skin that Hades had caused by glaring at her. Her secret smile stole Caterina's heart and made her miss her mother all the more. She whispered, "Although, it is fun sometimes."

"Fun for you." Marek edged towards them, closing ranks with Caterina as he warily watched Hades.

Persephone shrugged. "Your father will not lay a hand on her."

"I'll believe that when I see it."

"What are you talking about over there?" Hades growled.

Persephone smiled over her shoulder at him. "Come down from there and find out for yourself."

He sneered at Caterina, making it painfully clear he had no intention of getting anywhere near her.

Which was oddly reassuring.

Until she considered that he probably didn't have to get anywhere near her to kill her.

"This will not hurt." Persephone gently laid her hand on Caterina's forearm.

She steeled herself, because Keras digging around in her mind had hurt and she was sure that someone digging around in her body would be even more painful.

Only Persephone's touch was warm, gentle, and Caterina felt strength flowing into her, heat and light that pushed out the vile darkness she had been aware of from the moment the wraith had injected her with the daemon blood.

Her stomach turned.

That blood writhed in her veins, as if it feared Persephone.

Persephone stroked her hand upwards and the darkness swirled within Caterina, clearing her left side and pooling in her right leg, causing it to ache and burn. Sweat broke out on her brow and slid down her spine, and her vision wobbled as the ground pitched beneath her.

She swayed towards Marek.

He caught her right arm and held her. "That's enough."

Persephone released her.

Marek checked Caterina over, beautiful concern in his eyes as he palmed her arm and pressed his other hand to her forehead. "Are you all right?"

She swallowed and nodded as the darkness washed through her again, spreading out, and the fierce heat that had been building in her right leg abated.

Leaving her feeling as normal as she got these days.

She looked to Persephone, afraid to hear the verdict but needing to know.

"What has been done to you can be reversed," Persephone said, those words chasing the cold from Caterina's heart, restoring fragments of her hope. "You simply need to find a healer. Which is lucky for you."

She smiled, the sort of smile someone used when they made a joke.

Caterina didn't get it.

A healer? Where was she meant to find a healer?

"Megan."

Caterina looked at Marek. He stared into the distance, hope flaring in his eyes that quickly died as he shifted them to land on her.

"Ares would never allow it."

"Why not?" Persephone beat Caterina to asking that question. "He has allowed Megan to heal others. Why not this mortal? She cannot infect Megan."

But she was a daemon.

Caterina's shoulders sagged. She didn't want to, but she could understand why Ares would be reluctant to let Megan near her. Ares had come across as a tough son of a bitch when she had met him, one who fiercely protected those he loved. He had demanded she tell him what she wanted with Marek, why she was targeting him.

He had been convinced that she had still been out to hurt his brother.

Which meant he would never let her near the woman he loved.

"Ares is determined to keep Megan safe. He practically made it a vow when we discovered she's pregnant." The last word to leave Marek's lips fell heavily, ratcheting up the tension in the air.

Thick silence followed.

And then Persephone's green eyes shot wide. "Pregnant?"

Marek's own eyes widened and he cursed. "You haven't had a Messenger come?"

His mother shook her head.

Another curse pealed from his lips. "Then forget I said that. I said nothing. It was a mistake."

It was too late.

Persephone turned away from Caterina, revealing Hades where he now stood closer to them, his eyes completely blue and filled with surprise.

"We are going to be grandparents?" Persephone turned back to Marek.

Marek shoved his fingers through his wild brown hair, grimaced and then his shoulders sank.

He nodded.

"A baby." Persephone smiled at Hades, her emerald eyes glittering with unshed tears. "Our son is having a baby."

"Megan is having the baby," Marek muttered.

Persephone dismissed him with a wave of her slender hand, and then paused and looked at Caterina. "Speak to Megan anyway. Healing a mortal will be easy for her compared with healing a god."

Marek nodded, and that flicker of hope ignited in his eyes again, sparking it to life inside her.

His mother grinned at Hades, sending the tears tumbling down her cheeks. "A baby."

She laced her fingers together and brought her hands to her lips, her happiness shining in her eyes, seemingly infectious as the corners of Hades's lips curled into the semblance of a smile and his blue eyes shone with something akin to love as he looked at her.

"Oh, a baby. I want to build a nursery." She beamed at Hades.

He sighed. "Ares has his own house now."

She frowned and the earth around her feet sprouted thorny brambles. "But I want the baby to live here. They could have the east wing. It is quiet there and I can visit."

"If you have your way, you will be raising this child. I know that look in your eyes, my love."

"But…" She hurried to him and he held his hands out to her, looked down into her eyes as she slipped her hands into his and he curled his claws over them, holding them gently. "A baby."

There was a slight pout to her lower lip.

And apparently that was all it took to strip Hades of his power.

He raised his hand and cupped her cheek, smoothed his thumb across it and looked at her with so much love in his eyes that Caterina looked away, because she felt as if she was prying.

"I know you long for another," he murmured low. "But we talked about this. I cannot bear to see you hurt. When we lost her, it almost destroyed you. It destroyed me."

Caterina's gaze drifted back to them. They had lost a child?

It was there in Persephone's eyes as the happiness turned to fear and the brambles spread, becoming thick twisted branches as they encircled her.

Hades's brow furrowed as he cupped both of her cheeks in his palms, his face tilted towards her, and his eyes shifted to red.

"I swear, my love, nothing will happen to this child. We will keep him safe." Hades's voice darkened, dropping low to scrape over gravel as the ground shook beneath Caterina's feet. "Nothing will happen to any child brought into our family. I failed once. I will not fail again."

Persephone nodded and he wrapped his arms around her, lowered his head and closed his eyes as he kissed her crimson hair.

What had happened to a child of theirs?

She looked at Marek.

Tears laced his eyelashes as he looked at his parents, pain glittering in his eyes that told her the loss of that child had hurt everyone in their family.

Marek glanced at her out of the corner of his eye and swallowed hard, brushed the back of his hand across his nose and then scrubbed his neck. She wanted to ask him about the sibling he had lost, but she couldn't find her voice, and right now didn't seem like the appropriate time.

She didn't want to cause Persephone more pain. It was clear that she still felt the loss keenly, and Caterina felt sorry for her. She had been so happy when she had found out she was going to have a grandchild, but that happiness had turned to cold fear in the space of barely a minute. She should be excited about this time, enjoying every step of it, not fearing it.

Caterina looked at Hades and then Marek. Persephone wasn't alone in her fears. Hades and Marek both wore the same look, determination to keep that vow Ares had made and keep Megan and the baby safe, and fear they would fail at that task.

She could understand why.

Their enemy would make Megan a priority target if they discovered her pregnancy.

Caterina wouldn't let it happen.

She turned to Marek, more eager than ever to help him, and in turn his family.

He held his hand out to her and she placed hers into it, warmth curling through her when he closed his fingers over hers and held it tightly.

"We should go." He looked at his parents.

Persephone emerged from Hades's arms and smiled despite her tears, aiming it at Caterina. "Be careful."

A trail of purest white tulips sprouted in a wave towards Caterina and bloomed around her feet, and Caterina looked down at them, afraid she would crush the delicate blooms.

She looked to Marek for an explanation.

"Apparently, white tulips are your flower." He bent and plucked one, and offered it to her. "Mother is a goddess of nature. We each have a flower."

"What's yours?" She kept still as he tucked the bloom behind her ear.

"That's a secret." He smiled. "Maybe you'll find out one day."

She looked at the black earth, hoping the flower would blossom from it and reveal it to her, but apparently Persephone wasn't on her side and wanted her to find it out from Marek.

"Relay a message to Ares," Hades said. "I wish to speak with him."

Marek nodded.

Hades slid her a look, not a disgusted one as she expected, but one that stayed with her as darkness swirled around her and Marek pulled her into his embrace, tucking her against him.

His father had almost looked hopeful.

And she had the feeling that if Megan could reverse what had been done to her, that he would welcome Caterina into his family.

She looked up into Marek's eyes as they appeared back in the cell.

Seeing the hope that blossomed inside her reflected in them.

She could save her brother. She could become human again.

And then she could have the thing her heart wanted most of all.

A life with Marek.

CHAPTER 27

Marek wasn't alone with Caterina. He looked over her head to Keras where he stood in the doorway of the cell, Valen just behind him.

"Where did you take her?" Keras stepped into the room, a shadow flitting across his face as he stared Marek down, leaving him in no doubt of his brother's anger.

Because he thought he had tried to take Caterina away from them to stop her from carrying out the mission Keras wanted her to take on.

"Nowhere." Marek slowly released her and checked her over again, all of the fear that had been building inside him, the tension that had brought him close to snapping more than once, flooding from him as he saw she was fine and she had come out of the meeting with his parents unscathed. "Mother summoned us so she could take a look at Caterina."

Keras just stared at him.

Valen whistled low. "Well, shit. Was Dad there?"

Marek nodded.

Keras and Valen exchanged a look, one that echoed the shock that still flowed through Marek.

Because he had honestly expected Hades to kill her.

"How'd he take it?" Valen looked at Caterina, as if Marek needed a clue to know what he was really asking.

How had Hades handled a daemon in his domain?

"Mother talked him down." As Marek's fear gave way, anger filled the space it left inside him. "She could have just come here to see her. It's summer."

Which meant Persephone could leave his father's side without causing the seasons to spin out of control.

"She wanted Dad to see her." Valen leaned against the doorframe.

"Why?" Marek looked at him, and he shrugged.

"Maybe she wanted him to see Caterina wasn't the enemy. Maybe she wanted him to see how you feel about her. I don't know. Mum works in mysterious ways."

He really hadn't needed Valen bringing up his feelings, not in front of Caterina. He could feel her looking at him now, studying his profile as he diligently kept it towards her. If he looked at her, she would see that Valen was right, and he had feelings for her.

Deep ones.

The sort that made a man do crazy things.

Like shielding her from a god-king who could obliterate him.

Hades didn't need anyone pushing his buttons, not since Esher had breached the Underworld to save Aiko and had ended up fighting him, and had come close to getting himself killed in the process.

"She's meddling." Valen scuffed the stone floor with his boot and muttered, "Told you about meddling."

He was right. Persephone was meddling. She was always aware of them, more so than Hades was. She knew their innermost feelings.

She knew when they were in turmoil.

And she always tried to make things better for them.

She must have felt Marek's confusion and conflict, and his love for Caterina, and his desperate need to save her, and how he had lost hope.

Not because he feared Caterina couldn't be cured, but because he feared his family would exile him and turn on him when they discovered what had dawned on him.

If Caterina became a daemon, he would still choose to be with her.

So Persephone had summoned him, not only to see if she could find a way to cure Caterina for him, but because she had wanted Hades to see him with her. She had wanted his father to see that he loved Caterina and nothing would change that.

"At least he let you leave." Valen pushed away from the wall. "Which is good."

"It means our plan can go ahead." Keras's green eyes held a subtle note of concern as he looked at Caterina.

"I'm ready." She straightened to her full height and tipped her chin up. "I can do this."

Marek looked at her. "What Mother said... about Megan being able to reverse what's happening to you. I want to take you to her now."

"But you can't." She smiled softly, understanding in her eyes. "I know. For this to work, I have to be the same as when I left."

"I worry he would be able to sense the difference in you." He lifted his hand and stroked her right arm, aching with a need to go against what he had just said and take her to Megan. "I don't want you to do this."

She raised her hand and placed it over his, cupping it to her shoulder over her T-shirt. "I want to do it. I might be able to see my brother. I might be able to get him away from them."

Hope flared in her eyes and he was glad to see it after how resigned she had been, her hazel gaze dull and sombre.

"Are you sure you're strong enough?" He looked her over, from her caramel hair, over the T-shirt that swamped her frame, to her dark sweats and her small feet.

She looked so delicate, so easily breakable, even when he knew she was a fighter at heart, and her skills had been honed in battle against creatures far stronger than she was.

She nodded. "When Persephone touched me, I felt strength flowing into me."

Strength that Marek could sense as he held her, and could see in her returning colour and the brightness of her eyes.

Yet he still didn't want to let her go and face their enemy alone.

He didn't want to have to stand by and let her fight Eva.

"I'm not sure *I* can do this." He frowned and shook his head. "The thought of you fighting…"

Her smile stole his heart. "Don't worry. I have this. It won't be the first time I've taken a beating and I'll make it look convincing."

He wasn't worried about that. He was worried about what came after. He was worried about what the daemons might do to her.

All of that worry condensed inside him, compounding into a need to be alone with her, to hold her without his brothers watching and judging him.

To show her that even when she was alone, she wasn't really alone. He was right there with her.

Because he loved her.

"I'll join you all in Tokyo." He gave Valen and Keras a pointed look, one he felt sure would make it clear he wouldn't change his mind, no matter what they said against the delay.

Surprisingly, Keras just sighed and stepped, leaving black vapour behind. Valen smirked, waggled his fair eyebrows and disappeared.

He hadn't meant to give his brothers the impression that he wanted to be alone with Caterina so he could be intimate with her, but now that Valen had put it in his mind, he couldn't think about anything else.

That desperate need to be close to her latched onto it, had him leading her from the cell and up the stairs to the ground floor, and then up the wooden staircase to his room.

She nervously glanced around it as she entered ahead of him, her eyes straying to the four-poster bed that took up most of the room.

"I thought you might want to wash. The water is warm now. I could run a bath?" He tamped down the nerves that tried to rise inside him as he moved past her, heading for the bathroom.

"That would be nice." She padded around his room, taking it all in, even going as far as peeking in his drawers.

He didn't call her out on it. She could be nosy all she wanted, as long as it took her mind off things. He wanted her to have a moment to breathe, away from the craziness. He wanted things to be as they had been between them, back in Barcelona, before his enemy had set their sights on her.

The relief on her face, the calm that washed over it as she moved to the leaded window and looked out, at the loch and the mountains, said that she needed it.

She needed a moment of normality.

Marek focused on running the bath, giving her some time to enjoy the scenery, aware that she needed to erase the image of the Underworld from her mind and that the lush green of the Scottish countryside would help her do it.

He peeked back in on her as the water thundered into the old clawfoot tub.

And wasn't surprised that there were three white tulips blooming around her feet.

His mother's way of offering comfort and showing Caterina that she wasn't alone.

It was a relief that his mother had taken a shine to Caterina, would be keeping an eye on her from the Underworld, and hopefully working on his father to make him see that Caterina wasn't the enemy or someone to despise.

When the bath was full, he switched the water off and gathered soap and a washcloth for her, setting them on a shelf near it. He went to her where she still stood at the window, watching the seabirds.

Or at least he thought she had been watching them.

He stopped beside her and tracked the line of her gaze, and smiled.

A seal bobbed in the water near the rocks, just its head breaking above the surface.

"There's so much wildlife here." She watched the seal, smiled as it dove beneath the surface, and kept her eyes on the water. "I think I saw a deer across the water too."

"It wouldn't surprise me." His arm brushed hers as he moved closer, and he couldn't resist the urge to take hold of her. He stepped behind her and wrapped his arms around her, looping them over her shoulders and drawing her back against his chest. "We're miles from any roads here and we own the land as far as the eye can see. Plenty of deer out there, as well as other things. I saw a pine marten once. I swear it was going to swim to the island to raid the larder."

She lifted both hands and curled them over his, and gods, it felt comfortable to hold her like this.

Right.

Her back pressed against his chest as she leaned her weight on him, and he settled his chin on top of her head and just held her, savouring how she felt in his arms, relishing the quiet of the moment and the feelings it stirred in him.

"I wish we could just stay here." Marek let the words fall from his lips.

And waited.

Caterina didn't keep him waiting long. She brushed her hands over his and sighed as she leaned more of her weight against him.

"I wish we could too."

Those words were ambrosia to him, the sweet taste of heaven.

"But we can't." She clutched his hand and he sensed her mood shifting, darkening in a way that had him wanting to pull her back into the light and vanquish her doubts and fears, and keep her here with him.

In this moment.

"I know." He held her tighter. "Just let me have this for a while. I need it."

She turned in his arms and pressed her palms to his chest, her eyes on the space between them, where his heart beat for her. "I need it too."

Her hands shook against him and doubt filled her eyes as she tilted her head back and looked up at him, edged with fear, and then pain as she looked away, turning her cheek to him.

She tried to push out of his arms but he held her closer, refusing to let her go, unwilling to let her believe whatever was spinning around her mind and tormenting her.

"Caterina," he murmured.

When she lifted her head to look at him, he swooped on her lips and kissed her. She tensed, going rigid against him, but then she melted in his arms and her lips started a fevered dance over his. He groaned and twisted her loose T-shirt into his fists and clutched her to him as he angled his head and deepened the kiss, brushing her tongue with his and eliciting a soft moan from her.

"We shouldn't." She broke away from him and pushed against his chest when he tried to pull her back to him.

He loosened his hold as she locked her elbows, afraid of hurting her with his strength. "Why not?"

Her eyebrows furrowed and she looked away from him, and he knew what she wouldn't say.

Because she hadn't been cured yet, and she thought he would only really want her if that happened, and he would break her heart if she remained a daemon.

Well, she was mistaken.

He would never do anything to hurt her. She had become his entire world, vital to him, and he would move all the realms to keep her at his side and make her see that she belonged with him, no matter what happened.

He loved her.

He wanted to tell her that, but he could see that she wasn't ready to hear it, and she wouldn't believe him if he did say it. Not until Megan had reversed what had been done to her.

He would tell her then, when he was sure that hearing it wouldn't hurt her and she would believe that he was sincere and wasn't just saying something to make her feel better.

"Kiss me," he husked and tried to coax her to him.

She resisted. "Why?"

He frowned at her lips, aching to take them again. "Because I need to kiss you. I need you, Caterina. You might not be afraid of what's going to happen, but I'm going out of my mind with worry."

And not only about what was ahead of them.

He worried about how he might react to her, that the darkness in his veins might rise to the fore and have him lashing out at her again when he didn't want to do such a thing. He stared down at her, studied his feelings and picked them apart, and mulled over that night on the beach.

It dawned on him that he hadn't reacted that way to her since that night and hope built inside him. Was it possible that the shock of sensing she was a daemon and his past had combined to cause that reaction?

He would still be on his guard, because he didn't want to hurt Caterina. Just the thought of hurting her caused him pain.

And the thought of her in danger had him needing to hold her close, to savour every moment he had with her and deepen the connection they shared so she would know she wasn't alone.

So she would know how he felt about her.

He removed his left arm from her waist and captured her cheek with his palm, ran his fingers along her jaw and brushed his thumb over her lower lip.

"Gods, Caterina, I need this. I need you. Being pulled to the Underworld… facing my father… knowing what's about to happen. I can't handle it. I don't know whether I'm coming or going, but this…" He stroked her lip. "You… you ground me, and I need to feel this again… I need this."

He wasn't explaining it very well.

He cursed, gritted his teeth and growled, because he couldn't translate the feeling in his heart into words.

"Déu… I need you too." Caterina threw her arms around his neck and kissed him as she leaped into his embrace.

He caught her and clutched her to him, kissed her hard as the need building inside him reached a crescendo, surging through his veins to obliterate all reason and control.

Marek twisted with her and carried her to the bed as she kissed him, her lips playing on his, tongue teasing and stroking, driving him wild. He set her down on the mattress and covered her, caging her with his body.

Her thighs fell open, welcoming him into the cradle of them, and he groaned as she wrapped her legs around him and pressed her heels into his backside, forcing him down into contact with her.

Her heat scalded him through their sweats, had him grinding his erection against her as he mastered her mouth, a slave to the need she had awoken in him.

She tangled her fingers in his hair and pulled his head up, gazed into his eyes with ones full of passion, need that burned inside him too.

"What about my bath?" she murmured and stroked her hands down his throat, teasing his nape and then his shoulders.

"What about it?" He lowered his gaze from her lips to her neck, dropped his head and kissed it as she tilted her head back, arching her breasts into his chest.

"It'll get cold if we don't use it." Her hands drifted down his spine and he groaned and licked her throat, teasing the spot below her earlobe as she tugged his T-shirt up.

"We won't fit in there together." He skimmed his hands down her side and mirrored her, pushing her T-shirt up to reveal the smooth plane of her stomach.

He broke away from her lips and growled as he pushed to his knees between her thighs and took her in. Her hair cascaded across the dark covers, her rosy lips beckoning him for another kiss, and her eyes were dark, hungry as they dropped to his chest.

Marek pulled his T-shirt off, obeying her unspoken command, and savoured the way her face crumpled and she bit her lower lip, as if the sight of him had just completely undone her.

Or deeply satisfied her.

Her legs lowered from his hips and her feet pressed against his thighs, pushing him backwards.

He slid off the edge of the mattress and landed on his feet, forced himself to stand there and keep still as she moved onto her hands and knees and crawled towards him, the hunger in her eyes building as she raked them over him.

A shiver tripped through him as she stroked her fingers down his chest and his stomach, swirled them around his muscles and kept tracking downwards. She leaned towards him and pressed wet kisses to each muscle on his stomach, following her hands lower.

He swallowed when they hit the waistband of his sweats, tipped his head back and groaned as she ran her fingers along it and the heel of her palms met his cock. She dipped her fingers behind the waistband and her sweet moan as she brushed the blunt head had his hips jerking towards her, hot need rushing through his veins, a desire to hear her moaning like that as he filled her.

She swirled her tongue around his navel and then disappeared. By the time he caught up and opened his eyes, she was kneeling on the bed in just her sweats, pushing them down her slender hips.

His throat worked on another hard swallow as he watched her, as she teased him with a glimpse of her before she tugged the soft material back up. He frowned and groaned as he reached for her, the ache to see her naked building into something fierce and controlling.

She smiled and a hint of blush coloured her cheeks as her eyes darkened, as if she had seen that need she had created inside him and knew he was on the verge of losing himself to it.

Rather than pulling her own sweats down, she reached for his, tugging them down his hips, freeing his cock. The cool air hit it and it kicked against his stomach as he imagined the warmth of her hand on it, and burned with a need to feel it.

She didn't make him wait long. She stroked her hand down the length of him, from the blunt crown to his balls. He closed his eyes, lost in the way her hand felt, the softness of her touch as she explored him. It was too much.

He gripped her wrist when she curled her fingers around him, not sure he would withstand such torment, not without making a fool of himself.

Her eyes met his as he looked down at her, the wickedness in them saying he wasn't going to get his way. There would be no stopping her.

Gods, he loved this woman.

She had strength, knew what she wanted and wasn't afraid to take it, or fight him on it. She had stood up to his father, and had stood up to him more than once. She had courage and fire.

And, damn, her mouth was wicked.

He groaned as she wrapped her lips around him, as she suckled the head of his shaft in a way that had his eyes rolling back in his head. He sank forwards, until his knees hit the edge of the mattress, giving him some support as she went to war on him.

She gripped him with her hand, holding him at her mercy as she moved her mouth on him, slow teasing pulls that propelled him to the edge of control, had him skirting the point where need would take over, leaving him a slave to his hungers.

He wanted her right there with him.

He pushed his fingers into her hair, twisted the spun caramel around them and gripped her as he worked his hips, lost in the pleasure building inside him as she started to stroke him, obliterating his plans to push her to the edge.

He groaned and frowned, clenched his jaw and told himself to pull back on the reins, but he couldn't convince his body to listen to him. Not when Caterina was stroking him, sucking him, her wet heat gloving him.

Release climbed to the base of his shaft.

The urge to spill was strong, but somehow he forced himself to move, to push her backwards and break contact between them.

He breathed hard as he stared down into her eyes, fighting for control over his body, slowly easing the tempest within him.

Caterina lowered her hazel gaze to his cock, the look in her eyes warning she didn't intend to give him the moment he needed.

He swept her up into his arms before she could take him back into her mouth and kissed her as he kicked his sweats off.

She twisted in his arms, looped her legs around his waist and rubbed against him, the feel of her breasts brushing his chest and the heat of her against his aching length almost pushing him over the edge.

"Caterina," he moaned, begging her to give him just a few seconds.

Enough time to get her out of her sweats.

He lifted her, placed her over his shoulder and weathered her frustrated grunt as she shoved her hands against his backside and pushed herself up. That grunt became a moan as he pulled her sweats down and off over her feet.

Her panties followed them.

Marek skimmed his hand over her bottom and gave it a light tap when she wriggled, just enough to leave a handprint on her right buttock.

She huffed and smacked his arse hard enough that it stung.

"It's like that is it?" He hefted her, intending to toss her onto the bed.

Only she twisted in his arms, wrapped her leg around his neck and heaved backwards, sending him off balance. He tipped over her, his back hit the mattress and she landed on top of him.

Good gods.

He wasn't sure he had ever been so turned on.

He growled, seized her backside and pulled her to him before she could make her next move, delving between her thighs. She moaned and shuddered above him as he stroked between her plush lips, tasting her sweetness.

Her hands came down on his head and she arched, another trembling sigh escaping her as she rocked on his tongue, riding each stroke of it over her sensitive flesh.

Marek was right there with her, moaning as he licked her, as he suckled and swirled his tongue around her bead, unable to get enough of her.

Her sweet cries rose in pitch, her rocking growing more frantic, and he grinned as he pushed her higher still, towards that edge of losing control.

She suddenly lifted her hips and slapped at his head when he pulled her back to him, refusing to release her. When she wriggled and loosed a frustrated noise, he reluctantly eased his grip on her, because he didn't want her angry with him.

"What's—" He didn't get a chance to finish asking her what was wrong.

She took hold of his length and eased back, guiding him into her and destroying his ability to think.

Feeling took over, had him seizing hold of her hips as she sank onto him, as he filled her and her warmth gloved him.

She pressed her hands to his chest and rose off him, setting a pace that had his heart thundering and hips rising to meet hers. Her fingertips dug into his pectorals, short nails scoring his skin as she rode him, as she tipped her head back and moaned.

Marek palmed her nape and pulled her down to him, kissed her hard as he worked his hips, matching her frantic pace. Ripples of pleasure collided and built into waves that crashed over him with each thrust of his hips, each plunge of his cock into her. She moaned and rocked, her desperate strokes pushing him to take her faster, harder, until that need that gripped her was satisfied.

"Marek," she murmured against his lips, painting them with his name spoken in a way that he would always remember.

She seared it on his heart as she clutched him to her, as she clung to him and he rolled her onto her back, wedging himself between her thighs.

She surrendered to him, her head tipping back as he braced himself above her, planting one hand onto the mattress and the other beneath her lower back. He lifted her from the bed and angled his hips, filled her and stole the sweet cry of bliss that left her lips in a kiss.

Her breaths came faster, mingling with his as he sank into her, as he curled his hand around her shoulder and shifted his knees, pressing them into the bed and using them as leverage. He groaned and lost himself in her, in the storm building between them, a wild tempest that would break at any moment.

But one that would leave them forever changed.

She clawed his shoulders, leaving her mark on him again, and kissed him deeper. Her hips rocked up to meet his as she ploughed the fingers of her right hand into his hair and clutched him, and he groaned and shuddered as a hot shiver cascaded down his spine and his shaft grew harder.

Caterina tightened around him as he filled her again.

She jerked up against him and cried into his mouth, her thighs quivering against his hips as her body pulsed around him, propelling him over the edge with her. He groaned and shuddered as release swept through him, so swift and powerful that he could only hold Caterina as it took him, as every inch of him shook in response as he spilled inside her.

She peppered his lips with kisses that had warmth following in the wake of his climax, feelings flowing through him that filled him with a need to hold her and never let her go. To keep her with him and not let her carry out their plan.

He couldn't do that to her though. She needed to do this—for him and for her brother. All he could do was keep her safe, and he would do that. Whatever happened, he would be there for her. He would see her through it all.

Marek pulled back and looked down at her, stroked her cheek as he stared into her hazy, warm eyes that revealed more than she probably wanted him to see.

She didn't have to fear.

He couldn't get enough of her either.

There was no one in this world more perfect for him than she was.

He wrestled with the words again, even when he knew now wasn't the time.

He would tell her later, when she was safely back in his arms.

When she would believe that the heart pounding in his chest belonged to her, and it would forever.

No matter what happened.

Because she was it for him.

CHAPTER 28

Marek checked Caterina over for what felt like the millionth time as she stood in the kitchen of the castle reciting the plan for Keras, because apparently his brother wouldn't be satisfied until they had gone over it at least a hundred times.

Whenever Caterina got to the part about being taken by the wraith, his gut churned and his pulse picked up, adrenaline flooding his veins in preparation for a fight he knew he couldn't let happen.

As much as he hated it, he had to let the wraith take her. He had to trust that she would be able to get away from him if necessary, using her newfound powers.

Although, he could have lived without her admitting this morning that her ability to teleport was flaky and she had only managed it once, when she had run from him.

Valen fussed over Eva in the corner, as if she was the one about to get snatched by their enemy, risking her life to get them intel.

"I still say you should just let me step to the house where they held me." Marek scowled at Keras, unable to keep a lid on his temper as a thousand ways this could go wrong crowded his mind, tormenting him.

"They will not be there anymore." Keras offered him a look that Marek supposed was meant to be consoling, as if he would believe Keras felt bad about what he was asking Caterina to do.

Or that she might end up dead.

"I could take a look." Marek paused and looked down at Caterina as her hand came to lightly rest on his arm.

Confidence shone in her eyes, mingled with determination that ignited the spark he had always found so alluring.

"I can do this." She stroked her palm down his arm, sending a warm shiver skating over his skin. "I'll be fine."

She wouldn't be.

He knew that in his gut.

He didn't believe in omens, but gods, he was starting to.

As much as he tried not to do it, he couldn't stop himself from thinking that skull he had watched sliding down his shower screen in Seville had been a portent, a sign that he was going to lose someone close to him.

Someone he loved with all of his heart.

He stared down into her eyes, wishing that strength that blazed in them would ease his mind, but it wouldn't. He wouldn't be satisfied until she was back in his arms again, safe from his enemy.

She smiled, one that hit him hard in his heart, and trailed her fingers off his hand as her gaze flicked to Keras.

Whatever she saw there had her toying with the hem of her dirty cream camisole, smoothing it down over her jeans.

Marek looked at his brother and his mood took a sharp downwards turn, something he hadn't thought possible since he was already on the verge of unleashing an earthquake across the Northern Hemisphere.

Keras's green eyes remained cold and hard as they slid from Caterina to Marek.

Damn, his brother really resembled their father when he wore that look, the one that revealed how disgusted he was that Marek was allowing Caterina to touch him, that they were close to each other despite what she was becoming.

Marek didn't care.

He turned to Caterina, fighting for the words again, aware of Keras's gaze on him, and Valen's too now as the room fell quiet.

He wanted to tell her now, before she threw herself into danger for him, that he had feelings for her that wouldn't change, no matter what.

In the end, he settled for pressing a soft kiss to her dirty forehead, and whispering in Catalan, "Be careful. I will be there to keep an eye on you."

She nodded against his lips, touched his hand and then broke away from him.

Watching her go to Keras twisted him in knots, filling him with an urge to steal his brother's part in this so he could remain in contact with her and so his brother couldn't lay a hand on her.

Keras took hold of her before he could make a move and disappeared.

Marek stepped, following him and trying to tamp down the black urge to rip his brother to pieces.

That urge only intensified as he landed in the elegant front garden of the Tokyo mansion and found Keras shoving Caterina towards the wooden porch.

Making far too big a show of it.

Caterina struggled against his hold and every instinct Marek possessed roared at him to fight his brother and stop him from harming her.

He fought it as he stormed after them with Valen hot on his heels as Eva lingered in the garden, waiting to play her part.

Keras disappeared into the mansion with Caterina, and someone snarled. Esher. Marek had wanted him away from the mansion when this went down, but Keras had insisted he remain to make it look more realistic. Marek was beginning to think Keras just wanted to frighten Caterina, showing her what sort of reception some members of his family would always give her until they managed to reverse what had been done to her.

Marek didn't bother to take his boots off at the door. He strode into the old building, quickly scanned it and banked left when he spotted Keras shoving Caterina towards the bathhouse.

And the small building beyond it that housed Esher's cage.

"What the fuck is happening?" Esher bit out, his voice a black snarl as he shirked Aiko's soft touch and took swift strides across the tatami mats, closing the gap between him and Keras.

And Caterina.

Keras looked back at his brother, his grip on Caterina's arm tightening to the point where her skin blanched and she flinched.

Marek bit back a growl, somehow managing to hold it at bay as he glared at Keras.

The growl did leave his lips when Keras spoke.

"We have captured a spy and need to question her. Are you up for it?" His cold green eyes remained fixed on Esher, even as Marek shook his head and stormed towards him.

He changed course when Esher's blue eyes brightened dangerously and his brother smiled slowly.

No. No way. They needed to make it look convincing in case the wraith was watching just as expected, but he was damned if he was going to let Esher lay a finger on Caterina.

Esher doubled his pace, practically running to keep up with Keras as he reached the space between the shower stalls and the hot spring bath that looked out onto the zen garden.

Marek raced to intervene.

He hit the corridor that ran alongside the kitchen area just as Caterina turned and shoved Keras in the chest, catching him off guard and sending him falling into the bath.

What the hell was she doing?

She threw a panicked look at Esher.

The fear Marek could sense in her spiked.

Genuine.

He knew what she could see as Esher rushed her. Claws and fangs. Black eyes flooded with a terrible hunger for violence.

Edged with crimson.

Because she had just dared to hurt Keras.

Marek launched himself at Esher, no longer giving a damn whether the wraith saw his desire to protect her, because this was no longer a game. It had become real the moment Caterina had attacked Keras. Esher would kill her for it.

Before he could tackle his brother, Esher hit an invisible wall and fell on his backside.

Blue hexagonal glyphs shimmered across the air between Caterina and Esher.

She had developed more than one succubus talent.

Caterina's hazel gaze landed on him, a myriad of feelings swimming in it, and then she disappeared.

Outside, Eva yelled an obscenity and gravel crunched in a rapid beat, telling him that the assassin was giving chase and their plan was somewhat back on track.

He pivoted on his heel and shoved past Valen as his brother did the same, rushing for the door. Behind him, Keras bit out a curse and Esher growled.

Marek hit the porch.

Spotted Caterina near the broad wooden gate in the white wall that surrounded the mansion.

Eva lunged at Caterina.

Caterina dodged the blow, grabbed Eva's arm and teleported with her.

Marek cursed this time.

"That wasn't the fucking plan," Valen snarled beside him.

"I know that." Marek turned on him, his temper spiking right back up as he faced off against his brother, because Valen wasn't the only one frantic to find his woman.

He stepped to beyond the wall, into the street between the box-shaped houses that filled the quiet suburb of the city. He scanned the roads around him, fought to breathe slowly to bring his racing heart back under control as he struggled to hear over the thundering beat of it.

"Damn it, Caterina." He twisted this way and that, searching for her.

To his left, Valen appeared at another crossroads, one that had a small group of trees near it. A square?

His brother yelled, "Eva."

Pivoted and kicked off.

Marek sprinted as hard as he could, and when that wasn't fast enough, he stepped again, draining more of his strength. He landed in a dead run beside Valen, his pulse pounding again as they streaked across the square.

Valen must have seen something.

It was all Marek could think as a desperate need to find Caterina flooded him.

They hit another road and then Valen broke right down a smaller one, and Marek heard it.

A muffled grunt and a ripe curse.

In Catalan.

He doubled his effort, pushing himself towards his limit, outpacing Valen. But not for long. Valen caught up with him and together they broke into another square, this one little more than a few trees in each corner of a dusty patch of land.

In the middle of it, Caterina and Eva were fighting, their moves looking almost as if they had been perfectly choreographed and practiced a thousand times. Caterina dodged and ducked, sweeping under Eva's arm as she attempted to land a blow, and swung her leg out towards Eva's ankles. Eva leaped over Caterina's foot, landed on one leg and brought her other one around in a swift arc.

Caterina raised both hands and managed to block it, grabbed Eva's ankle and twisted hard, sending the black-haired assassin into the dirt.

Caterina shuffled backwards and onto her feet.

Eva leaned back, pressed her hands into the dirt, and pushed off, springing onto hers and straight into an attack that Caterina must have seen coming.

But she took the blow to her left cheek like a champion.

Staggered to her right and whipped back to face Eva.

Caterina wiped the back of her hand across her mouth and looked down at it.

At the near-black blood on it.

On a vicious yell, she launched herself at the assassin.

Marek wasn't sure he could watch as she failed to land half of her blows and left herself open to most of Eva's. It took all his will to keep his boots planted to the road and not intervene.

As she fought Eva, a feeling built inside him, that sense of doom returning.

"I can't let her do this," Marek murmured as she took a blow to her gut and doubled over.

Not the fight, but what came after.

She would be in too much danger. One false move on her part and he would lose her forever.

When Eva delivered a hard-right hook that landed Caterina on her backside, Marek lunged forwards.

Violet smoke spilled from the air behind her, swirling in the gentle breeze and turning black in places as it spread. Sparks of green and violet chased across it as it formed an oval at least four feet wide and seven feet tall.

A bare leg appeared out of it, long and shapely, and Marek readied himself as the illusionist stepped from the portal. The high slit in her slinky black strapless dress caused the material to fall away from her left leg as she moved towards Caterina and Eva, her silver eyes swirling as she assessed both women.

She casually flicked her long fall of dark violet hair over her right shoulder.

Her black lips curled into a wretched smile.

Eva grunted, dug her fingers into her black jaw-length hair, clawing it back to flash the electric blue streaks in it, and went down.

Hard.

"Eva!" Valen threw his right hand forwards, unleashing a white-blue bolt of lightning that shot towards the daemon as he raced towards Eva.

The illusionist stepped back into the portal. It rapidly dissipated and Valen's attack went straight through it and out the other side. It struck a tree in the corner of the square and wooden splinters exploded from it, flames swift to engulf it as the lightning ravaged it.

Caterina flinched away, curling forwards with her hands over her head as she gave her back to the blast. Marek was swift to raise his hand, to pull up a wall of earth between her and the shards of wood.

The portal reappeared on the other side of Caterina and the illusionist stepped out again, her smile cold as she looked at Valen where he knelt on the ground, holding Eva as she rocked and muttered things under her breath.

When the daemon turned that cold smile on Caterina, Marek knew in his gut that their plan had failed.

Caterina seemed to know it too.

She flung herself at the daemon. "Take me with you. I need to see my brother. I have information to give you."

The daemon curled a lip at her and brushed Caterina's hands away as she looked down her nose at her.

"Whatever information you have, it is of little consequence now." The daemon waved Caterina away. When that didn't deter Caterina and she seized her arm, the daemon scowled at her, grabbed her wrist and twisted her arm, forcing her to release her and sending her to her knees on a pained cry. The illusionist narrowed her silver eyes on Caterina. "Your role in this play is over. Eli no longer has a use for you. You have played your part."

"My brother." Caterina tried to grab her again, desperation washing across her face as she reached for the daemon's leg.

"Eli still has a use for him." The illusionist lifted her left foot, pressed her heeled shoe to Caterina's chest and shoved her backwards as she sneered.

Caterina's back hit the dirt, but she was swift to recover, scrambling onto her knees and kicking off as the daemon backed towards the portal.

Marek kicked off too, sprinting across the dirt on an intercept course. If they couldn't get Caterina to infiltrate the enemy to bring them information, then he would get it out of this daemon.

He lunged for the illusionist as she stepped into the shimmering oval.

And collided with Caterina.

"He will be safe with us."

Those words drifted from the violet and black smoke as it began to thin and dissipate, and Marek couldn't hold back the growl that rumbled up his throat. Keras was not going to be happy. He should have reacted faster, the moment the daemon had made it clear that they were done with Caterina.

But part of him had believed she could convince the daemon to take her to the wraith.

Caterina stumbled through the lingering tendrils of the portal, pivoted and tried again, disturbing the remnants until they were no more. "I have to reach my brother. I have to reach him. Let me through."

Marek's heart went out to her as she desperately tried to capture tiny wisps of the portal.

To his right, Valen helped Eva onto her feet, every other word that left his lips a curse.

A light entered Caterina's eyes.

"Don't you do it." Marek seized her before she could follow through with that thought. "We'll find another way."

She tried to wrestle free of him, but he tightened his grip on her, refusing to let her go, using all of his will and every drop of his power to keep her in place and make her listen to him.

"Your teleporting skills might land you way off the mark. It might land you somewhere that could kill you." He lowered his head and willed her to look at him, but she was too busy trying to escape his hold. "Don't, Caterina. I'll take you wherever you need to go. We'll get Guillem back together."

He had no love for vampires, but Caterina loved this one deeply.

So he would do all in his power to save him.

"I have to help him, Marek." Her struggles suddenly ceased and he could see it in her eyes as her strength leached from her. "I need to see him. I need him."

She sagged against him, and he released her and gently wrapped his arms around her.

"We'll find him." He bent his head and kissed her hair as he stroked her back. He looked at his brother. "How's Eva?"

Valen stopped fussing over her for barely a second. "Recovering. What did the bitch mean? Caterina has played her role?"

He wasn't sure.

"Caterina was meant as bait for me. Maybe she served her purpose when I was captured... but I escaped." He frowned as he looked at that from all the angles, considering every possibility. "The daemons didn't really get what they wanted from me."

As those words left his lips, a sense of dread loomed inside him.

Gods.

A shiver shot down his spine.

An ache bloomed in his shoulder.

"What is it?" Valen twisted to face him, his pale eyebrows knitting hard above his bright golden eyes.

"The wraith knocked me out by stabbing me with a blade." He stared straight through his brother, reeling as the implications of that hit him and they hit him hard.

"Yeah, you said that before. What about it?"

He didn't have time to explain.

"Grab everyone and meet me at the villa. I have to go back to Seville." He pulled Caterina against him and focused.

"Why?" Valen hollered, halting him in his tracks.

If his brother needed a reason, something to motivate him into moving his arse and doing what Marek wanted, he would give him one.

"The wraith has my memories. He knows the protective wards on my villa," Marek barked and understanding dawned in Valen's eyes.

Capturing him hadn't been the objective.

Stealing his memories had been.

The wraith had been after his amulet the whole time.

"He's going to try to open the gate."

CHAPTER 29

Marek landed in his villa with Caterina to find the entire place had been turned upside down. He released her and stepped down from the overturned couch he had landed on and ran his hands over his hair as he looked around at the mess.

He took swift steps across the terracotta tiles, heading straight for his office and the cupboard there, some stupid part of him hoping that it was going to be all right.

The doors were open.

He eased towards the cupboard and stared at the circular shield hanging at the back of it.

And the place where his amulet should have been.

"Damn it!" He grabbed the fallen lamp from his desk and hurled it across the room.

It hit the wall near the window opposite the door and smashed into pieces.

Caterina gasped behind him.

Marek shoved his fingers through his hair and growled in frustration as he clawed it back. Maybe it wasn't too late. Maybe there was still time.

He looked out of the window at the darkness.

Maybe he was fucked.

Instinct said to move now, but he was already in enough trouble. If he went to the gates alone, Keras would kill him. The wraith wouldn't be there alone, and Marek wasn't talking about just the illusionist being with him. The daemon was clever.

There was no way he hadn't mustered an army of daemons to keep Marek and his brothers occupied while he interfered with the gate, using them as cannon fodder to ensure he and the illusionist were able to complete their mission without coming under attack.

"I'm sorry," Caterina said and slowly approached him. She slid her hand over his back as he leaned forwards and braced his palms against the edge of his desk, anger and disappointment colliding inside him. "Whatever it was he took, we can get it back."

"It's not your fault," he muttered. "This mess is on me. All of this mess is on me. What happened to you... what happened tonight. It's all on me. I should have considered the implications of what the bastard did to me, but I was too focused on my hurt... my anger."

He pushed up and huffed as he looked at the cupboard, as he focused on the villa and felt that every ward had been disabled.

"I knew the wraith must have taken my memories through the blade, as he did with Esher." He turned and sank onto his arse on the desk. "I'm an idiot for not realising it earlier."

"Nah, don't be too hard on yourself. If you're an idiot, what does that make most of us?" Valen appeared in the middle of the room with Eva tucked close to him, both of them armed for war.

The onyx leather holster over Valen's black T-shirt held rows of small throwing knives against his ribs, and a short blade hung from the waist of his combat trousers.

The holster over Eva's own black T-shirt held guns, a weapon Marek had learned she preferred over knives, although she did have one of those strapped to the waist of her tight black jeans.

"We all fuck up at some point." Valen boxed him on the arm.

That wasn't a comfort.

So far, none of them had messed up this badly. The enemy had managed to seize an amulet more than once before, but the brothers involved had felt the wards on their homes trigger and had returned quickly enough to stop the enemy from realising the amulets weren't the Keys of Hades.

Marek had a sinking feeling that wouldn't be the case this time.

He wasn't sure how long the wraith had been in possession of his amulet.

But he was assuming it had been with him from the moment Marek had come around in that country house to find himself a prisoner of his enemy.

Which meant there was a chance the wraith had already made an attempt on the gate and knew the amulets didn't control them.

And if the wraith knew that, how long would it be before the male realised he and his brothers were the keys to the gates and their blood could open it for him?

Daimon and Calistos arrived, both of them geared up for a battle. Daimon wore a similar holster to Valen over his long-sleeved navy roll-neck he had paired with his jeans. Calistos had a wicked pair of knives the length of his forearms strapped to his hips and was wearing black leather vambraces over his forearms.

Keras appeared barely a second later.

Not a single weapon on him.

"Esher and Ares have agreed to protect the other gates." Keras adjusted the sleeve of his crisp black shirt and scowled at the open cupboard, at the leather and bronze shield hung on the back wall of it. "Any idea how long it has been missing?"

Marek shook his head. "The wards were disabled. Some of them were complicated and might have taken time to break, but it's highly probable that the wraith has been in possession of my amulet since the night I went missing."

Valen whistled low.

Daimon cursed.

"You think they know?" Calistos looked from Marek to Keras, his stormy blue eyes growing darker as the tips of his blond ponytail fluttered.

"How about we find out?" Valen touched Cal's shoulder, pulled Eva against him and smiled. "Race you to the twin gate?"

Cal nodded and stepped.

"I'll check the main gate. I'll text if something is wrong." Daimon disappeared before Marek could tell him to be careful.

"Sorry," Marek muttered as he looked at Keras.

Keras shrugged it off. "Sooner or later the ruse would end. We are more than prepared for that. We are strong enough to face whatever they dare to throw at us."

Marek wasn't sure they were, but he nodded and waited for Keras to step before he slid his arm around Caterina's waist.

"I thought you wouldn't want me there." Her hazel eyes searched his, and he cursed the doubts in them.

"I want you right where I can see you." He stroked the fingers of his free hand down her cheek. "I need to know you're safe."

He stepped before she could answer him, landing at the main gate.

Daimon stood in the middle of the beautiful garden in the heart of Seville, staring at the low fountain that stood in the middle of a crossroads in the gravel path that intersected the shrubs and trees.

He looked up from his phone, the screen making his irises appear as white as snow ringed with black. "Nothing here."

Marek tightened his grip on Caterina and teleported again, landing on the hill overlooking the dusty valley basin.

And around four dozen daemons.

He immediately crouched behind a bush and pulled Caterina down with him. Maybe they weren't too late after all. The wraith hadn't attempted to open the gate yet. They could turn this around and keep the enemy under the illusion that the amulets controlled the gate, keeping their focus on getting hold of them.

And off his brothers' weaknesses.

His gaze slid to Caterina. His own weakness. Just as Megan was Ares's weakness and Eva was Valen's, and, well, everyone was Esher's weakness but if Aiko was hurt again, the world would pay for it.

Which meant Marek needed to get his hands on that amulet before the wraith realised all it did was protect him from the gatekeeper on the other side.

Valen lay prone on the ground beside him, frowning at the gathered daemons.

"Someone arrange a party?" he hissed with a smile in his voice that was out of place in such a grave situation.

It earned him a sigh from Keras.

"You take the left and I'll take the right?" Cal whispered, and Marek wanted to cuff him for taking this so lightly.

Marek wished Keras hadn't brought him. Whatever went down tonight, Calistos was going to take it personally. The Seville gates had been built when Calistos and Calindria had been born.

Meaning Calistos and Calindria were the keys to them, bound by blood to the gates in secret during their construction. Calistos had ultimate power over the gate bound to him, and there was a chance he could control the gate that had been bound to their sister too.

Marek kept a close eye on him, watching that storm brewing in his eyes.

He hated to admit it, but Keras had been right to bring him. If the gate needed to be closed, Calistos might be able to do it.

Emphasis on the *might*.

It was just as likely that Calistos would push himself too hard attempting it and would blackout.

Marek surveyed the daemons as they moved, parting to allow two figures through the crowd.

The wraith and the illusionist.

The daemons spread, moving as one to form a ring around the area where the gate would form, all of them facing outwards and all of them armed with swords.

Marek's eyebrows drew down as he charted the location of the gate in relation to the wall of daemons and calculated the space the disc of the gate would occupy once it opened. The daemons had been placed in a perfect ring around the gate, leaving only a few feet of bare land between their backs and the edge of the disc.

He narrowed his gaze on the wraith where he stood, near one side of the ring, his long black coat making him almost blend with the illusionist as she came to stand beside him. The bastard must have noted the width and position of the edges in relation to the terrain when Marek had been called here before.

This had been his plan all along.

The wraith lifted his right arm and the amulet dangling from it caught the slender moonlight.

Any moment now, the wraith was going to realise that the amulet didn't control the gate.

Marek needed to get down there and fast.

He went to move.

Froze.

Marek's eyes slowly widened as the amulet began to shine.

"What the fuck?" Valen muttered, echoing Marek's thoughts perfectly.

Marek gritted his teeth as something tugged at his chest.

The gate.

Someone was on the other side.

That was why the amulet was reacting.

He could use it to his advantage.

He kicked off and skidded down the dusty hill, using his arms to keep his balance as he plunged towards the daemons waiting at the bottom of it. One hissed as it noticed him, drawing the attention of the illusionist.

And then the wraith.

Marek barrelled towards the wall of daemons.

Keras beat him to it.

His brother appeared before him, a shadow in the night, black tendrils of smoke rising from his short onyx hair like a twisted crown as he launched a hand out at the first daemon, closed it around his throat and snapped his neck in one brutal move.

Two daemons next to the fallen male shook themselves out of their stupor and attacked as one. Shadows raced from the trees, leaving the ground beneath them eerily void of them, and shot upwards as they reached the first daemon. The male panicked, slapping at the black spreading up his legs, clawing himself in the process as he tried to get the shadows off him. He spun away from the group, shrieking as he twisted in circles, desperately attempting to stop the shadows.

That high keening noise shut off as the shadows engulfed him.

Just as quickly as they had swallowed him, they fell away.

The daemon dropped to the ground, his skin a sickly shade of grey and eyes white as he stared into nothing.

Marek shuddered.

Once upon a time, he had been envious of Keras's power. Then he had seen it in action, sucking the life from things, a black malevolent force that seemed to have a mind of its own.

The shadows rushed past him and he stepped back, giving them a wide berth as they skittered towards the wall of daemons.

Caterina slammed into his back, breathing hard.

"That was—" Her words died as she looked beyond him.

Marek tracked the line of her gaze.

Keras cut through the daemons, slashing throats with his claws and snapping necks, leaving a trail of bodies in his wake.

All with an empty look in his eyes and no trace of emotion on his face.

His brother was a cold, merciless killer as he decimated daemon after daemon, never slowing, not even when the more foolish ones tried to attack him rather than flee.

Marek made a mental note to keep Caterina far away from his brother.

To his left, Valen and Eva were working in tandem to breach the wall of daemons. Beyond them, Calistos and Daimon were cutting a path, combining their powers to form short spears of ice and propel them at high speeds at their enemies.

Marek cursed as light flickered in the centre of the collapsing ring of daemons, a bright purple spark that illuminated the entire area in blinding flashes. It grew rapidly, forming an orb that twisted, filling the air with a low hum as the sense of power built inside Marek.

The gate.

The orb flattened into a disc that grew as it rotated, and then another ring formed in a flash of yellow light, slowly turning in the opposite direction to the first one. A blue wave rippled from that ring as symbols appeared around it and another one formed, this one rotating in the same direction as the centre, but slower.

The wraith looked from the growing gate to Keras and the others, and then finally Marek.

A slow smile curled his lips.

Sent a chill down Marek's spine.

The bastard knew the amulet wasn't the key. It was right there in his violet eyes, in that satisfied glow they held. Marek's first intuition had been right and they were too late. This wasn't the first attempt to open the gate. This was a trap.

The wraith had been waiting here, aware that Marek would realise what had happened at some point and would come to this place to try and stop him.

And in doing so, Marek had exposed the gate to danger.

The wraith twisted the amulet into his fists and crushed it.

The gate remained.

One of his brothers cursed. Probably Valen.

He looked towards him and cursed too as a violet and black portal formed in the midst of the daemons and then another one followed it, and another, until there were six of them. As soon as they were large enough, daemons poured from them.

There was no way his brothers and Eva could handle so many.

Marek looked between them and the wraith where he approached the gate. He needed to help his brothers, but he needed to protect the gate too. Maybe he could do both.

He focused on the gate as he summoned his powers and the ground shook beneath his boots.

Caterina grabbed one of the fallen swords from the dirt and battled the daemons as they turned their sights on him, clearly sensing the rising threat coming from him.

He fought to keep his focus on the gate, on stopping it from opening completely. He dug deep into the ground, past the earth to the rock below, and pictured a ring around the gate.

Towering slabs of hard earth and huge monoliths of rock burst from the ground in a wave, running anti-clockwise from beyond the wraith and the gate, towards Valen and everyone to his left, and past him.

A vicious snarl left Keras's lips as he twisted and slammed his fist against one of the walls that sprung up right beside him, shattering it with a single blow, despite the strength of it.

His brother was formidable.

Marek had never seen anyone break one of his walls before, not with such ease at least.

Marek stepped to the other side of the wall of earth and rock and looked to his right, commanding it to continue to form.

Several dozen daemons poured into the inner ring before he could close it. They ran through the gate, and the rings sparked and blackened, the power it emitted pulsing in a strong wave through Marek. One of the daemons lingered too long and went down screaming as the gate reacted more severely, a wave of colourful light bursting across it as it tried to purge the taint and reset itself.

The wraith eased a step back from it and guided the illusionist behind him.

Keras appeared within the wall and cut through the daemons, taking two down with a single blow before he turned his sights on a third and then a fourth. He wasn't alone.

Caterina suddenly appeared to Marek's left, looked around herself and then sprang into action, her blade a silver blur as she attacked the daemons, driving them back and buying Marek time.

He wouldn't waste it.

Marek focused on the gate rather than the daemons, trusting Caterina to deal with them and keep them from him. The rings began to slow and the disc began to shrink.

The wraith unleashed an unholy snarl.

"Marek?" A soft female voice invaded his mind.

Marek ignored it. It wasn't real. She wasn't real. He refused to look at Airlea but he was aware of her beside him, moving towards him. He kept his gaze on the gate, his focus on his duty as the wraith raised his hands.

Five points of light appeared around the outer ring of the gate, swirling violet orbs streaked with green, and they grew as the wraith murmured low words. Power charged the air around Marek and he fought the gate as it slowed to a halt and then began to open again.

"Shit," he muttered and redoubled his effort, attempting to push back against whatever power was in the incantation the wraith was chanting. He risked a glance away from the gate, trying to find his brother. "Keras."

Keras appeared beside him, took one look at the gate as the five points of light moved outwards and the discs grew larger, another ring appearing.

Not Marek's doing.

Keras raised his hand and shadows shrouded the gate. The power humming in the air weakened and Marek focused everything he had on the gate, on convincing the damned thing that it wanted to close.

Purple beams shot up from amidst the shadows, curved towards each other and twisted around to form a dome above the gate. The shadows separated.

Keras grunted and stretched his hand out to them, his arm shaking as he splayed his fingers and the shadows writhed.

Attempting to obey him.

Holes began to appear in them, patches where the colours of the gate shone through, chasing back the darkness.

And then they began to close.

Keras was winning.

His brother stiffened, stared wide-eyed directly ahead of him, and his shoulders slackened as his arm fell to his side.

The shadows evaporated, revealing the gate, and the power contained in the violet orbs and the words the wraith was chanting rose again, pushing down on Marek as he fought the gate, trying to force it closed before it opened enough that someone could pass through it safely.

"Keras," he snapped, but his brother didn't move, just kept staring.

Staring at something that wasn't there.

"Daimon," Marek hollered. "Take her down!"

Before that pain that was steadily building in Keras's green eyes reached a crescendo and he unleashed it all on the world.

Whatever the illusionist was showing his brother, it was tearing him apart.

Daimon appeared beside him, took one look at Keras, and said, "Has to be Enyo."

Cal came thundering out of the black vapour trail of his teleport and grabbed Keras, pulling him around to face him. Keras snarled and tried to look back at the empty space where whatever he was seeing was playing out for him.

"Get him out of here," Marek bit out.

Cal's eyes widened. "I'm not that strong. He isn't going to budge."

Damn it.

"Do something," Marek snapped at Daimon.

His brother grabbed Calistos and pulled him away from Keras, towards the illusionist where she stood behind the wraith, her silver eyes glassy. Was attempting to control more than one illusion taking its toll on her?

He looked around and found no sign of Airlea. The daemon was putting all of her effort into destroying Keras.

Keras slowly reached for the ring around his thumb.

Marek frowned as he didn't spin it.

He started to pull it off.

"Don't do it." Marek grabbed his arm and shook him. "Whatever you're seeing, it's not real. It's a lie, Keras."

His brother slowly turned empty green eyes on him.

"Shut her down!" Marek hollered to Daimon and Calistos, and slapped Keras. "Snap out of it."

Keras's eyes went pitch black.

He lashed out at Marek with his claws.

This wasn't good.

Either striking his brother had really pissed him off, or the illusionist was attempting to pull him into whatever Keras was seeing, turning him against Marek.

He raised his arm to block Keras's next blow and the sense of power in the air grew stronger as his focus shifted away from the gate. Panic lanced him. If he didn't do something, it was going to open, and he had the dreadful feeling that it would stay open.

He needed to break those points of light. Somehow. He just wasn't sure how.

Keras lashed out at him again and Marek had to step to avoid his shadows as they attacked, shooting towards his legs. He reappeared in a clearing on the other side of the gate.

His brother's gaze whipped to him.

A vicious snarl pealed from his lips as he bared his fangs.

Keras swept his arm up and Marek realised his mistake too late to stop it.

A wave of shadows erupted from the ground, cutting in a line straight towards him.

Right through the heart of the gate.

His lungs seized as he threw himself to his left, as he hit the dirt and barely avoided being struck by the shadows. His eyes leaped to the gate and widened.

Several of the glyphs in the rings sparked and stuttered, little more than shattered pieces now. The rings halted.

Not good.

Marek looked through the gate to his brothers.

Daimon and Cal both stopped fighting the daemons and looked at the gate, and then at Keras, their wide eyes reflecting the colourful light it emanated as it slowly began to glow brighter.

Cal's blue eyes met Marek's and resolve filled them.

He wanted to tell his brother not to do it, but they had no other option. They needed to close the gate before the daemons could destroy it now it was seized open, and the only way to do that was to seal it.

Shutting it down completely and removing all power from it.

A process that might kill Calistos.

His brother didn't hesitate.

He sprinted for the gate, ripping his vambraces from his forearms as he ran at it, his blond hair streaming behind him.

The wraith signalled the illusionist and she turned her sights on Cal.

Marek's stomach fell.

They were going to use illusions against Calistos to buy themselves time to destroy the gate.

Valen appeared with Eva, and Daimon joined him as he launched himself at the daemons swarming around the illusionist and the wraith, a living shield that his brothers would be able to tear through if they had enough time.

But time was against them.

His gaze flickered past the daemons to Keras as his brother staggered backwards and looked around himself, shock rippling across his face as his green eyes landed on the gate. The illusionist had released him.

To focus all of her power on Cal?

Marek met Keras's gaze across the shimmering gate. "We need those two away from here right now or it's over."

Keras's gaze zipped to Cal and then the wraith and illusionist.

Marek kicked off, intending to join him when he teleported to reach them.

Only it wasn't his brother who appeared behind the two daemons.

Caterina was suddenly there.

She grabbed both of them and his heart lunged into his throat and slammed to a halt. No. Not her. It was suicide. The daemons would kill her for interfering with their plans when they had been on the cusp of a victory.

"Caterina!"

She looked across at him.

Gave him a sorrowful smile that told him she was well aware of what was going to happen to her.

And disappeared.

CHAPTER 30

Calistos had never heard anything as terrifying as the mournful, vicious sound that ripped from Marek as he sprinted through the flat glowing disc of the gate and skidded to a halt where Caterina had been.

And was now gone.

The ground shook and bucked beneath Cal's boots, sending Eva to her knees and Valen cursing as he went down with her when he attempted to help her. Marek tore through the daemons they had been fighting with Daimon, the scent of spilled black blood flooding the air as it ran in a river across the dry ground, soaking into the cracks that formed as the tremors continued. The olive trees around the grove swayed, and rocks tumbled down the hillsides.

Cal kicked off as his senses blared a warning, narrowly avoiding being hit by one of the boulders. A daemon beyond him wasn't so lucky. The rock crushed him beneath its weight, and knocked several more flying before it hit the hill on the other side and rolled back, slowing to a halt before it could cause any more mayhem.

"Anyone care to get him under control?" Cal kept his focus on the gate as he held his palms out facing it, focusing on it to assess the damage.

The moment Keras's shadows had torn through it, pain had ripped through Calistos, stealing his breath and leaving him feeling as if he was the one that had been damaged by his brother's attack.

He wasn't sure he had the strength to do what was necessary, not after the fight against the daemons, but he was going to give it everything he had.

If he could concentrate.

He leaped aside again as a huge fissure formed in the ground, the side he landed on in a low crouch dropping as the other one rose to tower over him.

"Fucking hell," Valen growled. "Dial it back."

His brother appeared on the other side of Cal with Eva tucked against him, his glare levelled on Marek as he ripped apart a daemon and tossed the body into the crevasse.

"Marek," Keras snapped, his deep voice a commanding snarl that had Marek finally stopping his assault.

Cal glanced at his blood-soaked brother.

Or maybe he had stopped because all the daemons were dead now.

Marek leaned over, braced his hands against his knees and breathed hard, his back straining as he fought for air, his eyes as black as night.

"Can you think of anywhere she might have taken them, or they would have taken her?" Keras moved to stand beside Cal, his voice level and calm.

It had the desired effect on Marek, pulling him back from the darkness.

Marek grumbled, "I can think of a few places."

"Take Daimon. I don't want you going alone." Keras didn't take his eyes off the gate as Marek grabbed Daimon and stepped. "Godsdammit."

The fact his brother had cursed made the gravity of the situation hit home.

If Cal couldn't seal the gate, there was a danger the mortal world and the Underworld would bleed together through it, and that would be the beginning of the end.

After Keras had revealed they were the Keys of Hades, bound to the gates through blood, they'd had several meetings to discuss what that might mean, and what they might have to do to seal a gate if it came down to that.

In the end, the only solid guess they agreed on was spilling their blood on the gate. Blood bound them to the gate, so maybe blood could control it.

None of them knew what to expect if they managed to forge a connection with a gate though, or how they were supposed to close it. Something told him it was going to be painful, and it wasn't going to be easy.

He let his gaze lose focus as he looked at the gate, summoned that feeling that brewed inside him whenever he was seeing the otherworld.

The sky turned blood red, streaked with flaming boulders that rained down on the land, tearing up huge tracts of the black earth as they impacted. Trees blazed around him. Smoke filled the air, together with the distant sound of screams. Some human. Some other things.

The acrid stench of burning flesh filled his nostrils and ahead of him, an enormous red tower speared the sky, flanked by smaller black ones. At their wide jagged bases, shadows swirled, a legion of daemons illuminated by pyres on which mortals burned.

Cal squeezed his eyes shut, not needing to see any more.

His glimpse of the otherworld, the future of this one should the enemy succeed, did its job.

Strength surged through him, determination to do his duty and not fail in his mission driving it higher as he opened his eyes and focused on the shattered, colourful horizontal disc of the gate that hovered a few feet above the earth before him.

He could do this.

He pulled one of his knives from the sheath on his hip, took a deep breath and drew the blade across his left palm. He curled his fingers over into a fist as he sheathed the blade, ignoring the sting of the cut as he squeezed it, because he was sure he was about to experience far worse pain, and strode towards the gate.

When he reached it, he turned his hand on its side and sucked down another breath as he waited. A bead of blood pooled on the side of his hand and he swallowed and braced himself as it trembled and fell.

It hit the gate.

Cal held his breath.

Either this would work or it wouldn't and they would be in even deeper shit, trying to come up with something on the fly.

Colours shimmered across the disc, chased by a wave of red that rapidly spread to cover every ring and glyph of the gate.

Was it working?

Pain cut through him, a white-hot bolt of lightning that tore a grunt from his lips as he gritted his teeth and bore it.

He knew the great rip through the middle of the gate hurt.

He could feel everything about the gate as a strange connection formed between them. It danced across his skin at first, a wave of prickles that made him aware of the power of the gate, how that line of shattered glyphs was painful, and left him feeling as if it was a living thing.

Maybe it was.

They were forged from blood after all.

Cal wasn't sure it would be a good thing if the gate was more than just a portal, if the blood had given it a strange sort of life. He had always wondered if they were sentient, from the day he had seen one react to a daemon, shimmering black where the daemon had passed through it and sparking violently, as if it despised the creatures as much as he and his brothers did.

If the gate was sentient in a way, it might not like what he intended to do to it.

He got his answer when he focused on the thought of closing it, on the fresh blood he had spilled on it that now coated the surface, dimming the light of it further with each drop he fed to it.

The prickling became a thousand white-hot needles that sank deep into his bones.

The pain that washed through him was so intense, he bent forwards and vomited.

"Cal?" Valen lunged towards him.

Cal managed to hold his free hand out and shake his head.

Because he had the sudden urge to lash out at his brother to keep him away, to protect himself.

"I don't think…" He swallowed and breathed through another wave of nausea. "It likes it."

Valen slowly looked from him to the gate. The colours tried to break through, writhing beneath the crimson, turning black in places.

"It's fighting you?" Keras looked as if he wanted to reach for him too, but held himself back as he looked between Cal and the gate.

Something slowly filled his brother's eyes.

"Doing this," Cal muttered and straightened as he finally tamped down the pain, bringing it to a more manageable level, one where he could move without wanting to vomit. "Don't try… to… stop me."

Keras's jaw flexed and he pivoted away from Cal on a low curse.

The second of the night.

Cal wiped his clean hand across his mouth and then motioned for his brothers to back off, because the connection between him and the gate calmed as Keras distanced himself.

Either it hated his brothers near it now it was damaged, or it really didn't like Keras anymore.

It was probably the latter since Keras had attacked it, but there was no harm in gaining himself some space in which to work.

His brothers backed off and he focused back on the gate.

Pain rippled through him, a streak right up his front and back. He focused on that line as he squeezed his hand, dripping more blood onto the gate, building the connection between them. The blood gathered along the line of the fracture and then parted as he stared at it, wanting to see beyond the crimson to the glyphs and rings. Sparks of colour emanated from the shattered glyphs.

Could he repair them and restore the gate?

That weird connection between him and it coaxed him into doing it.

Because the gate wanted to be fixed?

He looked at Keras where he had stopped near Valen and Eva. The look in his brother's eyes was right. The gate had to be sealed.

Pain shot up his chest in a fierce wave and he gritted his teeth against it as the connection wavered and the colours sparked brighter, turning black as they arced down to land on the crimson. He clenched his jaw and focused through the pain, but his connection began to slip, his control fading with it.

He looked down at his hand.

The offering of blood he was making wasn't enough. Not if he wanted complete control over the gate. Not if he wanted to seal it. He had to give it more.

He drew the knife from the sheath.

Looked at his wrist.

"Don't," Keras barked.

Cal drew it across his left wrist.

His head turned as blood spilled in a waterfall onto the gate and he blinked hard, fighting to keep his focus as he watched it hit the disc and spread across it in a thick layer, one that muted all the colours.

The connection ran deeper, another thousand hot needles piercing his bones, and he swallowed down the bile that rose up his throat.

The world blurred but he kept it together, kept his eyes on the gate and his mind on not only closing it, but sealing it shut.

Marek's voice swam in his ears, something about not being able to find Caterina.

And then something that sounded a lot like a demand to know what the hell Cal was doing.

Cal leaned forwards as heaviness invaded his body, blinked again and tried to focus on the gate. The connection between him and it seemed to disappear, blurring like the world around him, and he couldn't distinguish himself from the gate. It was as if they were one.

A familiar feeling built inside him.

A sense that he wasn't alone.

That part of him that had been missing, the other half of his soul, was right there before him.

Tears filled his eyes as he reached for it. For her.

Her sweet laughter chased around his mind. Her teasing words. Her scolding ones. He sank into it all, let it wash over him as he reached harder, stretching further, sure that if he could just make it another inch that he could touch her again.

An image of a young girl holding his hand and pulling him through a field of daisies and poppies sprang into his mind, her blue eyes filled with laughter as she looked back at him, golden hair bouncing with each stride as she told him it was fine and they wouldn't get into trouble for playing in the Elysian Fields.

Calindria.

She stopped and turned, beamed at him, and his heart ached.

"Gods, I miss you." He shook his head when her hand slipped from his, as she backed away from him. He reached for her, silently begging her to come back. "Don't leave me."

She turned away and disappeared. The lush green world around him withered and blackened, the blue sky darkening to dull red and the river that snaked through the land turning to blood.

Because there was no light in this world without her in it.

"Cal." Marek's voice was distant and watery in his ears.

He shook his head. He didn't want to go. He could find her. Wherever she had gone, he would find her.

Or he would follow her.

"What's wrong with him?" Daimon this time.

"Calindria's blood was used to create the gate." Keras's voice was louder. Had he moved closer?

A firm hand landed on his left shoulder and another gripped his right, and something solid pressed against his back.

Just as his knees buckled.

"I have you," Keras whispered close to his ear. "Focus on the gate, on what you want it to do. Focus on the present. We will find Calindria, I promise you."

Cal sucked down a deep breath that burned his lungs, as if he had forgotten to breathe and had been on the verge of suffocating. Maybe he had. Maybe that was why he always blacked out whenever he remembered something about his sister.

Because he wanted to follow her.

And the only way to do that was through dying.

Keras eased him back onto his feet. "She would want you to live. You know that."

Cal did.

Calindria would scold him if she knew he was even thinking about following her. She would be hurt by it. She would blame herself for his demise, and it would destroy her.

He didn't want her to be sad.

He wanted her to be happy.

He wanted her to run in those fields again.

To laugh and smile as she had then.

"But it's her," he croaked as he looked at the gate. "I can feel her there."

"It's her blood, Cal," Marek said, closer to him too now. "It's not her. We will find out what happened to her and we will make sure she can rest at last."

Cal focused and realised that Marek and Keras weren't the only ones around him. Valen and Eva were there too, and Daimon. Everyone was there at his back. At his side. Lending him their strength.

He pulled down another breath.

Told himself that Marek was right and it was her blood he could feel in the gate. It wasn't her. She was out there somewhere and they would get her to the Elysian Fields.

But that wouldn't happen unless he sealed this gate.

He pushed deeper into the connection between him and the gate and focused on sealing it. If he had to seal something, how would he do it?

Probably with wards.

What were wards?

Symbols that held power.

Like the glyphs on the gate.

He closed his eyes, inhaled slowly, and pictured the glyphs that filled each ring of the disc and how he might change them in order to shut it down. As the first glyph altered, he sensed a difference, and the pain lessened.

Encouraged by what had happened, he moved on to the next glyph and then the next one. He lost track of the world again as he altered one after the other, and lost track of himself in the process. It was only when his head turned and darkness encroached at the edges of his mind that he realised he was running out of time.

Losing too much blood.

He moved faster, pushing himself to keep going, even as the darkness spread and began to crowd his mind. He had to keep going. He changed another glyph, and felt the gate weakening, the connection fading with it. One last push.

Cal pictured the remaining symbols, the five that filled the central disc of the gate. Someone propped him up, slipping an arm around his waist. Someone else gripped his arm for him, keeping it above the gate. He silently thanked his brothers as the first glyph changed to a ward.

One designed to keep things hidden.

It was the closest to sealing as he could get and it was powerful, bound to the one who created it. It would prevent the gate from appearing to anyone and no one but him would be able to undo it.

He changed the second and third glyphs to the same ward.

Started to change the fourth and then stopped as an idea hit him.

Three wards would be enough to hide the gate. The remaining two could be changed to something stronger.

Something liable to drain the last of his strength from him.

But he would do it.

He focused on both remaining glyphs at once, because the darkness was spreading faster now and he wasn't an idiot. He had one shot at this, and he couldn't risk leaving even one glyph unchanged.

Cal pictured the ward, imagined drawing it in his blood on the gate, overwriting the glyphs with it. One line formed and then another, and a dash and a circle. He slowly built the symbol, imbuing it with the last of his strength, with every shred of his power.

"Whatever he's doing, it's working," Daimon muttered.

Cal pushed through the pain and the darkness, holding on to consciousness and refusing to lose his grip on it. Just a few more lines and he would be done, the wards completed.

The last curved spikes and slashes were the hardest, slow to form as they drained the last of his power.

When they were done, he waited, barely breathing, and willed the wards to take effect.

If he had done it right, they would be enough to bind the power the gate contained, and in conjunction with the ones designed to hide it, the gate would be rendered inactive.

Sealed permanently.

The twin wards shone, golden light chasing over their surfaces, and he felt it when the gate disappeared, the connection between them severing, leaving him missing part of himself again.

Relief washed through him, stripping him of his remaining strength and he sagged in Keras's arms as his legs gave out.

"It's done?" Marek sounded as if he couldn't believe his eyes.

"Rome gate feels different," Valen muttered, a thoughtful edge to his voice.

"Hong Kong too." Daimon sounded distant.

"You will have to tell us what you did later." Keras gently lifted him into his arms and Cal didn't have the strength to make his brother put him down and stop coddling him.

Just this once, he wouldn't fight his big brother. He was too damned tired.

He sank against Keras's chest and mumbled, "After I've slept for like... forever."

Coolness embraced him as they stepped, a brief connection to the Underworld that soothed him and eased some of the pain burning in his heart, and then more voices rose around him.

"What happened?" Esher's shocked voice became a snarl and Cal knew he had seen the state of him. "Who did this?"

Cal peeled his eyes open as someone touched his wrist. Aiko was there beside him, her dark eyes filled with concern as she assessed his injuries, and then she was springing into action, her black hair bobbing in its pigtails as she raced from the room.

She returned with a medical kit and set it on the low dining table that occupied one side of the room. Keras turned away from her, carrying Cal like a damned princess in front of all of his brothers, and set him down on the couch that faced the TV.

Aiko hurried over to him, sank to her knees beside him and applied a white square piece of padding to his wrist before she carefully wrapped a bandage around it. She did the same with his hand, and he didn't have the strength to tell her that wound was fine and already healing.

"I asked who did this," Esher snarled.

"I did it." Cal pushed the words out, not about to let his brother go over the edge and flip his switch because he thought someone had slashed his wrist for him. "I needed blood to seal the gate."

Esher's dark blue eyes landed on him. "You sealed a gate?"

"The twin one." Marek gently placed his hand on Esher's shoulder, over his dull grey shirt.

Esher's black eyebrows dipped low. "I felt a shift. I thought I was just being weird."

"We all felt it. Sealing one gate appears to have distributed the power it once contained to the remaining ones." Keras came to stand over Cal, his green eyes holding concern as he looked down at him. "Will you be all right?"

Cal tried to give him a thumbs-up, but he didn't have the strength.

"Quit coddling," he murmured and sighed as he closed his eyes. "Just gonna nap."

Sleep rose up on him, swift to claim him.

"We'll keep you safe." Valen sat on the arm of the couch above his head, his presence a comfort as Cal slipped into the darkness.

His brother's voice echoed in the black as he succumbed to it.

"You two have a wraith to hunt and a woman to save."

CHAPTER 31

Caterina didn't get a chance to see where she landed as she came out of the teleport still clutching Eli and Lisabeta. The second her feet touched the ground, and her legs turned to noodles beneath her, she was hurled into a portal by the wraith. Had she wasted the last of her strength teleporting him and Lisabeta only for him to immediately take her back to the fight?

She stumbled out of it and tripped, landing hard on golden gravel that told her she wasn't back at the gate and breathing heavily as her entire body quaked, every inch of her trembling and weak. Teleporting before had left her shaky, but nothing like this. She felt on the verge of passing out, and that was something she couldn't allow to happen. She had to be on her guard.

Fear pressed down on her, but she fought it as she mustered her strength, gathering the tattered remains of it for when she needed to defend herself. It wasn't a case of *if*. Eli and Lisabeta had brought her to a place other than the gate for a reason, and every fibre of her being was screaming that it was to kill her.

She tried to lift her head as the wraith casually stepped out of the violet and black swirling smoke, his shoes appearing in view beside her.

They halted.

Caterina managed to edge her eyes upwards.

Lisabeta helped her by kicking her in the gut and flipping her onto her back, ripping a cry from her as pain blazed outwards from her side.

She lay there a moment, Eli staring down at her, his violet eyes bright in the low light that came from in front of him, casting shadows in his sculpted cheeks and golden highlights in his short onyx hair. The buttons that ran in a line down the front of his tight black cotton coat, from his Mandarin collar to his waist, glinted in the light as he moved to face her.

Canted his head.

Sighed.

"I commend you." His low voice sent a tremor through her as his eyes narrowed on hers, brightening in a way that said he wasn't as impressed as his words sounded. He was angry. "It is rather noble of you to sacrifice yourself for the sake of those wretched gods, but I do not appreciate it... and I do not think they will either."

"We should have returned to the gate," Lisabeta said as she scowled down at Caterina.

Eli cast her a withering look and Lisabeta lowered her head, settling her gaze on the gravel, making it clear who was in charge between them.

"The gate is useless to us now." Eli's tone was hard as diamonds, black as night. "We would be outnumbered if we returned now and there is no guarantee we could open the gate enough to cause the necessary break down of the barrier between this world and the Underworld even if we did manage to defeat the wretches."

"Marek will be looking for her." Lisabeta sidled up to him and ran her hands over his shoulders, her breasts threatening to spill from her elegant black dress as she pressed against his arm. "Perhaps we can use that to our advantage."

The wraith frowned and his jaw flexed as he stared at Caterina for what felt like forever and she fought her racing heart, trying to calm it.

It was impossible when she felt sure she was about to die.

Eli wanted her dead. It blazed in his eyes. She had known that would be her fate for interfering with their plans and buying Marek and his brothers time, but now that she was facing death, she wanted to live.

Could she muster a barrier if he attacked her? She doubted that she could right now, and what good would it be if she managed it anyway? She was no match for Lisabeta and Eli, not if they worked together. Not when she was alone.

Part of her clung to what Lisabeta had said to her lover, hoping that he would listen to reason.

The rest of her was strong enough to face whatever fate awaited her, because it was better she died than Marek came under attack again. If her sacrifice could buy him time to protect the gates and keep this world safe, she would gladly go through with it.

"Very well. For now, we will keep her alive." Eli turned away from her.

Caterina felt as if he had just announced her sentence, each word falling like a gavel as she sank against the gravel, head spinning and heart racing. She would have accepted death, but she couldn't accept this.

She couldn't let him use her against Marek. Not again. She had to do something.

She had teleported them away from Marek and his brothers in the hope of saving them, and this world.

She hadn't considered that Marek would come after her, or that the wraith would so easily turn this to his advantage, making her his captive again.

Bait.

She focused, trying to summon that feeling she had whenever she managed to teleport. Her body shook, muscles turning to liquid as she tried to force it, and she sagged when it was too much, had her heart labouring and breath sawing from her lips. Maybe if she had more time. She hated the thought of them using her as leverage against Marek, but it would give her the time she needed to regain her strength so she could teleport away from them, ruining their plans again.

He nodded towards someone, dipping his head as they approached, gravel crunching beneath their feet. More than one pair of feet. How many had come to greet him?

How many more were under his command?

Caterina managed to muster enough strength to roll onto her front. Her vision grew hazy from the effort of moving, and when it cleared, she was looking at an enormous sandstone mansion with lights glowing in most of the windows on the three floors.

And her brother.

He was alive.

She shoved to her knees and then her feet, regretted it when her head turned and she stumbled, somehow making it to the wall around the base of a circular fountain that stood in the middle of the driveway.

"Guillem," she breathed, her eyes darting over him, relief flooding her to give her strength as she saw that he was all right.

He was more than all right.

His cheeks had colour and he was no longer gaunt, and the shadows around his eyes were gone, and she swore his hair was black now. Maybe it was just the light.

He slowly shifted his gaze from Eli to her where she sank against the wall of the fountain.

Caterina looked at Eli as he walked towards her. Towards Guillem.

"Let him go." She tried to grab Eli when he drew close to her and he cast her a black look, one that had her lowering her hand to her lap because it promised pain and retribution if she touched him, and she didn't want Guillem caught in the crossfire. "You have me and that's what Marek will respond to. Guillem is of no use to you. Make him better as you promised and let him go."

The smile that curled Eli's lips chilled her to the bone.

"I made him better." His deep voice rolled over her, each word ratcheting up the feeling inside her. Something wasn't right. Something was very wrong. Eli's violet gaze slid to Guillem. "I do not think he wishes to go anywhere though."

She slowly looked from Eli to Guillem, and a shiver raced down her spine, spreading over her arms and thighs as she noticed something.

There was a violet corona around his hazel irises.

"Your first error was believing your brother to be a vampire." Eli kept his gaze on her, drilling into the side of her face as she stared at her brother in disbelief. "It is not blood his fangs desire. It is a soul they crave. A soul his hunger needs to feed it."

Guillem's lips parted to reveal the barest hint of his fangs.

Fangs that seemed longer now.

Dread pooled in her stomach.

Because he had fed.

He was a wraith, and Eli had always known it. He had never meant to make her brother better. At least not in the way she had interpreted his words, the way she had wanted, freeing him of this curse.

"Your second error was imposing your desires upon him." Eli's words sent another icy chill down her spine.

She looked at Guillem, into his eyes, and all of her hope died as she saw in them that Eli was right.

"I never wanted what you did." Guillem came to her and eased down into a crouch, but his eyes remained cold, devoid of the love they had once shown her. Disgust laced his voice as he stared at her. "I was so sick of you trying to fix me... like I was broken."

"No, it wasn't like that." She tried to touch him, but he reared back, rising to his full height to tower over her. "I wanted it because I love you, Guillem."

His eyes narrowed and the violet grew brighter as he bit out, "If you truly loved me, you would have helped me as Eli did. He made me whole, Caterina... and I'm glad of it. He set me free."

"He didn't set you free, Guillem. He's using you."

"You don't know that," Guillem snapped and his face darkened. "He helped me."

And she hadn't.

All this time, she had believed she had been helping him, but as she looked at him now, she could see all she had been doing was hurting him.

She sank against the wall and fought the tears that wanted to come.

"I have so much to learn about what I am, and Eli will teach me." For a moment, Guillem looked as if he might soften towards her, but then all the warmth that had been building in his eyes vanished.

And it was like she was looking at another person.

And that sucked the soul right out of her.

"I will." Eli came to stand before Guillem, his expression holding a hint of pride as he looked at her brother. "Once we have dealt with the immediate threat. Your sister has one final use. She will lure the god to his doom and this world there with it. Then, we shall be truly free."

The part of her that wanted to live, that wanted to protect this world, and Marek and his brothers, rose to the fore and she shot to her feet, coming to face Eli.

"No." She lunged for him, managed to land a blow on his right cheek before he could react.

He swayed to his left, his jaw clenched and she cocked her fist again, ready to deliver another blow.

Guillem grabbed her from behind and hauled her backwards as he hooked his arms under hers and pressed his hands to the back of her head, forcing it down.

Immobilising her in a way she had taught him.

"Damn you!" she spat at Eli as she struggled against Guillem's hold, even when she knew it was futile. He was stronger than she was, the pressure of his grip crushing as he tightened it. Her fight fled her as the pain caught up with her, the thought that she had been hurting her brother all these years, and that now he was turning against her stealing her strength. She sagged in his arms and whispered, "I'm sorry... I'm so sorry."

"We will take her to the gate in Seville." Eli straightened and she felt his glare on her, a dark malevolence that said he wanted to lash out at her as payment for what she had done.

"Guillem, don't do this. Don't listen to them. Please?" She tried to turn her head to see her brother. "I'm sorry. Please, don't do this."

Guillem tightened his grip to the point of pain and she cried out and arched forwards as much as she could when it felt as if her spine would snap.

When he eased the pressure, she sagged again, hanging limp from his arms. Seville? Gate?

They were taking her back to where she had just been even when Eli had said he wouldn't do such a thing?

Violet and green flashes lit her boots and the gravel. The wraith was summoning a portal.

She mustered her strength and struggled again, and when that got her nowhere, she bit out, "What use is a damaged gate to you?"

She had seen it take a direct hit, and that look in Marek's eyes and the way his brother had leaped into action had told her they meant to do something to the gate. Heal it? Close it? She wasn't sure, but she knew by now they'd had enough time to do whatever it was they had intended to do to it.

"A damaged gate?" Eli's black leather riding boots appeared in her view, the tails of his coat settling around them as he halted. He chuckled, a cold and sinister sound. "The gate in Seville is perfectly sound. The one we had hoped to penetrate was damaged. I admit, it will be more difficult to succeed with the main gate, but when I drew up my plans for our operation here, I did not have you."

Another gate?

Eli leaned over and Guillem eased his grip enough that she could lift her head and look at him, right into his violet eyes.

He smiled, lifted his hand and pinched her chin between his fingers and thumb, keeping her gaze on his. "Now I have seen how he reacts to you... I know the god will open it to save your life."

She twisted her head out of his grip and scowled at him.

Being bait was bad enough. Being a hostage was entirely another thing and she wouldn't go through with it.

She focused on her body, on the strength that was slowly returning, and how she had felt when she had teleported, trying to build that same sensation inside her as she focused on Barcelona.

On the cathedral there.

Just as the image completed and the world around her wavered, as if it was about to disappear, Eli lifted a hand to her forehead and fire blazed across it. She cried out as the world grew solid again, as hot liquid ran down her nose and her cheeks, the coppery odour of it turning her stomach.

Blood.

Eli withdrew his hand and she stared at his crimson-stained claws as she fought to stop herself from throwing up, battled the pain and tried to push through it so she could teleport.

Nothing happened.

Eli cleaned his fingers on a crisp black handkerchief. "It is a most useful ward."

She reared back when he raised that same handkerchief to her face, but couldn't escape him. He dabbed around her forehead and she flinched with each sharp stab of pain, each sting that had her stomach turning because she had the sickening feeling that he had drawn something on her forehead using his claws.

"I admit, this development does cause a few difficulties." He lowered the cloth and tucked it back into his pocket as his eyes turned colder. "Not for us... but for you."

She stilled and stared at him, dread filling her again, pulling her insides down.

"You bloomed faster than I anticipated. Perhaps it was the stress of the situation?" He looked to Lisabeta, who gracefully shrugged, and his gaze shifted back to Caterina.

Caterina shook her head, refusing to believe what he was implying. "I can be healed. A healer—"

"It may have been possible once. Perhaps a few days ago. No more." He looked her over, no remorse touching his features as he studied her. "Now, the remains of your life will play out as the ultimate, beautiful tragedy. The god will foolishly open the gate to save you, damning this world and his one, and then he will forsake you once he realises you will always be a daemon."

Caterina's heart sank at that.

She told herself not to believe him. Tried to push his words out of her mind and tell herself he was lying, and that even if he wasn't, it wouldn't turn out as he predicted.

But she couldn't deny the truth.

She had heard the hatred in Marek's voice when he had been fighting daemons.

She had seen it in his eyes when he had realised what she was.

The hope that had ignited inside her when Persephone had announced she could be saved withered and died.

Even if she could stop Eli and Lisabeta, and save this world, she would end up with nothing.

She had lost Guillem.

And she would lose Marek too.

Everything worth fighting for in this world was gone.

And she wasn't sure she could face seeing hatred in Marek's eyes again.

Not when she had seen something else in them.
Something that burned inside her too.
Love.

CHAPTER 32

Esher appeared from the corridor that led towards the bedrooms on one side of the Tokyo mansion, adjusting the cuffs of his dove-grey shirt. Marek had wanted to head off right away to find Caterina by using his and his brother's new ability to sense when they were close to the wraith, but Esher had needed a moment.

Seeing Cal hurt, and knowing that they were going after the wraith and the illusionist, two daemons who had almost taken everything from Esher when they had killed Aiko, had sent his older brother skirting dangerously close to the edge.

When Marek lost it, daemons died and the earth shook, causing a minor quake in his locale. When Esher lost it, the seas ravaged the coasts, the rivers burst their banks, and torrential rain battered the lands, and not only in the locale.

Esher losing it tended to result in the entire world suffering.

So, despite how desperately Marek wanted to find Caterina, he had given his brother a precious few minutes alone with Aiko.

He had used the time to wash some of the blood off him, and then pace and go over everything, seeking a starting point for their hunt, one that might cut back on how much time it was going to take them to find Caterina.

He needed her back in his arms—right this moment. He needed to know she was safe, because his chest felt too tight and he couldn't breathe without her.

"Ready?" Esher drew down a deep breath and Marek could see in his blue eyes that his brother wasn't ready, not yet, but he was willing to do this to help him.

Marek went to nod.

Shook his head instead as that tight feeling became a tugging, irritating burn.

He grimaced.

"What's wrong?" Keras looked across at him, over the cream couch where Valen and Eva were slumped together, both resting after the fight.

"A summons." Marek ground his teeth, because he didn't need this, not right now. "It isn't the gate either."

"Penitence?" Daimon looked less than happy about that, his pale eyebrows knitting hard above ice-blue eyes that verged on white as he stared at Marek. "Bitch goddess."

The bitch goddess in question was Nemesis, a woman he and every one of his brothers despised. She took pleasure in punishing them whenever they broke a rule, her position as what amounted to the resident torturer on Mount Olympus giving her power over them that they couldn't deny. She held it over everyone in his world. Even the slightest indiscretion was met with a turn in her dark chamber, and a thousand lashes of her barbed whip.

Ares paid penitence every other week just because he couldn't keep his foul mouth in order and had a bad habit of cursing in the language of the Underworld.

Speaking it was forbidden in the mortal world and Olympus.

Marek had somehow managed to wind up paying penitence only a few times since leaving the Underworld.

"I can go." Keras took a step away from Calistos where he slept soundly on the couch that faced the enormous TV. "You go and find her."

Marek shook his head. He appreciated his brother's offer, but he was responsible for what had happened. This summons for punishment was because he had lost the twin gate. It rested on his shoulders. It had been his duty to protect the Seville gates, and he had failed.

Keras looked as if he wanted to argue, his green eyes revealing emotions for once. Because Keras had been the one to damage the gate when the illusionist had shown him something featuring Enyo?

It wasn't Keras's fault and Marek wouldn't let him take the blame for it.

"I won't be long." Marek looked to Esher. "Be ready. We're leaving as soon as I get back."

He stepped before anyone could argue, not bothering to go to Seville for his sword and vambraces, something that was usually required by Nemesis. She liked to see them in what armour they were allowed to have in the mortal world. Marek had long ago decided it was a sick quirk of hers. She liked knowing she had a son of Hades at her mercy, and that he was powerless to stop her from meting out her punishment, even with his sword and shield.

He landed in a dark chamber, under a weak beam of light that made it even more difficult to see into the shadows.

Marek looked down at the thick metal ring attached to the dark ground.

Metal of the gods.

He and Ares had bonded once about how much they hated that ring, because when he was bound to it, it wouldn't move, no matter how much he struggled.

It was another device, a method used by Nemesis to make him feel weak, and to make herself feel strong.

He sucked down a steadying breath and kneeled before it, but no attempt to calm his nerves and the adrenaline flooding his veins would work. He knew it.

Gods, he hated this.

He had to do it, though. Ignoring a summons was a recipe for making his punishment worse, and the tugging, weakening sensation inside him wouldn't abate until Nemesis was satisfied he had paid his due. He couldn't go into battle with it niggling at him, stealing his focus.

"How many lashes are a suitable punishment for failing to uphold a duty?" The haughty female voice rang in the darkness around him and he kept his focus on that infernal metal ring before him, waiting for her to announce his sentence. "Five thousand?"

His brows drew down and he couldn't stop himself from speaking, because that many lashes would leave him critically weakened, unable to go after Caterina.

"One thousand," he countered, and knew he was on thin ice when she laughed, the empty sound echoing around the chamber.

He had only ever heard her laugh when she was dealing pain, or thinking about dealing it.

He waited for her to increase the amount as payment for his insolence in thinking he could negotiate the terms of his punishment.

"Two thousand. It seems reasonable. I give your brother a thousand lashes for that black tongue of his." Nemesis stepped into the sphere of pale light, her blood-red sandals a contrast against the black earth and the sheer layers of her onyx robe.

He slowly lifted his head, needing to see that she was serious and was happy with that amount.

A chill breeze swept from her, causing her black robes to flutter, the layers reaching towards him like tendrils of darkness. The gold filigree that formed a corset over her torso glinted in the light, the black fabric beneath it so thin he could almost see her nipples.

She stepped closer, forcing him to tilt his head back, to look up at her where he knelt at her feet.

At her mercy.

Her cold red eyes glowed as she locked gazes with him, her crimson hair spilling around her slender shoulders as she slowly leaned over.

"Perhaps three thousand?"

"Two." He should have leaped on the offer when she had made it.

He wanted to say he had somewhere to be, but that would be a mistake. She would probably end up tripling the number of lashes just to detain him, punishing him for thinking something was more important than her.

"Two thousand it is." She eased to a crouch before him and thick brown leather straps appeared in her delicate hands.

Marek obediently held his hands out to her, wrists together, and remained still as she bound them to the ring.

Her scarlet eyes glittered as she lifted them to meet his again, a flicker of pleasure that revealed how twisted she had become. She had probably been filled with glee when he had lost the gate, had probably been keeping track of the situation and urging him to fail.

Because she wanted to hurt him.

She wanted power over him.

He shifted on his knees to get more comfortable.

She moved around him, graceful slow steps that had him wanting to yell at her to get on with it. Her fingers skimmed across his shoulders, sending a chill down his back, and paused on his spine. He jerked backwards when she tore the black T-shirt from him.

Shuddered as she stroked his back and murmured. "It is almost a shame to ruin this."

She was talking about his favour mark, a gift from the primordial goddess Gaia when he had been born.

"It will heal," he grunted.

Except for one scar. Nemesis would ensure one remained to remind him of his failure.

When she touched him again, it was with cold metal, and he closed his eyes and bent his head, twisted the leather straps in his wrists and held on to them, steeling himself for her first strike.

She stepped back.

A whirr sliced through the thick silence.

And then his back.

Lightning streaked up it where the metal whip had struck, and he gritted his teeth and muttered his first apology.

She was quick to strike again, not giving him a chance to finish before another wave of fire ripped through him.

Marek focused on the ring before him, on his hands where he gripped the leather, on what he needed to do when he escaped this torment. He muttered an apology whenever the whip lashed at him, counting each one, keeping track of them because Ares had warned him Nemesis had started to sneak in extra.

The pain was bearable during the first five hundred lashes, while Caterina filled his mind and he could think straight, focusing on his mission.

But as they neared one thousand, his thoughts began to blur. The anticipation as the whip whistled and cut through the air, the agony as it slashed his back, and the fierce sting as sweat seeped into the cut all had his focus slipping.

Caterina slipped away with it.

He muttered another apology, unsure how many it was now as the pain made it impossible to keep track. His head swam with it and it took him several more lashes of the razor-sharp whip to realise the goddess was speaking to him.

Her words wobbled in his ears, distorted at first, until he pieced them together.

"The daemons destroyed your amulet."

He swallowed and nodded.

"They revealed they are not the keys."

He frowned but nodded again, admitting that he had failed in his duty and revealed that to the daemons. His thoughts blurred together as the whip cut up his back, catching him in his ribs this time. He wavered, his grip slackening before he roused himself. He couldn't pass out.

"It was your duty to keep it hidden that you and your brothers are the Keys of Hades."

Another nod.

He sagged forwards as she struck again, the force of it blinding him, and grunted this time, unable to hold it back as pain ricocheted through his aching body.

"You are far more amiable than your brother Ares." She struck him again, making her words distort in his ears. "And far less difficult than Keras."

Another strike.

He sucked down a breath and issued an apology, the words slurred as they left his lips.

It seemed enough for her.

She struck him again, and he slurred another one.

"Getting a reaction from Keras often proves difficult. He does not respond to physical pain."

Another lash, another grunt ripped from his lips, this one accompanied by a wave of nausea that rolled up on him so swiftly he was sure he was going to vomit.

When the wave receded, Marek made sense of her words and uttered another apology.

Keras didn't respond to physical pain? What sort of punishment did she give him then?

What pain did she deliver?

The whip whistled through the air and he arched forwards as it lashed him, cutting over his right shoulder and down to his left hip, shattering his ability to think. He apologised on auto-pilot and waited for the next blow.

It didn't come.

"We are done." Nemesis rounded him, her scarlet eyes glowing with satisfaction, pleasure he had given her with his pain.

He gritted his teeth, clenching them so hard they creaked under the pressure, and tried to pull his wrists apart to break his bonds.

His arms shook, every muscle on his body tensing and flexing, trembling as he tried harder.

They didn't give.

Nemesis crouched before him, no trace of sympathy in her eyes. "You seem weaker than usual."

Weaker than usual?

That barb cut deeper than the two thousand lashes she had delivered and he growled as darkness surged through him.

The ground trembled beneath him as he clenched his fists and pulled his wrists apart. The worn leather gave this time, one strap ripping open, and he twisted his arm free and tore at the other strap, pulling it off his other arm.

He staggered to his feet and glared at the goddess. "Do not question my strength again."

She rose to her feet and a hint of a smile tugged at her lips, the satisfaction that glowed in her crimson eyes deepening. She was pleased she had angered him, provoking a reaction. If she hoped it would get him back at her mercy for another thousand lashes, she was mistaken. His penitence was done.

He could say whatever he liked to her at this point and there was nothing she could do about it.

But he had nothing to say to her.

He mustered his strength and stepped, teleporting back to the Tokyo mansion.

Rather than landing inside the main living space, he landed in the courtyard nestled between the three sides of the building, close to the broad stone steps that led up onto the covered wooden deck that ran around it.

Esher growled the moment his blue eyes landed on him.

"I'm fine." Marek wasn't, but he needed to keep his brother from slipping into the darkness.

Ares stood just beyond Esher, his brown eyes awash with concern that only increased as Megan bustled past him, her deep scarlet T-shirt and blue jeans a contrast to his all-black clothing.

Her chocolate eyes widened as they landed on Marek and her dark ponytail bounced as she hurried towards him.

Marek held his hand up to stop her.

She scowled at him in a way that said that wasn't going to happen. "I know all about penitence and I'm damned if I'm going to let you go out like this. It's barbaric."

"It's the rules," he countered.

Beyond her, Ares rolled his eyes in a way that warned he wasn't going to get his way. None of them were.

"Sweetheart," Ares started but she turned her glare on him, and he sighed deeply. His voice dropped low as he reached for her, worry creasing his brow. "Healing us weakens you."

"The babe?" Esher looked from Ares to Megan, and his eyes darkened, black edging out the blue. "You cannot. The babe..."

The determination in Megan's eyes wavered and she crossed the short span of wooden deck to Esher, looked as if she wanted to touch his arm and glanced at Ares. Ares frowned at her hand, sparks of red and gold flickering in his eyes.

She settled for smiling at Esher instead of touching him. A wise move. Ares was feeling protective enough without her provoking his darker side, the one that was liable to make him attack Esher if she laid a finger on him.

"The baby will be fine," she said to Esher and then looked at Ares and Marek. "It will be fine. I'll only heal the deeper wounds. You can't let Marek go after Caterina like this."

A war erupted in Esher's eyes. Not what Marek needed. His brother felt deeply protective of his family, and now Megan was asking him to choose between endangering the baby by allowing her to heal Marek, or endangering Marek by allowing him to go into what was bound to be a battle while he was injured and weakened.

"I'm making a decision here, and no one is going to change my mind. I know the rules. I'll only heal the deepest wounds. If I feel anything is wrong, I'll stop." She planted her hands on her hips and stared each of them down in turn. "But I am doing this."

Ares looked as if he wanted to argue.

Or possibly teleport her away so she couldn't go through with her plan.

"Won't you rest a while?" Ares said, hope building in his eyes.

Marek destroyed it by shaking his head. He didn't want Megan risking herself by healing him either, and resting would heal the worst of his wounds, but only if he slept for a few hours.

"I've lost too much time already." Marek looked from Ares to Megan. "I don't need to be healed. I'll be fine."

Esher looked as if he wanted to argue and force him to either rest or allow Megan to heal him. He stopped his brother with a well-aimed glare and stepped onto the deck. He banked right, following the path towards the wing of the building where the showers were.

"Oh, you overbearing—" Megan's voice came from behind him.

Ares rumbled, "I'm not letting you see my brother naked. You want to heal him, you wait here."

Marek took a left when he reached the first bedroom and followed the wall around it to the bathhouse. He stripped off, set the shower running and stepped under the spray, flinching as the warming water hit the lacerations on his back and sides.

He stared down at his bare feet, watching the crimson water swirling around them into the drain. The moment it ran clear, he switched the water off, dried himself as best he could without disturbing the healing wounds, and pulled his clothes back on.

He stormed back through the main living area of the house, passing the kitchen and the long low dining table, his gaze fixed on the corridor to the left of the TV area. He just needed to grab a T-shirt and then he and Esher could go.

Megan and Aiko stepped into his path, a formidable wall despite the difference in height and build between him and them. The hard edge to their matching dark eyes said he wasn't going to get past them, not without using what little energy he had to teleport.

He looked at Ares and Esher, silently asking his brothers to weigh in. Ares just shrugged. Clearly, whatever war he had waged while Marek had been in the shower, Megan had been the victor.

"Make it quick." Marek turned his back to the two women. "Only the deepest cuts."

"And you stop if you feel tired." Ares stomped past him, heading for Megan.

She huffed. "I already said I would. Stop coddling me."

Ares grumbled, "Never going to happen. Get used to it."

She sighed and her voice softened. "I know. I know. Just, lend me some strength."

"You got it, baby."

Marek could picture his brother behind Megan, kneading her shoulders in that way he always did when she was healing one of them, monitoring her vitals and offering encouragement, support that she seemed to relish.

They made a good team.

Marek's thoughts turned to Caterina. They made a good team too. The way they had fought against the vampires together had been incredible, working as a unit to swiftly deal with them. It wasn't only fighting beside her that felt right, though. All of it did. She was the perfect partner for him, one who enjoyed tracking and surveillance, fighting and working to protect something. To save something.

Like he should be working to save her right now.

He needed her back in his life, safe in his arms.

"Are you done?" He was sure Megan had only managed to heal a few of his wounds in the time he had been lost in his thoughts, and Aiko had cleaned some of the others in preparation, but he needed to get going.

He couldn't stand idle any longer.

"Let me just do this one." Megan sounded tired already.

Guilt lanced him and he turned away from her, breaking contact before she could funnel her power into him.

She looked pale.

But fire shone in her eyes as she frowned at him.

"No more." He put it out there before she could protest and lifted his eyes to Ares where he towered behind her, silently asking him to stop her if she tried.

Because he didn't want her to endanger herself or the baby on his account.

Ares nodded and palmed her shoulders through her red T-shirt. "Let him go. You did good, sweetheart."

She huffed. "I could do more, but I'm starting to get the impression you're not the only overbearing man I have to put up with for the next few months."

"I'm not the only overbearing man you'll be putting up with for the next few decades." Ares grinned and wrapped his arms around her. "You think I'm bad now. Wait until you deliver this baby. Father is going to lock you and the kid in a padded room under around a thousand layers of wards."

She pulled a face. "That is so not happening. No one is going to dictate what I do. Not even Hades."

The ground beneath them trembled.

Everyone looked at Marek.

He shook his head. "Not me. Mother was a little upset when she realised you were pregnant. Father wants to see you and Megan."

"When the hell did you see them and how long have I not known this?" Ares waved him away, closed his eyes and sighed as he shook his head. "Gods, I'm going to be in a world of trouble. You know he'll think I've been ignoring his summons."

"Things were a bit crazy." Marek rubbed his forehead. "I forgot, all right?"

"Go." Keras nodded towards him. "We can handle things here."

Ares sighed again, gathered Megan into his arms and looked down into her eyes. "Maybe he can wait a little longer."

He was stalling. Marek could understand why. Megan was tired from healing him and the teleport to the Underworld would drain her further. Not only that, but Ares probably didn't want to be the one to explain what had happened to the twin gate, not when Megan meeting their parents and officially announcing her pregnancy should be a happy occasion.

"Go after I've had time to explain what happened." Marek stepped up to his brother and laid a hand on his shoulder, not looking forward to the prospect of using a Messenger to tell his father about what had happened to the gate, or the inevitable summons that would follow. "We could use Megan here for now, just in case."

There was no just in case about it.

It was going to come down to a fight.

And he was going to win it.

CHAPTER 33

Marek tried to ignore the dark things Esher grumbled under his breath as they came out of the teleport on the hill above the twin gate. He was losing patience too. So far, they had visited the house where Marek had been held again, had been to Caterina's apartment in Barcelona, and had tried several other locations.

They hadn't found even a trace of the wraith.

And the night was wearing on.

It had been just before sunset when they had started their search. Now it was after midnight. In only a few more hours, it would be daylight and his chances of finding the wraith would be reduced to zero. The daemon would go into hiding until night fell again.

Esher had noticed his unease and had announced he was sure he would be able to sense him even if he had moved on recently, so they had agreed to return to the twin gate to see if that was true.

It had been twenty-four hours since they had been here. If Esher could feel the wraith's presence still, there was a chance they could somehow decipher where he had gone.

Could they track him? The bastard's portal didn't leave any trace of him behind, but it had been Caterina who had teleported him and the illusionist away from the battle.

Maybe it had left a trail they could follow.

He approached the brow of the hill and his senses sparked, his internal radar warning him that they weren't alone.

Marek eased forwards, not wanting to alert whoever was below them to their presence.

Esher walked right to the edge of the bushes and glared down into the dusty valley below.

There went the element of surprise.

But then Esher didn't need to be subtle when he could command blood to do his bidding. It took a powerful being to resist Esher's control over water. Whoever was in the valley below wasn't strong enough to do that. If Esher wanted them dead, they wouldn't stand a chance.

Marek came up beside him.

Frowned at the lone figure clad in tight black trousers, polished leather riding boots, and a short black tunic that hugged his lean frame.

"What's a Messenger doing here?" Esher said, loud enough the male heard.

His shoulders stiffened as his head whipped towards them, his mismatched eyes widening before they narrowed and he cautiously eased back a step. Everything in Marek said the male was going to run.

He stepped before it could happen, landing right behind him.

The male pivoted to face him and stumbled back a step.

"Did Father send you?" Marek looked him over, avoiding his green and blue eyes. He was dressed like a Messenger in Marek's family's service, the silver detailing on the cuffs and around the fastenings of his tunic unique to Hades's team of them.

He hadn't sent word about the gate to his father yet, but Hades was linked to them, was probably already aware of what had happened. He stared at the male, hoping he was wrong and he wasn't about to be delivered a demand from his father to return to the Underworld to explain himself, because he didn't need another delay.

He needed to find Caterina.

The male shook his head.

Backed off a step only to go rigid when he bumped into Esher.

Esher canted his head, curiosity shimmering in his dark blue gaze as he studied the back of the male's head.

"Not sent by our father but wearing the finery of our family." Esher stepped around him, each slow one seeming to ratchet up the Messenger's tension.

The more Marek looked at him, the more familiar he felt, which was ridiculous. All of the creepy bastards looked like each other. Of course he would appear familiar.

The sensation he had seen this one in particular before, stayed with him though as the Messenger glanced at the gate.

Or where it had been.

Marek couldn't feel it anymore.

And that was unsettling.

It felt as if he had lost something. A part of him.

"Who do you work for?" Marek closed ranks with Esher, forming a wall before the Messenger.

The male's gaze darted to his boots. "No one."

Marek frowned at that. "Messengers work for someone. All of you have owners. I've never heard of one of your kind not having one."

His words slowed as a reason the male might not have a master hit him.

Esher beat him to it.

"You were one of Calindria's."

Marek looked the Messenger over again, this time noticing how he kept glancing at where the gate had been, his mismatched eyes holding something surprising.

Emotions.

Pain was there. Sorrow too. And anger.

Marek had never seen a Messenger with emotions.

And he had never considered what had happened to the ones who had been in Calindria's service when she had died.

"We had to close it." He caught the flare of hurt in the male's eyes just before he shut them.

"I know. I felt it." His words were quiet, a bare whisper that Marek's heightened hearing struggled to catch.

He could understand the male's reluctance to talk. Messengers were only supposed to relay whatever had been told to them, and no more. They weren't meant to feel, or speak their own thoughts. It was part of the reason they had always made him feel uneasy.

They had felt soulless.

An automaton.

But this one was different.

"Where have you been since Calindria died?" He had an inkling he knew where.

The Messenger confirmed it when he snapped, "She did not die. She was *murdered*."

And it had sent this male off the rails for some reason.

He turned away from Marek and stared at where the gate had been, his perfect features darkening for a heartbeat before sorrow swamped them.

Marek knew that feeling. He felt as if they had just lost her all over again too.

"Who do you serve now?" Marek braced himself when the male turned on him, his green and blue irises bright in the darkness.

"I serve Calindria," he barked and curled his hands into fists. "I will only ever serve her."

It dawned on Marek that he and his brothers weren't the only ones searching for a way to bring her back.

The rage Marek could see building inside the Messenger deflated again as the male looked back at the empty ground where the gate had once been hidden.

"She was the only person who viewed me as something with worth," the male murmured, his voice distant and quiet. "She was meant for me. We were meant to be together. We will be together."

The male disappeared before Marek could stop him.

He looked at Esher.

Esher's black eyes remained fixed on where the male had been and Marek could easily read his thoughts in them.

How was a Messenger going to achieve that?

And like hell would they let one end up with their sister.

"You think he stands a chance?" Esher's blue eyes slid to him.

Marek shook his head.

"But what if we could do more for her?" Those blue eyes began to brighten, turning the colour of a summer's sky.

"If we can somehow do more than just find her soul and see it safely to the Elysian Fields, then she won't be allowed out of the house for at least a century, and even then, either me, you or one of our brothers will be going with her everywhere." Because Marek was damned if he was going to let anything happen to her again.

He took a step towards the fractured ground where the gate had been and froze when he felt a tug in his chest.

"Not now." He reached for his pocket, intending to fire off a message to one of his brothers, asking them to deal with the Seville gate for him, and stopped as a feeling went through him.

"What is it?" Esher closed ranks with him again.

"The gate is calling." He lifted his head and locked gazes with his brother, seeing in them that he'd had the same thought.

It wasn't a Hellspawn wanting to travel to or from the Underworld.

It was a trap.

Light flared across his vision, dimming as Esher turned his phone towards him. It cast a cold glow in his brother's eyes as his thumb danced over the screen, the charms that hung from one corner of the device swaying with each word he typed.

It took Esher only a few seconds to finish his message, send it and pocket his phone. His brother had become an expert typist over the last few weeks, since meeting Aiko. Apparently, when the full and new moon had him in its grip and Esher was confined to the house, Aiko often stayed with her parents.

And they messaged each other like it was a competition to see who could send the most during their time apart.

Esher gripped Marek's wrist before he could say anything and stepped with him. Marek appreciated the assist. He needed to conserve his strength in case his gut feeling was right and they were heading into a battle. His pulse picked up pace as the darkness whirled around him, adrenaline pouring through his veins as he steeled himself, attempting to prepare for whatever lay ahead.

Even the worst he could imagine.

His boots hit solid ground and the darkness evaporated to reveal the shadowy park and he was glad Esher had chosen to teleport them into a corner of the square, away from where the gate was hiding. At this distance, it wouldn't respond to him.

He looked beyond Esher.

Relief and dread hit him in equal measure.

Caterina stood beside the elegant low octagonal fountain in the middle of the open square in the Parque de María Luisa, her back to it and the palms and deciduous trees that enclosed the large space.

She wasn't alone.

Guillem stood beside her, clutching her arm so tightly that her skin blanched where his fingers pressed in to her flesh.

Her eyes were puffy. Her cheeks glistened with tears.

On her forehead, some bastard had carved a ward.

Her dull gaze remained fixed on the golden path at her feet even as Eli moved around her, his long black coat swirling around his ankles as he paced.

Who had done this to her? The wraith or her brother?

Marek was familiar with betrayal, could spot when someone else was feeling it. Guillem had turned against her. It was the only reason she would look so crushed.

So... broken.

So ready to give up on life, and accept death.

Her brother lifted one booted foot to rest on the brown and white chevron tiles that covered the base of the fountain, leaned close to Caterina's ear and brushed the tangled strands of her caramel hair from it.

She tensed and flinched as he hissed into her ear.

"Be thankful we aren't killing you now you've outlived your usefulness and failed us."

It took all of Marek's strength to resist the urge to sprint along the path that led to the fountain, one of many that formed rays coming from it, and attack him for that.

Esher laid a hand on his arm. His brother had sensed Marek's rising fury and meant to hold him back. Well, it wasn't going to happen. Sense told him to wait for his brothers, but his heart roared at him to save Caterina.

He shirked Esher's grip and stepped out onto the broad box-hedge-lined path that cut straight towards the fountain. Esher muttered something and followed him, and he appreciated the backup because he was going to need it.

Eli slowed to a halt and casually turned to face Marek as he approached.

"You know how this will go." The wraith shifted his gaze to Caterina.

Guillem squeezed her arm so hard she cried out, the sound echoing around the park and ripping a hole in Marek's chest as he fought the instinct to lunge for her and tear her from her brother's grasp.

Eli's cold smile said he had seen through Marek's façade and knew he wanted to save her.

That he would do anything to achieve that.

The wraith's violet gaze drifted from her to Marek.

"Open the gate, or she dies."

CHAPTER 34

"Open the gate, or she dies."

Caterina's dull eyes suddenly widened and she came to life, going from a compliant doll to a fierce tigress in the blink of an eye.

"Don't do it." She kicked forwards and glared over her shoulder at Guillem when he yanked her back. She struggled against his hold, her heart racing in Marek's ears as she turned her wild gaze on him and his brother. "There's no saving me. It's too late. We can't reverse what was done."

He stared at her in disbelief as those words sank in and he saw in her eyes that she meant them.

She truly believed that she would be a daemon forever.

He could also see she believed it meant that whatever they had together was now over.

What poison had Eli been dripping in her ears since she had interfered with his plans and teleported him and Lisabeta away from the battle at the twin gate?

Whatever it had been, it had had the desired effect on Caterina, stealing all hope from her.

"It's pointless." She shook her head, her hazel eyes pleading him to listen. "They want to ruin this world... your world... I can't let them do that."

Her brother slapped a hand over her mouth and dragged her back against him. She wrestled with him, but her eyes quickly glazed over, her cheeks reddening as she struggled for air. She slumped against his chest and Marek bit back a growl as he focused all of his senses on her to check she was all right.

"The female will do much to protect you it seems... even lie... and I can see she means something to you. Are you really willing to sacrifice her to protect the gates?" Eli's baritone rolled over him like thunder.

A storm built inside Marek in response.

His mind ran at a million miles per hour, calculating outcomes and looking at the situation from every angle imaginable. Where he stood now was far away enough that the gate wouldn't open. The daemons needed him closer so they could attack the gate once it appeared.

They were banking on him or his brother attempting to take Caterina.

He guessed the ward on her forehead prevented her from teleporting, but she had other powers at her disposal, ones that could provide her with protection in a battle if he could get her free of her brother.

Esher was already on edge beside him, probably because the illusionist was nowhere to be seen. Marek, like his antsy brother, refused to believe that meant she wasn't going to be involved in the fight and remained on guard, ready for anything she might construct to use against him and Esher.

As soon as it looked like he or his brother would attack or the daemons were in danger of losing, Eli would build a portal for her to appear through and take them down with an illusion.

Or was Eli waiting for the gate to appear before he did it?

Illusions would keep him and Esher occupied, and his proximity to the gate would keep it visible.

Vulnerable.

The sensible thing to do was leave.

But he couldn't.

He stared at Caterina, across the distance that felt vast between them.

The wraith was right—she meant something to him.

And he needed her back in his arms.

It would happen, but she wasn't going to be happy about his means of getting her there.

He shrugged, aiming for casual. "She's a daemon now. What do I want with a daemon?"

He couldn't bring himself to call her filthy, not when his gaze met hers.

Her eyes widened and tears lined them, and he cursed himself, hating having to do this to her. He would make it up to her when he had her safely away from his enemy. He would make her see that this was all a lie, a ploy to keep her and the gate safe.

He took a step back. "The only reason I came here was to open the gate for someone worthy of being in my presence, but now that you are in my way, I think I will make them wait. They will probably go to another gate."

Another step.

Unless whoever was waiting on the other side was in on things, of course. It was tempting to open the gate to see if anyone came through. It couldn't be a coincidence that the gate had summoned him, and Eli had been waiting here. The suspicion that they were working with someone on the inside, someone who could move through the Underworld with ease, deepened.

He took another step backwards.

Eli's violet eyes brightened, anger flaring in them. Marek wanted to grin at the fact he had finally provoked a response, was on his way to tipping the scales in his favour by making the daemon lose his temper.

The air behind Marek cooled.

The hair on his nape rose in response.

Or maybe he was only tipping it more in the daemon's favour by forcing his hand.

Darkness built around him, a black mansion constructing itself stone by stone before him, blotting out the park and Caterina.

And his enemy.

Before the final stone could fall into place, an unholy shriek pierced his ears and it exploded. He flinched away, bringing his arms up to shield his face as he twisted, waiting for the rubble to hit him.

When it didn't, and another black snarl pealed through the air like thunder, he lowered his arms and looked at Eli.

The daemon's eyes were bright violet as he bared his fangs, his eyes fixed on something to Marek's right.

Marek looked there.

Esher held Lisabeta to the floor, pinning her beneath him, his left hand closed around her throat. Her cheeks were red and blotchy as she struggled, legs kicking wildly, heels tearing at the satiny material of her black dress. Her silver eyes swirled, wide and desperate as she clawed at Esher's arms and battered his face, trying to force his brother off her.

Esher didn't even react.

He bore down on her, pressing more weight on her throat, his expression devoid of emotion as he grinned, flashing his own long fangs as his black eyes gained a crimson corona.

Esher lifted his head and fixed his gaze on Eli.

"I can see she means something to you." His brother parroted Eli's words. "Are you really willing to sacrifice her?"

Lisabeta's struggles increased, her legs thrashing as she raked claws down Esher's arms, drawing blood.

Eli stared down at her, his face slack and eyes empty.

He was going to let Esher kill her.

She seemed to sense it and started kneeing Esher in the back as her silver eyes brightened. Pieces of scenery built and collapsed around Marek as she desperately tried to conjure an illusion, none of it holding as she desperately tried to breathe.

Eli was suddenly behind Esher, digging claws into his shoulder and hauling him off the dark-violet-haired female. She gasped in air, her chest bowing off the dirt as her arms fell to her sides.

"Kill her," Eli snapped.

Caterina cried out.

Marek burst into action when he realised the daemon had been talking to Guillem. Trusting his brother would keep Eli and Lisabeta distracted so he could save Caterina. He turned towards her, intending to sprint to her, cursing the fact he couldn't muster another teleport right now, not without dramatically weakening himself and making himself vulnerable.

He froze when he caught sight of her, his heart aching as fiercely as hers must have been.

Hurt shone in Caterina's eyes. "Please, don't do this."

She struggled against her brother's hold, and Guillem looked down at her, hesitation etched on his face and something flaring in his eyes. Something that looked a lot like regret.

For a heartbeat, Marek felt sure her brother wouldn't go through with it.

"I said kill her!" Eli barked, more force behind those two words this time, enough to jolt Guillem into action.

Guillem tensed, swallowed hard and gripped her caramel hair with one hand. He pulled her head to her left as she frantically fought him and raised his claws to strike.

Marek's heart lodged in his throat and he kicked off.

Esher appeared behind Guillem in a swirl of black smoke and tore him backwards as he shoved Caterina forwards, separating the two and sending her stumbling towards Marek. Both Esher and Guillem disappeared.

He heard them land behind him.

Caught Caterina as she sank to her knees and eased her down.

"Stay here." He smoothed his hand across her forehead, over the ward, the fire burning in his blood blazing hotter at the sight of it.

He risked a teleport just as a bright purple light pierced the darkness, stepping away from the gate so it wouldn't have a chance to start opening.

He appeared in front of Eli as the daemon looked in the direction of the gate and used as much of his power as he could spare to summon a dome over it. The baked earth walls were thin as it went up, weak enough that the daemons could break through it given the chance, but it would protect the gate and might stop it from reacting to him if he got too close to it.

Esher held his hand out and the pipes beneath the park burst. Water shot into the air all around them, saturating Marek in a heartbeat, soaking the ground and turning the path to slippery mud. The water droplets swirled together, gathering into one long stream that suddenly sped towards the dome.

And Caterina.

He cursed his brother as icy claws sank into his heart and looked over his shoulder, taking his eyes off Guillem and Eli as his chest tightened.

The fear pounding through him eased as he saw the water curving around Caterina, avoiding her as it formed another protective wall around the gate. Using his powers in such a way and having to constantly control the water would drain Esher. They would have to end this fight quickly, before Esher ran out of strength or his focus shattered and the water dropped to hit the earth dome, weakening it.

Caterina crawled away from it and it lowered to cover where she had been, sealing the dome in completely. The water picked up speed as it grew deeper, ripped at the blue and white chevron tiles on the benches set into the box hedges. Debris swirled within the water, the dirt it picked up turning it murky.

Guillem leaped onto Marek's back and he turned with him, grabbed his arm and threw him over his head, sending him flying into one of the statues that stood at four corners of the park. The male dropped to the dirt and didn't move.

Esher seized hold of the illusionist again, his short black claws sinking deep into her throat as he held her in front of him, between him and the wraith.

Eli bared his fangs and a short black and violet blade appeared in his hand.

Marek raised his hand and thick shards of rock shot from the ground like spikes. Eli leaped backwards, glaring at him as he evaded each one. His violet eyes flared brighter as the distance between him and Lisabeta grew.

She struggled in Esher's grip and whatever illusion she was casting, it was angering his brother. Crimson invaded his black eyes. His lips peeled off his razor-sharp fangs.

Was she trying to push him over the edge?

"Whatever she is putting in your mind, it is all lies, brother." Marek grabbed his shoulder and shook him.

When that didn't rouse him, Marek risked it.

He seized Lisabeta and yanked her from his brother's grip, twisted her into his arms and into a chokehold that had her gasping for air as his forearm closed over the front of her throat.

Esher turned crimson-edged eyes on him. They narrowed and Marek gritted his teeth as he felt the blood slowing in his veins, his heart labouring as the flow of it became dangerously weak.

"Esher," he gritted and struggled to keep his grip on Lisabeta as she lashed out at him, clawing and kicking him.

Esher snarled low.

Marek's vision wobbled.

Maybe taking Lisabeta had been a terrible mistake.

It might have freed his brother of the illusion, but it had also pushed him close to the edge of losing control.

Because he had taken Esher's prey from him.

"Esher." He tried again.

When his blood felt as if it was growing thicker in his veins and Esher looked ready to finish him off, he hurled Lisabeta at his brother, hoping it would appease him and stop him from killing him.

Esher grinned and caught her, sank claws into her shoulders and stared deep into her eyes.

Whatever she saw there, it tore a scream from her throat.

"Lisabeta." Eli lunged for her.

Marek backhanded him. He wanted to kill him, but they needed one of them alive for questioning, and Eli was higher up the chain of command.

Plus, Esher had a score to settle with Lisabeta.

"You... killed... her." Esher snarled, his voice darker than Marek had ever heard it as he struggled to speak. He sucked down one ragged breath and then another, the crimson in his eyes spreading as his countenance changed, all of the light leaving it as his other side, the vicious and terrible one that had been born centuries ago in the wake of Esher being held captive and tortured, rose to the fore. "You... killed... Aiko."

Eli lunged for Lisabeta again, ducked and disappeared as Marek lashed out at him to stop him from interfering.

Esher bellowed.

Eli loomed behind him, grinning as he pulled the dagger from Esher's shoulder and raised it to strike again.

Marek stepped and pulled Esher to one side.

The blade struck.

Lisabeta screamed.

Eli staggered backwards, his hand slipping from the hilt of the dagger as his eyes widened, his lips parting as he stared at her.

She sank to her knees, raised trembling hands and clutched the hilt where it protruded from the left side of her chest.

"Lisabeta." Eli recovered and reached for her.

She grunted and inched the blade from her flesh, her gasping cries filling the night.

Esher didn't give her a chance to remove it.

He broke free of Marek's grip and slammed his palm against it, driving it deeper into her chest.

Eli yelled, "Lisabeta!"

He kicked off, his eyes blazing with fury as they landed on Esher's back.

Esher hauled Lisabeta onto her feet and twisted to face Eli, using her as a shield as she weakly fumbled with the hilt of the blade, her fingers slipping in all the black blood as it cascaded from the wound.

"Talk, and maybe I will spare her." Esher cupped her jaw, keeping her head up as it lolled.

Her hand slipped from her chest, falling lax at her side.

Esher angled his head away from her and looked down at her face. He jostled her, frowning when she didn't respond, a flicker of confusion in his near-crimson eyes.

"Esher." Marek edged towards him.

He kept shaking her, harder and harder when she didn't respond.

"Esher."

His brother looked at him.

Too far gone to comprehend what he had done.

Eli understood it all too well.

On a vicious roar, he launched at Esher while his brother was distracted, another blade materialising in his hands. Marek pulled Esher backwards and tried to teleport.

Nothing happened.

He had used too much of his power already.

All he could do was watch as Eli sailed towards his brother, murder in his eyes, and Esher refused to budge, kept looking at Lisabeta where she hung limp from his arms, as if she was miraculously going to spring back to life as he wanted.

Marek focused on the earth and put all of his strength into summoning a wall, his heart racing as time slowed, as Eli plunged the blade towards Esher and his heart lurched into his throat.

Too late.

His heart felt as if it would stop as the blade met Esher's chest.

It did stop when a wall of blue hexagonal glyphs shimmered across the air, spreading outwards from the point of the blade where it had halted just an inch from Esher's body.

Esher finally roused himself, a low growl rumbling through him as he discarded the dead daemon and narrowed his eyes on the wall of glyphs, and then turned his glare on Caterina.

Marek leaped into his path before he could even think about attacking her. "She's on our side."

Esher's crimson-to-black eyes pierced right through him, remaining fixed on Caterina.

Eli rallied and attacked again.

Esher shot his right hand out, closed it around Eli's throat before he could land a blow, and twisted with him, slamming his back into the ground. The daemon's breath left him on impact and he disappeared. Esher's knee hit the dirt where the daemon had been, another dissatisfied snarl leaving him as he realised his quarry had escaped.

Marek intercepted Eli as he appeared again, sweeping in between him and Esher before he could attack his brother. He blocked the arm Eli held the blade in as he lunged at him, knocking it aside and gaining some space, and reared back as a blade flew between them, cutting across his vision.

It snapped into Esher's hand and he kicked off, swiping at the daemon, driving him back past Lisabeta's body. Eli's eyes dropped to her and he snarled, the pained sound filling the thick night air. The wraith stopped evading Esher and attacked, his strikes swift and vicious as his lips peeled back off his teeth and his eyes glowed violet.

Marek joined his brother, working with him to block blows and wear the daemon down, waiting for the right opening, one where he could land a blow without being cut with the daemon's blade.

But it was Esher who began to slow as they danced around the square, his movements growing sluggish, each swipe with the blade he had pulled from Lisabeta's body weaker than the last.

Blood tracked down Esher's back from his shoulder.

Cold realisation slid down Marek's spine.

"Go home," Marek shouted as he moved around behind Eli, trying to keep the daemon away from his brother.

Even when he was aware it was too late.

Esher's eyes verged on scarlet, his other side rising to the fore as the wound the wraith had dealt him continued to weaken him. He needed to get his brother away from the wraith, before the poison the blade had delivered could kill him. The last time the wraith had stabbed Esher, it had taken all of Megan's strength to reverse the damage and save him.

"Esher."

When his brother didn't listen, Marek pulled his phone from his pocket and fired off a message as quickly as he could manage.

Esher lunged for Eli, landing a hard blow on the daemon, one that staggered him. His brother followed it with another, slashing across the male's chest and carving a line through the breast of his black coat. He attacked again as Eli struggled to shake off the blow to his head, but stumbled at the last second, his left knee giving out and sending him to the ground.

Eli slowly smiled.

The blade tumbled from Esher's hand as he shook his head, the finger-length strands of his black hair falling to cover one side of his face. He sank forwards, planting his hands against the golden dirt, and swallowed hard.

Marek whipped his hand out and focused on the fallen dagger. It shot into his palm and he closed his fingers over it as he kicked off, lunging at Eli. The wraith was swift to leap backwards, evading the strike Marek aimed at his neck.

He just needed to buy more time.

He willed Daimon to move his arse.

Marek struck with all of his strength at every opportunity he got, driving Eli away from Esher as his brother began to move again, low growls and snarls rumbling from him as he clawed at the earth.

"Hurry, Daimon," Marek muttered and lashed out at Eli, catching him across his left shoulder.

He twisted and spun around the daemon, landing another blow that cut up his back, slowly weakening him.

He sensed it when his brother appeared.

Esher must have felt it too.

Because an unholy roar left him and he barrelled into Marek, knocking him aside, and lunged at Eli.

"Fucking hell," Daimon bit out. "Esher's message said he had this. This is *not* having it."

"Damn it." Marek tried to get up but hit the dirt again when Esher slammed a boot into his chest, knocking the wind from him. He wheezed as it felt as if someone had just caved his ribs in on his lungs and fought for air.

He had thought Esher had messaged for backup.

He should have known his brother would see this as an opportunity to hunt, his other side driven to claim his prey without anyone interfering.

"Thought... he called... for backup." Marek eased onto his knees.

Daimon scowled at Esher's back as he fought the wraith, landing blows with his claws and bare fists, battering the daemon.

"He'll kill him." Marek staggered onto his feet. "Stop him."

Daimon's ice-blue eyes widened and slid to Marek. "I don't really fancy my chances."

"We need him alive. Calindria..." It was all Marek needed to say.

Daimon was moving in a split-second. He disappeared and reappeared behind Esher as their brother brought his claws down in a fast arc towards the daemon's neck. Daimon grabbed him from behind, throwing his aim off.

"Esher," Daimon murmured, his voice soft despite how violently he was wrestling with Esher, trying to get him under control as he fought to break free.

Marek shoved off, moving as quickly as he could towards Eli.

"We need him alive." Daimon edged his hand up.

Esher snarled and snapped his fangs at it when it came close to his face, twisted and elbowed Daimon in the side of his head, knocking him away.

"Wraith... dies." Esher turned cold eyes on Daimon. "You die... if you interfere."

Daimon planted his hands on his hips and his white eyebrows met hard above his glittering frosty eyes. "You gonna kill me? I don't think so. Maybe you need to take a nap."

Esher bared his fangs and kicked off, springing away from Daimon.

Towards Eli.

Marek leaped into his path and took the blow meant for the daemon, gritting his teeth as Esher's claws slashed across his chest, fire erupting in the wake of them.

Esher stilled.

His red eyes regained a sliver of black as he stared at the wounds on Marek's chest.

Eli made a break for it.

"Damn it." Marek pushed through the agony searing his chest and went after him.

"Kill the wraith. Free her soul." Esher's plan was solid.

But killing Eli meant destroying their chance to get information from him, intel that might prove vital in the fight ahead.

Eli gave him a better reason not to kill him when he caught the bastard.

"I might have taken her soul, but I gave it to another, made him the owner of it and you will never find it… I will make sure of that," Eli spat and stopped running.

And turned to face Marek.

Plan A it was then. Capturing him. He just needed Daimon to keep Esher under control for a few seconds more and he would be on the daemon, taking him down.

Eli kept perfectly still as Marek sprinted towards him, and Marek wanted to grin.

Eli did grin.

"You took Lisabeta from me. I will keep your sister from you."

Marek threw himself at Eli.

Something hit him like a truck from the side, sending him crashing to the ground. He rolled into one of the low hedges and grunted as a fist struck his jaw, knocking his head into the dirt. Weight pressed down on him and he bucked it off, wanted to growl when he saw who it was.

Guillem.

His eyes were bright violet.

The bastard was a wraith, not a vampire.

Marek twisted with him, pinning him beneath him as he rolled back onto the path and looked up at Eli.

Dark purple and black smoke rapidly spread behind him.

Eli stepped backwards towards it.

Esher blazed past Marek, on a collision course with the daemon.

Even with his other side at the helm, his brother was too slow, the effect of the wraith's blade taking its toll on him.

Esher reached the portal just as it dissipated, disturbing the remaining smoke as he twisted in all directions, flashing fangs and snarling as he tried to find the wraith.

His prey.

Daimon slammed into him, taking him down. "Time to sleep."

Esher lurched, attempting to buck Daimon off him, but Daimon pressed his hands to the sides of Esher's head. Esher's struggles slowed as frost glittered over Daimon's hands, his skin paling as their brother's ability took effect, the cold sapping his strength.

This time, Daimon broke away before he went too far, leaving Esher breathing softly and slowly as he shuddered, wracked with shivers.

Daimon looked across at Marek, sorrow crossing his features.

It echoed in Marek too, but he refused to lose hope.

He was sure that whoever Eli had given Calindria's soul to was involved in this plot too.

They would have their shot at the bastard and the wraith.

And they would kill both of them.

Once they knew how to find Calindria's soul.

He looked across at Caterina where she knelt in the middle of the path, holding herself as sweat dotted her brow and she trembled, shaking violently.

But for now, he had a daemon to take care of.

CHAPTER 35

Caterina was too weak to fight Marek as he scooped her onto her feet, wrapped an arm around her ribs and walked her towards her brother. Guillem hissed and snapped fangs at Marek's white-haired brother, earning a glare from him that had his eyes turning glacial, like a winter storm.

She trudged along beside Marek, heart growing heavier with each step as the look he had given her and what he had said to Eli ran around her head. She was a daemon. What did he want with a daemon?

She swallowed hard as an answer came to her.

Information.

She was sure that it was the only reason she was alive now, being led towards her brother. Marek wanted information from her. She had seen another of the wraith's safehouses. There was a chance she could explain to him where to find it. Would that be enough to buy her freedom?

She couldn't teleport him there, not with whatever Eli had carved into her forehead still active.

The white-haired god towering over her brother grew bored of his constant threatening and she flinched as he placed a gloved hand on Guillem's head. He paled and slumped to the ground, out cold just like Esher.

"I can take them, Daimon." Marek stopped at Esher's booted feet.

Daimon glanced down at Esher, a wealth of love in his eyes, conflict that told her how deeply he wanted to be the one to take care of their brother.

"You're weak. You can't teleport him in your condition. I'll make it quick." Daimon crouched beside Esher, hovering a hand over his arm, and looked up at Marek, as if waiting for permission.

The moment Marek nodded, Daimon laid a hand on Esher and they were gone, only wisps of black smoke left behind them.

Marek tugged her to her brother, stooped and did the same, teleporting the moment he made contact with Guillem.

The black whirled around them, her head twirling with it, stomach rebelling as she squeezed her eyes shut and tried to endure the effect of the teleport as it ravaged her tired aching body. When they landed, she kept her eyes closed, waiting for the spinning to slow before she dared risked opening them.

"Take him to the castle." Marek's deep voice curled around her, and the ache inside her worsened, because she still found it comforting.

"Sure," Valen answered, and in the background, she heard Marek's other brothers.

"I cannot believe he would do such a reckless thing." Keras sounded close to snapping at someone.

Marek?

Was he angry because Marek had brought her to this place, their sanctuary?

She opened her eyes, instinct pushing her to react, to defend him even when she knew it wouldn't help him, or make a difference. A flash of his cold eyes danced across her mind, his words still echoing in her ears.

She was a daemon.

When she looked at Keras, she found him gazing down at Esher where he rested in his arms, cradled against his chest.

"Megan, Ares, I will need your help. If what Daimon has said is true, Esher's other side is in control. We need to make sure he cannot teleport when he comes around." Keras's green eyes flooded with concern.

The entire room fell silent and the tension in the air rose to an unbearable degree.

Caterina looked at Esher. Were they going to carve a ward on him like the one Eli had placed on her?

Ares's voice was gruff as he said, "He won't be happy if he comes around in the cage."

A cage? They meant to place their own brother in a cell? Like the one they had placed her in? She looked at everyone, taking in their grim faces, and it struck her that this cell they spoke of was far worse than the one she had been held in.

Marek sighed. "I agree with Keras. I don't want to do this to him either, but Esher was close to losing control. He turned against me... almost killed me with his powers."

That had everyone staring at Marek, and Caterina squirmed as more than one of them levelled a black look on her.

"I'm sorry," Marek continued. "We lost Lisabeta and Eli escaped, but we can still get information from our prisoner."

She squirmed even harder as those words left his lips. Their prisoner. Her.

A pretty petite woman with black pigtails fussed over Esher, worry written in every line of her face. Caterina looked away, unable to bear seeing the love she held for Esher, not when her own heart was breaking.

Her eyes fell on Guillem where Valen was hauling his dead-weight into his arms as if he weighed nothing.

The heart that was already aching in her chest burned deeper, the pain spreading through her as she gazed at her brother, despair mounting inside her. She hadn't meant to hurt him, had only ever wanted to help him. She loved him with all of her heart, even though he had broken it. She wasn't sure anything could ever stop her from loving him. He had betrayed her, had hurt her, but still she couldn't quell the love she had for him.

He was her brother.

She closed her eyes again.

He had been her brother.

Now he despised her, was an agent of evil, a member of Eli's forces. If she had been more supportive of him, if she had listened to him rather than trying to impose what she wanted on him, would he have still been her brother?

Would he still love her?

Marek's fingers flexed against her arm, drawing her back to him.

She opened her eyes and looked at them were they pressed into her dirty skin, her heart sinking lower as dread mingled with despair inside her.

"Are you going to take me to the castle too?" she whispered, unable to get her voice above a murmur.

Marek's gaze landed on her. "Do you want to go with your brother?"

She shook her head. She didn't want to go back to that cell, and she didn't want to be near Guillem, not right now. It hurt too much. She needed time to come to terms with everything and then maybe she would be strong enough to face her brother. Although, she wasn't sure that time was something she had.

"Why do you want to go to the castle then?" His fingers flexed against her arm, almost a caress.

She wanted to cry and rip her arm from his grip, but wanted to lean into him at the same time, stealing every moment of contact between them.

"Because I'm your prisoner too." She lifted her gaze enough to land on the deep lacerations that cut across his broad chest as he turned towards her, but wasn't brave enough to risk going any higher.

When Esher had attacked him, she had been terrified, had thought she was going to lose him.

She had lost him. She knew that deep in her heart and it was the reason she couldn't bring her eyes up to meet his.

She was bone-deep afraid of what she would see in them.

She wanted to see warmth in them again. Love.

But all she would see was hate.

"No."

That word held force, enough that his brother with the blond ponytail stopped talking to Daimon and looked across at them.

She squirmed under his scrutiny, aware of what she was, how wretched she had to be in their eyes.

She wanted to believe that Marek's answer had meant she wasn't their prisoner, but she was tired and refused to let herself read into things, finding meanings in his words that weren't true just because she didn't want to part from him.

"Will you take me home then?" She inched her gaze higher, to his collarbones.

He swallowed, his Adam's apple bobbing, luring her eyes higher still.

"No." He paused and his deep voice held a regretful edge to it when he said, "I can't do that."

Cold slid down her spine.

Her mind went blank.

And then a single question spun in it.

"Are you going to kill me?" she blurted and her eyes leaped to his.

She had been ready to accept death just hours ago, but now she was afraid of it. She wanted to live even when she knew it would be a struggle to go on alone in this world.

Marek's right eyebrow hiked up.

"You have some weird and wild ideas." His eyebrows dipped low, narrowing his rich-brown eyes. "I'm not going to kill you. I'm taking you with me."

"Where?"

If he wasn't taking her to the castle, and he wasn't taking her home, where did he intend to go with her?

His answer hit her hard, had that dread pooling deeper inside her until she felt as if she might drown in it.

"The Underworld."

Her eyes widened and she backed off a step, but he tightened his grip, stopping her from escaping.

"So your father can kill me?" She searched his eyes, hers leaping between them as her heart raced. She tried to call on her power to see emotions, but it refused to come, leaving her in the dark and increasing the panic that swept through her on tingling waves.

"Good gods, no," he barked and scowled, his earthy eyes revealing how deeply she was offending him, and annoying him apparently.

She didn't need to be able to see his emotional aura to see that.

It wasn't her fault. She didn't know what was happening or what to think, and he wasn't exactly being clear with her. They had carted her brother away. She was a daemon. It wasn't unreasonable that she expected the same treatment, but Marek looked as if she was being just that.

His handsome features softened as he gentled his grip. "I'm taking you there so Mother can check you over. I want to know if you really are a daemon now."

That wasn't really a comfort.

What happened when Persephone announced she was a daemon and it was irreversible?

Were they going to have this conversation again with far different answers?

Marek shifted his gaze to the blond with the ponytail. "Cal. I know what your favour mark does."

Shock danced in Cal's blue eyes.

"It's no secret." Marek led her over to his brother. "I need a portal to the Underworld for two."

"It's not easy, you know." Cal frowned at him. "A portal for just you isn't a problem, but a portal for you and her… that's pushing it. I'm not sure I have enough strength to cast that."

The world suddenly went black.

And then her feet hit onyx dirt.

Marek stared straight ahead, surprise lighting his eyes. Evidently, this wasn't how Cal's portal worked.

Which meant they had been summoned again.

And that had more ice inching down her spine.

That dark malevolent power she had felt during their last visit to the Underworld washed over her, fiercer this time. It pressed down on her, had her legs weakening beneath her as she tried to fight it and remain standing. Marek palmed her arm, his grip on her tightening again as he pulled her closer to him. He wrapped his arm around her, supporting her, a flicker of what might have been concern in his eyes as she struggled against the oppressive weight of that power.

Hades.

She didn't need to look to know he was standing on the steps of the enormous black Grecian temple. She could feel him there, could sense him as a dark presence, one that had her wanting to run in the other direction, as far from him as her wobbly legs would carry her.

Warmth spread upwards from her feet, chasing away the cold that washed through her.

She felt Persephone's presence before the goddess came into view, circling her, her long black robes brushing the ground, parting to reveal her bare feet. Wherever she stepped, green stems curled from the ground and budded, bloomed into colourful flowers, a carpet of them that separated her from the bleak earth as she came to a halt in front of Caterina.

Between her and Hades.

Persephone's soft green eyes held hers, and Caterina felt as if the goddess was reaching into her. Her blood writhed in response, nausea rolling through her as Persephone slowly approached her and lifted her hand.

She meant to touch her.

Caterina recoiled on instinct, but Marek was there, a solid wall at her back.

His hands came down on her shoulders, holding her in place as the goddess closed the distance between them down to only inches.

Caterina flinched away when Persephone's hand neared her.

And melted against Marek's chest when her palm landed on Caterina's forehead.

Warmth spread outwards from her touch, the weird heavy feeling that had been a constant presence on her brow since Eli had carved the symbol on it lifting.

"A nasty mark." Persephone stroked fingers across Caterina's brow, and Caterina's head grew hazy, strangely light. "Is that better?"

She nodded in a daze.

"Why is she here again?" Hades's voice boomed from the temple, shattering the calming warmth.

Marek's grip on her tightened and he drew her closer to his chest. Afraid his father would do as she had expected and kill her? She shoved that feeling out of her head and her heart, refusing to believe it.

"I think—"

Hades cut her off. "It dares speak in my presence?"

Persephone sighed, and even that was gentle and soft, but somehow managed to relay her irritation.

"Caterina is not an it, my love." Persephone's emerald eyes remained fixed on Caterina's.

She lowered her hand to Caterina's cheek and then her chest, settling it over her heart. Her eyes brightened and the flowers that bloomed around her withered.

Caterina's hope died with them.

"I know what you're going to say." She shook her head, not wanting to hear it. "It's fine. Really."

Marek palmed her shoulders and she tensed, wanted to beg him not to let go of her.

He released her and cold immediately rolled across her back in a frigid wave as he broke contact with her. She looked down at her feet, at the dead blooms, feeling as if she was withering inside too.

Could she teleport away from here now that mark was gone?

She wanted to escape.

Before Marek broke her heart.

"Deal with her." Hades's black demand had that need to flee rising faster.

She took a step back.

Marek seized her arm. "Don't run."

Because it would only make it harder for him to kill her?

Her eyes leaped up to his and she braced herself, sure she would see that cold look in them again.

But there was only warmth.

She didn't understand.

"I'm a daemon," she whispered. "I know it. I can feel it. You can feel it."

She needed to hear him admit that he knew what she was, and that whatever foolish thoughts were beginning to creep into her mind and her heart, they were wrong. His family despised daemons.

It was his duty to kill them.

And his father had just issued an order.

He looked her over, his gaze gaining an almost clinical edge to it as he studied every inch of her.

Shock rippled through her when he lifted his hand and gently stroked her cheek.

"You don't feel like a daemon." He brushed her hair back, clearing it from her face, his gaze sincere.

"But I am one." She fought the need to lean into his soft touch and couldn't stop her mouth from moving, spilling words that she used as a shield around her heart and an attempt to provoke a reaction. Something that would give her a clear sign of what her future held. "I'm a daemon... in the Underworld... and I think your father just gave you an order."

"And I will obey it." He palmed her cheek, his touch painfully gentle, threatening to draw tears from her.

"Son." Persephone's voice carried around them like a light warming breeze. "Carry out your duty."

He nodded.

Caterina braced herself.

Squeezed her eyes shut.

Waited.

Nothing happened.

And then Marek tilted her head up and kissed her.

Hades growled. Persephone made a small gleeful sound.

"I win." Amusement and victory laced those two words as they left Persephone's lips. "First duty always trumps the second. It is your blood in his veins after all."

Another, lower and darker growl sounded from the direction of the temple, and then a huff.

Marek didn't stop kissing her, and Caterina felt as if she was spinning as she struggled to catch up, her mind swimming with confusion.

When Marek finally released her lips, but not the rest of her, keeping her pinned against his chest, she opened her eyes and stared at her surroundings.

They were back where they had been, standing in the middle of the Japanese mansion.

"What did your mother mean?" She lifted her eyes to meet Marek's and the warmth in them hit her hard, curled around her and eased some of the fear from her heart. "First duty beats second or something like that. What's the first duty?"

"First duty is to our heart. Mother's rules." Marek brushed his knuckles across her cheek.

"What does that mean?" A shiver raced over her arms and she didn't dare believe it meant what she thought it did.

"It means that I'm picking you. I'll always pick you over the duty my father gave to me."

He kissed her again and her head spun, thoughts racing as she tried to make that sink in.

For a moment, she had thought she had lost everything. Discovering that she hadn't, that she wasn't going to be alone in this world, and that Marek wasn't going to turn his back on her, was too much. It overwhelmed her.

She wrapped her arms around his neck and kissed him, relishing the way he banded one arm around her back, tucked the other beneath her backside and lifted her, so their faces were level.

So she could kiss him deeper.

Déu, it felt good to be held by him like this. It felt right.

She wanted this forever, even when she feared it wasn't possible, was afraid that one day he would wake up to what she was and he would leave her. His brothers were watching them, and none of them were saying a word now, but what about when she wasn't here? What if they secretly hated her? Poisoned Marek against her?

Marek murmured against her lips, "You think too loud. It's never going to happen."

"How do you know that?" She pressed her cheek to his as he peppered her face with kisses.

As he held her closer still, making her feel as if she wasn't the only one who wanted to hold on to the other forever.

He whispered the sweetest words she had ever heard in her ear, ones that stole her heart, and made everything right.

Perfect.

"Because I love you."

CHAPTER 36

Insects buzzed, filling the thick hot air with their song. Birds chirruped as they darted between the olive trees that surrounded Marek's villa, seeking the shade and relief from the afternoon heat.

That heat seeped deep into Marek's bones, caressed his bare chest and lower legs, soaking into his black shorts, as comforting as the feel of the hand that gently clutched his left one.

He tucked his right hand behind his head, propping himself up on the wooden recliner so he could see Caterina.

She lay beside him on her own recliner, tucked in the shade of the ribbed terracotta roof that extended out over the patio, covering the dining area that overlooked the valley.

Strands of her spun-caramel hair had come loose from the twisted knot at the back of her head, caressed her cheek in ways he wanted to imitate.

But he didn't want to disturb her.

Keras had sent them away from Tokyo with strict orders to rest after they had held a meeting, insisting that he would cover Paris and Seville while Marek recovered. Valen had offered to take care of London and Rome, giving Cal a chance to recoup his strength too. Daimon was covering Tokyo and Hong Kong, although Esher was apparently fine again now, back on his feet and grumpy if the weather everyone had experienced in their cities a few days back was anything to go by.

The rain had been so heavy, it had almost caused a flood in Marek's valley, and when Caterina had realised it was caused by Esher, she had begged Marek to speak to him.

The fact that she feared Esher didn't sit well with Marek.

He had gone to see his brother in person, and rather than giving him a verbal beating for scaring her and making her think it was because she was a daemon and he hated her, he had ended up talking Esher down.

His brother had felt everyone was angry with him for not summoning them to help with their enemy at the main Seville gate.

They had been at first, but as always, that anger had quickly faded, because as testing as he could be, everyone understood Esher and his reasons for doing the things he did.

Although, if he so much as looked at Caterina wrong, he was going to get a beating from Marek.

She was still finding it hard to believe he wanted to be with her, mentioning several times a day that she was a daemon.

The most recent had been this morning, when she had dropped a mug during another episode, and had cut herself on the pieces. She had seen how dark her blood was now, verging on black, and had lashed out at him when he had tried to help her. He had weathered her blows, letting her get it all out because he knew how hard this was for her.

It was hard for him too.

Not because she was a daemon.

But because he hated seeing her hurting.

He hated feeling powerless to help her.

He had swept her into his arms, kissed her and carried her out onto the patio, into the sunlight.

Proving that she wasn't entirely daemon.

He wasn't sure what she was yet, but he would call her a hybrid. She was still human, with some human limitations, but she was part daemon too.

A fact she had proven last night by suddenly sprouting fangs.

Which had made dinner interesting.

She had panicked so hard, she had fallen backwards off her chair and almost tumbled down the hill on the other side of the patio. Marek had calmed her by showing her his own fangs, and it had gone down well with her.

He smiled and brushed his thumb across her fingers.

He liked having something in common too. They could both teleport. They both had fangs. They both still loved hunting vampires.

Although, Keras had ripped him a new one about that little penchant of his. He planned to dial it back and see if he could cope with no longer hunting vampires. He stared at Caterina, feeling as if he could now that she was his and had made him realise his past was just that. It was over. Now, he had a future to look forward to, and someone who loved him as much as he loved her.

Tonight, he had intended to take her out to the city, to stroll around it and maybe test some of her abilities. She had been practicing with them, and could teleport half of the times she attempted it now, and had managed to form a barrier a few times as well.

After their date, he had planned to take her to see her brother. His brothers had tried to get information out of their captive, but Guillem was proving to be as stubborn as his sister. The wraith wasn't being cooperative at all, so two days ago, Keras had visited to ask Caterina to attempt to get her brother to talk.

Caterina had been reluctant to agree to it, and Marek knew why. She felt guilty about her part in what had happened, ashamed that she had driven Guillem to turn on her and side with their enemy, and hurt that her brother had changed so dramatically.

Marek didn't think the change had been as dramatic as she imagined, or that all hope was lost. He had seen Guillem hesitate. There was a chance she could reach her brother.

That feeling had strengthened when she had agreed and he had taken her to see Guillem.

Rather than being motionless and distant, he had reacted in an instant to the sight of her, and Marek had caught the brief flare of relief in his eyes before he had shut down his feelings.

During their last few visits, Caterina had managed to get a handful of words out of her brother by talking about their past and happier times. Guillem hadn't offered any information yet, but Marek was confident that he would soon, if Caterina was allowed to keep rebuilding their relationship and reminding him of better days, and that she still loved him.

She had talked about getting some photographs from her home in Barcelona to take with her to their next meeting with Guillem, and Marek had wanted to see how the male would react.

Keras had called a meeting though. His brother wanted reports. Marek didn't really have much to offer, unless his brother wanted to know how Caterina was doing.

And how much he loved her.

He gazed at her, every inch of him aware of her.

He loved her with every fibre of his being, to the depths of his soul, and with all of his heart.

He had thought what he had felt for Airlea had been love, but it was a shadow of what he felt for Caterina. She stirred his blood, the dark possessive and protective side of him, and roused a fierce need inside him.

One he knew would never die.

She was perfect for him too.

An invaluable partner.

It wasn't just how well they fought together that had him feeling they had been made for one another. She had revealed another side of herself when she had found him in his office one morning, and had insisted she help him. It turned out that she loved researching as much as he did.

Which was a major turn on.

He shifted, trying to get comfortable as his shorts pinched.

They had spent most of the time they hadn't been practicing with her powers deep in research mode, uncovering everything they could about wraiths and the gates, and hunting for a possible connection between the daemons and Hellspawn.

He hadn't dared to take her back to the mansion since she had developed one ability he wished she didn't have. He had wanted her to spend time with his brothers now that everyone had confirmed they had no problem with her and she didn't trigger their darker sides just as she didn't trigger his. She didn't feel like a daemon to them either.

He had been quick to change his mind about her attending meetings when they had landed in the mansion only for every single one of them to look at her with hunger in their eyes.

Even Keras.

It turned out she had inherited more than just the ability to see emotions and cast barriers from the succubus.

She could emit a sort of pheromone too.

One that messed with his brothers.

When he had asked her why it was happening, she had admitted with a blush she had been thinking about him. He had wanted to kiss her for that, but he had also wanted to get her the hell away from his brothers.

Valen had seconded that, labelling it as disgusting and gross. None of his brothers wanted to know when she was thinking dirty things about Marek apparently—Marek didn't want them to know either. So, he had been training her, trying to get her to master her ability. Which had ended with several serious make out sessions.

The sun disappeared behind the horizon.

Caterina's nose wrinkled.

Her lashes fluttered and then her eyes opened, sleepy hazel depths locking with his.

She smiled, rolled onto her back and stretched like a cat, stirring his blood.

"I was having a wonderful dream." A hint of crimson coloured her cheeks.

Maybe that need stirring in his blood was courtesy of her. It was hard to tell when he wanted her every time he looked at her, ached for her if they were apart for even just a few minutes.

"You're adapting well to sleeping throughout the day." He rolled onto his side to face her.

"It's not hard when my body wants it."

He groaned. "My body wants something."

She grinned, pushed him onto his back and mounted him, tearing another moan from him as she settled back on him, her tiny black shorts and cropped tank doing him in, flashing far too much skin.

He skimmed his hands up her bare thighs. "We have a meeting tonight."

She pouted, pressed her palms to his chest, and leaned over him, giving him a view down her top, rousing that heat until it licked at him like fire, had him shifting his hands to her backside and holding her in place as he ground his hips against her.

Sparks lit her hazel irises. "I wanted to re-enact my dream."

Marek tipped his head back into the padded seat and frowned as he groaned. "We can do that. I'm not taking you anywhere near my brothers when you want me… I might kill them."

"Oh, well, if it will stop you from doing that." She leaned over and kissed him.

He lifted his head, craning his neck, and claimed her mouth, seizing control of the kiss as he clutched her backside.

Frigid cold washed over him.

"Do you know there's a daemon on your lap?"

That haughty female voice dampened his libido and had Caterina scooting backwards.

Marek tightened his grip on her hips, stopping her from escaping, and she tensed. He eased her down so she was lying beside him, her left leg mercifully draped over his hips, concealing the evidence of his arousal from the goddess towering over him.

"What do you want so badly that you're wrecking my personal time?" Marek looked up at her, into her pale green eyes.

Enyo preened the glossy twisted braids of her black hair, frowned and dabbed at a splotch of crimson on her left cheek. She brought her fingers away from her and frowned at them. It wasn't the only blood on her. There were streaks of it over her black and silver armour too.

"I heard what happened with the gate." Enyo wiped her fingers on her cloak.

Caterina gave him a look.

One Marek heeded like a sensible male.

"This is Enyo, goddess of war, sister of the real Ares. Not my brother." He turned his gaze on the goddess again. "Look, I have a fantastic idea. Keras asked me to ask you if you have any new information for us. We could cut out the middleman and you could just talk to my brother yourself."

That cold swirling around him turned glacial and she glared down at him.

"Doesn't she like Keras?" Caterina whispered as she curled closer to him.

"Something like that," he muttered.

The goddess didn't disappear as expected.

She lingered, the black look on her face fading into one of concern.

"How is... He fought..." Enyo took a breath, looked as if she wanted to finish one of those sentences, and averted her gaze instead.

"He's fine." Marek wanted to say more than that, wanted to tell her that he was beginning to suspect something was seriously wrong with his brother, but he also didn't want Keras to make another attempt at killing him. Once a century was enough for Marek. Last time he had been lucky in a way and the gate had taken the hit for him. "We need information, Enyo. The night we had to seal the gate, it wanted to be opened. We all know that gate is off-limits."

"Have you asked Hades about it?"

"No, and that isn't going to happen. I can't bring up Calindria, not until we're sure we can get her soul back." Marek sagged against the seat and blew out his breath. "I don't know how possible that is though. The wraith said he gave her soul to someone else, passing ownership of it to them."

Enyo stiffened.

"What is it?" Marek sat up, moving Caterina onto his lap as he got the feeling the goddess knew something.

"Transferring ownership of a soul would be complicated. The new master would need to be more powerful than the previous one, a creature capable of holding and controlling a soul... and that narrows it down to one species."

Marek felt as if he couldn't breathe. He told himself not to pin any hopes on this information, that it might turn out Enyo was wrong, but he couldn't help himself. She was a goddess three times his age, who had been everywhere and seen everything. Her position as a goddess of war meant she had spent most of her life honing her knowledge of every species.

If she could only think of one species, then that had to be the one they were looking for.

She hesitated.

Sent a chill through him when she finally spoke.

"Not a daemon. I might be wrong, Marek. It is possible... I would need to look into it."

"Tell me what species, Enyo. I can research too. I have to do something, even if it turns out to be another dead end. I need to give my brothers some hope." Being able to tell them even just the name of a species capable of doing what the wraith had said would keep their spirits up.

It would keep them strong.

"It might also help us arm ourselves against the next threat. We all suspect whoever has her soul is involved in this plot against this world and our own."

That had the goddess relenting, concern flittering across her face as she toyed with her braids again.

"I have not seen one in centuries, but once I met a descendant of a god of the Underworld your family knows well. Thanatos."

The god of death who had helped his father crush the rebellions.

"Thanatos bred, seeding a demigod offspring who inherited some of his powers. In turn, that demigod created an entire breed of Hellspawn." Enyo's jade eyes gained a glimmer of worry. "As I said, I have not seen one in many years. Perhaps even before Calistos and Calindria were born. It is entirely possible I am wrong, but if I am not... Marek... you all need to be on your guard."

A shiver spread down his arms and over his thighs, the graveness of her words and the concern in her eyes filling him with a sense of dread far worse than what he had experienced that day in the shower.

This one ran soul-deep.

He stared at Enyo, needing her to say it, because he wouldn't believe the word running around his mind until she spoke it aloud, confirming his suspicions.

"Necromancers are dangerous, Marek. Never trust one. Never. They are nefarious, devious creatures, driven by a powerful need to harvest souls."

He felt Caterina's gaze on him but he couldn't bring himself to look at her as he absorbed that, what little he knew about the elusive and rare breed of Hellspawn flying around his mind.

This required some serious research.

And he needed to tell his brothers.

"I must go." Enyo pressed a hand to her chest. "Brother is calling. He will be furious I slipped away from the battle while he was occupied."

Marek nodded. "Any information you can give me about this breed would be appreciated, Enyo."

She dipped her chin and disappeared, leaving a trail of white-blue smoke where she had been.

"I don't like her," Caterina muttered.

Marek wrapped his arms around her and kissed her cheek as she glared at the vapour trail. "I'm not interested in Enyo. She is a pain in my backside. Every time she visits me to help us, Keras ends up furious with me."

"Because they hate each other?" Caterina finally looked at him, right into his eyes.

"Quite the contrary I think."

"So why doesn't she go to see him. He's the leader." Caterina frowned at him, all the fires of the Underworld in her eyes. "I don't like her hanging around you."

"Someone is jealous." He pressed a kiss to her lips, a brief one that only served to reignite the fire in his veins and remind him what they had been doing before Enyo had crashed their private party. "There's history there. They haven't seen each other since Keras left the Underworld. I don't know why, but neither of them seems inclined to see each other."

Caterina glanced back to where the goddess had stood.

"That's odd. She was clearly worried about Keras. I would go as far as saying she was interested in him in an emotional and physical way judging by her aura. I caught flares of pink and red. I've figured out those colours together reveals desire." Caterina grinned cheekily. "I can't blame her. He is a looker."

Marek scowled at her. "I don't want to talk about my brother anymore, or I'll be the one getting jealous."

What he wanted to do was step inside with her and make love with her, but he needed to talk to his brothers about what he had just learned to make sure they would be on guard around the Hellspawn they encountered at the gates.

He teleported Caterina inside, but set her down in the bedroom and tossed her jeans and a T-shirt at her. She dressed without fuss, casually removing her tank and shorts, inflaming him without even trying as he paused to watch her.

"Stop it, or I will get kicked out of your family home again." She pinned him with a look. "It's hard enough controlling myself right now. I don't need you giving me the come-get-me eyes."

He tamped down his needs, because fitting in with his family meant a lot to her and she was making progress, beginning to feel as if she could be a part of it. He didn't want to do anything to jeopardise that.

He wanted his brothers to accept and include her.

He threw on his black linens and a grey shirt, and didn't bother with shoes. Caterina remained barefoot too. He crossed the room to her, pulled her into his arms and teleported.

He would have to send a message to the others, calling them to the meeting early.

When the darkness dissipated to reveal the TV area of the Tokyo mansion, he scrubbed that thought.

His brothers lounged on the cream couches, watching Valen and Esher racing each other in some video game on the enormous flat-screen television. Eva and Aiko were cheering them on, squeezed next to them at either end of the couch.

On the one that stood with its back to Marek, Daimon muttered something to Ares, and Megan laughed.

Keras rose from the seat on the other side of Daimon, nearest the television, and turned to look at Marek.

His brother's green irises darkened, blackening around the edges. He knew Enyo had visited him. Marek waited for the fallout as his brother held up his hand and the TV switched off, drawing everyone's focus to Marek.

"Did something happen?" The storm that had been building in Keras's eyes abated. "Did she have new information?"

Marek nodded.

Everyone stood now, and he frowned as he spotted one of his brothers was missing.

He looked at Keras.

"I thought it best Calistos remained at the gate for this meeting because I wanted to discuss what the wraith told you."

Marek was glad his brother hadn't included Cal. He didn't like keeping things from their youngest brother, but he also didn't want to hurt him. There was always a danger that hearing them talk about Calindria would be too hard on him and would cause an episode.

And right now, Cal was more susceptible to his affliction than ever.

Sealing the gate had taken more than a physical toll on Calistos. That gate had represented their sister, had been bound to her before her death, forged with her blood.

Losing it was like losing her all over again.

Or losing all hope of saving her.

Marek pushed that thought from his head and faced his brothers, because there was hope.

"Enyo believes the only breed powerful enough to take ownership of Calindria's soul is one straight out of the Underworld, born of Thanatos."

Keras's black eyebrows lowered. "A necromancer?"

Marek nodded and looked at each of his brothers. "A Hellspawn."

"Shit." Valen tossed the controller on the couch. "Suddenly I don't feel like playing anymore."

Neither did Marek. It felt as if they had all been playing, not treating this as if it was a game, but not taking it entirely seriously. Daemons were weaker than they were, and could be defeated. They had proven that with the illusionist and the valkyrie, and the incubus and succubus, and had almost taken down the wraith too. The power of a daemon was no match for them, not if they worked together.

But the power of a Hellspawn?

And a breed that used harnessed souls to feed its strength?

One that drew power from death?

That wasn't good.

For all they knew, they had been feeding the Hellspawn by killing the daemons, making it stronger, a formidable foe that was going to prove a challenge.

And what if it didn't stop there?

What if more than Hellspawn were involved in this?

"We have a lead to go on," Keras said, pulling him out of his thoughts. "Look into this breed. I will help with whatever information I can give you. I met one once, so we have that to our advantage."

"We'll be on guard at the gates." Daimon looked at Megan and Ares. "You be extra careful."

Ares nodded. "You know me. I'm always careful."

Valen snorted at that. "We'll get Calindria's soul back. One way or another. We'll turn over every damned rock until we find where the wraith is hiding."

"I'll scout any locations with you, places he might have been." Esher stepped out from behind Valen.

"I'll help." Caterina didn't shrink back when everyone looked at her. She stood by Marek's side, her chin tipped up and resolve in her hazel eyes. "He took me to a different mansion. A lot of daemons were there. It'll be a good place to start. And I'll try to get through to Guillem too and see what he knows. I think he'll start talking to me soon. I just need a little more time."

Everyone murmured in agreement.

The hope that had been leaching from him grew again, filling his heart as he looked at his brothers and they all started talking, discussing what they would do next, forming a plan.

Working together to face this rising threat.

Marek ushered Caterina over to them where they formed a wall, shoulder to shoulder.

As his brothers included her in the conversation, and Megan, Aiko and Eva joined in, Marek looked off to his left, over her head to the opened screens and the garden beyond it.

The sky turned crimson, smoke billowing across it, but no shrieks reached his ears and some of the buildings he could see were no longer crumbling and in ruins.

The otherworld was stable, possibly even improved.

They had taken a knock by losing Calindria's gate, but sealing it and taking out the illusionist had reversed some of the damage done in the otherworld.

He slipped his arm around Caterina's shoulders and tucked her against his side as he turned back to his brothers, and smiled as she wrapped her arm around his waist.

The stakes were getting higher, but whatever the enemy was going to throw at them, they could take it.

Their team was growing stronger as the enemy's grew weaker.

He looked at Caterina.

She was part of this fight now, like Megan, Eva, and Aiko, and he knew that like them, she wouldn't be sitting on the side lines during this war.

She would be right there in the thick of it.

Fighting at his side.

Watching his back as he watched hers.

Together, they would make it through whatever fate had to throw at them.

Because there was no one in his world more perfect for him.

And no one he loved more.

Caterina lifted her head and looked up at him, her hazel eyes meeting his, reflecting the love that beat in his heart.

A heart that beat for her.

She smiled, tiptoed and whispered against his mouth.

"You think too loud."

She brushed her lips across his in a brief kiss.

"Or maybe that's my thoughts echoing in your head."

The black looks his brothers levelled on him said the thoughts in her head were nothing but wicked.

Marek wrapped her in his arms.

And stepped.

Because he was damned if he was going to let her near his brothers, or let his brothers near her when she was projecting her feelings. The darker part of him growled as he claimed her mouth in a fierce kiss.

She was his and his alone.

And he was hers.

Forever.

The End

ABOUT THE AUTHOR

Felicity Heaton is a New York Times and USA Today best-selling author who writes passionate paranormal romance books. In her books she creates detailed worlds, twisting plots, mind-blowing action, intense emotion and heart-stopping romances with leading men that vary from dark deadly vampires to sexy shape-shifters and wicked werewolves, to sinful angels and hot demons!

If you're a fan of paranormal romance authors Lara Adrian, J R Ward, Sherrilyn Kenyon, Kresley Cole, Gena Showalter, Larissa Ione and Christine Feehan then you will enjoy her books too.

If you love your angels a little dark and wicked, her best-selling Her Angel romance series is for you. If you like strong, powerful, and dark vampires then try the Vampires Realm romance series or any of her stand alone vampire romance books. If you're looking for vampire romances that are sinful, passionate and erotic then try her London Vampires romance series. Or if you like hot-blooded alpha heroes who will let nothing stand in the way of them claiming their destined woman then try her Eternal Mates series. It's packed with sexy heroes in a world populated by elves, vampires, fae, demons, shifters, and more. If sexy Greek gods with incredible powers battling to save our world and their home in the Underworld are more your thing, then be sure to step into the world of Guardians of Hades.

If you have enjoyed this story, please take a moment to contact the author at **author@felicityheaton.com** or to post a review of the book online

Connect with Felicity:
Website – http://www.felicityheaton.com
Blog – http://www.felicityheaton.com/blog/
Twitter – http://twitter.com/felicityheaton
Facebook – http://www.facebook.com/felicityheaton
Goodreads – http://www.goodreads.com/felicityheaton
Mailing List – http://www.felicityheaton.com/newsletter.php

FIND OUT MORE ABOUT HER BOOKS AT:
http://www.felicityheaton.com

Made in the USA
Las Vegas, NV
17 January 2024

84471745R10194